ALL THE TEACHER'S PRISONERS

N.J. ADEL

ALL THE TEACHER'S PRISONERS

THIS IS A WORK OF FICTION. ALL INCIDENTS AND DIALOGUE, AND ALL CHARACTERS ARE PRODUCTS OF THE AUTHOR'S IMAGINATION. ANY RESEMBLANCE TO PERSONS LIVING OR DEAD IS ENTIRELY COINCIDENTAL.

ALL CHARACTERS DEPICTED ARE OVER THE AGE OF 18.

NO PART OF THIS PUBLICATION MAY BE REPRODUCED, DISTRIBUTED OR TRANSMITTED IN ANY FORM OR BY ANY MEANS, INCLUDING PHOTOCOPYING, RECORDING, OR OTHER ELECTRONIC OR MECHANICAL METHODS, WITHOUT THE PRIOR WRITTEN PERMISSION OF THE AUTHOR, EXCEPT IN THE CASE OF BRIEF QUOTATIONS EMBODIED IN CRITICAL REVIEWS AND CERTAIN OTHER NONCOMMERCIAL USES PERMITTED BY COPYRIGHT LAW. FOR PERMISSION REQUESTS, WRITE TO THE AUTHOR AT THE E-MAIL ADDRESS BELOW.

N.J.ADEL.MAJESTY@GMAIL.COM

Copyright © 2019 N.J. Adel
All rights reserved.
ISBN: 9798621747756
Salacious Queen Publishing

DEDICATION

To the darkness that never ends,
I accept

CONTENTS

ALSO BY N.J. ADEL XI
BEFORE YOU READ XIII
ONE 1
   DIVINA **1**
TWO 14
   DIVINA **14**
THREE 24
   DIVINA **24**
FOUR 34
   DIVINA **34**
FIVE 43
   DIVINA **43**
SIX 53
   RONAN **53**
SEVEN 65
   FLYNN **65**
EIGHT 79
   DIVINA **79**

NINE	88
AEDAN	**88**
TEN	103
GIANMARCO	**103**
ELEVEN	112
DIVINA	**112**
TWELVE	121
DIVINA	**121**
THIRTEEN	130
RONAN	**130**
FOURTEEN	147
DEREK	**147**
FIFTEEN	162
RONAN	**162**
SIXTEEN	170
DIVINA	**170**
SEVENTEEN	179
DIVINA	**179**
EIGHTEEN	191
DIVINA	**191**
NINETEEN	207
AEDAN	**207**

TWENTY	210
AEDAN	**210**
TWENTY-ONE	216
AEDAN	**216**
TWENTY-TWO	219
RONAN	**219**
TWENTY-THREE	233
RONAN	**233**
TWENTY-FOUR	249
DIVINA	**249**
TWENTY-FIVE	275
RONAN	**275**
TWENTY-SIX	283
DEREK	**283**
TWENTY-SEVEN	300
GIANMARCO	**300**
TWENTY-EIGHT	311
FLYNN	**311**
TWENTY-NINE	320
DIVINA	**320**
THIRTY	336
AEDAN	**336**

THIRTY-ONE	347
DIVINA	**347**
THIRTY-TWO	355
RONAN	**355**
THIRTY-THREE	362
GIANMARCO	**362**
THIRTY-FOUR	367
DIVINA	**367**
THIRTY-FIVE	382
GIANMARCO	**382**
THIRTY-SIX	393
FLYNN	**393**
THIRTY-SEVEN	413
RONAN	**413**
THIRTY-EIGHT	425
DIVINA	**425**
THIRTY-NINE	444
DIVINA	**444**
FORTY	453
RONAN	**453**
FORTY-ONE	459
FLYNN	**459**

FORTY-TWO	466
DIVINA	**466**
FORTY-THREE	472
RONAN	**472**
FORTY-FOUR	481
DIVINA	**481**
FORTY-FIVE	487
DEREK	**487**
FORTY-SIX	502
GIANMARCO	**502**
FORTY-SEVEN	511
DIVINA	**511**
FORTY-EIGHT	515
AEDAN	**515**
FORTY-NINE	526
DEREK	**526**
FIFTY	536
DIVINA	**536**
ALSO BY N.J. ADEL	546
ACKNOWLEDGMENTS	548
ABOUT THE AUTHOR	549

ALL THE TEACHER'S PRISONERS

Also by N.J. Adel

Paranormal Reverse Harem

All the Teacher's Pet Beasts

All the Teacher's Little Belles

All the Teacher's Bad Boys

Reverse Harem Erotic Romance
Her Royal Harem Series

Her Royal Harem: Complete Box Set

Contemporary Romance

The Italian Heartthrob

The Italian Marriage

The Italian Obsession

Dark MC and Mafia Romance
I Hate You then I Love You Collection

Darkness Between Us

Nine Minutes Later

Nine Minutes Xtra

Nine Minutes Forever

BEFORE YOU READ

No catchy phrase here, only a warning. This is prison.
There is blood. Lots of it.
There is crime. Kidnapping. Torture. Attempted rape. Murder.
As much as I love that you're reading, I love it more when you take care of yourself.
Not backing down? Good because there is sex. Lots of it.

ONE

DIVINA

The longer I stare at the murder photos, the stronger my beasts howl and claw at me. I bite the end of my pen and chew on my bottom lip, fidgeting in my seat, as I study the angle from which the killer has murdered his friend's girlfriend.

Instead of studying Derek's smell and the pounding of his blood.

I crook my neck and rub the back in a feeble attempt to ease the tension. Derek leans back in his chair away from my desk and looks up from the file. Then he flashes me a tender smile. I bury my gaze in the gory pictures, but I feel his eyes on me.

He smells so damn good. So delicious I want to eat him. Literally.

"You look tense," he finally says.

"That's because I am." It's never easy, working around crime scenes, interrogating vicious criminals while a wolf and a reindeer are fighting constantly to break free from my human cage.

Especially with all the blood. The reindeer gets squeamish. The wolf gets hungry. It's a hot mess.

But I love my job as a criminal psychologist—what movies and TV shows like to call a profiler—even more than my teaching. Putting my Psychology degree to good use, locking up murderers and rapists where they belong, makes me…human. The way I should be.

"Want me to massage it for you?" he asks.

I blink up at him, at the smile that always melts my insides. The thought of his big hands rubbing my skin... "I…" I shake my head, wanting to say yes so much, "I'm good. Thanks."

Derek sets down the file on the desk and

comes around to my seat. "It's just a neck rub, Divina, from a friend."

A friend who wants to be a lot more than just a friend. A friend with a smell that sends shivers to my spine and hardens my nipples.

My hands move on their own and pull my hair to the side, letting it all dangle and rest on my thigh. "Okay. Just this once."

What in the actual fuck?

"Did I ever tell you your hair is so beautiful?"

That's Dad's dark brown hair. I wear it long and keep the natural curls, but I'd kill for Mom's soft, blond hair. Now, that hair was really beautiful.

That is beside the point.

What matters now is how Derek murmurs that question in my ears. I tense some more, my heart pounding.

Before I can say anything, his hands find the back of my neck. "Dear God. Tense is an understatement. Your poor neck feels like one huge knot."

I close my eyes and hold in a sigh. His strong, warm hands feel so good over my skin. If I'm not careful, a moan will slip out and give him the wrong idea. Since Uncle Carter helped me get this job, Derek and I have worked together. We've become good partners and friends despite the sexual tension that never eases between us. He's so handsome with dark blond hair and kind, gray eyes. I never get tired of seeing his face. He might even star in a few of my wet dreams, but that's as far as the fantasy will ever go.

Apart from casual one—sometimes two—night stands, I've been single most of my life. That isn't going to change anytime soon. I've long forsaken my shifter side, which screws my chances to find my fated mate. And as a human…being a shifter doesn't exactly help the dating process. As hard as I try to hide my beasts and act like a normal human being, Wolf and Reindeer will always be there, lying underneath the surface, waiting to break free. And worse, to be found.

It's a risk I just can't take.

Derek is nice, amazing and so handsome, but he must forever be in the friendzone.

Besides, between my two jobs, I don't have time to date. Solving cases as a profiler and discrediting fake paranormal incidents and theories as a parapsychologist are the things that truly matter to me.

It might be weird I ridicule Parapsychology instead of supporting it, considering my whole family and I are supernatural. Just because we are, doesn't mean I have to be okay with it. In fact, I've fully adopted my human side. Sometimes, I even forget I'm a shifter at all.

Until either Wolf or Reindeer begs to run free.

The thing with the beast is, if I keep it caged too long, it goes wild and drives me crazy, until I give in and let it out. That doesn't change the remorse I feel afterward. I'm always a mess of emotions after I shift back into my human form, fighting a battle with my supernatural side I haven't won yet.

"Did you fall asleep on me?" Derek's fingers swipe along the length of my neck. "You got awful quiet there for a bit."

I open my eyes, back to reality. "Nope, I'm still awake. Just thinking about the profile, the motive, what steps we need to take tomorrow to get the rest of the answers we need."

"The killer is in custody with a full written confession, Divina. No more profiling needed. He's just another crazy fuck of the bunch we stumble upon every day. All we need to do now is get the evidence tight for the DA. Relax a bit."

This is why Derek is not a profiler. The suspect has described the crime in accurate and consistent details, yet his motive doesn't add up. The stabs on the victim's body aren't made in the spree of a crime of passion. They are slow and deliberate. A man who secretly loves his friend's girlfriend, confesses it to her and gets laughed at for it won't slowly and cold-heartedly torture her to death like that. It will be swift and violent and reckless.

"I am relaxing," I lie. "I feel much better already. Thank you."

My cellphone chimes, and he steps back. "My pleasure."

I lean forward and look at the screen. Then I swipe it to ignore and focus on the pictures.

"Let me guess." He gestures at the phone. "Your family?"

I purse my lips and grunt.

"You can't ignore them forever, D."

I hate that nickname, but when it comes from him it's cute. "I can, and I will." My office phone rings. "Beastly," I answer.

"Before you hang up on me, I have something important I have to talk to you about." Dad's voice makes me roll my eyes.

I place a hand over the receiver, shaking my head. "Derek, would you mind giving me a few minutes to take this?"

"Sure thing. It's time for a coffee break anyways. You want something?"

"The usual. Thank you." I watch him walk out with a smile, appreciating how nice his ass looks in his slacks. But when he shuts the door, I frown as I take my hand off the speaker. "You couldn't just text me instead of breaking my rule of never calling my office?"

"I wouldn't have to if you actually pick up or text back. But the only way to reach you is to call the line you can't screen and has no caller ID."

"Whatever. What do you need? Bail out a Blood Demons' prospect? Cover up a murder? 'Cause I'm not going to do any of that. I think we've established that I don't answer family calls because I really don't want to have anything to do with beasts or the motorcycle club or—"

"Always so sweet. I don't know how I'd act if you were nice from time to time."

I twirl the phone cord in my fingers. "Wonder where I got that from."

He sighs. "I'm not calling about the club, Divina. Have you heard about today's murder yet?"

"You're going to have to be a little more specific."

"The one at Forest Grove Penitentiary."

"Doesn't ring any bells. What does that have to do with me, *Terror*?" I call him by his road name as I already know what this must be about. He says it's not club related, but the Road Captain only calls when it is. The Blood

Demons hunt the bad guys of the supernatural world. This new murder must hold some interest for them. If they are not the ones who have done it in the first place.

"We think it took place on a secret ward where they hold supes. From what we've gathered so far, it has every mark of a cover up. I'm hoping you can get on the team that works the case. I need eyes inside the penitentiary to see firsthand what is going on. We need to know whether the killer is human or supernatural, and for what reason he made the kill."

"What... There are no... Nobody knows about our kind to lock them up, Dad," I whisper. "How do *you* know about the secret ward?"

"It's MC business to know."

That's it? That's all I get? Fine. I'll bite. "Why does it matter who or what killed them?"

"It matters," his voice lowers, "because the government is building a new prison in Mount Hood that is being specially outfitted to hold supes. Several have already been arrested and mysteriously disappeared. We think they've been taken to that prison, and this murder is being staged to make our kind look dangerous. An excuse to illegally arrest anyone and everyone and send them to the new prison as a way of population control."

I chuckle. "Seriously? A conspiracy theory? Dad, none of this can be true. In my line of work, ninety-nine percent of reported paranormal incidents are fake, and the one percent that is real doesn't get discovered. The real supernatural learns well how to hide among humans."

"Like you?"

"Yes." I clench my teeth, hating this conversation and everything it reminds me of. "Answer me this one question. How is it that they manage to keep supernatural inmates at a regular penitentiary that isn't specifically prepared to keep them like the new one claims to be?"

"That's where you come in."

I twist the phone cord a little more. "What exactly do you want from me, Dad?"

"Get on the team that investigates the murder. Report back to me everything, and I mean everything. No detail is too big or too small. I can't stress enough how important this is, Divina."

I roll my eyes. "Why don't you ask Uncle Carter? You do know I'm full-time busy with two jobs, right?"

"Mad Dog has retired since he's got the

looks of a twenty-year-old when he's supposed to be fifty, and you know it. And don't get me started on your second career choice!" He huffs. "Why are you always chasing answers when they're right in front of you? You are a supernatural creature, and someday you'll finally accept that and be done with all of this parapsychology war nonsense."

"When will you accept that what I do in that domain is important to me?"

"When you start defending it instead of opposing it, not a moment before."

My jaws hurt from clenching them too hard. He goes silent, thinking I'll be the one to give in. Not today, Terror. I remain quiet until I hear it. His sigh. His defeat.

"Baby, we need to know who the true murderer is so that we can protect ourselves. If what we suspect the government is planning turns out to be true, our kind is at risk here, the whole family, you included." The edge of his voice, the way it cracks with real fear alarms me.

I might not have the best relationship with the family, considering I have completely different viewpoints than them, and the major fact I've denied my beast side all together. At the end of the day, though, they are still my family.

I take a deep breath, twisting my lips. "I'll see what I can do, but no guarantees. Most likely they already have a team picked out."

"I'm sure you'll find a way. And Divina…thank you."

"Don't thank me. If I do this, it's not for free."

"You want something in return?" His voice rises in disbelief and…pride.

"Yes."

"What's that?"

"A promise that this is the last thing I ever do for the Blood Demons. No matter what, none of you will ever ask me to do anything supe related. I love my life as a human, and I intend to keep it that way for as long as possible."

For a few seconds, all I hear is his breath and the thrumming of my heart in anticipation. Then he sighs. "I promise. Please take care of yourself, baby girl." He hangs up.

I stare at the phone, my brows shot high, a strange mix of emotions washing over me. Talking to my family always makes me feel awful, which is why I don't like to answer their calls. No matter what, the conversation always circles back to my work as a parapsychologist. They will never accept what I stand for. And I will never accept their true nature even though I share it with them. The curse they've given me.

Now, I've just made a deal that can finally give me the peace I long for. Away from everything supe. From the world and the family I'll never fit in. With my beasts under control, I can live my life as a human. Fully. In peace.

But first, I have one last weird crime to solve and rub the answers in Terror's face. It's going to be super easy as I'm sure no supes are held in that pen, and it's just another *normal* psycho doing what they do best.

There's a small knock on the door as Derek comes inside, carrying two coffees. He has his perfect smile on. Just looking at him makes me feel better.

"Perfect timing." I hold out my hand for the coffee. A pleasant tingle shoots down my spine when his fingers touch mine. But, quickly, I withdraw my fingers, reminding myself of everything I cannot have. Yet.

I wait until he sits down. "Have you heard anything about a murder at Forest Grove Penitentiary this morning?"

He blows on his coffee and takes a sip before answering. "Yep. Someone was saying something about putting a team together. It's a priority case, all of a sudden. I'm not sure why. Why do you ask?"

I rise to my feet, shrugging into my jacket. "It feels like a propaganda piece to me."

"My thoughts exactly." He chuckles. "Where the hell are you going?"

"Chief's office. I want in."

"What?"

I hurry to the door before he asks more questions, groping for the best lie to silence his forming doubts. "You know me. Love to expose false shit. And I've been dying to get into that penitentiary in particular to interview a few inmates for my next article, but it's almost impossible to get a pass. Wish me luck."

Marching to the Chief's office, I slow down. The enthusiasm I should be feeling is slipping away, replaced by something more…dark. Suddenly, I don't know what to hope for. That he has already sent a team or that he hasn't.

TWO
DIVINA

Chief Wainwright is sitting at his desk when I knock once and walk in. He looks up as if he's not surprised to see me, holds up a hand to Detectives Papadakis and Hobbs in front of him and smirks at me. "Beastly."

The too-bright lights hanging from the ceiling irritate my supernatural sight. My gaze wanders from the white walls covered in crime stats to the duo he's most likely assembling for the investigation. Damn, Papadakis and Hobbs are two of the most experienced detectives in the precinct. My odds have just slimmed to zilch.

"Chief," I say with a nod, taking a glance at the picture of his kids on the desk. They're cute, I must admit. I don't know how he does this job with kids waiting at home. "You were expecting me?"

Wainwright laughs. "Who told you? Bright?"

Derek hasn't told me anything, but I can't just tell the truth. "Told me what?"

"About the mysterious penitentiary murder. I knew it would get your skeptic's instincts all hot and bothered. Tickle that parapsychology funny bone. I had a bet with Tracy about how long it would take for you to march in here." Chief nods to the corner, where his assistant, Tracy, watches me over the work she's pretending to do. She barely smiles and gives me a little wave. She hates me. I'm not really sure why.

Chief is a study in her opposite, dark where she's blonde, tall where she's about five foot four like me, age lines showing his experience as much as her smooth skin shows her youth. She's at least five years younger than I am. It makes her what? Twenty-three, twenty-four?

I focus back on Chief. "How mysterious are we talking?"

"They're saying a ghost did it."

I want to snort, but I manage to keep my expression neutral. People come up with the most ridiculous ideas. "Are we talking Casper or *A Christmas Carol* style?"

Only Chief chuckles at my joke.

I shrug at the two detectives. They're both in their forties, maybe closer to fifties. Hobbs is black, with deep brown eyes and a permanent serious expression. Papadakis looks as Greek as his name, with wild dark curls and a straight nose that could slice paper, just above his cocky little smirk. I return my gaze to Chief. "Why a ghost?"

He swivels a little in his chair. "Nobody knows who got in or out. No alarms went off. Nothing on the cameras. A ghost. But if Jacob Marley's been rattling his chains, he certainly made a mess of things while doing it. The crime scene is chaotic."

I cock a brow. "You have pics?"

"'Course I do. These two gentlemen have them. Because they'll need them to go investigate the murder."

I open my mouth, but he holds up a hand to stop me. "Beastly, you're excellent at what you do. But you already have three open cases, and I don't see you looking at this one objectively. You can get in on it the next time one of these lowlifes offs his buddy, all right?"

"Chief…"

He waves a hand, dismissing me. Chief Wainwright isn't a bad guy, but when he gets an idea into his head, he can be stubborn. If he believes I shouldn't go, it's game over.

Unsubtly, Tracy gets up from her seat and walks over to open the door, looking pointedly at me. Wolf growls. Even my reindeer wants to give her the antler.

I should fight for this case. I can't give up on that awesome deal so quickly. I need this.

Run.

My chest heaves at the abrupt voice in my head. The nagging feeling I've got on the way here comes crushing back. Are these my instincts? Why are they kicking in so strongly?

Run.

Tracy clears her throat, and Chief follows with a dismissive order. Fuck it. It's not like I can change his mind now. Dad will have to find someone else to be his spy.

I will have to wait for another deal to put me out of my misery.

Fuck.

As I walk toward the door, an unexpected wave of relief washes over me. I don't need that bullshit case. All I need is to get back to the real, human assholes. Especially the sadist girlfriend killer. I'll find out why he is lying about…

My eyes fall on one of the crime scene photos peeking from the file in Hobbs' hands. Before he can stop me, I step forward and grab the photo. Wolf reacts instantly, practically slavering at the jaws. I curse my rotten luck as Hobbs yells at me.

I'm used to gruesome murders. I've seen blood in places no one has ever dreamed. I've seen beheadings and quarterings, hangings and drownings. All kinds of bloodbaths.

But this? This is a massacre.

The body is barely recognizable. The room seems to be painted with the vic's blood. There is a mess of confused footsteps all around him, and—are those hoof prints? Paw prints? It's too grainy and too muddled to tell. His hand is clenched around something, which on closer inspection looks like a wad of fur. The floor is littered with scales. His head lies several feet away from his arm. His face is gaunt, as though someone has drained the life from him before the slaughter.

I snort. I've never seen such a perfect setup. With all this evidence. Someone has gone overboard to convince the police something not human is involved in this.

Shit. Can Dad be right?

My instincts are spot on to roil like that. This case is not what I've expected at all.

I look up at the door, cursing my luck again. *Why do I have to catch every fucking detail? I was one step away from leaving this shit.*

Now, I can't just drop it. I have to be on that team.

Great, just great.

I should be happy, though. I'll get my long-sought freedom from the Blood Demons after all.

My head turns to Chief. "How many are on the team you're sending?"

He points at the photo in my hands. "None of your business. Give that back to Hobbs."

"With all due respect, sir, you really need me on the team."

"You're overstepping, Beastly. These detectives—"

"Can close high-profile crimes of passion from three cities away, I know, but how many cases that involved occult rituals have they solved or even come across?"

Chief's stern face twists with interest. "You think this is what…a sacrifice to the devil?"

I shrug, continuing to lie. I have to. If my father is right, none of my fellow human detectives can get into the supposed supe's head like I can. I need to find out the truth myself to protect my family...and to get them off my back. That's why I'm doing this.

"I don't know exactly, but this," I slam the photo on the desk, "is a ritual kill. Look, does a ghost have claws? Fur? Does it suck the life out of a person like this? Unless it's the ghost of a wolf…"

My eyes shift toward Papadakis, whose cocky smirk has left him. His eyes keep flicking to the photo in my hand, and his throat bobs with a swallow.

He's scared, and I know what I have to do. "You need someone on this case who's not scared of *the devil and his demons*, who knows what they're doing. Someone who exposes this crap for a living."

Chief shakes his head at Papadakis, frowns and leans back in his chair. Then he fiddles with the tie resting on his small pot belly, and I know he's considering it.

That window of doubt I push wide open. "Papadakis and Hobbs are great cops, but we're not talking about some ass who murdered his friend's girlfriend."

"What more could you know about the devil than we already do, Beastly?" Hobbs scoffs.

I stare right back into his eyes. "More than you think." It's all I volunteer, but my tone is firm and low enough to strike a line of fear that makes Hobbs back off.

I can't exactly tell him what I know about Damien Pattison. The devil himself, who has tried to kill my mother on the day I was born. He practically delivered me, snatching me and my sister out of her womb to steal us away for his infertile bride. He thinks my sister and I are beautifully evil and belong in his kingdom forever.

Does that make him my godfather? Or is it the devilfather?

"She's right, Chief," Papadakis says gruffly. "If this is really a satanic ritual, she has more experience in that field. And if the ghost thing is a rumor, you need someone who knows how to smother it."

I press my lips on a smirk, shooting a grateful glance at Papadakis, even though he isn't doing me any favors. He's only afraid.

The Chief is still fidgeting, so I play my trump card. "That's me. Someone who can smother these rumors. You don't want a repeat of the 'I'm A Vampire' scandal from nearly thirty years ago, do you?"

Wainwright's eyes widen at me. "How do you even know about that? That must have been before you were born. Before even your uncle joined the force."

Actually, it happened on the day I was born, but I say nothing. No one needs to know a literal acolyte of the devil nearly exposed all supes to the world the same night I was born. *Because* I was born.

I shudder, failing to suppress the sudden feeling of guilt. I've been told my whole life it isn't my fault, but I can still see the pictures I've managed to find of those carved up bodies. They would never have died if the devil didn't order that lowlife to create a distraction so that the whole MC would go to the rescue, leaving my mom alone and unprotected.

All those innocent lives wasted, all this damage because the devil wanted to raise me and my sister as his children.

I don't know why. What is so appealing about a simple shifter Beastly twin?

Dad and the MC barely stopped the vampire in time, made it look like it was some lunatic slaughtering people, and came back to save us.

I should be grateful to him, to the whole family, to our supernatural side even, but that's not how I feel. None of this would have happened if we were just human.

Wolf grumbles a protest, and Chief is still watching me. "I'll even take it out of my overtime this month." I press on, even though I just want to go back to my desk and forget my dad has ever called me this morning. "What do you say, Chief?"

THREE
DIVINA

Derek is waiting when I get back, though I nearly walk into him, busy flipping through the file Tracy reluctantly has handed me on my way out. The only reason I don't is his scent, that delicious familiar smell that causes me to pause and take a second before my fangs find his neck.

His easy smile makes my lips stretch in return. He hands me the coffee I've left behind on the desk. He's warmed it for me, and my heart flutters at the tiny gesture.

"Well? Did you get fired?" he asks.

"Yep. No severance pay, either. God knows how I'm going to keep my twelve hungry children from starving."

He grins. "So you're in?"

"So are you. Wainwright insisted. Something about having someone to stop me from using that smart mouth on the wrong prisoner and getting shanked."

He cackles. "All right then. Guess we're going to see which of the murderers is more murdery than the rest. When?"

I look at the photos on my desk, but there's no way I can focus on that crime scene now. I have to go to solve the penitentiary murder before it gets any worse. "No time like the present?"

He blinks, but he reaches for his coat. "Fine. I'll buy you some street meat on the way. I've had stranger first dates."

"This is work, Derek," I say firmly, ignoring the tight feeling in my stomach as I grab my bag. "Not a date."

"I'm just teasing you, Beastly."

Do I imagine the undertone to his voice? Maybe. I push it out of my mind. I have more pressing matters to focus on now.

Derek drives. I don't pay attention to how small his car is, the one he lovingly names the Millennium Sparrow after the *Millennium Falcon* from *Star Wars*.

I, especially, don't pay attention to how close we are to each other inside it. His arm keeps brushing against me every time he changes gears—of course, he drives stick—and I struggle not to moan at every little contact. Instead, I focus on the file, studying the horrible pictures and the detailed information inside.

"What are you expecting to find when we get there, D?"

"A signed confession would be nice."

He snorts. "That would always be nice. What do you think of the ghost rumor?"

I roll my eyes at him. "There's no ghost here. It's just some psycho assholes killing each other. Ghost stories are for children. That's what I'm here to prove."

He gives me a quizzical look. "Do you really believe that?"

"You don't?"

"Well…it does make you wonder."

"What does?"

"If it really is some criminal wiping out his buddy, then isn't he doing us a favor?"

I cock a brow. "If? You think there's really

a ghost, Bright?"

"I've never seen an ordinary human leave such a mess. Even in your worst voodoo cases you brag to me about after you call them on their bullshit. I think it's unwise to assume we know everything that exists in the world."

All this time, I've never thought Derek believes in superstition or the existence of my world. "You're such a nerd. Life is not one of your comic books, Detective."

"Hey, don't kinkshame me."

I chuckle. Then I chew on my lip, holding my breath. "Hypothetically, if there were supernatural creatures living among us, what would you do about it?" I dare ask, but I look away from his eyes.

"What do you mean?"

"Would you try to befriend them? Hunt them down?"

"You want to know if I'd try to befriend Teen Wolf?" he asks, amused. "Divina, if some magical bloodsucking creature comes up to me, I'm running as fast as I can. I like being alive."

I purse my lips, using the file as an excuse to not answer.

We finish the rest of the drive in silence, my mind on the conversation with my father this morning. I don't remember ever hearing him quite so taken aback by anything. The longer I study this case, the more concerned I become.

No. Terror can't be right.

That's why I'm here. To prove him wrong. Get him off my back and go back to my normal life. My human life. The life where there is no such thing as monstrous supes or secret government conspiracies. After all, this is another fake. A convincing one. A horrible one. But a fake. Ninety nine percent of reported supernatural incidents are false. I'm not about to lose my sanity, or my years of expertise, because of a ghost story.

The photos stare back at me, calling me stupid. They scream at me, at my instincts. *It's a setup!*

I slam the file shut and shove it in my bag. Even if it is a setup, my job is to expose it and end this game before it starts. Our world has to remain in the dark. Not just for the safety of my family.

But for the sake of all humanity.

We arrive at the penitentiary about twenty minutes later. Derek shivers in his coat, and the snow, while not pelting down, is lazily making its way to the pile already building on the ground. I don't feel the freezing cold. My wolf thrives in these temperatures, but as

Derek rubs his hands together, I pull my jacket closed so he won't notice.

The penitentiary itself is a stark building, and the armed guards who let us in aren't exactly chatty. The green barbed wire has been copper once, but the rust just makes it look more menacing. All of the metal and barbed wire fences put my beasts on high alert. Animals don't like to be caged and the thought of being here sets me on edge.

Other guards are keeping watch all around the premises and even more are stationed in the yard, even though there are no prisoners there. At first glance, everything looks secure.

It's not much different inside, with the monotonous gray walls and tiny windows. We flash our badges, and once we've made it past all the security checkpoints, we're shown directly to the warden's office.

The walls are wood panel. The desk is mahogany. No personal pictures whatsoever on it. Secretive or protective? Perhaps even detached?

Warden Collins sits in a red leather chair, a huge window at his back. There's an oil painting on the wall of a farmer in the fields, and a wall of books nobody here has ever read.

My mind works a profile swiftly. If the

government is setting this up, the warden is my first suspect.

He's come from a poor family. Hasn't received an esteemed education as he's hoped. He overcompensates with the fake library and expensive furniture. Grandiose thoughts?

I consider what I know about him from what has circulated at work since his arrival. Warden Collins used to work out in Texas, but he moved to Forest Grove less than a year ago with his family and took over the penitentiary. He must have been offered a substantial raise to come from one of the hottest states to one of the coldest.

However, since he took hold of this place, efficiency has skyrocketed. Divisions in the prison are clearer, and there is less in-house crime—which of course makes this murder all the more baffling. I wonder how such an overachiever is taking this hit to his reputation.

He stands in greeting. "Welcome to Forest Grove Penitentiary. I wish you could be visiting under different circumstances, but it is what it is."

Derek holds out a hand. "Detective Bright, and this is Beastly, criminal psychologist."

"I do believe I'm somewhat acquainted with Ms. Beastly already," the warden says.

My instincts flare. I can't recall having ever met him in person before.

"I've read your Parapsychology articles, and I feel as if I know you already," he explains, a sly smile on his face. "Very fascinating."

My bullshit detector is through the roof, my senses on high alert, as if I am in the jaws of a predator. Wolf is primed, ready to attack. Reindeer, too. I don't know if it's the prison or the warden, but something is wrong here, and my two sides are in a conflict about whether I should dig deeper or run far away.

I growl silently, but I won't let this stupid animalistic reaction cloud my judgment. This man is hiding a lot of secrets. I'm not sure if I want to find them out.

"Thank you for your support, I love to hear that my work is being appreciated," I lie—about the first part, at least—filing that little piece of information he's given me in my head, using my training to calm down and keep everything underneath.

Collins sits back in his chair. "I hear you asked specifically to be put on our case."

So Warden has ears at the precinct? Or has Chief decided to give him a call and tell him? Derek glances at me, but he knows better than to try to speak for me and leaves me to handle Warden myself.

"I did." I sit, too, keeping my tone neutral, taking in Collins. His hair is salt-and-pepper shaded, and his eyes are dark brown and seem to laser focus on me. I wouldn't want to be a prisoner under that gaze. "I'm here to get to the truth. The wild stories going around—"

"Wild?" Warden interrupts, cocking an eyebrow. "You don't believe in any paranormal influence on this murder?"

I keep my voice level, speaking carefully. "I believe we shouldn't jump to conclusions until we have all the facts."

"Excellent." He reaches for an envelope sitting on his desk and hands it to me. "Perhaps these can help you."

I flip through the photos inside the envelope. There are several pictures of the victim while he was alive, surrounded by different inmates at various parts of the prison. My heart thuds, completely at odds with the situation, when I notice how attractive the inmates are. I guess there isn't much to do in prison except work out, but jeez. My eyes linger on one face that somehow seems familiar to me. I can't see him clearly, and though it nags at me, I move on. "Who are these inmates?"

"The suspects. It's definitely one of these four. I'm sure of it."

I stare at him for a second before I smirk. "I thought a ghost did it."

Warden's hard face doesn't change, which tells me exactly what he's trying to hide; there's a big fat lie here.

I glance back at Derek, who leans his elbow on the desk and peers at Collins. "This isn't how it works. We need to interview everyone, interrogate the guards—"

"There's no need for that," Warden interrupts, a little sharply. "Do you want to come down into the prison?"

"Crime scene first, Warden Collins," I correct him. "If I'm going to build a profile, I need to see where the murder happened."

"You already have the photos—"

"You asked the police for help, Warden. Let us do our job," I say firmly.

Collins's jaws tighten for a moment, but then he nods. "Very well then." He rises to his feet. "This way, if you please."

Derek chuckles behind me as we march outside, but I don't share his humor.

Something awful is definitely going on in this prison.

Something human.

FOUR

DIVINA

Derek and I follow Warden and his two guards through the gray-walled halls. I can't fathom how they know their way in this maze. Each corridor looks identical to the last. The only distinction is the faded yellow letters and numbers painted on the walls that label the wards.

We pass a few cell blocks. All prisoners are locked inside, the whole pen on lockdown after the murder. The wolf-whistles, rattling cages and bangs on the bars as I walk along the cells don't bother me. They expect me to flinch so they can get a kick out of it, but I march steadily, keeping my eyes straight ahead. They think they are the animals and I'm the prey. If only they knew.

Derek goes to my left so he will be on the cell side. The protectiveness, even though I don't need it, sends a warm, fuzzy feeling through me. I can't help the smile forcing itself on my lips.

I take mental notes of the surrounding details. The high-tech locking system. The cameras pointing at every door. The whole ghost story is nonsense, but I see now where it's coming from.

Derek nudges me as Collins puts in a code and scans his fingerprint to get into the next division of the prison. "Nobody is sneaking past all of that, not unless they have Lex Luthor locked up here somewhere. Do you think a supervillain did it?"

"It's more likely than a ghost," I deadpan.

We turn at one intersection and go down another hallway until we come to a heavily locked door. It looks to be made completely out of iron. The only decoration is a keypad and a fingerprint scanner.

A couple more guards are standing on

either side. The smell of blood fills my nostrils, and I use all my strength to silence the beast. This must be where the murder has taken place.

I slow down, prompting Derek to do the same. As the guards and Collins get busy unlocking the room, I glance at my partner and whisper, "When we get inside, distract him, hammer him with questions about the body and the scene. I'm going to try to sneak off and get some interviews. He doesn't want us talking to anyone, and I want to know why."

Derek nods as Collins turns back to us.

"I warn you now." Collins scowls. "This isn't pretty. I don't know what you'll find here that you couldn't find in the photographs."

"An actual body, probably," Derek says, and one of the guards snickers, quickly covering it with a cough when Collins glares at him.

Collins folds his arms. "The body is already with the coroner, Detective Bright."

"What?" Derek and I demand at the same time, his surprise mirroring mine.

"I didn't want it just lying there in my prison. I hired a specialist to come and take it away, see what they can find out. You two aren't CSU, I figured you wouldn't mind."

"We do mind," Derek says irritably. "Have you mopped up all the blood, too, because it ain't pretty for your precious prison?"

Warden just rolls his eyes and pushes open the door. No, he hasn't cleaned up the blood.

The coppery stench dizzies me as my two conflicting bestial reactions battle with each other. I stay outside while Derek steps in. For a moment, I can't even see, so focused on the wild tang of the blood. So much blood. So much…

"It's an exercise room," Warden says, and I almost snarl at him. Damn it. I keep my eyes down, hoping no one notices the gold that must be flickering in the blue of them now. The fucking *strikes*. The mark of a shifter. The reaction to anything…feral.

I place a hand over my jaws, blocking my nose as well. Then I make sure no one is looking at me—they are all inside anyway—when I glance back up. Warden points up to a metal hoop—without a basket—on the upper wall, and then to the heavy-looking weights in the corner. "Single occupancy, obviously. They go stir crazy otherwise."

That is…odd. I've never been in a prison with such a strict rule about something as small as exercising. Whatever their reasons for it, it hasn't worked. Somebody has gone stir crazy anyway.

The photos aren't wrong. The vic's blood soaks the walls, sinking into the stone. There is so much it hasn't even dried yet, half-red, half-brown, muddied against the gray. There's a chalk outline on the floor where the body used to be, and another, a little farther away, for the head.

Traces of scales and fur litter the floor. Deep gouges mark where claws have scraped along and taken some of the floor with them. The weights are all in a perfect pile, and nothing else is out of place. There's no sign of anything that may have been used as a weapon.

I take a couple of steps back, pretending to be pinching the bridge of my nose rather than covering my nostrils, my eyes shut just in case. "Warden, who was the first to discover the scene?"

"Me," one of the guards replies. "I was bringing the next prisoner for his turn and collecting the victim… Chisholm…to take him back to his cell. I walked in and found him like…well, you've seen the pictures, ma'am."

I have. It disturbs me how much they fill me with a deep hunger as much as they horrify me. I bring myself to look at the guard. He's young. Early twenties. Round face, dark blue eyes. Cropped black hair. He has the aura of someone who has gotten into this job for the good of it. His excessive blinking, swallowing and face touching tell me it hasn't turned out exactly how he's hoped.

"What's your name?" I ask.

"Wilder, ma'am. Graham."

My glance shifts to Derek, who is getting latex gloves out of his pocket. He catches my glance and launches into a million questions with Warden while Wilder and I walk farther out of earshot.

I smile at the guard. "Graham, how many ways in or out of this room are there?"

"Just this door, and it locks automatically and can't be opened from the inside." He points at it. "There aren't any windows. Those little vents at the top ceiling let air circulate, but they're too tiny for any human no matter how small they are to get in or out."

A grunt that is more of a snort escapes me. The guard thinks a ghost did it too. Awesome.

I circle back to the exercise room and look up at the small slits. He's right, though; those aren't fit for an escape route. He points out the cameras, too. Four of them, all fully operational, covering every inch of the room and the hall. There's no sneaking in the shadows here. "I need the surveillance tapes."

"They're wiped out, ma'am. Whoever did this tampered with them beforehand."

Wonder who has the power to do just that. I lure Graham back away from the room—from Warden. "Were you alone when you found the body?"

He shakes his head. "I was with another prisoner like I said, ma'am. Roger Smythe. He's in Ward D, the one we came through to get here."

I remember a yellow D painted on some of the walls we've passed. "Right. And what's Chisholm's ward?"

"Also D, ma'am. This exercise room serves the inmates in D and…"

The way he's chopped his words alarms me. "D and what?"

"Just that."

There's something he's not supposed to say. The click of his jaws as they snap shut confirms it. "So there are four wards in the pen, right? A, B, C, D? Or are there more?"

His face tightens, and something crosses his eyes.

"Graham?"

His eyes flick at Warden, but Derek has Collins' full attention.

"Do you believe that truth and justice are

above everything, Graham? Or is it just me?"

Graham hesitates a little more and then nods. "There are five. Wards A through D, those have been here forever. But Ward E...is new."

Holy shit. Is it the secret ward Terror has mentioned? "How new?"

His gaze flicks to Collins again. "Less than a year, ma'am," he admits.

"I see. The inmates in E must be special to have a new ward built just for them, right?"

His hands settle on his hips, clutching his belt. Then he shoves them in his pockets.

I nod slowly. "Who's in Ward E, Graham?

"They're sick," he answers earnestly. "I don't... I haven't had Ward E duty yet, but the other guards say these people are dangerous. They can't control themselves. They're on a ton of... I don't know for sure, but everyone thinks whoever or whatever did this came from E. They're occasionally allowed to exercise in this room."

I firmly believe no supernatural creature has committed this crime. What would that be anyway? A mythical monster with scales, fur, claws and a blood thirst? But I understand why my Dad is worried. I can't ignore his theory about a potential conspiracy anymore. There is something terrible going on here, and

I am going to have to get to the bottom of it, one way or the other.

I hold Graham's gaze, staring him down. "Can you take me there?"

Graham pauses, shifting on his feet, but then nods.

FIVE
DIVINA

Graham and I go back the way we've come, and then he takes a hard-left turn from Ward D. He types a complicated code into a keypad, and the lock opens with a pneumatic hiss.

Through the door, Ward E does not look like the rest of the wards. The walls aren't the dull concrete gray. They're a bright, blinding white, more like a hospital than anything else. There are more guards patrolling here than

I've seen anywhere else in the pen. Their uniforms carry a patch the others don't.

There's a weird hush to the area when we pass the doors to the cells. The bars aren't dark metal like the rest of the prison, but strong, corrugated steel. Prisoners are inside, but they barely even look up at me, making none of the usual inmate seeing a woman ruckus, not even approaching the bars.

This can't be right. No matter how ugly I am. I still own the parts they don't see much of around here. When Graham says they're sick, I originally think he means mentally. But now, I think he's a homophobe, and by sick he means they're gay.

Not cool, Graham. "What's the sexual orientation of the inmates here?" I ask him.

"Some are straight, some are gay. But it's a prison, ma'am. Even if they're not gay…" He shrugs with a chuckle.

He doesn't blink, no dilation in his pupils. I'm sorry I've judged him too quickly. He's telling the truth, and I have to accept the fact I'm too ugly for the inmates in E. Ouch.

In here, I feel something odd myself, too. My sight and hearing are lessened; still better than a human's, but it's like my beasts are knocked out.

My heart thrashes at the thought. I never

miss Wolf or Reindeer. If anything, I want them gone. Now that they're quiet—too quiet—I am...painfully empty.

What is happening to me? What is happening here?

I approach one of the guards on the ward, a man in his fifties with green eyes and a distant expression. "Excuse me, sir. My name is Beastly. I'm here with the police." I show him my badge. "Do you have time to answer a few questions?"

He folds his arms over his chest. "Is it about Chisholm?"

"Yes. I'd like to know the names of any other guards who were working on the night shift and the ones working this morning when the murder took place. Along with those of any of the prisoners who have been displaying strange behavior lately."

He snorts. "Everyone on Ward E displays strange behavior, ma'am. But sure. Let's go have a chat." He gestures, and Graham and I follow him along to a small office at the end of the cell block.

It takes me around an hour to systematically work through all the guards on today's shift in a brief initial interview, and then file the names of the ones from last night for later.

The stories are all the same. It's been a quiet night. Nothing unusual, no alerts, nothing on the log for the morning shift. The prisoners have been following their regular routines, except for—and here the story varies, but every guard mentions one of four names—Killian, O'Shea, Connelly and Oakberry.

Each of the guards tells a version of a day where one or more of those four high-profile prisoners have been acting strange in some way. One guard describes Oakberry's overwhelming aggression. Another tells of Killian's suspicious silence. Connelly has been found giggling to himself and won't explain why. The ones who mention O'Shea are much vaguer, though. Whatever he has done, it freaks them out. However, the guards' eyes are shifty, and I can't get them to give me a straight answer.

As the guards leave, and only Graham is left with me in the office, he offers to take me back to the crime scene, but I ask him for one more favor. "I need to see those inmates." I have to interrogate those four prisoners myself. I have no doubt they are the same inmates Collins is forcing me to believe are the only suspects.

"Ma'am…" He shakes his head. "Warden

Collins needs to approve of that."

"I just want to see them in their cells. I won't talk to them. Not yet. I promise," I urge.

He sighs. "If anyone asks, you went there on your own. I could get into a lot of trouble for this."

"Of course." I gather my things quickly, beating him outside the office. He takes a few corners before we come to two cells at the end of a row, directly across from each other.

The eerie quiet is here, too. Nobody makes a sound when we pass the cells, which unnerves me. Where are the wolf-whistles, catcalls and pounding at the bars? The unusual silence hanging over Ward E throws me off as much as that of my beasts, and not just because it makes me feel absurdly unattractive.

"Oakberry and O'Shea," Graham announces, pointing to the cell on our right. Then across the hall. "Connelly and Killian. The warden's favorite four."

I study the prisoners on my right first, not surprised to recognize them from the photographs Collins has shown me. Oakberry and O'Shea are playing cards, and while I feel like they are watching me, neither looks up.

What surprises me, even takes my breath

away, is how attractive they are—even more surprised I'm taking the time to notice it on such terms.

This is supposed to be a murder investigation, not a dating site. I still need to take in their appearances if I'm going to profile them, though. Right?

The smaller of the two—only because the other one is a giant—has black skin like the bark of a willow tree. Long, lustrous, raven black hair falls past his shoulders, creating a striking contrast with the bright green jumpsuit. His eyes are strange, not quite blue. I could swear they're…violet? He has thin, elfin features. An incomprehensible tattoo around his wrist. Some sort of letters, not drawings, in a language I've never read or seen before.

Something about him fills me with adrenaline, and it isn't just that he's ridiculously sexy or the strong, tantalizing scent coming from the cell I can't place or recognize. For once, my beasts, though drowsy, are in tandem. Danger. Run away. But, at the same time, an even more irresistible voice begs me to draw closer.

I tear my eyes away. Oakberry sits across from him, studying his cards. He's got one up his sleeve. Can O'Shea see it, too?

Oakberry's eyes are coal black. Unlike O'Shea, he's lily-white, with red hair cut short. His shoulders are wider than O'Shea's whole body, and his muscles... They're huge. His forehead, cheeks and neck have faded scars. Freckles cover his nose and face, and for one crazy moment, despite his crude looks, I think he's kind of cute.

Then he growls and swears at the next hand O'Shea deals, and I change my mind. Yet the growl vibrates in me to my very core. In more ways than one.

"Well, well, what have you brought for us, Guard?" a smooth, silky voice asks from behind us.

I spin around to find the source, ignoring the heat wave warming my cheeks. One of the prisoners opposite has a languishing grin on his full lips as he leans against the bars. My heart thuds at the sight of him; I can't help it. He's unbearably beautiful.

His dark blond hair and its effortless waves glisten with a gorgeous sheen. His emerald eyes, which seem familiar somehow, hold me in place as if hypnotizing me.

He's tall, but not lanky, the well-toned muscles of his arms beneath the prison jumpsuit visible. Strong and proud features. Bronzed skin, the kind of bronze people spend weeks on the beach trying to perfect and are never quite successful.

I drag my gaze back to those eyes, my breath catching. I can't remember where I've seen them before, and it's driving me crazy.

Everything about these inmates is. Especially their scents. They're nothing like I've smelled before. Not on humans or supes. I've thought prisoners are supposed to be stinky, fat, bald, toothless and ugly. Not hotter than movie stars and male strippers, and definitely not with scents that make me crave a gangbang.

Now, *I* feel stinky, fat, bald, toothless and ugly. No wonder they haven't even bothered to lift their eyes and look at me.

Except for this one. I like him already.

"Back from the bars, Connelly," Graham instructs.

Connelly ignores him, looking curiously at me. "We don't get many women in here, darling. What a fine woman you seem to be," he drawls, and his lips quirk with a seductive smirk.

Would he be talking in such a way if it was any other guard than Graham? I get the feeling most of the guards on E duty aren't as pleasant as my new friend.

Graham narrows his eyes, and his hand

hovers over his baton. "Last warning."

"Don't get possessive." Connelly smirks again, eating me with his stare. "I can share. You can join us, if you like. You're not my usual type, but I'd give you a go."

Graham blushes bright red. I want to snicker, but I open my mouth to tell the prisoner to shut the fuck up, only because I'm feeling bad for Graham's green ass—the picture Connelly has painted isn't entirely an unpleasant one. I'd love to feel those lips on various places of my body. Graham is cool, too.

"Stop being an ass, Marco," his cellmate says coldly from behind him, interrupting me before I say anything. He's lounging on his bunk. When my eyes flick to him, my heart thuds again, in a different way this time, because I recognize him. I *know* him.

Flynn *Killian*.

How the fuck have I missed that?

He has olive skin he once told me he got from his Native American mother. I can't see his eyes from here, but I remember a clear summer sky staring back at me. He has beautiful, brown hair, tied back right now, emphasizing his square jawline. His arms are up behind his head, his jumpsuit too small, his muscles rippling beneath it.

The Flynn Killian I know, the student in my Psych class, doesn't look like that. He's never been so muscled in my Parapsychology lectures, either. He's always been handsome, but this Flynn is rock-hard, built up into someone I barely recognize. When I first saw his photos in Warden's office, I couldn't place him. Now I know why.

He looks up at me, finally. He freezes for a second, but then he sits up. "Divina Beastly," he says in a quiet voice. "Fancy meeting you here."

SIX

RONAN

My cellmate Aedan and I are playing cards when a girl walks by the cells. Aedan is cheating, and I pretend not to notice, just like we do every day. We're not playing for anything. It's not like we have anything to bet on.

She looks so young, but she carries herself with the confidence of a mature woman. It's fake, though. I can feel it. There's a guard with her I don't recall seeing here before.

She's studying us, but as far as she knows Aedan and I are focused on the game, not on her. I don't need to gape at her the way she gapes at me to get her measure.

Calm features, ice blue eyes that are near-translucent, long brown hair. So long it hides the swell of her tits and almost does the same to her ass. She has these sexy, pouty lips, but her too-serious expression is just making them pouty now. What really is attractive about this little shorty—other than the ass and lips and maybe even the tits if she lifts that hair—is the mystery in her aura. A mystery I don't mind solving immediately. It's been too long since I've seen any woman, much less one so…interesting.

And non-human.

Aedan growls and swears at my next card. I don't know why. I always let him win in the end. Then Gianmarco Connelly makes a flirtatious comment. It's crass but effective, like everything he does. Gianmarco Connelly and Flynn Killian are our neighbors across the hall. They can get a little rowdy at such rare treats.

The girl turns immediately at the Italian's voice, gifting me with the whole outline of her ass now. Even Aedan steals a glance. Those curvy globes will be the main attraction in each of our solo performances today. And so many days to come.

Her breath hitches. I roll my eyes, but I understand. Apart from me—I'm not bragging, it's just a fact—Gianmarco Connelly is the most likely to capture a heart at a glance in this dump. He's tall in general, but not compared to me or Aedan. Lean, too, but he makes up for it in sheer swagger.

I suspect he is a vampire or a demon, but I can't be sure; Marco, as he likes to be called, isn't exactly known for sharing his secrets. He is affable and could charm the hind legs off a cow if he wants to. Yet he has a gift for sharing absolutely nothing when he speaks. I appreciate that about him. He'll make a good ally, if it ever comes to that.

His cellmate, I know less about. He's the kind of quiet that only happens when you don't give a shit anymore. The dangerous kind. The rare times he graces us with a glance through the bars, his eyes are cold and dead. What has stolen his soul? Can I put it to use if I need to?

I take the opportunity of them distracting her to enjoy the rear view. She's a pretty doll. One I'd enjoy dressing and undressing repeatedly. Fragile? I don't think so. Insecure maybe, but not fragile. I'm not sure what it is about her, but there's a strength in the way she holds herself…and a weakness, too. An uncertainty.

Yes, that's it. She's uncertain. A struggle between her human side and her other one, whatever that is.

No wonder Connelly is so immediately taken with her. Then Flynn Killian says her name. Divina Beastly. It sounds… Well, it's familiar. I know I should know it, but I can't remember from where. It irritates me. Names are what I do, and such a slip is unforgivable.

She looks back at me, but my eyes are already on my cards. Then she leaves with the guard.

"That was unexpected," I say.

Aedan grunts. "Focus on the game," he instructs me, which is the opposite of what he actually wants me to do. I don't say anything about it.

About an hour later, the click of her heels echoes back on the block. My skin tingles at the sound, but the other heavy steps dull the pleasant sensation.

She's back with the warden in tow, along with a man in a suit and coat—a cop—and a couple of big guards I don't recognize. No doubt, the guards are here for the warden's protection.

Our cell door swings open. "On your feet, O'Shea. Oakberry," the warden commands.

I sigh, and put down my cards, lithely rising to my feet. Aedan is significantly less graceful as he gets up, and one of the guards recoils.

I smile. Aedan is intimidating. Six and a half feet tall, with a build strong enough to squeeze a car. His eyes alone are enough to instill fear in any human with their extreme darkness in contrast to the golden sheen going through them.

He keeps his dark red hair cropped close to his skull, and the buzz cut and scars do nothing to soften the frightening aura. Nor does his conversational habit of preferring grunts to answers with words in them, or his way of looking at a person like they're going to be his dinner.

Aedan is a good friend to have in here, though. His arson charge, the fire that has us both locked up, should probably make us hate each other. Instead, we've forged an unspoken bond. We have each other's backs. It's extremely useful to me.

"Warden, have you come for a chat?" My eyes scan the others. The girl is watching me. I smile at her. An adorable pink shade crosses her cheeks, and my smile grows.

"Shut your smart mouth, O'Shea," Collins

snaps. Aedan growls.

My eyes don't leave the girl's. "Manners cost nothing, you know? What can my friend and I do for you?"

"You two are suspects in the murder of Sean Chisholm," he says without any preamble.

It's not surprising at all this murder will be pinned on us. The warden has had Aedan and me in his crosshairs since we got here, along with the other two across the hall.

"Detective Bright and Ms. Beastly here are from the police department. We're here to escort you to the holding cell for your interrogations," he adds.

I grin at him. "Lovely."

When I glance at Beastly—Divina, such a beautiful, twisted name—I'm a little baffled that, while she looks back and forth between the two of us, she seems more scared of me, not Aedan.

Interesting. That makes her rather clever.

I know what I look like. Perfectly handsome. My black hair allows me to blend in wherever I like. Less so in its natural silver color, of course, but I haven't walked around with it silver in many, many years. She can't see the point to my ears, hidden under both my hair and the misdirection glamor. And since Aedan and I are wearing matching prison uniforms, it's not my usual sense of style that's got her attention.

So maybe in some deep, dark, secret place inside, she senses what I can do when I'm uninhibited. The thought excites me. I can't wait to unravel what kind of creature she really is.

I switch my grin toward her, showing my teeth. Her eyes narrow at me, but she doesn't look away.

"You haven't even checked if we've taken our medicine like good boys yet," Aedan says, and we're both satisfied as the warden flinches.

One of the guards steps forward, his hand moving to his baton, and I hold up my hands in peace. "Relax. Of course we took it." Aedan and I line up to swallow those disgusting pills every day, just the same as everyone else on the ward. Vitamins, they say. Psych drugs say some others.

Everybody here knows what they really are. Magic suppressants. Which makes sense; if you're going to lock up creatures like us, the last thing you want is to give them full access to their powers.

Like me, Aedan does better than most on the meds. His magic is dulled, and he can't shift, but his mind is much clearer than some of the other poor bastards walking about like zombies every day of their immortal lives. It's one of the upsides of being a dragon. I'm grateful he can't shift in here. No cell can fit that, and the last time he's shifted we both ended up in here.

As for me, I barely feel the effects at all. They muddle my head a little, but they can't touch my magic. My people aren't like the others. For a shifter, or even a vampire, the magic is something they have. For me? I am the magic. Without it, I can't exist. You can't take away fae magic and leave a human behind. It's my breath, my life, my soul.

But whoever is making sure we never leave this hole either doesn't know or doesn't care, and either is to my advantage. I play the zombie along with everyone else and blend in.

For now.

The guards approach with the handcuffs. Every time I see those, I suspect they're made of iron. I'm sure all inmates have the same feeling. Vampires think they're made of Vetala. Shifters think they're made of silver or iridium. But not once have Aedan or I been burned by handcuffs. Which makes me certain they know absolutely nothing about how to kill us. That's why they're locking us up. Keep us caged until they figure that part out.

Although it's annoying, we let them cuff us so they don't feel threatened as they lead us out of the cell. I make sure to stay away from the bars as I step out. Those are made of fortified iron. I don't think it's deliberate. They just put it there because it's strong. I don't want to give them any tips if it accidently touches my skin and burns it.

We head to the holding area outside of interrogations. It's neither Aedan's nor my first time; we barely need the guiding, but we stay quiet. Unsurprisingly, we stop across the hall to collect Marco and Flynn. Flynn says nothing at all as his cuffs are put on. Marco's gaze unsubtly trains on the girl the entire time. She tries so hard not to look in his direction. It's rather endearing.

We all follow the warden and the cops to the holding room. The guards make sure we're inside and Flynn is the first to be taken out to be interrogated. The warden goes off to hide in his office or whatever burrow the coward likes to bury himself under.

The holding room is small, but not terribly uncomfortable. An empty table lies in the middle surrounded by long benches. They do us the favor of unlocking our cuffs. They don't care so much if we attack and kill each other, maybe even encourage it.

I lounge on the bench next to Aedan as we wait in silence, my mind drifting toward the girl, her name that I should know, and her strange allure. That look in those big, translucent eyes that makes me feel as if she sees right through me.

"You felt it too, faerie, didn't you?" Gianmarco asks.

Aedan growls, and I sit up, shaking my head as though a fly is irritating me. I'm not annoyed Gianmarco knows what I am. I'm not exactly trying to hide it, not here. What would be the point? What does annoy me is his word choice. By the curl of his lip, I say he does it on purpose. "Fae," I correct politely. "Faerie is a realm. Fairies are children's stories. We are fae."

Gianmarco snorts. "Indeed. I forgot how touchy your kind is about your words."

"Words are what we have, demon," I reply, satisfied at the flicker of surprise in his eyes. I've guessed right. He must think he's been hiding it better. "My kind cannot speak lies, so we must be very careful about what passes our lips."

Gianmarco grunts with practiced disinterest. "What about you, big guy? You smelled it?"

Aedan glares at him, and then he shrugs. "The girl? Yeah, I smelled it."

My mouth twists. I'm not used to being the only one in a room who does not know what is going on. "Smelled what?"

"Her scent," Aedan grumbles. "She's a shifter. Don't know what beast."

Shifter? That can't be. It's too…simple. "What about that cop?"

"As human as they come, though an exceptionally good-looking specimen." Gianmarco grins.

I ignore the comment. Everything with the demon has to be sexual. I admit the cop is good-looking, but she's far prettier. "Shifters have a strong sense of smell. Do you think she knows what we are?"

Gianmarco winks. "We shall see."

My eyes scrutinize him. "How did *you* know she's a shifter?" He doesn't have the same strong sense of smell as Aedan, and the miserable suppressants should be affecting his magic.

The demon just smirks at me.

I won't waste my time with him. He won't give me anything he doesn't want to give. His kind is the worst. I lean my back on the cold wall behind me, thinking of the girl and her eyes, not letting the whirling in my brain show on my face.

Half human, half shifter. It doesn't explain any of the strong feelings I'm sensing from her. It doesn't explain why I feel like I should know her.

No. She's a lot more than just that. She has to be.

SEVEN

FLYNN

I thought I'd never see her again.
Professor Beastly in all her glory.
Her drowning eyes. Her full lips. Her wild hair I've always wanted to grab while tapping her tight ass.

Having her near me is a cruel punishment. A thousand times worse than prison time. I'm in here to pay for what I did. Seeing her reminds me of my past, and now I feel I'm being punished for what I am. What I've become.

The Flynn that used to be Divina's student is dead. He died the moment he followed Carline and Leopold up to that bedroom that night. He was already dead when he stabbed that ancient dagger into Carline's rotten vampire heart. And more dead when he tracked Leopold down and yanked his out of his lion's ribs.

The thing that's left, the thing that pretends to be Flynn Killian when I wake up every morning, is only still alive because even death doesn't seem to want it.

Frankly, I don't care. I don't care about anything anymore. When Leopold bit me, and Carline couldn't hold her thirst and sank her fangs in my wound after him, they sucked it all. The care. The emotions. The good. Anything that has ever made me human.

But seeing Divina makes me... I just want her away from me.

I'm the first to be led to the interrogation room. Is she going to take her time? Or does she want it over with quickly? Maybe she doesn't even recognize me.

Why would she? I've only been one of her students. Even though I've been quite taken by her, she's never responded to my flirtations with more than an eye roll. Again, why would she? Everybody has flirted with the hot teacher that barely ever smiles hoping she would for them. I've never been more than just another number in that pile.

Besides, I look different now. My eyes have been stolen from me, replaced with these silver things that shine with gold lines and mark me out as double a monster. My body is different, too. I work hard on this body. Every moment I get, I exercise it, tone it. I have nothing else to do.

What would the professor who denies the existence of the supernatural do if she knew what I am? I'd kill again to see that look on her face when she does. If she ever does.

Divina is whispering with the other detective nearby while I sit handcuffed to the cold metal table. She thinks she's far away enough in the corner of the room that I can't make out what she's saying, but I do. She's telling him she knows me. So she does recognize me after all.

Does that mean the detective is going to do my interrogation instead? He's offered. The protective way he stands near her, the look in his eyes… She's caught him in her charms, too. Are they fucking? Is that more ethical than fucking a student? Divina has always been one for ethics.

She, not the detective, walks over, sits across from me and sets a yellow file on the table. Whatever past connection we used to have doesn't matter to her to be considered a conflict. It stings more than it has any right to. I scowl at myself for my idiocy.

"Hello, Flynn," she says calmly.

Hearing my name from her lips after all this time makes me shudder, shooting an awful warm feeling through my chest. I scowl deeper. "Professor Beastly."

Her hand covers her nose, and a sadness crosses her eyes. She pities me. I hate it. I want her to stop. "Do you know why you're here?"

I laugh bitterly. "Because you think I killed Chisholm."

"Did you?"

"No. I'm not sorry he's dead though. Scum."

She exchanges a glance with that detective. "What was your relationship with the victim, Flynn? You don't sound like you liked him very much."

"What makes you think I had a relationship with that piece of shit?" I snap.

She tilts her head, her hair falling to the side, and my mouth waters at the way it exposes the curve of her neck and her throbbing veins. "You just told me you weren't sorry he was dead. You called him scum."

"This is prison. We're all scum." Me most of all.

She taps her fingers on the table, and then reaches into her file and draws something out. I flinch, even though she can't be hiding anything terrifying in that little Manila folder. I want to smack myself. What, she'll give me an F?

She draws out some pictures and extracts one. Then she puts it on my side of the table, the back of her hand on her nose. It's me, sitting next to that bastard Chisholm at the cafeteria a few days ago. Looks like Warden Chickenfuck has been preparing well for this bullshit.

I look up from the picture. She's watching me silently, waiting for my response. I shrug. "Well, you caught me, Professor. He stole my dessert that day and deserved to die. Didn't he know how much I loved those rubbery muffins? He knew better than to put his filthy hands on the muffins of a psycho son of a bitch like me. He had it coming. Do you need me to sign the confession now or later?"

Rolling her eyes, she smacks the file closed. "Flynn, I'm trying to help you."

I ignore the sincerity I detect in her tone so my expression won't change. She cares. It's the last thing I need right now. I glance down at the photo. "We ate together. That's all."

She probably doesn't believe me. She shouldn't. But she doesn't need to know the two-bit smuggler has—had—been getting me some beer. A lot of beer, actually, over the time I've been here. The fucking pills they give us dull the magic but don't take the edge off. Alcohol helps.

She doesn't speak, waiting for me to dig my way into a trap. I know her game. She's taught it to me in her classes. But I don't say anything else, and she doesn't push it as though my lack of an answer is enough for her. She writes something down before she holds my gaze. "Where were you at the time of the murder?"

"What time is that?"

"Seven-thirty this morning."

"In my cell, same as I am every day except for meal and shower times and around five in the p.m. when I get my exercise turn."

Her eyes flick to my arms, checking out my muscles, which makes me unreasonably smug. "You spend a lot of time in the exercise room?"

"Yes, as many other inmates do. And a

guard leads me to the room and after my half hour is finished a guard leads me back to my cell. Even if my exercise time was right before Chisholm's I wouldn't have the time to gut the piece of shit."

"Gut him? So you know how Sean Chisholm died? How—"

"It's a prison, Professor. Word spreads in here."

"Not that word. As far as anyone else I've questioned, Chisholm was strangled. Or stabbed. Or hit with a blunt object."

I pause, pondering my options. I'm telling the truth; I didn't kill him, but that doesn't mean she's not right. I have information I shouldn't. Marco and I make a point of knowing things around here, but if I reveal that, I'll reveal my sources. If I reveal my sources, I'll lose them. I shake my head. "Lucky guess."

Her eyes glance over at that detective before they catch my gaze once more. "So if you didn't kill him, who did?"

The question drops flat on my ears. I don't bother with an answer. Instead, I study her eyes. They are as drowning as they've always been. However, now, there's something I've never noticed before. Could she be... No fucking way.

"You know who did it. Who killed Sean Chisholm, Flynn?" she presses.

"How the hell should I know? Maybe he chopped his own head off." I regret the words as soon as they fall off my mouth. Fuck. I'm not supposed to know about that chopped off head part either. How does she do that? Is she doing it on purpose? Distracting me with that inhuman stare so I spill it all?

Does that mean she knows what I am?

She still stares at me with those calm blue eyes, the golden lines that look a lot like mine gleaming now. "I take it that's another lucky guess."

A wave of resentment toward Carline and Leopold threatens to waken my monsters. If they'd left me human, maybe I'd be the one questioning prisoners now. I had a whole life ahead of me, and they took it, leaving me as this.

"Can anyone corroborate your whereabouts this morning and last night?" she asks.

"The guards. My cellmate. The surveillance tapes."

"The tapes were wiped. I'm surprised you didn't guess that, too."

"You caught me again. I made an invisible

clone of myself while I was in the exercise room, left it behind to murder that useless bastard and gave another clone an electrical engineering degree to mess with the footage. Do you read me my rights now?"

The detective dashes forth and slams the table. "Is this a joke to you, Killian?"

I laugh. "Everything is a joke to me, Detective."

He's about to say something else, but Divina holds up her hand for silence. "What's the name of the guard who escorted you to and from the exercise room?" she asks me.

"No idea. Quick with his baton, though."

"That's a lie," one of the guards interrupts angrily. It's not the same guard from yesterday, but I guess they talk. "There isn't a single mark on him. You can check."

I'm half a vampire, half a lion shifter. I fucking heal fast, asshole.

Divina doesn't take her eyes off me. "He beat you? Why?"

I shrug. "I looked at him funny. I threatened him. I'm the wrong color. I don't know. You'd have to ask him."

"And how will I ask him if I don't have his name?"

"That sounds like your problem, Professor."

"Why the hell won't you let me help you?"

A snort vibrates through my nose. "We both know you're not here to help me or any other inmate. Not that we need any help from you."

"I'm not the enemy, Flynn. Believe it or not, I'm here to find out the truth. If you didn't kill Chisholm, then you sure need my help."

I'm not falling for this shit again. The truth my ass. She's playing a game. For Warden Collins? For the police? For the government? I don't know or care. The gentleness in her voice, and the way she says my first name enrage me. His name. The name of a dead boy. "Like I said, I don't want it," I hiss, gritting my teeth.

A somber shadow crosses her expression. "Flynn, why are you in prison?"

My eyes tighten at her. She can't be asking about my charges. She must have read my file. She must know I'm in for double homicide. What she wants to know is why I did it, why I'm in prison when I should be thriving in some office and having hot orgies in my condo. "Vacation."

She takes a short breath, but it's enough for her tits to stick up. I stare as she goes through her file, her hand on her nose for the umpteenth time. "My notes say two counts of aggravated homicide."

"Damn right."

She looks back up at me. I don't stop staring, and she doesn't make me. From the corner of my eye, I see a murderous glare in her boyfriend's eyes.

"Are you innocent?" she asks.

"Hell no." I don't see any point in hiding it. "I killed them both. Loved every second of it. It doesn't mean I offed this bastard."

She rises to her feet. "You're right, it doesn't."

Pursing my lips, I nod. "Does that mean you got what you need for the profile?"

"For now." She puts the stupid picture back in her file, not looking at me at all. "One of the guards will return you to the holding cell. I'll call you back if I have any follow up questions."

"Wonderful."

The other guard, not the one who has spoken before, grabs me roughly by the shoulder and pulls me to my feet after unlocking me from the table. He tries to propel me out of the room, but I shrug him off. "I can walk."

As soon as we're out of the door, he kicks me hard in the shin. "Watch your mouth, you piece of shit."

I want to hit him back, but I don't. Not yet. He pushes me into the holding cell, and Marco catches me as I stumble, sitting me down on the bench next to him.

"Always so pleasant, Rivera," Marco scoffs. "Who's next?"

Rivera—I don't remember seeing that guard before, but Marco does make a point of knowing everything—scowls at him and waves his baton in a warning. He doesn't like the easy way Marco talks to him. "Oakberry," He nods at Aedan. "You're next. Move it."

The dragon grunts, but he follows without protest the fucker I can't wait to drain dead. When the door closes, Marco chuckles at me. "Had fun?"

"I think she's… Her eyes…"

"Spent a lot of time looking into her eyes, didn't you?"

I shove at Marco, and though he lets out a pained breath, he seems amused.

"She is what you think she is." Ronan O'Shea leans on the table. "But how do *you* know her?"

Divina Beastly is a shifter? That doesn't make any sense. Maybe I can't smell her beast because of the fucking meds, but she dedicates half of her time proving anything supernatural a hoax. How can she be one herself?

And how the fuck does a shifter walk among humans with such ease, with that status, with that…perfect life? A life that could have been mine.

The image of Flynn from long ago flashes in my head, the easy-going party boy with a crush on the teacher. I remember her rare smile when she has given me an A+ on my essay, the smile that has made my heart skip a beat. Then I think of the heart that no longer beats.

She must know what I am now. Must have smelled it. That's why she kept covering her nose. My bloodsucker disgusts the shifter professor.

Fuck you, Divina Beastly. I've been completely fine before you set foot in the prison, accepted my life in oblivion, cared about nothing. Then you come, parade the life that could have been mine just like this, show me I've been living a lie, ruining everything.

My fists clench, and I squeeze my eyes shut.

"How do you know the shifter, Flynn?" Marco repeats.

"I don't." I swallow my anger as I stare at nothing, my chest heaving with a blaze of emotions I've long smothered. "You should be careful around that bitch, though. She's dangerous…with an agenda of her own."

Marco and Ronan exchange looks, but I ignore them. All I want is to forget I ever saw Divina Beastly today and go back to the blissful silence.

EIGHT
DIVINA

My eyes flick at Derek. Concern radiates off him as his kind gaze trains on me. The interrogation with Flynn has been more...challenging than I've anticipated. I don't let my emotions show on my face, but Derek knows me better than this. He must see it in my eyes. The sorrow.

I wish he'd stop. When he cares about me too much, it makes this whole thing we have, whatever that is, much more difficult. His beautiful face, policeman-toned body, and scent that challenges my very nature every day are bad enough. It's unbearable when he shows what a genuinely good guy he is, too.

If I allow myself to fall for someone, Derek is exactly who it should be. But I can't. For my sake, and for his. So instead of asking for a hug or confessing how shaken the confrontation with Flynn has left me inside, I say, "You don't need to look at me like that, Detective Bright."

My tone is harsher than I intend, and hurt flashes across Derek's face. Shit. I hate when I have to be cold to him, but it's really the best for both of us.

"I'm not looking at you like anything, Divina. But are you sure you're all right? It can't be easy. He was your student."

I shrug, trying to look nonchalant, though I'm not sure how successful I am. "The job is the job." I'm thankful the harshness has retreated a little. I don't want to make him hate me. His friendship is one of the most valuable things in my life. It's one of the few things that keeps me sane. Keeps me human. "Killian was a suspect. I interrogated him. That's all there is to it."

The remaining guard coughs. "I need to go to the bathroom. Sit tight. Rivera and the next inmate won't get back before I do, but if they are, don't start until I am here, all right?"

What in the actual fuck? Why should we wait for a guard? So he can report back everything we say to Warden? I'm surprised this room hasn't been wired before we got in. God knows what they do in here that they keep it camera free.

I give the guard a distracted nod, not that I approve of his demand, and Derek waits a beat until he's gone. Then Derek leans back on the table edge, too close to me. "You don't have to be strong all the time, you know?"

Yes, I do. I fidget in my seat, holding my breath. "I'm all right," I say hoarsely. So I clear my throat and repeat, more businesslike this time, "I'm all right."

"Of course you are." He wears an ironic little half-smile, and it hurts. But he reaches over and takes my hand. A sigh escapes me as I look up at him. The feeling of his warm skin against mine makes me crave more. I imagine his fingers running up the skin of my arm, down my shoulders, his hands caressing my back.

His gray eyes are intense as they look into mine. It forces me to lower my gaze. There's nothing magical about Derek—he's the most human person I know, and I mean that as a compliment—but when I see the concern, the care, the jumble of feeling in his eyes, he enchants me. All I want to do is melt into them, to lose myself, to—

I pull my hand away and leave my seat.

His sigh falls heavy on me as he, too, shuffles away. "You said *was*."

I barely glance at him over my shoulder. "What?"

"You said Killian *was* a suspect. He isn't anymore?"

Nothing Flynn has said should lead me to that conclusion. In fact, it's suspicious how much he knows about the murder. The gutting, the decapitation…the guards who are aware of the crime scene all have assured me it's top secret during my questioning, especially from the prisoners, and Warden insists the exact method of death is not public knowledge. And yet, and yet…I don't just listen to words from suspects. I would be a poor profiler if I did.

Flynn, that easy-going student who used to flirt with me at the end of the class, is not an innocent man. Not anymore. He's killed before, freely admits to it, and maybe even relishes it. That thought disturbs me, but it doesn't cloud my judgment.

His tone and body language during the

interrogation tell me a lot more than words do. And his eyes…reveal a secret even I shouldn't have known.

I face Derek. "Killian has been upright and honest the entire time. He isn't cagey. Yes, he knows more than he should and is hiding things, but it's more like protecting his sources, not lying about a murder."

"What about his open distaste for the victim?"

"If he is the killer, he'll try to be more subtle about it. He could be trying to throw me off, but…Killian has got nothing to lose." A pang sets in my chest. "To a man like him, what's another life sentence?"

Besides, my instincts say he has nothing to do with this crime. I resent my family for cursing me with what I am, but one benefit is that, more than most people, I know I can rely on my instincts.

That's something I can't say to Derek. Nor can I tell him my former student's smell is completely different from the one I used to know. It is headier, muskier, more bestial, yet under the animalistic aroma lies one colder and more repugnant. Not only are his eyes silver, but they also have the *strikes*. I don't fail to recognize the gold flicks that mark a beast like me. Or the silver that screams bloodsucker.

Flynn Killian has changed from a carefree party boy with an interest in Psychology to a murderer and a hybrid monster.

Fuck, I hate this. Every second of it. Every discovery. Every piece of evidence. Each and every lead that drives me to conclude Dad might be right.

Derek interrupts my thoughts, clearing his throat. "Have you ruled him out already?"

I don't like his tone. "I haven't ruled out anyone. Officially, he's still a suspect, and so is everyone in this place."

"But you don't think he did it."

"You're right. I don't."

"Okay. You know I trust you on this. But Divina, are you sure your past—"

My eyes widen at him. "Excuse me?"

He shakes his head and shoves a hand in his pocket. "I'm sorry."

"Derek, why don't you lure the guards out and go to the crime scene again? I have a feeling the suspects will talk freely without them in the room, and you have a better chance to find something more helpful when Warden isn't breathing down your neck back at the scene."

"Divina…I said I'm sorry."

"I'm only thinking about the best way to

solve this case. Nothing personal here."

He glares at me, his jaws and eyes hard. "Of course."

The door opens, and the two guards walk back in with the big, white inmate. Oakberry. The guards must have met in the hallway and come back together. Or the whole bathroom thing has been an excuse to have two guards escort this giant instead of one without making themselves look like pathetic chickenshits.

Oakberry is intimidating, I won't lie. He's huge. Muscly, at least six and a half feet if I'm guessing correctly. Now that he's close, I can see his eyes clearly. They're jet black, except for…the fucking strikes. Another shifter, then. Thanks for getting me involved in this, Dad.

In here, like Flynn, Oakberry's scent is more obvious than it's been at the cells. I can't understand why I haven't recognized it back at the ward, but I will find out.

Oakberry grunts, pulling his arms away from the guards as he takes the empty seat. They chain him to the table and retreat to the wall. The look he's giving them tells me he's more than capable of snapping their necks without a second of regret if he really wants to.

However, Aedan Oakberry doesn't intimidate me at all. Beyond all logic, I still think he's cute, and his smell does the same things Derek's does to me.

I take my seat, hiding a swallow. Then I glance at Derek, but he shakes his head, folding his arms across his chest. "No way. Not now."

Here is that smoldering overprotectiveness again. My hand covers my snicker as my eyes roll toward Oakberry. What beast is he? I've never seen one that huge.

"Afternoon, Princess," he drawls in a gruff voice, looking at me like I'm a particularly tasty burger. "Are you going to ask some questions, or do you just want to stare into my eyes? Not that I mind a staring contest with a pretty lass like you."

Princess? I'd rather be called a bitch than this. I haven't heard that title since I left the MC. Does he know who I am, the MC Princess? Or is he just trying to rile me? "Professor or Ms. Beastly is how you address me."

"Oh, to be sure, your highness." He grins, leaning forward in his seat.

It's a challenge. He's baiting me. I chuckle. "Is that an Irish accent I detect?" It's faint, but it's there. "Scottish?"

"Right the first time, love." He winks at me. "Want to hear my tragic backstory?"

I do. I'm filled with the overwhelming urge to know everything about this hulking man. He reminds me of the fable my sister and I used to like a lot, the one with the lion with the thorn stuck in its paw. If I show him gentleness, will he be grateful like the beast in the tale? Or will he pounce and devour me?

Wolf likes that metaphor a little too much. My heart is racing, and my breath is coming quicker. I'm on high alert.

I take a few deep breaths, closing my eyes, focusing on the hammering of my heart. I don't let it take over and silence Wolf. I'm not here for a fight...or a quickie.

"As much as I love to stay and chat I only need you to answer a few questions."

"No nonsense, huh?"

"That's how I prefer it. Shall we?"

He leans back in his chair, and it creaks. I'm surprised it doesn't break underneath him. "Let's do."

NINE

AEDAN

Two things are obvious about this Beastly lass. One, she's sharp; sharp enough to be dangerous. Two, she'd make a wonderful wee snack. I take in her appearance, the grace of her neck, the softness of her skin, the swell of her tits, the curve of her arse. A truly wonderful snack. In either sense, really; I'd love to run my lips and tongue all over that skin. And take a bite or two.

I've kept to myself when she visited the cell earlier. Sure, I have a look at her backside since she's such a fine article, but I leave the rest to Ronan and his over-analysis of everything. I neither have much interest in people nor in his schemes. Unless it's about keeping his skinny fae arse safe.

Now that I'm alone with her, it's different. Her scent has been masked before by the dulling effect of that fucking ward and all the drugs and mix of stenches from the bastards I'm locked up beside. Her smell…makes me want to capture her in my claws and fly up into the sky. Take her to my nest and never give her back. God almighty above, it's been too long since I've been so close to a woman. And unlike Ronan, or Gianmarco and Flynn, the alternative does nothing for me.

Here I am, a big scary dragon all locked up in a cage, and here is Divina Beastly, a little princess delivered straight to my lair. These thoughts entertain me as I sit across from her in the interrogation room.

She doesn't like my pet names, I can tell, which makes me want to call her by them more. I'm not going to show a cop the respect of a title, but I'm not stupid enough to use her first name. She'll get mad about that too.

It's not just her smell or beauty that sends

these pulses straight to my cock. I know her type. She's got something to hide, a chip on her shoulder, and she makes up for it by being tough as nails. It's hot, and I plan on continuing to tease her because the reactions are golden.

Heh. Golden. Like my dragon. I'm hilarious.

"So no nonsense." She echoes my phrase back at me. "Did you kill Sean Chisholm?"

"Nope." I lean back in my seat to look as deliberately and annoyingly casual as I possibly can. "Is that it? Can I go?"

Behind her, the male detective chuckles. Her mouth twitches at the side, but she doesn't allow the smile. I don't think she's big on smiling in general. I know I've amused her, though. My hard skin tingles with satisfaction.

"Not quite, Mr. Oakberry," she says, proud and proper as Lady Muck. "I need a little more than that before I send you back to your friends. After all, you could be lying to me. Very easily."

"True. It could easily be a load of fibs," I agree. "I'm not O'Shea."

She raises her eyebrow but doesn't comment. Obviously, she isn't one who can be headed off on a tangent easily. "So do you lie?"

"Frequently," I grin, flashing my big teeth. "But not now."

Unimpressed, she stares at me. She looks small and delicate—most people do to me—but the hard look she's giving me makes me think she can kick my ass if she wants to. Or have me pinned for her satisfaction after a bit of wrestling. I'm down with either.

"Where were you this morning?" she asks.

"Oh, that's easy. I slept in."

"What about last night?"

I look away from her so I can wink at the guards. "Last night I was dealing in illegal contraband."

"Is that so? Like what?"

My eyes return to her. "Cigarettes. Phones. The shit from the outside that people will pay me a load for. Gotta have a hobby, right, Princess?"

"Contraband is a week in the hole. You sure that's what you want to go with?" the guard we've *accidentally* met on the way back snaps. I can't remember his name, but I know he's hurt Ronan once, before we've been moved to the new Ward E away from gen pop. I'm going to kill him for that one day.

I let out a low growl to make him flinch. "And how long in the hole is admitting to murdering an inmate?"

"So you did—" he starts.

"Please, leave the interrogation to me," Beastly interrupts. She's polite, but there's steel in her voice that forces the guard to shut his fucking hole and obey. She turns her attention back to me. "Is there someone who can vouch for what you're saying?"

"O'Shea was there, too. He's the brains. I'm the muscle." I flex my arm. "I'm sure you noticed."

Her mouthwatering lips purse. Is she hiding another smile? "Anyone who isn't your friend? Do you and O'Shea work alone?"

I smirk. Fair play to her. "No, we have an…ally, who works the gen pop. Outside of the crazy, high-risk ward."

"Have? Or had?"

I actually laugh. Yeah, I'd take her to my dragon cave. She'd be the jewel at the top of my pile. "Had indeed. Clever lass, aren't you?"

She doesn't deign to answer that. Instead, she takes out a photograph to show me. "Is that why you, your cellmate, and Sean Chisholm are in multiple photos together?"

"Or maybe Warden thinks I photograph well." I grin again. "Don't you? I see you gawking."

"So there was nobody else with you last night? Or this morning?"

"I can't rat out my customers. That's bad for business. And you won't see me on the cameras either. I make a point of that. But really, do I look like the kind of person who can sneak about? Have you seen the size of me?"

The way her pupils are dilating implies she has. She doesn't let it show on her expression, though. What does it take to get her to admit I make her wet?

"Appearances can be deceiving, Mr. Oakberry."

"They can indeed. Do you think I'm secretly a gentle flower then, your highness?"

She writes something down. "What time do you visit the exercise room?"

"Never. It's too small for me," I say, and she tosses the pen on the file in disapproval. "I know it's hard to believe this body is naturally fit," my chains rattle as I gesture at myself, "but any of the pleasant guards or even Warden can tell you I'm not lying."

"I see. Do you have any idea how Sean Chisholm died during his exercise slot this morning?"

"Horribly, I hope. He was a right gack. But if he wasn't burned alive, it wasn't me. I kind of have an M.O."

"He wasn't burned. He was strangled."

Who the fuck cares? "I bet he went out like a little bitch, too."

She goes back to her scribbling, unfazed by what I say. "Do you burn a lot of people alive, Aedan?"

"Not as many as I hope."

She consults her precious file. "It says here that when you burned down the clinic and were thrown in here for arson, nobody actually died. In fact, it seems like you saved someone's life."

Most people don't bother to correct me when I play the scary, arsonist killer card. After all, I look the part. And I don't like how she's painting me as a hero. That's not what happened. "I saved O'Shea. I knew he'd be useful to me. Nobody else."

"There was nobody else in the clinic." She keeps reading. "It looks like you waited until you thought all the patients and nurses had left."

She gives me too much credit. I didn't wait for anything. They were all just lucky it was after closing hours. The fact that Ronan was there was a coincidence, and even then, I didn't exactly save him out of the goodness of my heart. "If that's what it looks like in your file, then it's wrong."

She tilts her head, examining me. "You've

been in trouble with the warden a lot, haven't you?"

"Not nearly enough for either of us."

"And the guards?"

I show my teeth, not quite a grin. "They've been known to try to have a square go. Or more of a triangle, where I'm the pointy end."

"Try?" she asks.

This time I do grin, but I don't say anything.

She watches me for a moment, and I have the uncomfortable feeling of being x-rayed. "Who do you think would want to kill your *ally*?"

I roll my eyes. "Not me."

"He was entirely alone in that room, which doesn't make much sense. Can you think of any way someone might have gotten into such a secure room?"

Damn. She's really dangerous. And impressive with her calmness and determination to stay on topic and set her traps. "Not a clue, Princess." I can't quite figure out her game, but she doesn't fear me at all. I know that much. It excites me, and my cock pulses again.

Can she feel it, too? I'm not imagining the tension in the room, the heat slowly building. I want to ask her if she wants to have a go right now, just to see her reaction.

Part of me tells me to just go for it, launch myself over and kiss those full lips out of that concentrated frown. I won't make her if she doesn't want to, but my instincts tell me she does. A lot.

She does a good job at hiding it, but her quickened pulse, the rise in her temperature, the way she looks at my arms, my lips, my teeth…

I growl with the big twitch in my cock.

Here it is again. That move with her lips when she conceals her smile. She likes it when I growl? Looks like Divina Beastly does have a thing for beasts after all.

She glances down at her file. "Thank you, Mr. Oakberry."

"Is this the part where I'm carted back to sit with the rest of the cattle?"

"Pretty much." She nods at the guards, and they unchain me from the table and escort me to the door.

"Aedan?" she calls.

Stopping in my tracks, I can't help the smirk on my lips. That's the second time she's called me by my first name. Things are getting intimate with the pretty, little lass. I bet she's soaking her panties right now.

I turn, grinning. "Can't have enough of me

already, Princess?"

Her lips stretch into a small smile. Finally. I knew it. She fucking likes me. I let out another growl for her pleasure, hoping to see her nipples harden, too.

She tilts in her seat, her eyes holding mine. "Who's Bethany?"

I freeze, my head banging as if struck by a baton. A painful jolt zaps through me. "How do you know that name?" I snarl.

She doesn't shiver at the tone of my voice, but her eyes gleam gold, and her tits fall and rise with every rapid breath. I can't even enjoy it. All I can think of is my little Bethie.

My own hands are shaking, and all of a sudden my dragon is roaring inside like he hasn't since I started taking these godforsaken pills. He wants out. He wants to burn. I want to let him.

The hard scales scrape at the underside of my skin. My nostrils flare. Fire burns my chest. But she...

She stares at me with a warning. Beast to beast. Not the *beware, I can tear you apart, too* warning. But a *beware, you can't shift in here* warning. It smothers my heat, and I snap me out of it.

Another picture flashes in her hand. "The tattoo on your chest. Who is she? Or should I say *was* she?"

Bethany.

My baby sister. We never knew either of our dads, and our mother died when I was just fourteen, a couple years after we moved to this country. Bethie was only ten. She was terrified.

There was no way in hell I was going to let them take her away from me. They sent us between foster homes, but Bethany wasn't like I am. She wasn't tough. She was young, lonely. And human. There was no dragon inside her, just like Mum. I guess my dad, whoever he is, is to blame for that part. Or to thank, depending on the day. I don't know for sure, Mum never talked about mine or Bethie's. Probably thought the three of us were inseparable and didn't need anyone else. So did Bethie and I.

They kept trying to split us up. Turns out the kind of families who want a sweet little ten-year-old girl don't want a big, brawny, pyromaniac teenager with anger problems. And the kind of place that does want a lad like that isn't exactly the safest place in the world for an innocent, quiet little girl with health issues.

So one day, I just took her. I was fifteen, and as far as I was concerned, that was old enough to protect her on my own. We found somewhere to squat, I got involved with people I shouldn't have, but I didn't care as long as she was safe.

We found other shifters, too, but none of them were dragons, so they were suspicious and distanced themselves from me. I didn't have time for other humans. They'd shown me what they were really like when Bethany and I were thrown around like trash, and I wanted—I still want—nothing to do with them. The most important lesson I learned back then, the one I've held onto now, is that yourself is the only person you can really trust.

For years, I took care of my beautiful, little sister, managed to get her into a school, and we were fine on our own.

When she finished high school, she got a job in a shop. I was trying to get the money together to let her go to college, though who the fuck knows how I'd have managed that. I would have though. For her. She was clever, my Bethie. She deserved the best in life. Had she lived, she could have been great.

But Bethie got sick. She'd been sick before, but this...this was different. She needed help. So I scraped together any money I could get from anyone who'd hire me, as well as a few thefts and casual dealing, and took her to that fucking clinic.

My fists clench at the memory. My wrist collides with the cold metal as my muscles flex.

Divina's eyes are on me. "Was she your girlfriend? Your sister? Your daughter?"

An urge to snap my teeth in her face burns me. Nobody gets to talk about Bethany. Nobody. That fucking bitch is lucky my hands are chained, and I'm being suppressed by these meds.

"Aedan? Do you hear me?" she presses.

I grunt. I don't want to answer her. She doesn't get to know. "Bethany couldn't have killed your Chisholm. She's as dead as him. Are we done?"

She waits a beat, and then tucks the photo back into her file. "Until I need you again, yes."

I don't resist as the guards shove at me to get me to walk out of the room. They don't try any of their usual shit on the way back, though. Maybe they see the way I'm holding myself and realize I'll happily bash their heads off the wall repeatedly, cuffs or no cuffs.

After reliving the events with Bethany, the quiet makes my fists clench. I want them to attack me. I want to fight. I want to shift and rip out their throats with my sharp teeth, and then burn what's left of the corpses until nobody can recognize them anymore.

The other three inmates are all sitting together, talking in low voices, when I walk back through the door to the holding cell.

I put my hard face on, pulling myself together. They don't get to know I'm upset either. "Gossiping, lads?" I ask as one of the guards undoes my cuffs. I hold my hands together to stop them from swinging.

Ronan looks up and gives me one of his patent wicked smiles. He's discovered something or thought of something. He's got a plan in the works; I know from his expression I've seen so many times before. "Just making friends, Aedan."

"Enough chatter," the guard barks, and all four of us turn to look at him. I growl, and he takes a step back. His face turns red, and he yells more to make up for it, as if that covers it up. "Connelly! On your feet!"

"You mean you won't carry me?" Gianmarco asks him in a musical twang. "What a shame. I was so looking forward to being carted around in your arms, Rivera."

"You are asking for the stick," he snarls, reaching for his baton.

Gianmarco raises an eyebrow. "Not usually until the third date, good sir. I have my pride." He stands.

Ronan lets out a low laugh. I sit beside him as Rivera cuffs Gianmarco, and the second guard leads him out of the room.

When the door closes, I snort. That demon has balls. "What a bunch of arseholes."

"How did your meeting with Ms. Beastly go?" Ronan asks.

"She's…a bitch like he said." I look over at Killian, who's sitting silent now that I'm here. "She gave you the third degree, too?"

"Something like that," Killian mumbles.

I wait for him to say more, but he doesn't. Eventually, I shrug, and go back to Ronan. "You're going to like her. She's a right clever clogs. She won't fall into your head-messing tricks so easily."

"Good. It won't be any fun without a challenge." He has a shit-eating grin on his face.

"What are you planning?" I demand.

He glances at Killian and leans forward. "Come closer, and I'll tell you."

TEN

GIANMARCO

Does she think I don't hear the low groan she lets out when I walk in? 'Cause I do, and it delights me. I can't be certain, but it looks to me like our very own dragon has gotten her all hot and bothered. Following it with me is the last thing she wants.

I practically flop into the chair, winking at Rivera, savoring the taste of his discomfort as he attaches my cuffs to the table. He backs off quickly before I can make another suggestive comment. My lip twitches in amusement. Homophobes are so *easy*.

As soon as he's away from me, I lean forward. "Well, there are certainly worse people to have me in cuffs."

"Mr. Connelly." She opens a page in her file. "Thank you for joining us."

"Careful who you thank around here, Ms. Beastly. You don't want to be throwing a *thank you* around when it's dear Ronan's turn. His kind will take advantage of that sort of thing."

The guards don't react at all to what I've said. Are they in the know? Or are they just too stupid to notice? She, on the other hand, flinches, giving me the reaction I want, even if she manages to cover it up as she brushes her hair to the side.

She peers at her detective friend, who doesn't seem to have noticed. His eyes are narrowed and glaring at me instead. Possessive boyfriend? No, no, the taste in the air around them is wonderfully unrequited. I love it. This is going to make things so much easier for me.

"Derek." There's a tenderness to her tone when she says his name. Ah, not unrequited, just unconsummated. She's torn up by something. It's stopping her from going ahead with this handsome fellow. How delectably tragic. This is the kind of petty drama I've been missing locked up in this shit hole.

Perhaps she thinks her supernatural identity means he's off limits? I suppose she's not entirely wrong, given who she is.

Divina Beastly herself.

The aura of darkness she carries around wherever she goes takes my breath away. The second Flynn has said her name, a delectable chill runs through me and quickly turns into a throb in my dick.

Do you even know who you really are? What you really are?

I can't wait to get inside that pretty, dark head of yours.

It's not as easy as when I'm not held back by the ugly pills, but all I need to do is find an entrance. Once I'm in her head, I'll find a veritable feast. She's wound tighter than a watch; it won't be too difficult once I get started. "You have such pretty eyes. Is that a fleck of *gold* I see?"

She doesn't blink, but Detective Bright— no, *Derek*—gives me a hard look before glancing uncertainly at her. "You sure you don't need me here?"

She does a convincing job with her poker

face as she nods, but I can feel the flavor of her nervousness in my bones. Does she hate it that I know she has a supe side or has the Ronan comment shaken her?

Maybe it's only sparked her curiosity. She wants to know more, but she doesn't want her pet human to know what's happening. To protect him? How sweet. "Yes, Detective," I drawl. "Why don't you go? I promise I won't bite. Not unless she asks me to."

He clenches his fists, and Divina gets up from her seat, nodding at the far corner of the room. They talk to each other in low voices out of earshot. I don't know what she says to convince him, but he doesn't look happy about it as he and one of the two meathead guards leave the room.

Divina sits down again, her hands folded on the table. "What do you mean *his kind*, Mr. Connelly?"

"Please. My friends call me Gianmarco."

"We're not friends. Answer the question."

I wink. "Well, my lovers call me Marco."

She blushes. For the love of my fucking unholy father, she blushes. I bite my lip, devouring her beauty, and breathe out slowly. Her throat dips with a swallow as she holds her hands steady, pressing them down on the table to keep her dignity intact. There's my window. That moment of weakness. Of forbidden desire. It's not hard now to make my way inside. Even if, with the drugs, I can only scratch the surface.

It's *dark* in here. In her mind. In her soul. I can feast on Divina Beastly for weeks and never go hungry. She hates being a shifter. She hates her family. She loves her family. She doesn't know how to reconcile these two diametric opposites, and like the way it is with her human yearnings and her beasts, the opposition is tearing her apart. She makes herself cold, distant to overcome it.

But…there's something else in here, deeper, more hidden. Something that fills *me* with forbidden desire. Now, it's my turn to tremble and swallow.

"What do you know about O'Shea, *Marco*?" she demands.

Oh, fuck me sideways and call me Nasty Bitch. Marco? She is trying to manipulate me right back. Or is she actually flirting? Fuck, now I understand what my father wanted—wants—with her. *What the fuck is your game, D? Isn't that what your lover boy calls you?* "I can't just give away other people's secrets, Divina, dear. Or should I call you D?"

She twitches at my comeback. *Two can play this game, darling.*

"Fine." She tries to keep the quiver out of her voice, but I can still detect it. The confusion and the tension, mixed with a low, dark need. "Where were you last night and this morning?"

"The answer to both is the same. I was making sweet, tender love to my cellmate. You know him, don't you? Flynn Killian?"

I catch the look of disgust on the guard's face and give him another wink. To her credit, Divina barely reacts at all. Perhaps she already knows about Flynn's proclivities. Or perhaps she just wants to imagine all three of us having a tumble. Soft skin, hard muscle, three bodies writhing in pleasure. Flynn and Divina, naked, skin against skin, his lips giving me pleasure while mine see to hers. I moan. My aching dick needs an adjustment.

She picks up her pen. "You and Flynn are romantically involved?"

I let out a laugh, the kind that reverberates around the room and gets directly under her skin. "I'm not sure there's much *romantic* to what we do, but yes." I nod at the guard. "I'm sure Rivera can confirm, too; he's a bit of a voyeur, and he has access to the cameras."

He snarls at me, about to pounce, but she tilts in her seat, glancing at him. "Can you wait outside? I won't be long."

He clenches his teeth at me. "That's not protocol, ma'am."

I wink at him again, and she shakes her head, coming back to me. "Unfortunately, the cameras were wiped that night. No guard can corroborate anything of the sort."

I don't know about the security cameras, and I make it my business to know everything. "That *is* unfortunate. Were you hoping to watch?"

"Reviewing evidence is part of my job."

Delighted by her smart answer, I grin. To her credit, she keeps her cool. I am really fond of this one. "You're quite the professional, darling. But don't worry. I like women too."

"Dandy." She takes out a picture from her file. It's me, with my arm slung around Chisholm's shoulder, whispering something in his ear. I remember that day. I have a very nice, shiny double ended dildo to remember it by. Sometimes, Flynn and I like to go cheek-to-cheek. "How did you know the victim, Sean Chisholm?"

"Intimately."

"You were also involved with Chisholm?"

"No, no, nothing so banal." I examine my fingernails, despite how difficult it is with these stupid cuffs. "He had services I required. In exchange, I'd sometimes offer some of my own."

Now she's surprised, her eyes wide, her eyebrows raised. "You prostituted yourself for contraband?"

I give another laugh and then shrug. "No, darling. He had something I wanted. I had something he wanted. It was a fair transaction."

She writes something down. "Mr. Connelly—"

"Marco."

"—can you please tell me—"

"How is Rina?"

She can't hide her flinch this time, and I smile, widely, locking my gaze with hers.

"What?" she asks in a low growl. The threat in it jerks my cock.

I just keep on smiling.

She stares at me for a moment, her eyes shining like a new coin. She inclines in her seat but barely looks at Rivera, growling louder.

"Easy, darling. You know he doesn't have to leave to do this privately."

Slowly, her eyes return to me.

"We can go somewhere really nice, if you'll let me," I add.

Her breaths hitch as her fingers squeeze that pen, almost smashing it. She's pondering it. Weighing her options. She's guarded herself for years. To let a demon inside her head is tricky business.

The risk sets my flesh in goosebumps. I can't let her think for too long or I'll miss my chance. "Scared, Ms. Beastly?"

She tosses her pen and closes the file, her lip curling up in a snarl. "No, *Marco*. I'm not scared of your kind."

A pleasurable moan seeps out of me. "Let's dance, darling."

ELEVEN

DIVINA

I must be crazy to let a demon in my head. After all I've been through with the devil himself.

I stay away from my family. Deny myself any joy of intimacy. Set barricade after barricade all my life to protect my mind, my heart and my soul from the darkness.

Now, I allow a fucking demon to a buffet of my secrets, memories, desires and sins.

My wits along with my instincts and beasts are bellowing at me like wailing sirens, but I don't heed their warnings. How can I? That fucker knows my sister's name. He knows who we are, which means he knows Damien Pattison.

Does Gianmarco work for him? Does he know what the fucking devil has seen in my sister and me to try to steal us the day we were born? To mark us for all eternity?

Taking a second look at Gianmarco Connelly, at his emerald eyes and dark blond hair… I'm such an idiot for not recognizing it right from the start. Must be the ward's strange inhibiting effect that has muddled my brains.

He's the devil's son. Another one of Damien Pattison's bastards.

"Ooooh. It's fucking cold in here." Connelly makes amused sounds as he finds his way inside my head. He snaps his fingers, his hands no longer cuffed, lighting the dark corner we're crammed in with a flame. "But I'm sure I can warm it up, and not just with my hellfire."

I shake my head, creating some noise of random, useless thoughts so he won't get cozy. And to distract myself from the seductive temptation he is. As much as I hate it, he's so incredibly sexy, and my body reacts in ways that confuse me when I'm around him. He probably feels it, too, and I can't confirm his doubts for him. I won't let him prey on something as stupid as my libido.

Because that's all there is. A chemical reaction to his beauty. Nothing else.

"Thank you, darling, for the invitation. I was barely able to scratch that surface. I don't think I could have gotten here on my own with all the fucking meds they pump in me every day." His bright eyes hover around, and he makes those sex sounds again. "I can live here forev—"

I grab his neck and squeeze, cornering him further, silencing his shit. "How do you know her name?"

"So aggressive," he rasps. "So hot."

The involuntary throbs between my legs as his breath fans my face, my fingers feel his skin, and my breasts brush his chest irritate me. I cling to my rage as a shield. "Answer the fucking question."

He chokes on a laugh. "You know I didn't kill Sean Chisholm. Nor did any of the other three. Why are you wasting your time and ours? I mean I get it you're here to profile us, know our stories. But you already know mine, don't you? It's in that file of yours. Poor, little, unloved, orphaned bastard, tossed from home to home, falling into petty thefts for attention.

Living on the edge every day until an armed robbery goes tragically wrong and my incredibly handsome ass ends up in here. It's nothing too original. But you? You're much more interesting."

My eyes widen. The beasts rumble in my chest. For various reasons. "How do you mean?"

"I understand your resentment." His voice lowers now, clear, soft, fucking melodic, as if my fist isn't fastened around his throat. "You can't even understand how you feel about your mother anymore. She has a lot to answer for, doesn't she? Mixing you up with all of this, when all you've ever wanted, what any child wants, is a normal life. And then she dies on you? What the fuck?" His eyes burn holes into me. "My mother left me too. It hurts. All you want to know is why. How could she act like she did in life? How could she just die?"

All the heat rushes from my body. A lump clogs my throat. Pain slashes my heart as if it's being ripped from my chest. "How do you know about my sister and my mother, you low fuck?"

"I liked it better when you called me Marco."

My hand tightens even harder around his neck, my other hand turning into a wolf paw.

"You're going to stop your bullshit now and fucking answer me."

"But you already know…about our common enemy, D."

My nose scrunches. "Warden Collins?"

"C'mon. That ass is just a tool."

"Then who is our common enemy…Marco?"

He blinks, but then he grins. "I was a toddler myself when my dad delivered you and your twin, but your story still shakes the underworld today."

Wolf bares her fangs, my eyes aglow. "Are you saying Collins works for the devil? The murder of Sean Chisholm is a part of Damien Pattison's screwed up plan to burn us all?"

"Not directly, but isn't everything horrible and evil a part of the devil's plan to burn us all?" He wets his lips in slow motion. Then his eyes dip to my own lips.

His gaze smolders with arousal even though my fangs are out. Reflexively, I stare at his mouth. At his so fucking kissable mouth. Damn it. I drag my eyes away, reminding myself this is the demon's doing. He's seducing me, but I'm not that weak. I'm not that…whatever the devil thinks I am. "Then who says you're not the tool who killed Chisholm? Damien Pattison is your father, not your enemy."

"Father of the year, I assure you." He snorts. "Is your father why you're here, Divina? You know, basically I'm your step-daddy. Or is it step-uncle? Depends on what you call the other three that raised you. Didn't your mother have four husbands? One of them is my half-brother. Inferno. Another rejected bastard of our beloved Damien."

Every time he mentions my family, my mother, I want to gouge his eyes out of their cavities. Every time he swipes or darts or does anything with his tongue, like he does now, an urge to swirl mine around his takes over me.

He leans in, his breaths blazing as they fall on my lips. "We shouldn't make a big deal out of that, though, considering the way you're looking at me."

A shudder runs through me for a split-second, and I close my eyes. I know he's playing me. For Damien? For himself? He's provoked me to let him into my head, and I've complied. He turns out to be stronger than I've thought. Is he going to kiss me? No, he's waiting for me to kiss him. To fall. To open another gate for him.

Why?

When I open my eyes, I summon all my energy to contain Wolf. I'm in better control as a human. And I need to be. In control. Can't let him win any longer.

"You've tricked me to be here. Is that part of the plan? Damien's plan?" I ask.

He flashes his teeth in a charming grin. Then the back of his hand brushes my cheek. I flinch, swallowing, throbbing. He swipes his thumb ever so slowly across my lower lip, and my lashes flutter.

Tell him to stop.
Break his fingers.
Rip him to shreds.

"The things I'd give for your kiss," he whispers.

He's taking advantage of me. He's lying through his ass. He's seducing me for a reason that can't be anything but horrific. Why am I just standing here? Why the fuck am I enjoying it this much?

"Because you can't help it. The darkness. Your attraction to it you keep denying," he answers me. "You can't do it forever. Just like the beasts, it has to come out at some point, or it will eat you up. Deep inside you, you know, don't you?"

I tremble. "Know what?"

"What he sees in you. Why he wants you."

I stare into his eyes, our lips an inch apart, my mind a big dark cloud, spinning with temptation. One kiss can't hurt. I'll feel his lips on mine just once, and then I'll stop.

My hand eases off his neck and slides to his chest. My other hand finds his waist and feels his abdomen. The shudder that runs through him under my touch pleases me, as much as how well-toned his body is under that jumpsuit. His hands slither to my hips and pull me to him. A moan slips off my mouth when I feel his erection poking my stomach.

"Kiss me, Divina."

"Marco…" My eyes train on his lips and back to his eyes. "Get the fuck out of my head."

His eyes twitch. Taken aback for a moment, he glares at me. Then he chuckles yet his expression dark. "Your dad has always blamed you for not accepting your supernatural side. He wants you to be like your mother, always telling you she was the most accepting person he's ever met. After all, she's the only one who loved him despite how monstrous he is. But if she's really that accepting, why didn't she become an immortal when she had four supernatural husbands who would gladly turn her? Why did she stay human when she could have lived forever with her children? Why did she prefer to die on you, D?"

I shove him off me with a loud growl. "Get the fuck out of my head!"

His laugh echoes inside me. I squeeze my eyes shut and place my hands on my ears, blocking away his face and voice, taking deep breaths.

"Are you all right, darling?"

My eyes snap open at the rattling chains. My head jerks right and left. I'm back in the interrogation room. Guard Rivera is staring at me like I'm nuts. And that fucking demon, chained to the table as he's ever been, is smirking at me.

Leaning forward, I even my breath. "Did you kill Sean Chisholm, Connelly?"

He leans forward, too, looking me directly in the eye. "I most certainly did not."

I believe him, but I don't let it show. "I'll call you back when I need you."

TWELVE
DIVINA

I need air.

Scratch that. I need to get out of here.

If I leave now, it's too suspicious, but I just can't stay in this room a second longer. I remember passing the bathrooms for visitors and staff on the way here. I can have a moment to myself there, at least.

I scribble a note for Guard Rivera in case he returns with O'Shea before I do. Then I push the door open. Luckily for me, it isn't on the same auto-lock the exercise room is.

The cool, tiled wall in the bathroom provides me a brief refuge from the searing cage my body has become. My entire body feels like skin after a bad sunburn, raw and oversensitive.

I enter a stall, lock the door, close the toilet's lid, and sit down. Then I bury my head in my hands and bid my sobs free.

A demon has seduced me, and I've let him, but that's not why I'm crying. Yes, he makes me feel exposed, naked, and not in a good way. But I've stopped him before the damage is done. I've been strong enough. At least, before he mentioned my mother.

I don't think about her, not ever, because when I do, I lose control. My feelings toward her are too complex to bear. My anger at her actions and my sadness at her death are in constant battle with each other, as different as Wolf and Reindeer and even less able to come together peacefully.

Vixen Legend. My mother.

The human who has danced with the devil.

She's the reason I live this life of conflict. Connelly is right about that. She and her harem of four, not one of them a human. Nothing satisfies her except the supernatural. Slasher, Inferno, Uncle Carter and my own father. Not just a bunch of vampires, demons and shifters. They're the devil's rejects. Members of a gang who live on the outside even amongst outsiders.

A fucked up, dysfunctional family that wouldn't be mine if she just chose to close her legs and run away before she had that threesome with my father and his own brother.

But no, she *spreads*—like Inferno says—for the two screwed up shifters, in the woods, next to a fucking dead vampire. Who in their right mind does that?

And the result? Uncle Carter fathers my twin sister the same night Dad fathers me; the mad blood-tinged werewolf and the deformed reinwolf, both give their love and their seed to my Mom. This human who can't have enough of supernatural dick and even invites two more supes to her bed.

I don't call them Daddy or Uncle, by the way. They are Slasher and Inferno. I only have one dad, Terror. And two uncles, his brother Carter Beastly, previously known as Mad Dog, and Mom's brother, Uncle Malcolm, or Dasher, the Blood Demons turned-vampire VP.

What child can grow up in this…? I don't even have a name for it. Of course, the devil will spare nothing to have Rina and I as his children.

He snatches us from Mom's womb, aiming to give us to his mate to raise as their own. It doesn't work out that way, obviously, but the devil doesn't just let his plans drop after a failure. He still wants me. He still wants Rina. He sees something in us, a darkness, and he won't stop until he possesses it.

Yet Vixen Legend doesn't choose to stay alive to protect us. Too selfish to even live for her daughters.

Accepting my ass. Connelly is right again. Having four messed up supes for mates isn't acceptance. It's just staying high on orgasms. If she really accepted them, she would be alive.

But she dies. She leaves us behind. All of us. Alone.

I sit up, wiping my fingers over my eyes quickly, angrily. This is her fault. It's *all* her fault.

If it weren't for her, I wouldn't be in this mess. I wouldn't let a demon in my head and enjoy it.

It's not just him. I've let them all into my head, though not in the same way. Flynn, and my illogical need to protect him and the guilt that roils in my belly for him, as if his turning into a hybrid monster is my mistake. Well, I've convinced him so damn well in my classes monsters don't exist. Maybe if I have warned him, given him a clue…

Then there's Oakberry. Another shifter, and one of the biggest, most intimidating men I've ever come across. He sets my instincts on a full blast, harboring on extreme edges. Reindeer and Wolf want to retreat around him, and when those two are on the same page, I can be sure the danger is real. Yet Aedan brings out a feral wildness in me I can barely keep under my skin.

I hope the mask I've been wearing during the interview is good enough, but something tells me he knows how he makes me feel. It isn't only the fear. He is dangerous, and I like it so much.

If my mom hasn't made me a fucking shifter….

No, I'm lying to myself. My attraction to these criminals isn't supernatural. The shivers that run through me as I picture the veins showing at the crook of Flynn's arms or Aedan's coal-black eyes or the devilish way Marco smiles at me, feel very…human. Deliciously human. Human in a way I haven't been in a while.

Human like her.

Tears sting my eyes again. God dammit. I miss her so fucking much.

I burst out of the stall and splash water over my face. Then I take out my phone, pushing all my feelings underneath—as I always do. There is a more pressing matter now. My dad is right, and he and the rest of the MC need to know about it.

I'm about to call him before I stop. I can't risk being overheard, so I text him instead.

Dad. You were right.

A few seconds later, my phone pings.

?

Always so eloquent, Terror. I text back, describing in short terms Ward E, and the way Collins is trying to pin the murder on these four particular supes. I neglect the part where I let a demon fuck my mind.

Dad's response is instant. I have to read it over a few times before I'm sure of what it says. *Get out of there, baby girl.*

What? No!

Chuck the case, Divina. It's not safe anymore. Leave it to us. You've done your part.

I don't just give up cases, no matter how much I want to be far, far away from the supernatural mess that keeps creeping back into my life every time I think it is gone.

My phone buzzes. *Please.*

My Dad—Terror—is saying please? Begging me to get off the case he's begged me to take in the first place? He must be really worried about what's going on here, and that's…

Well, fuck it. I'm only here because of him and our deal. If he thinks I've done my part, and he wants to take over the case, maybe I should let him. The thought makes me uncomfortable, but being here, getting involved in this mass conspiracy…it's not what I signed up for.

It's probably for the best anyway. My emotions are jumbled, and maybe Derek and Chief are right; my perspective on the supernatural and the way I'm allowing myself to get involved with the suspects are clouding my judgment.

With Aedan and his intense, dangerous stare, Flynn and the coldness that's taken over the boy I used to know, and Marco and how he is still messing around in my head long after our conversation is over…I'm too close to see things objectively.

My fingers hover over the button, and the tearing indecision inside me has— for once— nothing to do with my conflicting beasts. I know what this is. It's a conflict between the human and the supe. I need to choose a side.

Am I a supe with a duty to help my kind or am I a human who shouldn't give a shit about all this? Do I stay and help those inmates get the justice they deserve even if they're monsters, or do I take the out Terror has given me and go back to the human life I cherish so much?

My phone buzzes again. *D?*

I have one more suspect to interview, I text, unable to prevent the defiance that I always feel when Dad tells me what to do.

Fine. But then you get out of there, baby girl.

Ok, I text back, ignoring the bile in my throat, and then I pocket my phone. I'll do this final interrogation. Then I'm done. I'll get my ass and Derek's out of here and go get lectured by Chief and bear Tracy's gloating as I tell them I want off the case.

Perfect.

I have a better chance to solve the tortured girlfriend case than this one anyway.

After another moment to clean my face at the sink, erasing all evidence of my tears, I head back to the interrogation room.

Guard Rivera gives me a disapproving look when I open the door. "You can't just wander around the prison by yourself, ma'am. These people are dangerous."

I want to laugh. Does he have any idea just

how dangerous these people are? Or how dangerous I can be, if I let myself? Instead, I force an apologetic look on my face. "Yes. I'm sorry. I just really needed to go." I flutter my eyelashes. "Girl problems, you know."

He grunts, uncomfortable, and moves to the side to let me in.

Ronan O'Shea is sitting at the table, already cuffed, smiling up at me as if we've been best friends our whole lives. I remember Connelly warning me not to thank him and Oakberry's comment about lies. O'Shea's violet eyes—they are violet, there's no mistaking it now—lock on mine, and it's like every part of me is holding its breath.

"Hello, Divina." My heart thuds at the way he says my name, and a sharp twinkle echoes in my bones. His eyes are still on me, unblinking, and I feel like they're carving a tattoo on my soul, never to leave.

What the hell are you, O'Shea?

THIRTEEN
RONAN

The girl is watching me like I'm a particularly difficult math problem. It's flattering, but I'm used to it. She does a good job of appearing composed, especially since it's just her, me, and that guard Rivera now. Presumably, she's sent her detective friend and the other guard away on some errand so she can freely chat with Gianmarco.

Her composure is as real as the current

color of my hair. I can't read her mind like a demon can, but whatever has happened with Gianmarco has taken a toll on her. Her entire bearing is different. What words of his are spinning in her head? What information has he stolen from her lips in return?

I keep smiling at her, at the intense scrutiny in those bottomless, blue eyes. She's already building a profile of me in her head. Maybe some of it is close to true, but I doubt it. Mystery shrouds me, and I lean into that shroud, letting it envelop me. I don't intend to ever be clear to anyone.

"Hello, Ronan," she greets back.

A spark runs down my spine as she uses my first name. Clever girl. Does she know about the power of names? That's how my magic works. How all magic works. Know the names of all things, use them to interact with nature and convince it to do my bidding. And if I know people's names, I can commune with them, too.

Then anything is possible.

Like healing. My favorite fae power. I can use a name to anchor a person to this life while the physical magic works its way through their system, repairing their wounds, curing their sickness.

But not all our powers are favorable. A

name gives power, and it takes power. Does Divina Beastly know that as she looks at me and her lovely lips form my name once more?

I enjoy what it does to my body, the tingling it sends to all my extremities. She pronounces it with the long *oh* so common around here, *r-oeh-nen,* but from her it sounds lyrical. I've always loved music, though something tells me she doesn't want to sing with me now.

"Can you tell me where you were this morning from six to eight?"

"Yes," I reply.

She waits. I wait too.

Her elbows find the table as she smirks. "*Will* you tell me your whereabouts when one of your friends was being murdered?"

"I'd rather not, and Chisholm was not my friend."

"Do you always answer questions so…literally?"

"I am very careful with my words, Ms. Beastly."

It's just her last name, but it's enough to make her tremble, even if she doesn't know why. I doubt she gets the power that exists in words, especially the ones that are used to identify creatures. She doesn't know when I use her name in exactly the right cadence, I am commanding her attention, linking us together through my voice, imposing my will every time I say it. I look forward to what will happen the first time I name her fully.

She's flustered, caught off-guard by her own reaction. It's in her face as she suddenly can't hold my gaze and her eyes shift toward Rivera. "Can you…?"

He sighs. "It's not protocol, ma'am."

"I don't give a shit. Just wait outside please. I won't be long anyway."

He gives a resigned nod. Apparently, this is a repeat of a dance they've already done. "Your funeral," he mumbles, and then he glares at me. "I'll be right outside the door, inmate. Don't try anything stupid."

I don't even acknowledge him as he walks out of the room and closes the door behind him. He's visible outside the single tiny window in the room, but he can't hear us anymore.

"Do you want me all to yourself, Ms. Beastly?" I give her my most cryptic smile.

The gold in her eyes sparkles. Just being around me is affecting her, bringing her supernatural side to the forefront. It's not her fault. I am pure magic. "Why did Connelly warn me not to thank you?" she asks, her question about my whereabouts suddenly unimportant to her.

Interesting. "So you don't know what I am yet?"

"No. It would be helpful if I did. Are you going to tell me?"

"What will you give me for that information?"

She grimaces. "I'll work it out myself then. I ask the questions here. Explain what he meant."

I approve of her tenacity. "Thanking creates debt. My kind doesn't like debt left unpaid."

"And your kind is?"

"Powerful," I say softly, letting the word float in the air like a leaf on the wind. "Ancient. Beyond your comprehension."

"My comprehension may be better than you think…Ronan." She studies me. "What keeps happening to me when you say my name?"

"Huh?! You noticed?"

"I'm not an idiot."

"No, you're not. You're…" *Many things I can't fathom yet, but they're all wonderful.* "Names have power, Ms. Beastly. If I say it in just the right way, I can use your name to heal you or to hurt you, as I see fit. It takes energy, and I can't always do it with the suppressants, but I admit I've been playing with yours just a little bit."

A frown crosses her face—not an upset one, but the kind a chess master wears for her final tournament match. "You're not a demon…"

A demon! I'm offended by the very notion. Demons are forces of evil, even the *good* ones who try to improve their lot in life. I'm above such petty matters. My kind predates, outlives, any notions of human morality. "No, I am not," I stress. "Nor a vampire. Nor a shifter, like you. What is your beast?"

She flinches when I call her a shifter but otherwise doesn't react.

"Don't be coy." I keep my voice soft. "You're hiding a lot of power behind that human façade, aren't you?"

Her eyes dart to mine, as if she hates being reminded of what she is, then away again.

"You're observant. Your brains are unquestionable. But there's an animal there, too. What is it?"

Her glowing eyes meet mine again. The power that surges out of her stings like a slap to the face. There's more than one animal inhabiting her soul, and there's something else inside her that makes that power burn like a red-hot flame. I don't have time to examine it before it's gone. I don't know how she does it, but she shoves her magic back down, burying it in a heartbeat.

"So…" She taps her pen on the table. "With the name thing, the debt thing, the claim that you can't lie, and—"

"My eyes? My irresistible appearance? The draw you feel toward me?" I'm going to kill Aedan for telling her I can't lie. Idiot.

She keeps tapping, her eyes pensive, ignoring what I've said completely. "You're a wizard?"

She throws it out as a joke, but my belly clenches in annoyance. A *wizard* indeed. I've had my fill of humans pretending they are magic-sensitive over the generations. They're not; they're just charlatans in robes with no respect for the power of names, the power of nature. What they think of as magic is a poor excuse for the power my kind possesses. I don't need to listen to it from this girl. One of the only plus sides about living in this iron-infused hell of a time period is that nobody believes in magic anymore.

"Do you like children's stories?" I ask, even though I shouldn't let my pride get the better of me like this. Something in the way she asks questions makes me want to prove myself to her.

Her silence and nonchalance around me provoke me further.

"*Rumpelstiltskin*? A fine fellow who did a good job and was tricked by a cruel woman who reneged on her debt by using his true name against him?"

She doesn't utter a word. She keeps staring, unblinking, as if she were made of stone.

My jaws clench. "How about *Tam Lin*, where Janet steals a man who is rightfully in debt to a queen all for her own? Have you read Tolkien? The hobbit goes to rather extreme lengths not to give his name to the dragon, though of course apart from shifters the dragons died out long ago—"

"Are you saying you're a faerie?" Her eyebrows arch in something between shock and disbelief.

My pride, my stupid accursed pride, speaks for me. "I am not a *faerie*." I'm unable to keep the edge out of my tone, just like when I've had the same discussion with Gianmarco. "I am *fae*."

She snorts. "I don't believe in faeries."

My long fingers dig into my palm as I lean forward. "I am not Tinkerbell. I do not need your belief to thrive. My kind existed long before yours, and we will outlive you by millennia. We were made when Earth was born, when she first breathed her name. Our children first cried when the first leaf blossomed, and the first laugh of a fae baby brought the first rain. Our magic is the world. The world is our magic. We know the names of everything, and we live in harmony with it. Your kind—no, humankind—has corrupted our mother, poisoning her oceans, tainting her land, and my kind has been driven from our home. You are killing our connection. You are killing the planet. One day, we will all return to Faerie, and then your world will burn around your ears, shifter. Then we shall see what I care for your *beliefs*."

The cadence of my voice has toppled kings, but Divina Beastly observes me as though I am just a particularly interesting animal caged at a zoo. She writes something down, not in her file—in a separate notebook, which she slips back into her pocket.

"I appreciate the answer." She doesn't thank me, even though that would be the most common speech pattern. It fills me with a strange mixture of rage, pride and excitement. It's not often that I am matched in intelligence, but this lovely lady is a quick learner.

"Now, I need a different answer to a different question. Your whereabouts this morning. And last night, too, please." She picks up her pen, poising it over the paper in the file with a steely look in my direction.

Well now. This girl is…infuriating. I'm not sorry for what I'm going to do to her when the time comes. She deserves it and more. Yet I have this inexplicable affinity toward her. I do like her a lot. Perhaps I will play along for a bit after all.

I try to stretch my arms, but of course my wrists are bound, and I don't dare to move them too close to the iron laced hooks in the table at risk of injury. "I am sure in your questioning of my esteemed colleague Mr. Oakberry, you learned what we were doing last night. As for this morning, I was working on my novel. It's a trifle, really; a notebook with all my scribbling. I can show you if you like."

"In English?"

I blink. Hard. That throws me off. I lose my conversational footing for a second. "What…do you mean?"

She gestures at the ring of names around my wrist. "Those aren't English. I've never seen that language before."

I'm impressed and taken aback by her wits. My friends telling me about her skill is something, witnessing it in action is something else. I'm not used to people noticing that the ancient symbols are a language. It's as old as time itself, the language of my people, half-forgotten to history. My father loved it. He made sure my brothers and I were fluent, both in speaking and writing.

I pull my sleeve down to cover the tattoo, and my nostrils flare. "They're names." Four names, which I won't give to her. They are all I have left of my family. My brothers, Michael and Kiernan. My parents, Caoimhe and Lorcan. All gone, now.

She writes something down, more like checking something off a list. "Another question, how did you know the victim?"

"In passing, for business, as I'm sure Aedan has told you."

"Do you exercise?"

"Occasionally. Nothing like Killian and never in that room."

"Why not?"

"Have you seen its door?"

She blinks for a moment, but then she smirks. "Iron. Of course."

"Now you understand I was nowhere near the crime scene, and I didn't kill Sean Chisholm."

Her eyes narrow, the scrutiny in them holds my attention for what seems to be forever.

Has she analyzed the others so thoroughly? I can imagine how Aedan has reacted to her inspection. I am surprised they've finished their time fully clothed.

"And how do I know you're telling me the truth?" she asks.

"I always speak the truth." I can't speak an untruth even if I want to. None of my kind can say anything that isn't true. That doesn't mean we can't not tell the truth. I've gotten very, very good over my thousands of years at clever wordplay, and I can make people believe whatever I want them to without needing to utter any falsehoods. It's a much better use for my mind than making up stories anyway.

"If that's the case, do you know who killed Sean Chisholm?"

"Yes."

No shock on her face. Instead, her palms are on the table, sliding on the metal in my direction. She takes a deep breath and leans forward, so close I can feel her breaths on my skin. "Who did it, Ronan?"

I eye her hands that are a few inches away from my chains. Does she know what I can do if I just grab her hand? Of course not, or she won't come so close to me, move that freely around me without an ounce of fear. "I refuse to tell you. Not yet. Though I think you already have a suspicion."

That doesn't surprise her either. "Was it one of the four of you?"

"No."

"And I'm supposed to just take your word for it?"

"Yes…Divina."

We're both staring at each other, a little out of breath, like the first unexpected kiss with a new lover. She arranges her face into something serious and retreats to her file, but she fails to hide the shake to her hands from me.

She turns a page in her file, reading, keeping me waiting deliberately, in a power move that would work on most people very effectively. Not on me, though. With her elbows on the table, she props her chin on her hands. "Is Doctor Ian Nelson dead, Ronan?"

My lips press together. My soul rumbles in disgust. That's a name I haven't heard in a while. Ian Nelson—I won't call him a doctor—was a murderer. An abuser. I worked for him for a while, before I discovered what he was. And when I did, I dealt with it. He was human, but he was more monstrous than any of us. He used his clinic as a front, and what he would do to his patients…

He thought of himself as a scientist. He had a taste for young women. He would torture those girls, hurt them, but he'd do it in a way that didn't leave any obvious bruises or wounds. He knew how to get into their heads.

He'd give them the new *medicines* he was working up, the drugs he wanted to sell on the market, and observe the effects. He'd take notes on their pain, gleeful notes. I'm fairly certain he got off on them, too. He and his drugs would mess with their minds. He'd bruise them on the inside just to listen to them scream. He'd target the girls who had little and less, and he'd make them believe he was the only one who cared. The only one they could trust.

So many of them died, and my greatest regret will always be that it took me months to stop it.

Each of those girls was just another note in his file.

I'm not ashamed of what I did to him. I smile. Killing him is one of the greatest things I ever did in my thousands of years.

My nostrils flare. "Yes, he's dead. *Someone* killed him. Slaughtered him. Then I took his identity and his clinic. His life, really. I'd still be living as Ian Nelson now if Aedan didn't get so unfortunately upset that day."

The way she examines my reactions is peculiar because I'm not used to anyone outside of *us* paying so much attention to anything. "You don't like killing," she states.

My head jerks. She's right, but for the life of me I can't understand how she knows that.

"You don't like death," she continues. "How you hold yourself when you talk about it. How you look away and your nostrils flare. The same way you've reacted when I mentioned your tattoo. Those names belong to family members? Probably dead. Killed?"

My heart thrashes, and my jaws clench so hard they could shatter. "Enough."

"You killed Ian Nelson because you thought it was necessary."

I didn't *think*. It *was* necessary. "Unlike the death of Sean Chisholm. Now, you see I couldn't have been involved."

She closes her file and stands. "Very well then. You're going back to holding now."

That's it? No, I'm not done. "What about you, Ms. Beastly? What's your secret? What beast is living inside you?" I don't just mean her shifter form, though I'm curious about that too. I keep dwelling on that darkness, on that secret roiling in her heart that makes her so scared of who and what she is, and what she could do with it if she wanted to.

"Ronan." Her voice drips with something dark and tantalizing. Her gaze is intense, and suddenly I feel like *I* am the one bound by the power of my name. What *is* this girl? "What makes you think I have any intention of answering any of your questions?"

Caught in her eyes, it's my turn to be hypnotized. I want them to stay on me as long as possible. "Perhaps you don't, but do you not want to know more about the fae?"

She breaks the gaze, breaks the connection. "What makes me think you haven't given me everything I need?"

"Do you believe what I told you?" I still can't believe I've told her at all. Now, I must live with the consequences, whatever they may be. Suddenly, though, nothing is more important to my pride and to my happiness that she understands me, understands who I am and what I am.

"It doesn't matter what I believe." She meets my eyes once more, and there's that sudden, intense, powerful draw again. That same darkness. I don't understand what it is that I feel from this girl. I've met countless shifters in my life, but none, even the dragons, have made me react like this. I don't know what's so odd about her life essence, about her power, but it pulls me to her. I don't want to leave her side. I *need* her. I crave the sound of my name on her lips just one more time.

She has captured my soul, leaving me breathless once more, and then she looks away and calls the guard back into the room.

I am set off-balance by the confusion of what I've just felt, but the part of my mind that is still functioning is dancing in jubilation. The power radiating from her, the darkness, whatever it is, will be my salvation.

Rivera comes in and loosens me from the table. As we're walking away, I stop, turning to look at those eyes one more time. "I can't tell you how pleased I am to make your acquaintance, Divina. When will I see you again?"

"We're done, O'Shea." She sighs, looking away. "This is goodbye."

Reflexively, I rattle my chains as Rivera pushes me out. I want to break loose. To have one final word with her. To feel her hand in mine. Just once. One touch of hers is all I need.

No. She has to come back.

Or everything will fall apart.

FOURTEEN

DEREK

Divina has been my partner for four years. She isn't the chattiest of people. I get that. But not once has she been silent the whole drive home after an open case interrogation.

Staring out the window, she holds the case file, which has tripled in thickness since this morning, loosely on her lap as though she's trying to absorb it through like—what was that thing called, the water thing? Osmosis.

My biology teacher would be proud.

But that's not all.

Is she still mad at me? I don't think so. Even if she is, she's very professional. She will discuss the case with her partner.

Something has happened. Who knows what those fuckers have said or done? I should smack myself. Leaving her alone with those inmates… I know it's for the best. She has her way with mindfucks more than most people I've known, and she's definitely more skilled in that department than I'll ever be, but I should have stayed. I don't know what it is about her that makes me not able to say no to her. I need to get better at it.

Just as much as I need to be more persistent in asking her out.

I've been head over heels since first sight. The curl to her hair. The fullness of her lips. The hard look of determination in her eyes. Getting to know her has only made me fall even harder.

We've become friends easily, opening up to each other. Really good friends that can talk about anything. When it comes to us, there are no secrets. As I work cases with her, bring her coffees, take her on friendly lunches, she tells me things no one else knows. How she doesn't get on with her father. The complicated relationship with her polyamorous mother before she died. Her twin sister that she thinks was her mother's favorite. Her two half-brothers she never mentions to anyone because they're basically MC outlaws.

She knows about the disaster of my one-year marriage to a woman who has run off with my uncle. How my mother has been in hospital for the last six years. She even knows about my secret sci-fi and fantasy collection—the figurines, the comic books—which will not go over well with the rest of the boys on the force if they find out, and she knows I may or may not have cried after meeting LeVar Burton at a convention a while back. In my defense, I am now the proud owner of a signed VISOR from the guy who read me my childhood on his show. I'm not the only person whose eyes would get teary at that.

The bottom line is, she knows me better than anyone, and I like to think I can say the same about myself when it comes to her.

Like how I know she loves both her jobs with an equal, fiery passion that makes her a force to be reckoned with. And that she doesn't smile much, but sometimes she smiles for me.

And I know I'm in love with her.

A slow sigh stutters out of my chest. I'm pretty sure she knows I'm in love with her, too, though for whatever reason she doesn't want to move ahead with me. I won't pretend it doesn't hurt, but a guy can't be pushy about these things. That's called being an asshole. I try really, really hard not to be one of those.

However, I'm not an idiot. A woman like her knows how to draw a line, force a guy back if she truly doesn't want him to be more than just friends. I've seen her do it so many times with assholes at the precinct and hormonal kids in her classes. As much as I've always wanted to rearrange their faces, her words have been more intimidating and more efficient.

Why she doesn't want to either draw the line or take that step forward with me is beyond me.

As I drive, I keep stealing glances at her. The silence is too much. Even for her. She will at least examine her files or swear or…or something. I can't imagine what these inmates have said to her to have this effect.

"Divina?"

"Huh?" She jolts, as though she's surprised I'm there. "Sorry, I was just—what's up?"

That's what I want you to tell me. "The interrogations. After I left. Are we any further forward?" I ease into a conversation. Direct confrontation is never the best way to get through to her. It makes her close up, get defensive, like she's got a whole world inside of her that she doesn't want anyone to know about.

She grunts and looks back out the window again. She's silent for so long I think she's forgotten my question.

I shake my head in disbelief. "Are you still angry at me, D? Is that what this's all about?"

Her head tilts toward me tiredly. "What?"

She's either too distracted to remember or she's totally forgotten about it and moved on. I don't need to remind her and make her angry again. Better change the subject. "Do you think any of them did it?"

A terrible frown scrunches her face. "I *know* none of them did it. But I don't have the evidence to clear them. Don't think it will make any difference even if I do."

"Are you saying they're being framed? By whom?"

"Who do you think?"

My brows hook. "Collins?"

"I think he's been offered something big to do it."

That's a serious accusation Divina would never make unless she truly believes it's true.

However, this is the first time she does without having enough evidence to back it up.

The theory isn't unbelievable. Despite his reputation, there's something off about Warden Collins. He tries to block our investigation, leading us only to what he wants us to see. Moves the body before our arrival. Something is up, yes. But what is his motive? To kill a bug like Chisholm, stage a crime scene that looks like a sacrifice to the devil gone bad, and then leak it's a ghost who did it? Only to pin it on one of the four suspects whom he clearly hates?

It doesn't make any sense.

"Do you know anything about a new prison in Mount Hood?" she asks.

"No. Is it related to the case? I can look into it if you think it can lead us to something on Collins."

Her lips twist. "No. You shouldn't."

Now, that's weird. "Why not?"

"Derek…I think I'm going to recuse myself from the case."

I grip the steering wheel so we won't veer off-course in my shock. "What? Why? Did something happen? Did one of them say something to you? I'll—"

"I'm fine," she says, but no part of me believes her in the slightest. She's trying too hard to make me feel like nothing is wrong, which always means something is wrong. "I just... It's Killian. I'm too hurt to see him...and we got enough on our plate already. Maybe we should both get off it, let the original team take back over."

"You want me off the case, too?" I've never known Divina to run from a case. In fact, I spend most of my time begging her to take it easy after we've got the perp. She devotes herself to each and every matter entirely, in a way that is as impressive as it is terrifying. And that Killian shit, she's just saying it because she thinks it's what I want to hear to be convinced. "What the hell, D? You're scaring me. For real. What happened back there?"

"Nothing happened." Her eyes snap shut, and she pretends to sleep until I pull up outside the precinct.

I put the car into park but don't open the doors yet or unfasten my seatbelt. I place my hand over hers. "What's going on, D? I'm not going to drop it until you tell me."

She just looks at me. The instant heat between us as soon as our skin touches engulfs me. It takes everything I have not to move closer. Being alone in the car together, stationary like this, nobody else around...it's tempting. So tempting. What will she do if I lean over and kiss her? I haven't ever been so bold about my advances. Maybe this is what she's waiting for. Maybe I—

"I already told you. Nothing's wrong." She pulls her hand away, breaking the moment. I sigh because I know she feels it too, and I don't understand why she keeps denying me. Denying herself.

"Is this about your dad?"

Something crosses her eyes for a split-second. Fear? But then it's gone. Maybe I am imagining it. "What do you mean?" she asks carefully.

"He called you this morning. Is that what your mind is on, instead of the case? Because it's okay to be worried about your family. Is he sick?"

She looks at me for a moment, her mouth half-open. Then she shakes her head. "Oh. Right. I… No, he's not sick."

"Your sister? Your brothers?"

"They're fine. All of them. It was just one of those calls that are the reason I don't want anything to do with the family anymore."

I don't say what I want to say, same as every time we talk about her family. That she should try to reunite with them before it's too late. I don't know if my mother will ever wake up from the coma the car accident put her in, the same one that took my father from me. I'm an only child, and my only other family, my uncle, is now living somewhere tropical with my ex-wife.

Whatever the problem is that exists between her and her family—Divina is always vague about the details—her dad and her siblings really seem to want to make it up to her. Especially after the death of her mom. Now is the time to reunite.

But I don't say it this time. She's too upset to listen. "Do you need to take some time off? I can talk to Chief for you—"

She shakes her head immediately. "No, I want to work. Don't worry about me, Derek. I just don't think our little team needs to be spending all our time at Forest Grove Penitentiary when there are plenty of murders closer to town."

What does that even mean? I'll chop off my right arm if this has nothing to do with that call. Divina is the top analyst, of course, but I'm a detective for a reason. I know when something's up, and something is up here.

What exactly has her father said that is buzzing around her mind and distracting her from her work? I can't even imagine how her family can be connected to this case in any way. I'm not even sure if she's implying they are, or if wanting to get away from the prison and whatever is going on with her father are two unrelated incidents.

I know I'm going to regret this, but I have to ask. "D…do… Are your brothers involved in this?"

"Oh for fuck's sake, Derek. Yes, my notorious biker brothers killed Chisholm, and Dad called me to cover it up. I went in there to do just that, but now my conscious is fucking awake, and I can't take the horrible guilt. Happy, Detective Bright?"

"Why are you twisting everything I'm saying today? I'm your partner and friend. I'm worried about you. All I want is to make sure you're okay."

"Well, I am."

"No, you're not. And it's because of that call, this fucking case and those inmates." I don't like any of the suspects, and I don't like how she reacts toward them—Killian and the big one, Oakberry, especially—and I'm worried she's let them get into her head.

If she has, we have more to worry about than whatever is going on with her father. Divina is one of the strongest people I know. She's got nerves like a steel barrier, and I've never, not once in all the years we've worked together, seen any criminal manage to break through it.

Whether it's her family, or the case, or both, she clearly needs to step away from it.

"You know what? You want to stay on the fucking case and waste your breath, be my guest. Do whatever the fuck you want. Just don't drag my family into any of this shit."

Her hand falls on the handle, and the door opens a little. I grab her arm gently, only to stop her from leaving. I can't just see her so mad, so hurt without trying to fix it, make it better. "Divina, please—"

She shrugs me off, swearing, giving me another lecture. I barely listen because her cheeks, that color that rises to them when she's angry or shy, and her lips that are now red as she continuously bites them in rage, are blowing my fucking mind away.

Kiss her.
Kiss her.
Kiss her.

I just put my hands on either side of her face and silence her with my kiss. My eyes close in a reflex to the feel of these incredible, fleshy lips on mine. They're so soft and warm…scorching. My heart thumps as I lose myself in this moment I've been fantasizing about for years. Then I'm aware she's not kissing me back, and I expect a shove, a slap…anything. She just freezes, unmoving, unchanging.

What am I supposed to do now? Pull away? Continue to taste her lips, hoping she will yield? What the fuck should I do now? *Give me something, D. Anything.*

With my eyes still shut, I take my hands off her face, cursing myself to hell and beyond. I've screwed up. Big time.

Instantly, her hand is behind my neck, pulling me closer, mashing my mouth against hers. My heart skips a beat as her lips part, and her tongue pushes mine open.

My eyes snap open. I have to see it for myself. Divina is kissing me back.

I fist her hair just down the back of her neck, my other hand around her waist. My tongue dances with hers while I savor every inch of her lips. My breaths are catching, hitching, but I don't stop, afraid I'll lose her if I do. I don't want to stop. Ever. I want to do nothing in my life but to kiss and touch Divina Beastly.

She wants to pull away, gasping for breath. I suck her lower lip as she moves back, holding on to her as long as possible. Her breasts heave, and I do my best not to look. It's not that hard. As much as I'd love to explore her body, her eyes alone, with that look in them can hold my attention for hours.

"Say something," I whisper. "Or just close that door and tell me where to go. I will go to hell with you if that's what it takes to kiss you again."

That mesmerizing look blinks away, and her expression suddenly changes. Shit. Have I said something wrong?

"Derek…we can't—"

"No. Don't give me that shit. No. You know how I feel about you, and this kiss… You feel something, too."

A troubled sigh bursts out of her chest. Her eyes glisten as she swallows. "About the pen case… I don't… We make such a great team, and that case… Trust me when I tell you it's a setup. We're not powerful enough to intervene. Our efforts are pointless there." Her voice breaks at the end.

I pinch the bridge of my nose, unable to believe how she's steering this conversation. As a man, I want to silence her again with a kiss that makes her think about nothing but the need that aches inside both of us. As her friend, her closest friend, I owe it to her to help her with whatever she's struggling with. If that means we both get off that fucking case, then that's fine. I'll do anything I can to support her. "All right. If you want us working something else, I can do that. But we need to go back tomorrow. We need to formalize the hand-off of the investigation, if nothing else."

She smiles, that smile just for me that makes my heart flutter. Her whole body relaxes into the seat. She looks truly relieved. "Thank you, Derek."

"Yeah." I don't understand what has just happened, but the way she's smiling at me now makes my heart swell, and I can't believe anything that makes her look at me in that way, with those eyes, with that smile, can ever be a bad thing. If she looked at me like that and asked me to walk through fire, I'd do it without hesitation.

Man, I've got it bad.

I open the door and climb out of my car. Then I walk to the passenger side and hold hers open for her. I lock the door when she's out. "After the debriefing, do you want to go get something to eat?"

We're not touching, but her body tenses next to mine. "You mean like…a date?"

"Is that the worst thing in the world?"

She doesn't say anything, wavering, still uncertain.

"Come on, we can even go to that weird

veggie sushi place you like so much, I don't know about you but spending all day amongst criminals sure works up my appetite." I wheedle. "And I won't try to pay. I'll even let you pay for me, if you want."

The joke lands, and she laughs, shoving at my arm. "You're totally ridiculous, Bright."

"And charming?"

"You can say so."

"And handsome?"

She bites her lips, but then she frowns. "Don't push it."

I grin as we walk back into the precinct together, heading up to the office to drop off the files before we go to the chief to report. "So…dinner?"

She stops, turning to face me. She looks at me for a long time, and for a second I know how the inmates must feel under that gaze. Exposed, like my every secret is written on my face. Then she lets out a breath and nods. "It's a date."

FIFTEEN

RONAN

Aedan and I shuffle back to the cell. The second we're shoved inside by the fucking guards, and the door buzzes locked, Aedan stares at me. "What the fuck happened to you in that room?"

We go way back that he knows me better than most. He must see and feel her effect on me. The things she evokes inside me that I can't explain. The mess she leaves me in when she says I'll never see her again.

"Get it together, mate. That love-struck face doesn't suit you."

I scowl. Hard. Love? What fucking love? I'm not in love with Divina Beastly. If I feel anything for her, it's quite the opposite. I want to hurt her for the tricks she's pulled on me. And I want to use her as many times as I can.

To do my bidding.

Only my bidding.

Love? It's a mistake I've only made once.

Before Aedan, I've lived close to three thousand years. My story has a lot of ups and downs, and it flashes before my eyes now. It involves a family who love each other above all else for two thousand years. Then it moves to the small village where my brother and I fall for the same woman. Michael finds a way to give up his magic, his soul, to marry her. Even though she originally wants to be with me, she chooses the one who chooses her over what he is, something I could never do.

My brother dies after ten short years. The woman I love grows old and decays, and then her children, and then her children's children, until I can't take it anymore.

I run, and my parents and my other brother Kiernan run with me. We settle in the New World for centuries. But rumors of how our people are fading around the world spread, and Kiernan returns to the realm of Faerie. I never hear from him again.

Sixty years later, my mother is accused of witchcraft and is murdered in cold blood, burned and poisoned by iron at the bottom of a lake. My father's magic slowly fades. One day he is just gone like my brother. I don't know if either he or Kiernan still lives as I travel the world, eventually returning to this country only in the 1960s, but it's decades yet until I find the clinic that kills Aedan's sister.

Less than a year after I start my position as Ian Nelson's assistant, I find proof of how he's hurting those girls. One of them mistakes me for him and begs me for her next hit of the drug he's been plying her with. I find documents about how much he enjoys it. How he finds pleasure, entertainment, in induced pain and calls it science.

The moment I corner him in his office and make him admit to his crimes, beg for his life, promise me things, try to bargain for his pathetic soul, fills me with pride.

I can feel the syringes in my hand, one after the other as I inject him with his own poison. I see his blood streaming from his eyes, his screams turn to gurgles as pink foam pours from his mouth. His skin turns black and blue, blossoming like a field of macabre flowers. It's a terrible death. An awful one that I will savor forever.

My memories flash forward to when Aedan turns up at the clinic, while I'm there working alone, and suddenly flames rain down from the mouth of a towering dragon.

The debris is trapping me, and the smoke is choking me, taking my breath, making it hard to think or move or breathe. I'm dying. I cry out wordlessly – not seeking help, not expecting an answer, but then Aedan is in the room. He is no longer a dragon, but a man in the kind of anguish I remember from every time one more of my family vanishes. But he bears a devilish look in his eye. He wants to watch me die.

The doctor who has killed his only family left.

He watches me struggle for a while, and then he hunkers down and tells me about Bethany. I don't know about her. Hers is not one of the files which I find. Maybe if I have found it, I could have helped her, but instead she dies in another doctor's care. His anguish, his sorrow, makes me think of my brother's still body, of my nieces and nephews.

Aedan asks the question that changes our fate. Am I the one who has mistreated his sister? The very thought makes me want to expel my insides, sickening me in a way that has nothing to do with the smoke and ash. That anyone could tar me with that brush, associate Nelson's mad experiments and torture with me, with my kind, it burns worse than the flames do.

The reason my whole scheme has worked so well is because I already look like that fucking monster Ian. Not a lot, but we have a similar build, similar skin color, and similar apparent age. When he dies and I take his identity, it only involves the bare minimum of magic. A few cosmetics here and there. Dark hair instead of silver. Round blue eyes instead of violet with a feline cant. The slightest image of a false addition to my height. It's not hard to convince casual patients that I am who they think I am. For those closer, like friends and family, I have ways to influence them. Sex, magic, manipulation; I use whatever it takes to slip into the role of the dead man.

But as I lie dying under this debris and the magic is fading, Aedan can tell the difference. Since he's taken Bethany elsewhere for treatment, but she dies anyway, Ian Nelson's burning face is all he can think about. He is no mastermind, but he instantly recognizes that the man he is killing is not the enemy.

He roars at me to tell him who I am. I almost laugh in his face. I may die here, but pride is a terrible thing. As far as I am concerned, I need nobody's help. I will escape this on my own, somehow. I am more ancient than this idiot can even begin to conceive. He thinks he is a dragon, but he's just a shifter, a remnant of a beautiful creature lost to time. I do not need his help. I will not accept it.

So I tell him, in my arrogance, what I am. I want to make him see how inferior he is, even now when my life is in his hands. I tell him he is nothing to me, shifter or not, and I don't need him. I tell him how Ian Nelson screamed when I quite literally gave him a taste of his own medicine.

Aedan tries to help me, perhaps in response to my words, but I yell at him to leave. He shrugs, getting to his feet, and turns away.

The building creaks, and timber falls from the roof and crushes my leg. That's when I know for sure I'm going to die. My father has once told me it's the most peaceful feeling in the world, but that is a lie. It rankles at my soul. I am furious. I will not die. The universe will not have me. Does it know who I *am?*

Aedan's voice is calm and even when he walks back over and tells me fire doesn't hurt him. He offers to get me out, but he wants something in return or I can burn to death for all he cares.

A deal with the fae.

That's when I understand Aedan isn't such an idiot after all.

It's one of the other old rules that govern my people. Our deals are binding, unbreakable, and the terms must be met by both sides or the consequences can be deadly. Nothing irritates the fae more than being in someone's debt without a way to pay it back. The scales must always be balanced. When they're not, it feels like a physical burning on every inch of our skin, persistent, refusing to leave.

That's why Aedan proposes a deal. One that will bind our lives together irrevocably.

First he asks me to revive his sister, but of course that's beyond even my capabilities. I explain this to him, and for a moment I'm sure he's going to leave me to die. Then I offer to heal him, make up for the lack that dragon shifters have where they can't cure their wounds as fast as the others. I can keep him alive, keep him safe, if he does the same for me.

I don't realize, then, or when the police sirens come rushing in, just how tight our bond will be forever as a result.

And now here we are.

Yet he dares think I'm in love with a girl like Divina Beastly. A girl whose name and eyes haunt me for reasons I can't understand.

"Take your nap, dragon. You obviously need it."

SIXTEEN

DIVINA

Chief is less than understanding when I tell him I want off the case. He can't pass the opportunity to tell me off for getting so stubborn and strong-arming him into letting me on it in the first place.

I don't blame him. He has every right. He must think I'm PMSing hard or something. Part of me wants to scream my reasons to drop the case are more than legit, and I'm not some girl controlled by hormones, but I shut the fuck up and take it. Swallowing my hurt pride is the lesser evil. I prefer it to the alternative.

Telling him now I don't buy the confession in the Mains case—the girl whose death I've been investigating before Dad's call—and the guy we have isn't the perp isn't the smartest thing to do, considering how crimson his face has turned and how loud his voice is when he's practically kicking us out of the office.

Yeah, I'll leave that battle till tomorrow.

All I need to do tonight is eat with Derek, take my mind off the pen and its monstrously hot inmates, and prepare to crack the humanly monstrous asshole who's covering up for the real Cynthia Mains' murderer.

The idea of going back to my human psycho criminals and the beautiful horrors of their real bloody crime scenes and the awful fantasies in their non-supernatural minds… I smile, moaning with pleasure. I can't wait for the soothing peace all this brings to my life.

Derek smiles back at me. He must think I'm smiling because of our date. "You ready?"

I press the elevator button. "Sure. Um… Just let me swing by my place for five minutes so I can change."

"You look awesome in anything, D. You don't need to dress up for me."

I tuck my hair behind my ear as we get into the elevator. "That's sweet. But I really need to wash off the pen smell."

"What smell?"

The smell of other shifters, demons, vamps and faes. I chuckle. "A girl is allowed to take a shower before a date, Bright. Relax, I already said yes. Won't change my mind."

He grins. "Maybe it's me who's having second thoughts."

"Too late now. You're stuck with me for tonight. There's no way out of it."

He twines his fingers with mine. "Good."

The happiness Derek's every simple, sweet, loving, caring gesture brings to my heart is amazing. And when he steals a glance at me every now and then while he's driving us to my place, I don't know why I haven't been allowing myself such joy. I live my life as a human, and from now on, no more connections with supes. This can work.

This can really, really work.

"Just five minutes. Longer than that, and I'll come barging in." He turns the corner to my house, and my smile stops in its tracks when I see Dad's motorbike propped up against the curb. Damn it.

"Is that…" Derek's frustration seeps from his voice.

I barely look at him as I nod. "Dad's bike."

"So…that means…"

"I'm sorry," I sigh. I hate to do this to him. "Rain check?"

"Of course." A scowl contorts his handsome face. "Is tomorrow too soon?"

"No. It's perfect." I smile so he'll smile back. It works.

Dad hugs me when I walk in. I kick the door closed instantly so Derek won't see how my father looks as young as I am. Because, of course, Derek is waiting for me to get inside safely before he drives off.

"How are you doing, baby girl?"

Seeing Terror is always an ordeal, even when we're cordial. Being around him reminds me of too much. It makes me think of Mom. It makes me think of the beasts I'm trying so hard to keep down inside me.

Dealing with all this tonight isn't easy. Especially when he's just ruined what could have been a perfect date. I regret letting Terror keep the key for emergencies. At least, it makes this easier; I don't have to call him or meet him somewhere else later. I can do the hand-off now and be done with this whole thing forever.

"All good." That's all I say and go make us both some coffee.

We sit on the couch, and I take out my notebook—the one I've been keeping away from the official file that has all my notes about the strange goings-on at the penitentiary.

Dad flips through it, and I fill him in about Ward E. How the inmates, as much as I hate to acknowledge it, are supes, though the vic was not. How the inmates are being given suspicious medications. I describe in short form the four that Warden and his guards have singled out for me. Their species and surnames. I don't use their first names to distance myself from them.

He scowls. "One of them is a demon?"

"Yes," I say, deciding to omit the details of my little encounter with Marco. Dad will flip if I tell him I've let a demon in my head, who has activated something dark and carnal inside me just with his smile.

Or how Aedan inspires something animalistic inside me, making me want to shift and attack and bite and fuck.

Or how I want to examine all of Flynn's new muscle, to kiss away the pain until I find the boy I used to know.

Or how Ronan's playing with my name, body and mind like ivory on a piano, makes me want to overcome him, makes me want to show him what it's like when someone else has the power over him.

Wet heat gathers between my legs, and I swear under my breath, hating myself for feeling this way. I hand Dad the notebook, reluctantly admitting he may be on to something after all.

"What about Collins?"

Marco says he's a tool for Damien Pattison. And Ronan implies he's the killer. "He knows a lot more than he shows. He even knows who I am."

Dad's eyes gleam gold, and his lips tighten. "Son of a bitch. You can't ever go back in there, D. Not even for paperwork."

I nod, sighing. "I'm already off the case, but we have to check in tomorrow... Don't worry. I'll tell Derek to go on his own."

"Thank you. Slasher, your uncles and I will take it from there." He rises to his feet. "I guess that's it then."

"Yeah...no more supes...no more Blood Demons...no more—"

He yanks me up and squeezes me in a tight embrace. He breathes me in and then pulls away a little just to look at my face. "I love you, baby girl. More than I ever loved anyone my whole life."

Tears prick my eyes against my will, and his

eyes that look exactly like mine glisten, too. "I…I love you, too, Dad."

"You remind me so much of her."

I chew on my lip. "I look nothing like Mom."

"Maybe on the outside you're all me, but on the inside…you're just as smart and stubborn and kickass as she was. Even her resistance to our kind. The only difference is that she came around. She learned to accept."

The muscles around my heart contract. I slip out of his embrace. "Don't give me that speech. Vixen Legend never accepted anything."

"That's not true. The moment she saw me shift—"

"I've heard that story a thousand times before. Your twisted version of Beauty and the Beast. The human who didn't shudder at your screwed-up paw. That doesn't mean she accepted us. She fucking died."

He freezes for a moment, his jaws clenched. "First of all, language," he says, and I roll my eyes. "Second of all, you know why she didn't turn. Don't think it was easy. It was so hard on her, too."

I throw my hands in the air in exasperation. "Are you kidding me right now?"

"No, Divina. I'm dead serious. She refused

to live forever knowing there's a chance she can't control the darkness the devil saw in her. She decided to stay human so she wouldn't give him any power over her. Or you."

"Then why do you blame me for wanting to be human? She knew our kind is evil. She knew if she turned, she couldn't be good anymore. I'm my mother's daughter after all."

He cradles my face in his hands. "No, baby girl. You got it all backward. It's her—"

"Dad, please. I can't listen to this again. Today was…hard. I already made up my mind. I had enough. I'd like to go back to my human life and be left in peace."

"Peace? I have no clue how you think humans are better than supes when you see the horrors many of them can do every day. What peace are you talking about?"

"The ones I deal with are sick. The exception. None of them have to feed on other humans or kill so naturally."

"Have you ever fed on anyone, D?"

"No." I cringe. I've never taken a life. It doesn't mean I don't want to. All the time. "But you have. All of you."

"Yes, on low lives you send to be executed or rot in the slammer. We have our laws. The same for humans. Some still break those on both sides. Even if you think most of our kind can't help the kill, *you* don't. That only means you have a choice. Just like your wonderful humans."

What are you trying to do, Terror? Is this a trick to get out of our deal? Are you messing with my head on purpose? No. Not today, Terror. Not today. "Dad, you promised. I did my part. It's time you kept your end of the deal."

A long, troubled sigh escapes him. "Just know one thing, deal or no deal, we'll always be there for you." He kisses my forehead and drops his hands from my face. "We will all miss you, baby girl. Take care now."

He tears away from me. The sound of the door slamming behind him quakes inside of me.

This is it. It's finally over. I'm free.

It's all over.

SEVENTEEN

DIVINA

The next morning dawns, and I am firm with myself. I cannot think of the penitentiary anymore. Or the things Dad has said. Or the cruel loneliness gnashing at me after he's walked out of the door. I will not. No more O'Shea, no more Oakberry, no more Connelly. No more Flynn. No more Blood Demons.

There's just me, my students, my police work, and, hopefully, Derek.

You're lying to yourself.

No. I have made the choice not to get

involved in my father's world or allow it to eclipse the human life I've built for myself. This is the right decision. The way it should be.

Derek and I are back on the Mains case. Frank Goldstein, our main suspect is about to go to trial, but I insist on talking to him once more. Something isn't right about him, even with the confession.

"I don't understand why you're here," Frank repeats himself in a sullen voice that betrays how young he is. "I already confessed."

How does a nineteen-year-old kid end up tangled in this shit? Because Cynthia dates his friend rather than him? No fucking way. "Because I don't understand why *you're* here, Frank. At least, not like this."

His eyebrows furrow, enough that they meet above his nose. "What do you want from me? I signed the confession. I killed Cynthia because she was a bitch. I don't know what else you expect to find out by grilling me over and over."

I have a hunch, and no evidence beyond that hunch, but sometimes that's enough.

"I believe you that you killed Cynthia." I take out the photos from the crime scene and pass them across the table to him.

Her body is there, covered in blood from the many open wounds his knife has dotted all over her, the floor coated from her torture. The red has seeped into the expensive hardwood boards, taking over the whole room, creating a stain that will never leave unless they replace the whole floor.

He doesn't even flinch, which is what I expected, and what doesn't make any sense at all about this whole case. If he loved her, like he claims, then seeing her body after a crime of passion would evoke…something in him. A flinch. A tear. Maybe even a cruel smirk of satisfaction. But there's no reaction at all.

I let him take in the pictures for a moment. Then I keep my voice as neutral as possible as I deliver my wham line. "But I don't believe you did it alone."

That gets a reaction. It's quick, but I see it. The widening of the eyes, the tightening of the jaw, the flick in his mouth. The shake of his hands when he holds the pictures.

The blind panic that crosses his face is enough for me. I have him.

"Did he pay you? Did he hold her while you cut her? Did he watch while she screamed?" All gentleness is gone from my voice now. "Was him turning on you part of the plan?"

"Turning on me?"

There it is. "He's been talking about what a monster you are for weeks to the press." I draw something else out of my file. It's a newspaper clipping, an interview with Pete Yates, the boyfriend of the murdered girl. Frank's best friend.

Frank's eyes move quickly as he reads how his *friend* has been condemning him. Not just the heartbroken act of a boyfriend who misses his girlfriend, but calling for the death of her killer, claiming he's only been friends with him in the first place because he feels sorry for him. But now he calls Frank disgusting.

A laugh cracks out of Frank. High pitched, cold like ice, and it sets my teeth on edge. Suddenly he's not the nineteen-year-old kid I've been wondering about. I see him for what he is. A cold-blooded killer.

"Pete didn't *have* to pay me," he hisses. I exhale. The story all rushes out at once, like Frank has been waiting for the chance to confess, really confess. I let him rant, silently ensuring my recorder is running.

"He asked for my help, and I gave it. I didn't lie. I killed her because she was a bitch. She ruined him. It was all because of her. He'd have never left me in here to rot. He'd never have said any of this. Everything is her fault." He devours the sight of her blood like a hungry monster.

"How was she a bitch?"

"Cheated on him. With his *brother*. Pete was so broken up when he came to me. He didn't know what to do. He was going to hurt himself. I stopped him. He was so grateful for my help. I'm his best friend. Then he said we should do something about it. We should hurt *her*.

"I never thought of killing her, but Pete said it would be easy, and I'd be good at it. He let me choose how to do it, the when, the where, the knife. All he asked is that he could be there and watch." A sick smile crosses his face.

This kid is sick, but his friend is sicker. Pete knows how troubled Frank is, and he pushes him over the edge for his own gain, to get revenge on Cynthia.

"She never liked me. She let me in only because he was with me. He told her he wanted her back, and *he* gave her the spiked wine. I was going to kill her while she was unconscious, but he made me wait. He wanted her to be awake again. He wanted to see the pain in her eyes." His elbows rest on the table. "I loved the idea. That's why Pete and I are best friends. We understand each other."

He looks like he's remembering a sweet song as he closes his eyes, bobbing his head to some invisible melody. "Her screams were like music when she begged him to save her. He just stood there and watched. Then when the knife went in the first time, *slowly,* and the blood began to spread, she began to cry, too. She screamed for Pete to call an ambulance. He told me to stab her again."

His eyes are open now, and they're glittering, with excitement or tears or maybe both. "I didn't kill her straight away. Pete wanted her to suffer, and I wanted Pete to be happy. He told me where to carve, and I did. And the blood, her blood, it *whispered* to me. It was warm. So beautiful.

"Pete wiped it on her lips and made her kiss him, and then he wiped it on her face because she didn't deserve to be pretty anymore. Then I stabbed her over and over until he was satisfied."

My fists are clenching under the table. Wolf is slavering. The scent of Frank's body is coming strong now, the blood pulsing in his veins. All I want to do is shift, stomp him with Reindeer's hooves, catch him in Wolf's jaws, and see if his blood is as sweet as he claims Cynthia's has been for him. And then I will hunt down Pete, the mastermind behind the monster, and devour him, too.

"She'd messed with his head. That's why he's saying this shit about me. He'd have never done that if it hadn't been for her. After what I did for him, he's still in love with her."

My beast moment passes, as my professor brain sees the delusions this kid lives in. It's just me, Divina the psychologist, and this sick boy who has been manipulated into becoming a monster. Oh, he's stabbed Cynthia, that's true, but he's not the one responsible for her murder. Frank will go to prison, and there he'll get some help, but it's Pete that needs to be locked up and the key thrown away. Thanks to this recording, I have the proof I need to get that done.

I leave the room and take it straight to the Chief, explaining what I've discovered. He issues a warrant for Pete Yates immediately, and some of our best officers—led by Derek—file out to catch the sicko before he manipulates or hurts anyone else.

Everyone keeps congratulating me. They're proud of me for cracking it, for seeing what they couldn't, but I...I feel empty.

No, I feel torn.

Did Collins manipulate a guard to kill Chisholm while he'd watch? Or did he do it himself to get his rocks off later? Or did he and his guards all take turns, laughing and dancing to Chisholm's screams?

I need to go for a walk.

It's cold, even for me, but I don't care. Let it sting me. I deserve the pain.

I can't get the images of the mutilated bodies of Mains or Chisholm out of my mind. I keep imagining both victims scream, begging for their lives. I remember Pete during the initial interview. He cried. I *comforted* him. The thought makes me want to vomit. He's not a person. He's a monster, a fucking beast, a…

I stop in the middle of the sidewalk as the blinding truth hits me like a truck.

After the real confession, Wolf has surfaced, but not in an urge to taste Cynthia's blood. She wants justice. Reindeer wants to protect Cynthia, even though she's gone.

But the two who have hurt Cynthia, the sadist and psychopath who have made sure her death is long and torturous have had no interest in saving her. They are more bloodthirsty than me and the carnivore in my soul. Pete is sicker than any vampire who drinks for sustenance, using Cynthia's own blood to play with her more before the torture had killed her. He has enjoyed her suffering more than the demons who literally feed from it.

And he is—both of them are—human.

Wolf growls in agreement. Reindeer nudges at me. But I don't need their hints, not now. Nor can I bear Dad's words from yesterday that are bellowing in my head. The sudden understanding is more than I can take.

Frank, and especially Pete, are human, but they are monsters.

I am a monster, but I am more human than they'll ever be.

It's all about choice. We can only be rewarded or punished for what we do, not what we are. No one should be oppressed because of what they are.

And I am a double supernatural beast. I'm definitely more supe than human, which explains the horrible void in my soul since yesterday. I should be happy that I'm no longer attached to the side I've always loathed, but all I feel is like a part of me—a huge one—has been brutally ripped out of me.

I'm a supe, and I'm proud. I can't deny it anymore. I shouldn't run away from what I am. Or live in fear because of it.

The same goes for the prisoners of Ward E. They may be guilty of awful things, but they do not deserve to be set up. What they are, what *we* are, shouldn't condemn them to whatever awful destiny that is being cooked for all supes. If they're given a chance, they, too, can choose to be good.

I can't get the four inmates off my mind, and maybe it's because I'm not supposed to.

They need help. To get that help, they need me.

I turn back on my heel, heading with purpose back toward the precinct, and go straight into Chief's office.

"He's busy," Tracy says rudely as I enter.

I ignore her, marching right up to his desk. He's on the phone, and he waves at me impatiently to go away, but I ignore him too.

I stand in front of his desk, my hands leaning on the wood, staring at him. After a moment, he grunts and tells whoever is on the phone that he'll call them back. He puts down the receiver. "What, Beastly?"

"I need back on the pen case."

"Get out of my office. Go back to your desk. Celebrate the win, Professor. I'll send you some files in a bit. It will give you your fix. That Yates is a sick son-of-a-bitch. Go profile that."

"So is whoever killed Chisholm at the penitentiary. I need back on it to find out who."

He jumps to his feet. "Oh for God's sake. You think this is a playground where you come and play whenever you want? You beg me to be on the case, but by the end of the day you want off. Then the next day you want on again? What the hell are you on, Beastly?"

"Chief...with all due respect—"

"With all due respect, do you have any new leads?"

I swallow. I know Warden Collins killed Sean Chisholm, just like I knew Frank didn't kill Cynthia alone. I know deep in my gut, even without proof. Collins killed Chisholm, maybe with the help of some of the guards, and then he targeted the four supes he hated the most to blame it on. The whole thing is a setup, and he's going to get away with it unless I get back there and fix it. "I have a hunch. You know my instincts are—"

"I think you should take some time off."

I want to snarl at him. He thinks I'm not *capable*. "I don't need time off." I move my hands from the table, so he doesn't see my fists. "I need to work. I just solved a case where we were going to let a murderer walk free, Chief. I'm more than capable of—"

"I'm not questioning your capabilities." He looks me straight in the eye, and I suppress a growl at the challenge. "I am questioning whatever weird emotional connection you've formed to this pen case." He sits and picks up the phone receiver. "Pass your *hunch* onto Papadakis and Hobbs. And relax a bit, will ya? Now get out of my office before I put you on a mandatory leave."

A scream gurgles in my throat. Instead of letting it out in his face, I nod and stiffly turn my back. Tracy gives me a nasty smile as I walk out of the door.

I smile back, flashing my big teeth. "Eat you later, Tracy."

The horror in her expression soothes my rage a bit. "Excuse me?"

"I said see you later." Bitch.

I don't go back to my desk. I only stop in my office and grab my coat, thankful Derek isn't here. It's better he doesn't know what I'm going to do. Safer.

As I get in my car, I send a quick text to Dad. *He* needs to know.

His text back is immediate.
STAY OUT OF IT!!!!!!!!!!

Chewing on my bottom lip, I pocket my phone and start the drive to the penitentiary.

EIGHTEEN
DIVINA

Guard Graham greets me when I arrive at the penitentiary. Looks like Papadakis and Hobbs aren't here yet, and Graham doesn't realize I'm not technically supposed to be here anymore. Good.

He flashes a cute smile. "Good to see you again, ma'am. Are you here for another round of interrogation?"

I blink for a second. Is he...*flirting*? I

chuckle, but I don't have time for this. "Yes. Can we please…?"

"Sure." He starts. "All work no play. I get it."

I ignore him completely. My heart is racing as he leads me to Ward E, back to the place where supes are doomed.

Wolf and Reindeer are in sync again, which seems to happen more and more recently, and while it's much more peaceful for me it's incredibly disconcerting. Still, neither of them wants to be back here, and I can't blame them. The second we step through the heavy door and the atmosphere of E weighs down on us, they are both suppressed. Suffocating.

This place is a suppressant for magic. A suppressant for me.

Graham leads me to a guard with one of those patches only found here and tells him where to take me. Then Graham wishes me good luck and leaves. He seems like a good kid. I feel bad for him. It feels like he's locked up here just like those inmates.

The new guard doesn't give his name. He just grunts, and leads me along the now-familiar corridor, right to the end to the two cells facing each other. Where the men who haven't left my thoughts for a moment, no matter how much I wish they would, are held.

I fully intend to interrogate the prisoners once more. Partly to tell them I'm going to help them solve this case, but also, in a much deeper, darker part of my soul, because I realize now that I've been craving seeing them again.

"Back for more, Princess?" Aedan's low growling voice reverberates down my spine, deep into my core. He leans against the bars, grinning at me. As soon as our eyes meet, I want to pounce, to lock my teeth on his neck, to show him who is the dominant one amongst us. There's a deep pulsing in my lower belly at the thought, no matter how much I try to shake it off.

"Hello, Aedan," I greet as neutrally as possible.

He gives me an even bigger grin, showing all of his teeth. Behind him, Ronan is sitting on his bed, writing something in a notebook. He doesn't even look up at the sound of my voice.

I'm offended. Would it kill him to acknowledge me? Then again, why do I want the acknowledgement of a criminal? I hate this place and what it's doing to me.

"We did miss you, darling," Marco croons in his silken voice behind me, and when I turn my head, he's come to the bars. "I dreamed of you last night. Did you dream of me?"

The guard raps his baton against the metal, causing Marco to have to take a step back. "Shut the fuck up, Connelly."

I shouldn't intervene, but my mouth dislocates from my brain. "Easy. He's not hurting anyone."

"Only because of the cell, ma'am."

Marco gives me a searching look, and then he smiles widely, mouthing something like a thank you. My cheeks flame. I can't meet his eyes, looking behind him into the cell instead.

Flynn is standing farther back. When my eyes meet his, he gives a stiff nod. My heart flutters, that tiny greeting taking me back in time to a carefree boy who just wants to give me love. No matter how hard I convince myself what has happened to him is not my fault, seeing him locked up like this still fills me with a gnawing sense of guilt. All I want to do is take him into my arms, stroke his hair, and tell him that one day everything will be all right.

"Who do you want first?" the guard demands.

Marco is my first bet. With his mind powers, he knows a lot. He gathers information and uses it to his advantage. He must know every move that happens in this prison.

And he knows about me what I don't know about myself. *What* I am.

Marco cocks a brow. "Thinking of me?"

I take a step closer to the cell. Our bodies draw close, like every one of my cells yearns to be near his. He smiles, the enigmatic feline smile of a cat who's been served a prime salmon fillet.

He's starting a game again, and while that darkness in me responds and would like nothing better than to play with him, my head needs to be clear. My eyes linger on his lips a little longer than they should before I manage to drag my eyes away.

Marco isn't who I need to be questioning. Despite his information gathering skills, there are gaps. He didn't know about the footage being wiped yesterday. And if I grill him, he'll circle back to me, my family and Damien. I don't have the time for that now. This is not what I'm here for, and the detectives will be here soon.

And honestly…I'm not ready to have another confirmation about the darkness that lurks inside me.

Don't think I'll ever be.

I'm better off without ever finding out.

I glance back into Ronan's cell, his voice

from yesterday dances around my head, telling me he knows who killed Chisholm, but that he won't tell me, not yet.

Aedan and he are whispering. If my powers were functioning properly, I'd be able to pick up on the words easily. I catch a few, though, including my name.

These two are close. Not the same kind of bond between Marco and Flynn, but something equally powerful, if not more so. The way they stand around each other is…protective to say the least. It's not just about business. Some deal they have made perhaps?

Whatever it is, it's their weakness. They have each other's back. If I press on one, the other will break. And I'll get my truth.

"I'll take Ro—O'Shea and Oakberry together," I announce.

Marco lets out a wolf whistle, clearly amused by the innuendo. Heat rises to my face, and the tugging in my belly gets tighter.

"Why?" the guard asks.

"They work together." He doesn't need to know what I've realized. I won't give anyone in this prison more power over these men. "If one of them is guilty, then the other was likely involved somehow."

Also, I'm running out of time. Questioning

them both together will be faster before security arrests me.

The guard doesn't look convinced, but he calls for another guard over the radio. When he arrives, they both take one of the prisoners each and the five of us head to the interrogation room. Once the two prisoners are seated and cuffed, I insist the guards wait outside.

The guards don't want to, but I continue to insist for a valuable three minutes until they finally give up. They make a point of standing just outside the door again, both of them visible through the window.

Aedan and Ronan are staring at me. They look nothing alike—one slender and dark-skinned, the other brawny and pale—but right now the odd smirks on their faces somehow make them look like twins.

"We missed you, Divina, even though it was just one night." It happens instantly, just like it does before; the moment Ronan intones my name, my every cell activates with yearning, aching for me to move closer to him. He's using his fae magic to pull me to his will. Even though I know it, even though I want to fight it, it's intoxicating. "We were worried you wouldn't return."

"I wasn't," Aedan snorts. "I knew you'd be

back." His grin is dangerous. He wants to swallow me up. His lips on my skin, his teeth grazing my neck... I clutch the back of the chair, hastily covering my momentary weakness by making it look like I'm just leaning. "When we get out of here, lass, you and me will have a hell of a go."

"Enough." My voice is sharp. "I'm here to fucking help you, and I don't have much time. So you two are going to tell me everything I need to know right now. What—"

"Divina," Ronan says my name again, this time like a song. My heart speeds, and as if in a trance, I take a step toward him, unable to look away from those eyes. They're not violet anymore, but a dark, brilliant purple. My head is too hazy to figure out why. "Divina Beastly, come closer."

I'm not attached to my body anymore, like I'm watching it from a distance. A detached part of my mind knows what's going on. He's told me himself; he can use my name to control me. That's what he's doing. I'm under his spell—and worse, I want to be.

I can't figure out a single reason to deny the gentle urging of his voice as he draws me closer to him. A woman who looks like me steps ever-so-slightly closer to the fae, and though I know she shouldn't, all I want her to do is touch him.

He continues murmuring to her, to me, coaxing her, while Aedan watches with that same hungry grin. Then she reaches out, slowly, hesitantly, and her fingers brush his skin. The barest touch, hardly even a connection.

It's enough.

"I'm truly sorry, Divina," he murmurs.

Suddenly, my energy vanishes, all of it, pulsing out of my body like blood during a donation. My magic, that same detached part of my mind realizes. Ronan is siphoning my magic. He's taking it from me to use against me.

I'm shoved back in myself again, and the dizziness is making it hard to see, hard to stand. I feel like the last time I got a little too drunk, that unpleasant feeling when it stops being fun and starts feeling like you'll never balance again. I'm dimly aware of a snapping sound, followed by another, and then I'm in Ronan's arms and he's holding me.

How has he gotten out of the cuffs? How has he—

There's a roar. Not a human roar, but the kind of angry animalistic howl that sets Wolf on edge, wanting to join in. The kind of rumble that activates all of Reindeer's flight instincts, screaming at me to run.

Barely standing, I lean against the fae while the guards desperately bang the door, trying to get inside. Why can't they open it?

Through the haze, I see Ronan has his hand pointed at it, muttering something. Is he holding it closed? With his other hand, he reaches out and touches Aedan, saying something else. A purple glow wraps around from Ronan's hand to Aedan's, and I can feel the shift in the air.

A golden shine echoes from Aedan, so brightly I have to shut my eyes for a moment. When I look back, I can register the flash of gold, the unfurling wings, the sweep of a tail powerful enough to knock someone out with a flick.

A dragon stands before me, golden and fierce. At least, that's what I think I see, but when I blink it's Aedan once more.

It takes me a second or two to understand; it's Aedan's body, but he has wings erupting just under the tattoo of a golden dragon on his shoulder blade, a powerful tail, and patches of his skin are covered in glistening, golden scales. Exactly like the tattoo.

A dragon shifter. Aedan is a dragon shifter.

F-U-C-KKK! And Ronan…fucking Ronan is a fae who has just stolen my magic to use it on Aedan. To heal him from the suppressants so he can shift and…

Flames pour from Aedan's mouth. He seems to fill the entire room as he attacks the wall and burns it with a fucking breath.

Oh my God, they're going to break out of here.

I try to speak, but my words don't work. Ronan is whispering to me, telling me I'll be fine when the siphoning wears off. He apologizes once more as Aedan tears at the blazing wall with his bare hands, creating a hole.

Cold air rushes in as Ronan half-carries me toward the new exit. They're not just escaping. They're taking me with them.

"I had to heal him for this to work." Ronan's tone is conversational. "While I'm not affected as much as everyone else by those accursed drugs, I needed a boost before I could clear them from *his* system, too. So I siphoned your powers. I hope you don't mind."

Siphoned?! That's what this son of a bitch calls it? Well, I do fucking mind. A lot. I came here to help them, all of them, and they stole from me. And now they're trying to kidnap me?

I am not a ragdoll to be dragged around. I will not allow it.

The cold air whips against my face as we tumble outside; the two of them jump, Ronan pulling me along with them. That, combined with my rage, is enough to snap me out of the haze.

"No," I roar at Ronan, at Aedan. Wolf snarls, and my body jerks in Ronan's arms so violently that they fall away off me as I shift.

We pile in the snow in the yard just outside the building, the fences in the distance, the woods barely visible beyond. My clothes rip, the shreds flying everywhere, the buttons of my jacket clattering to the ground. Fur sprouts from my skin. It itches and burns as my arms stretch. My fingers retract and my feet twist into paws. Then my eyes contract, my vision sharper, clearer, and I know they are blazing gold. My whole body is vibrating as the tail sprouts, and the world tilts and then rights itself just as I straighten on my four legs.

I am Wolf. Wolf is me.

Ronan stumbles backward, thrown away by the power of my shift, and Aedan turns from his stride, staring at me as I come barreling toward them, my canine teeth the same color as the snow around us, my gray fur rising all around me, giving me an aura of the outrage in my heart.

Screaming and yelling blare as alarms shriek. Guards pour out of the building. I don't concentrate on any of it because all I can feel is the anger toward these two bastards.

"Surrender!" someone yells, but it falls mute on my ears.

I pounce, but Ronan dodges. I miss him by only an inch. Aedan, still half in dragon form, lunges, but I am too quick for him, darting out of the way. Then I wheel back to attack, my teeth bared, aiming for his throat.

That's when the gunfire starts.

I have to move to the side, skimming on my paws to avoid a bullet, my target momentarily forgotten. The three of us are moving farther away from the building but toward the high, barbed wire fence that towers over us.

It may be electrified, but the gate is too far away. We can't make it even if we run. I don't want to run anyway. I'm still ready to fight, still snarling, and I leap at Ronan once more.

Aedan intervenes and grabs me, his huge arms wrapped around me, and then his wings are flapping. Ronan is grabbing at me, too. The three of us are in the air until a bullet strikes off Aedan's scales.

We spiral to the ground again; he hasn't

gained his full powers yet, and I'm too heavy for him to keep flying and also defend himself in this form. Good.

The fence is behind us. He must have managed to get us over it, away from the guards as the shot rang out. I'm the first on my feet while Ronan and Aedan try to help each other up. I swoop down on them fast. They are prone, weak, and Wolf is ready to claim her victory.

"Divina!"

My fur stands on end as I freeze at the last voice I expect to hear right now. I howl and turn from these two fuckers, bolting toward my father.

He dashes toward us in horror. "Divina, I told you to stay away. I—"

The sound of the guns is heavier. What the fuck is he doing here? I shouldn't have told him I was coming here. I need to get him out, I need to—

Something hits my underbelly. I fall on the snow in a split-second, dizzy, human once more, stark naked. So fast. A bullet won't do that. *What the hell?*

When I look down, my belly is bleeding, and a dart is pointing upward from it.

"D!" Dad rushes to my side, and then he puts his arm under me. "Shit. Easy, D." His gaze widens at my wound, and then it bounces around in panic. "Fuck," he growls. "Okay. Easy, baby girl. I'll get you out of here."

"Dad," I slur. "Why are you here? Run. I—"

"It's okay. It's going to be okay. You just need to get out of here, baby girl." He looks over to where Aedan and Ronan have scrambled to their feet again, Aedan's wings curved protectively around them both as the bullets continue to fly.

A shout pierces my ears, and two guards run toward us from this side of the fence, rifles and crossbows in their hands.

Dad helps me to my feet and nods at Aedan. "Go with them. They'll help you."

"No!" I argue, ignoring the pounding in my head. "No, no, I need to help you. I need to get *you* out of here. You could be captured. You could die!" Panic stabs me. "Please, Dad, I can't lose you, too. We need to—"

Gunfire starts again, and he gives me a hard shove. I yelp as I stumble forward until I bounce off Aedan's side. He puts his arm around me instantly, and I don't understand what's happening because all I can see and feel is his massive bulk. As he holds me tight against him, I'm too weak to struggle.

Then the cold air blows at me as we fly away.

NINETEEN

AEDAN

I lose my concentration for a second, almost getting hit myself, as she goes tumbling to the ground in human form, the dart piercing her naked belly. I manage to sweep the dart coming at me away with my wing just in time. Fuck, that was close.

I scramble to my feet, helping Ronan up. Why is she acting dense? How has she seen this ending by fighting us? And they say she has brains.

She's one tough cookie, though. There are cuts and bruises all over her from the fall or the fight, a huge dart sticking out of her bloody belly, yet she's struggling to her feet. She never stops fighting, does she?

A bloke appears out of nowhere and runs to her side, helping her. "D! Shit. Easy, D." He darts a fearful glance my way. "Fuck. Okay. Easy, baby girl. I'll get you out of here."

"Dad," she slurs. "Why are you here? Run. I—"

That's her da? What the fuck is he doing here? What the hell is wrong with this family?

It looks like they're arguing when the next wave of gunfire starts. Then, all of a sudden, he shoves her toward me.

Without thinking, I catch her in one arm, holding her protectively against my side. Close to the approaching guards, he shifts, and it's... I have no fucking clue what that is. It's neither a wolf nor a deer. Something so fucked up and ugly even for a beast.

I've got a kinship with this deformed creature. Maybe he struggles just as much as I do to find someone who accepts him amongst the other bastard shifters.

This *thing* charges at the guards, roaring and braying and holding them back. Is he actually...?

Holy fuck. He's giving us a chance to get out of here.

There's a brief second where the beast looks around, and his eyes meet mine. I understand what he wants immediately. He doesn't like us. He doesn't trust us. But he needs us to get his girl out of here.

The girl I'm holding so close, enveloping her with my wings so she won't get hurt, instead of flying my ass and Ronan's out of here as soon as we can.

Against all instincts or sanity.

I give her da a quick, respectful nod, and then unfurl my wings once more. I grab Divina's arm, and then Ronan is next to me, holding her other one. His eyes go bright purple as he summons the see-through wings of his own. They glitter silver in the snow and look a bit girly for my taste, but there's no denying that they help as we both take off together, lifting the girl into the sky and toward the woods, as far from here as we can get.

"Dad," she slurs again as we leave the ground. I glance back at the guards overwhelming the creature. I feel a pang of guilt, but I can't stop now. I keep flying.

It's time we were free.

TWENTY

AEDAN

We fly as far as our out-of-practice wings can manage, deep into the woods and settle in a clearing next to a lake.

I shift fully back into a human, and Ronan starts to strip. It says something about our relationship that I don't even ask why.

Divina reels back, staring at Ronan in horror. "What the fuck?! What the fuck are you doing? Stop that! If you come near me,

I'll kill you. I'll *kill* you."

"Calm down, Divina," Ronan says. "Do you really think I'd do *this* to you? Don't be silly. I don't want to hurt you, I swear."

"And I'm supposed to buy that because you say you can't lie?" she shouts.

I put my hand on her shoulder. "Easy, lass."

She shakes me off, and gives me a look that could kill a lesser man. She's right pissed off, and I'm glad she can't shift again.

Ronan holds out his shoes and the jumpsuit he's been wearing. She stares at it for a moment and then snatches the clothes without a word of thanks.

"You're welcome," he teases.

She turns her back to me, to us, and there's a sharp gasp and the coppery tang of blood as she pulls the dart out of her own belly and drops it to the side. She cleans herself off with the lake water with one hand, her other applying pressure to the wound, even though the water must be freezing her tits off. I can't risk starting a fire, though, not even one I make myself.

I can't see her from the front now, but the naked skin on her back and how it curves down into that sweet arse, tangled with the coppery smell, has my cock ready for action. I want to go to her, show her how to get warm with my body, rough and hard and sweaty.

It's not just about sex. She's been naked in my arms for a while, and I've managed to control myself. But now she's covered in blood—from her injuries, and from the rough way she's removed the dart. Most of it isn't visible from here, except what's matted in her hair, but I can smell it. I have to stay back because if I don't, I might not be able to stop my dragon from coming out again, and this time it won't be to play. My teeth and my tongue yearn to taste her flesh, to suck, to bite, to fuck, to *kill…*

Then, as if she hasn't already given us a show, she disappears behind a tree, limping and wincing, her hand still on her stomach. When she returns, the too-big jumpsuit on her, she's still groaning. At least she looks warmer.

She's trying to be strong, but she grunts in pain every time she moves. While the blood is muted somewhat, I can still smell it, and I still want to have her for dinner.

We need to do something about that wound. Ronan isn't the only one here who doesn't want to hurt her.

He grins, and she gives him a questioning look. With a wink and a wave of his hand that

I know is absolutely not necessary, he glamors some fancy shit to preserve his own modesty. A jumper and some trousers would do, but no, that's not good enough for Ronan O'Shea. He's got this loud purple shirt with ruffles, and dark blue pants. There's a dark pink waistcoat and a matching tie artfully arranged on there too.

The show-off. He should look ridiculous, but against his skin, and with his eyes, the effect is kind of powerful, even for me. It's distracted me from all the hunger frenzy.

"You look lovely," he says, as though she's come to meet him for a date and not here in a prison uniform because we kidnapped her.

"Oh, I look *lovely*, do I?" Her anger flares so hot I can feel it like a flame on the side of my face just by being near her. "Is this how you dress all the girls you take advantage of?"

Ronan frowns, and when he speaks, I'm reminded of a teacher who patronizes the shit out of everyone. "Divina, please be reasonable."

"Keep my name out of your mouth! We need to go back right now to get my father! I should never have come back for you, you selfish bastards. I should kill you!"

"I'd like to see you try." There's a flicker of irritation in Ronan's voice right now.

Cináed, my dragon, snarls in agreement. He wants to see her try, too. He wants her to shift back into that wolf, and then we'll see which of us is stronger. Teeth and claws and panting and sweat—

"And we're not going to get your father," Ronan stresses. "He made his choice. He sacrificed himself to protect *you*. If we go back there, and you get caught, you'll make it all for nothing. Should it go to waste?"

"You are going to help me, and then I never want to see you again, you selfish fae bastard! Either of you. I hate you, do you understand? You and your powers and your tricks. I couldn't care less if you die out here or there. But I'm not going to let you leave my father to die!"

Ronan shakes his head. "Unfortunate though it may be, we can't simply walk back into hell."

She snarls and takes a few steps, clearly meaning to get as far from us as possible, though her injuries ruin the effect a bit. "I don't need you."

"You can't go anywhere like that." My voice is unusually quiet and gruff, and the care lacing it is shocking to me. Why do I care if she storms off wounded? Let her, if she wants. But somehow, the idea of her being overpowered by those guards, unable to shift, unable to heal, makes me claw at my own insides in anxiety and outrage. "You're hurt."

"Let me heal you," Ronan offers.

"I can heal myself," she growls, but it sounds more like a groan.

"You can't. You've been injected by the same suppressant we have, and from what I can tell, it was a massive dose. You changed back immediately. And you're still bleeding through my suit. You can't heal, and you can't shift. You need me to—"

"I don't need you to *anything!*" She turns and storms off into the woods. "Fuck both of you. I'm getting my dad back."

Ronan and I watch her go. Maybe it's for the best. Maybe she will just slow us down. Maybe—

Her scream bellows in my ears.

I don't even think. I run toward the sound.

TWENTY-ONE

AEDAN

She shivers on the ground, delirious. Ronan examines her, pulling up her trouser leg where she's clutching it. Two little holes are bleeding just above her ankle. The sweat is pouring off her, and it looks like her dander into the woods is about to cost her.

"It's a snake bite," Ronan declares as he puts a hand on her forehead. "Shit. She's burning up. The venom is acting fast."

"Heal her," I command.

Ronan folds his arms. "No. She doesn't want my help, she said so herself. She can get by without it. We need to leave."

That stung pride in his voice makes me growl. But he stares at me, unmoved. "Aedan. She's dangerous. She could get us thrown back in that pit."

He's not wrong. As I stare at her shaking body, smell the blood from her fresh wound, my hunger is awake again. I'm starving. I want to swallow her up. That would solve all our problems right now. I'd just have to shift, and with one snap of my teeth—

"You're right," I grumble, struggling to stay under control. "We need to get the fuck out of here. I can't be around her."

Because I want to kill her. I want to make a meal out of her. But I also have this overwhelming need to protect her, as strongly as I need to protect Ronan. As strongly as I once had the need to take care of Bethany.

I can't do both.

I need to go.

We turn away, but after a few steps he stops and looks back before turning away once more. He does this a couple of times. His eyes flick between me and Divina's struggling body.

Now *he's* having second thoughts?

"Let's go," I insist, letting all my confusion and anger and need to escape fill my voice. "Now. She's a distraction. What do we say about distractions?"

He gives a sharp nod, and we march out of here, leaving her on the ground in a pool of her own sweat. A few feet away, we both unleash our wings, ready to fly.

Behind us, her soft sobbing fills the air, so faint yet thundering through me. Now that we're gone, she finally allows herself to feel pain. She finally allows herself to cry.

Because she's going to die.

Because we're leaving her to die.

Ronan freezes next to me, and I stop to a halt. "Ah, fuck. Away 'n shite and may the divil damn us a' to hell." It's a nonsense curse, one my mother used before she passed when she realized there was no way out of a situation, but it feels horribly accurate here.

One look is all we exchange before we put our wings away, and as one unit we run back to save Divina's life.

TWENTY-TWO
RONAN

We're farther into the woods, next to a much smaller body of water, the sky a dark orange around an hour away from the shelter of night, when Divina finally wakes up. She's been sleeping off the healing magic, curled up on a piece of the ground that Aedan has cleared of snow for her.

Wild-eyed, she looks around before she stares at me. "Why am I alive?" Her voice is cautious and thick with sleep, but not slurred anymore.

I rise to my knees and approach to check her temperature. When my hand rests against her forehead, she flinches. My fingers retract as I squat a foot away. The fever is gone, though, thank nature. "I healed you."

"Oh." She raises her hand to her head, probably dizzy. My magic still isn't at one hundred percent, so it isn't a perfect healing, and the drugs are still in her system. "You came back for me?"

I had to. I don't know why, but I just had to. "I told you, the drug inhibits you. You would have died if I'd left you."

"And you don't like death." She nods to herself. "It fits the profile."

I cock a brow. Even in this situation, confused and exhausted, she's analyzing me still? She's…astounding.

"Than—I mean, I appreciate your healing me."

The corner of my mouth twitches. Clever girl, confused or not. "You're welcome."

"Where's Oakberry?"

"*Aedan* is getting some food, so just sit tight and let us look after you."

Her bottomless eyes inspect me for long moments. I don't dare look away. They hold me in place in the most pleasurable yet dangerous way. "I should never have come back to the pen for you."

"Probably not."

"But I did."

"Yes."

"And now you've saved me."

"That's right."

She keeps watching me carefully, and I remain struck by her expression. "So…does that mean …we're even?"

"How do you mean?"

"Your kind doesn't like debts. Does that mean we've saved each other, and now we don't have to worry about paying it back?"

Fuck me. I intake a sharp breath. If only she knew what that intelligence, that spark, is doing to me. I can't believe how quick she is to learn and how able she is to use each and every situation to her advantage. It's almost fae, but not quite. She's something else. Maybe even something more. "I suppose it does."

"Good." She stands, too quickly.

"Careful, you shouldn't—"

Before I finish, her foot slips in the ice, and she loses her balance. Quick as a flash, I jump to her side, catching her in my arms. She falls against me hard, pressed against my chest, her face a few inches from mine.

My gaze roams her face, those lips. I bite mine in a reflex, her warmth intoxicating. "Looks like I saved you again." My voice is a low murmur. "How will you pay me back?"

The silence stretches, wrapping around us, and there's nothing for a moment except me and Divina in my arms. She doesn't pull away from my body, and her lips part. All I want is to lean down and…

"You're up on your feet already," Aedan disrupts the moment.

Her lashes flutter as she breaks our embrace. "Almost."

I glare at him, and then my eyes fall on the couple of rabbits in his hands. He's already skinned them out of sight. Is this for her sake? Is he trying to protect her delicate eyes from his kills? How…sweet. How unlike him. I am right about one thing—Divina Beastly is dangerous for us.

He offers her a chunk of meat. "Here."

She moves away from him and sits back where she's slept.

"What, you're vegetarian, your howling highness?" he taunts.

"I don't need your help. I can feed myself."

"How? You'll run to a convenience store?

Dressed like that?" Aedan laughs, so loudly it scares the birds from the nearby trees.

She looks down at my too-big prison uniform on her body, and then she scowls at him.

He crouches next to her and shoves the rabbit leg closer to her nose. "You need food to heal."

For a second, the stubbornness is there again, but then her expression softens when she glances down at the snow. "I'm not hungry. But...thank you for saving me."

A brief look of surprise crosses Aedan's freckled face, but then he snorts. "If you want to thank me, then eat."

Who are you, and what did you do with my gruff dragon friend?

Finally, she accepts the food, chewing at the raw meat without a fuss. Then she takes another piece, and another. She *is* hungry; healing isn't exactly easy on the body at the best of times, much less when my magic is still less than it should be.

As we chomp our little dinner, Aedan doesn't shut up. I'm beyond surprised; I've never heard him say so many words all at the same time. He tells her about Collins and the changes he's brought with him. Throwing us in the new Ward E that sucks the life out of each and every one of our kind. Then not long after giving us the mandatory suppressing pills.

"But they don't affect you like they do the others, Ronan?" I get that familiar thrill when she uses my name. Her aggression is gone now. She's just…curious. Could it be the near-death experience that has made that change?

"That's right. You and Aedan, Gianmarco and Flynn, *have* magic. I *am* magic. Separating a fae from that is impossible. When that happens, the creature they become is…even less than human. My brother found a way to give the magic up, and it killed him after just ten years. His body simply couldn't sustain him any longer."

I can't believe I'm telling her this. That sharp look in her eyes, the clever way she talks to me, still compel me to tell her more.

They make me *want* to tell her more.

Aedan grunts, his black eyes wide, baffled by my opening up as I am by his endless chatter.

"I'm sorry for your loss." She seems like she wants to say something else, and for a wild moment I think she's going to embrace me. But she turns to Aedan. "You lost someone too, didn't you?"

"Bethany," he mumbles.

I tense. Talking about Bethany can get...dicey. But his voice is different than usual, less angry. "My little sister... She got really sick and died because I couldn't protect her." He stares out onto the water. "She was all I had."

"I'm sorry." There's a look of pity in her eyes. My heart races; I know Aedan hates pity.

He just shrugs. "Don't apologize."

She glances at him for a moment, then at me, looking like she's struggling with something. After a long moment, she says, "My mom died, too."

My heart squeezes, and I think of my own mother. Magic, supernatural or human, losing a family member is an ache that never goes away.

"My mother...she could have stayed alive, but she chose to die." Her head turns toward the water. "I guess her children weren't worth living for."

That is...disturbing, and out of character, coming from her. "Your mother was human. Humans die, Divina."

"Well, Dad, me, anyone of the family could have turned her, kept her alive, but she refused, again and again. She tangled my life up with this supernatural nonsense, vampires and demons and shifters and the literal fucking dev—"

Aedan and I exchange glances. Her glistening eyes catch us as her head jerks back in our direction. "Apparently, what she praised about all her life, how supes are just good enough, she didn't believe a fucking word of it. Being a supe wasn't good enough for the great Vixen Legend."

Vixen Legend.

I know that name. Just like I knew the Beastly name. But why can't I remember anything about them?

"She had four children… four husbands…and her brother, all supes, but she just let herself die. As a fucking human. Leaving me all alone. Leaving all of us so alone." Her voice cracks at the end, and a tear rolls down her face.

Aedan seems to have forgotten I exist, forgotten his hunger for this girl, as he reaches out and hugs her. He's a marvelous creature; strong as an ox, stubborn as a bear, more loyal than anyone or anything I've encountered in thousands of years, but emotions are far from his strong point.

"Wait a minute. Did you say four husbands?" I ask, not that it's any of my business, putting enough humor in my question. For some wicked reason, I hate to see her sad.

Divina sniffs and nods. "Mom knew how to have fun, at least. Did you know that even though we're twins, my sister and I have different dads?"

"Get away out of that." Aedan draws back, his accent stronger in his surprise.

She shakes her head. "It's true. And guess who my sister's dad is?"

"Who?" Aedan asks.

"My dad's brother. My own uncle."

He growls a laugh, and she slaps his arm. "Sorry." He laughs again.

Well, now, isn't that interesting? I know such a thing is *possible,* but it's far from *probable.* I must learn more about her father, about her sister's father. Perhaps it's connected to that dark power that is so intoxicating within her. Perhaps it's the reason her name nags me. "That sounds complicated."

For some reason, this makes her cheeks go pink. "A bit. Yeah. You could say that."

Aedan coughs over the laughter. "What about the other two?"

"A vampire and a demon," she answers. "The four of them are brothers, by blood or MC, possessive as it can get, but they were just…fine with it. Can you imagine?"

Aedan shrugs. "I've heard stranger things, lass. Whatever rocked their boats."

She shakes her head again, irritably this time as if she's not explaining properly, as if he doesn't understand. "No. It wasn't just a sex thing. They…they all loved her. And she claimed she loved them all too."

My eyes narrow at her. "But you don't believe she did because she *died*?"

Her jaw twists. She doesn't look at me, though; her eyes are on Aedan, and that makes my stomach constrict.

"I've seen your da, lass. If a human had sex with that, her heart must have something to do with it," he says. "Do you shift into…that creature, too?"

"That creature is a reinwolf, and no, I have two separate beasts, a wolf and reindeer. Lucky me." She scoffs at the end.

"You are lucky. You don't know what it feels like to be an ugly monster, rejected even by other monster bastards that think they're too pretty to hang with a reinwolf or a…dragon."

Her thin brows hitch. Her lips part, her tongue flicking nervously along them. "You're not ugly."

The gold in his gaze sparkles as he seems to be eating her now in his head. The tension and the heat building between them are undeniable. She watches him carefully, like she's scared he might snap, but her gold flares as well. Suddenly I feel like an intruder.

Aedan will sleep with any woman who crosses his path, and Divina is far too fine a specimen for him to pass up. Yet I can't pretend it's only his lust for her I'm feeling.

If I'm honest with myself, truly honest, the draw she has for me isn't only intellectual, isn't only magical. I'm curious about all of her. I want to know every inch of her mind, of her body, of her soul. I want to hear her whispering my name under the stars.

I believe my good friend wants the same.

"Do you think it's possible? To…feel things for more than one person like that at once?" she asks him.

My pride pushes me to move away, but I want to hear his answer. It's suddenly very, very important that I know what he thinks on this matter.

"I don't know," he says finally. "I mean, I was sure you were fucking that detective lad you brought to the pen the first day."

Her cheeks blush. "That's… Derek and I are just—"

"I think," Aedan interrupts, that needy growl in his voice, "that you can feel whatever you like about however many people you like at once. Fuck society. Who says otherwise? Who cares?"

"Who cares," she repeats, moving closer to him as he does the same.

Before their lips can meet, I clear my throat, and they both jump back. I've never seen Aedan's cheeks so red before.

He rubs the back of his ugly skull. "Do you…um…have names for your beasts?"

She shakes her head. "Just Wolf and Reindeer."

"That's gammy."

Her eyes dip to his mouth every time he uses his Irishisms. I bet he's playing them up deliberately. "Yeah? So what? Do you name your dragon?"

"Cináed," he says, smug.

"Is that what you call your penis, too?"

His jaw falls, and I chuckle. He does call his dick that. "Uh… No."

She smirks. "I think you do. And before you ask, I don't call my breasts Wolf and Reindeer nor do I call my vagina anything."

He growls before he grimaces at me. "That's exactly what I was going to ask. How the fuck does she do that? She's worse than you."

A chuckle escapes her, but she moans right

after when she touches her forehead. "I'm exhausted. And dizzy. Is your magic supposed to do that?"

Oh, she can still see me? For a second, I think I'm invisible. "My powers aren't at full capacity yet. You should just get more sleep. It will help cover the lack."

"What about my father?" Her tone as it matches mine captivates me. She's not going to easily play our game. In fact, I think we might be playing hers all along. The conversation, the sharing, even the sexual tension…

Even though I understand all that and how dangerous she is with her mind games, as she meets my eyes a frisson of understanding sparks between us. For the first time in my life, I don't know exactly how to proceed, and while it's terrifying, it's also…exciting?

"You're in no state to worry about him right now. Sleep some more. We can talk in the morning."

With a reluctant sigh, she nods. It doesn't take long before she dozes off. Her injuries have obviously exhausted her.

I clear a space for myself, glad I'm nowhere near as affected by the cold as she must be.

Aedan and I lie down on either side of her. He doesn't say anything to me, and I don't say anything to him. We stare at the horizon, at the sun setting on the day we are finally free, and then at the girl that just feeling her next to me fills me with an emotion I've long forgotten.

Happiness.

TWENTY-THREE
RONAN

As night falls, Aedan is restless and wanders off back into the trees, leaving us alone by the water. Divina is fast asleep. I check her temperature, listening to her breaths. Better but not fully healed yet. She will, though. I hope.

I take the opportunity to enjoy myself in the silence at last. I rid myself of the glamored clothes, done with them for now. The weather never affects our kind like it does others, and

I want to finally feel fresh air on my skin after being trapped inside for so long.

I close my eyes for a long moment, allowing the air to sing to me, the grass that is sleeping under the snow to brush my feet. My heart swells. The remnants of the drugs are gone already, faster than I have imagined. I am able to be myself, my full self, for the first time in years.

Time to put my full magic to the test. Touching the water, I whisper its name. It doesn't respond on my first go. A lancing of fear tingles my skin. What if I can't do it? What if that place has left me ruined?

What if I am less than fae now?

I say the name again, enticingly, flirting with it to rise. It wants to respond. I feel it bubbling, but it won't rise, not yet. The third time, I'm pleading, singing for the water to listen, wishing it to love my song.

As I open my eyes, the cold water rises to meet me. I step forward, so grateful, so happy, so full of the power of my magic that tears fill my eyes.

The water is icy when I plunge into its depths, but I tame it with the right cadence of its name. It welcomes me with love, cocooning me like a mother bringing her child into an embrace.

The waves wash the stench of the prison and the dullness of the suppressants from my body. Closing my eyes again, I let Mother Nature reclaim me, let the water invigorate me, let the feeling of belonging awaken my soul.

I stay under for a long time, longer than most creatures could survive. I know the names of the air and water and they respond to my call, working together to let me breathe and keep me under.

Abruptly, a heaviness on my arm disrupts the serenity and pulls me out of the water and onto the bank with surprising strength.

My heart hammers, but I'm ready to fight the unwelcome intruder. Then the softness of her hands soothes me more than the water itself.

She looks angelic as she leans over me, despite the darkness inside her she knows nothing of. Her brown curls brush my bare chest, and her lips are startlingly close to mine as she shakes me by the shoulders. "Ronan. What are you doing? You'll freeze to death! Where are your clothes? What happened? Ronan!"

I chuckle and raise my hand to her face. My dark fingers stand out against her pale skin when I run them down her cheek. "I thought you didn't care if we died. Isn't that what you said? If I were you, I'd want us to die."

She grimaces. "I… Why were you in the water?"

"I was just taking a swim, enjoying my freedom. The coldness doesn't affect me."

She pulls back, but she doesn't get up, doesn't move away. Her eyes are wide and blue and staring into mine as if she can read my soul. "You're not hurt?"

"I'm not." I look up into her face, as reassuring as I can. Her skin and eyes twinkle with the reflection of the bright moon and the sky above her. She belongs amongst the stars. I'm suddenly very aware of her beauty, how her legs are parted across me, how I am naked and she is holding me. I may be thousands of years old but she is still a girl with stellar allure, and fae or not, I still have a dick.

"For the record…I don't want you to die," she whispers. "Does that make me stupid? Because I think it does. I could have been home now, celebrating a win. But I came back to the pen for you anyway. I'm an idiot."

"You're far from an idiot." There's a deep irritation to my voice. I'm angry that she'll even associate that word with herself.

"If I'm not, then why did I come back? And even now, I tried to save you again, even though you have all that magic. That horrible thing that brought me here in the first place."

"It doesn't make you stupid. It makes you kind."

She looks right at me, not into my eyes, but at my lips. Does she like the shiver only she is causing? Does she want to taste them? Should I let her?

My hand is still resting against her cheek, and my other moves slowly, cautiously, to her back, holding her where she is leaning over me. "I didn't know you cared so much."

Color deepens in her cheeks, her lips hanging open. "I...I don't." She doesn't even attempt to sound convincing. "Well, I mean...your death will be an injustice. I know you're innocent."

"I didn't kill Sean Chisholm." My hand on her cheek moves as if it had a mind of its own, tangling in her hair, and she leans into the touch without resistance. "But that doesn't mean I'm innocent."

She doesn't say anything, her eyes still locked on my lips.

"Does that scare you, Divina?" I whisper. "Do I scare you?"

Her gaze inspects me with more interest, my face, my shoulders, my chest. She suddenly seems to be aware of my nakedness, too. "No. You don't scare me."

She shuffles her legs as though she's going to move away. Instead it just brings her closer. I feel the outside of my rough uniform on her as it brushes against my cock. It stiffens, longing for something that should never happen. My fingers tighten, hesitantly, applying the faintest pressure to the back of her head, bringing her mouth down to meet mine.

She gasps as my tongue touches her lips. "What are you doing?" she mumbles, her lips still against mine.

"Do you want me to stop?"

She doesn't answer, and I pull her down again. This time she parts her lips. Her tongue flicks out, exploring my mouth, exploring me. Kissing her is sweeter than a spring morning.

She lies over my exposed body now, supported only by her hands in the snow on either side of my head, my grip in her hair and on her back. I want more of her, all of her. My cock is harder than I can ever recall, fully awake in agreement, which I'm sure she can feel as she presses herself against me, deepening the kiss.

She moans when I finally end it, but then she draws back a little. "What are we doing? Are you—"

"I'm not compelling you. Won't. Not for this. Never for this."

Her lashes do that cute fluttering thing. "I believe you. It's the drugs… My father… I don't know what I'm feeling, Ronan."

The way she says my name makes me shiver, and her body responds, shuddering against mine. "I won't compel you. We can stop," I say again, but there's a thirst in my voice now, a deep need I won't hide. "But I want you. I've wanted you since the first second you showed me that brilliant mind of yours. I don't know what you are, Divina, but I want to know all of you, every part. I *need* you."

"You can't have me." Her voice is firm. She moves back so that she's sitting up, her legs straddling my hips.

My whole body slumps, except for my cock that jerks at the disappointment, protesting. "I'm sorry—"

"But I can have you." She reaches for the zip on the jumpsuit, that same hard look she had during interrogations blazing in her eyes now.

My heart and cock leap. I'm enthralled as she bares her shoulders, that enticing dip between her neck and collarbone. Then she reveals her breasts, the nipples already erect.

Is it from the cold, or is it because of me? "I will have you." It sounds like a decision. "You're not in control here, Ronan. I'm in control. This is mine. Right now, *you* are mine."

I've never belonged to *someone* before. I am used to being the one who does the owning. I control people with their names, I hold people by their souls. The people I sleep with, they are being granted a favor, giving themselves to me. But that isn't what she wants, isn't what she needs. She feels out of control, and she wants to take it back, and she's going to use me to do it.

My pride objects strongly, but now she shuffles out of the suit, briefly breaking contact to remove it. She stands over me as nude as I am, and I swallow, unable to utter a word.

It's not just her perfect nakedness. She has captivated me, more than I know, more than I understand. Despite what I am, I want to give into her. I *have* to give into her, and the less I understand it, the more I need it.

She's straddling me again, and I can't move away. There's no hesitation in her eyes as she leans down to kiss me again.

I give a low, hungry groan of pleasure as her white tits press against my dark chest. My hand trails down her spine, delighted when I find a spot that makes her squirm just to the left of it. I tease her there for a bit before moving farther, touching the flesh of her ass. She lets out a little yelp when I squeeze, and then her lips move from mine to my neck, my ears.

She pauses there. From the wideness of her eyes I realize my glamor has faded. All of my concentration is on her now, and there's nothing left for magic. She *is* the magic.

I look to the side. My hair falls silver down to my dark arms. The point must be showing clearly on my ears. She gazes at them. Is she scared? Has it unnerved her too much? Does she want to stop? Fuck.

But then she leans forward more, her lips brushing the sensitive point at the tip of my ear. It makes me harder, craving to be inside her. Now. My responding groan is guttural as she's wetter than she has been.

"You're beautiful," she whispers.

With that, my hand moves from her ass, accessing her pussy just below it, not dipping in yet but stroking, teasing. She squirms and presses against my fingers, impatient. It makes me slow down more, enjoying her need, reveling in how much she wants me, needs me, just like she's made me need her back in that prison. Like she makes me need her now.

Then I slip two fingers in her wetness, moving slowly at first, then faster. She moves along with me as her mouth runs across my body, her tongue on my chest, my nipples, her sharp teeth digging into my shoulder. She's claiming me, marking me as hers, making this about her, not about me at all.

I shouldn't allow this, and yet I'm spellbound. I don't know what magic she casts over me, but as her teeth sink into my skin, all I want is to give her more pleasure. I continue to with my fingers even as my cock pulses in desperation, needing to feel her.

She bites again, tasting my blood, moving against my hand, her clit rubbing against my thumb while my fingers explore deeper and deeper. "Harder," she commands, and I obey her, groaning, my hand moving faster, my thumb rubbing at her, making her feel everything I possibly can.

Her head whips back as she gasps wildly, my blood on her lips. The feral darkness in her eyes now isn't about the thrill of a beast with a claim. I can't understand what makes her so different from any shifter I've met before, but I am locked into her. I want nothing more than her. Though my pride wants me to be the one taking control, I *need* to give in to her, to let whatever magic she possesses wash over me.

"You're mine," she grunts, her eyes closed as she moves. "Mine."

It's enough to undo me, but I keep up my work as she's told me to until she cries out. It fills the forest, and Aedan must hear it. Maybe the whole world hears it, but I don't care. At this moment, I don't care about anything except her.

She explodes around me, the wetness soaking my hand, her breath coming heavy, and her heavy-lidded, golden eyes and parted mouth are the hottest thing I've ever seen. My cock is straining, my body begging me to take her, but I can't because she's holding me, and she isn't mine, just like she commanded. I'm hers.

Suddenly, her arms are holding my wrists, her hand caressing the names of my family, pinning my arms down. She holds them above my head, growling at me wordlessly to stay still, and I want nothing more than to be whatever she wants from me.

She positions herself, sliding onto my cock, and the feel of her around me is too much even before she starts moving. It's agonizingly slow at first, and I know she's getting back at me, teasing me, taunting me.

"You're killing me," I groan under my breath.

Her teeth find my lips this time, and I squeeze her ass, moaning. "Did I tell you to speak?"

I just shake my head, burning with all the need she's inducing inside me. She holds me steady as she moves faster, leaning forward to brush her clit against me, making my hardness work for her, making this about her own pleasure, not mine, until she's good and ready.

As she bounces, I thrust my hips, moving with her, deep inside of her. I'm trying so hard not to come and fill her pussy yet because I want to see that face she makes when she comes again, the face of ultimate pleasure, before I take my own. But fuck, it's hard not to come right away, especially after going so long without a woman's touch.

I have never known pleasure like this in my thousands of years of life. I've never been tamed like this, never allowed it, never wanted it. If she wants me to tell her I'm her slave right now I will.

She rides me, uses me, and I let her. Then she leans down, her lips grazing my ear once more. "*Ronan O'Shea.*"

"Oh fuck." The way she intones my name is exactly right to overpower me. To bend me to her will, not mine, but at the same time, it doesn't subdue me. It's quite the opposite.

How the fuck does she do it?

I don't have time to think about it because I'm soaring. Literally. My wings are out, lifting us into the sky. Silver glitter falls from them, sparkling onto the snow as we rise. It's my magic, connecting with her. At this moment, she is as much a part of the magic as I am.

She gasps, not a gasp for what I'm making her feel physically, but something amazed, wondrous, entranced. She stares at my wings as though she's never seen anything like them, and I want nothing more than for her to look at me like that forever.

As she lets go of my wrists and holds my shoulders for support instead, my arms wrap tight around her, keeping her safe, keeping her with me. The gold in her eyes flames, and she rides me harder in the air.

I push inside of her, and she moans for me. My eyes shut tight as unbelievable warmth rocks through me in waves, my cum spilling into her pussy. I am going to pull away, but she holds me tight by the legs, riding me still, elongating the pleasure, letting me finish inside of her. Then I can hear nothing but her crying out again.

When she crumbles and pants on my chest,

I gently dip us back to the ground. My head rests among the snow as I pant with her in a kiss.

She touches the glittering silver on my wings, mesmerized by my magic, the magic she's caused in me. Then she flops back, lying on my chest, her long hair all over me, my cock still inside of her. I wrap my hands around her back, holding her close, and we stay like that in sweet silence for a while.

"I can't believe I just did that," she mumbles.

My heart skips a beat. Our bodies separate, and it's like I've lost a part of myself. I want to tell her to come back, but she's already rinsing herself clean with the icy lake water.

"Divina," I start, not sure what I plan to follow it with. I'm not used to being unsure.

Quickly, she dresses to protect herself. From the cold or from me? She looks at me, not hurt or angry. She doesn't smile, but there's something softer about her face than before. "You should put some clothes on before you sleep. It's cold. I don't want you to freeze to death. No matter how magical you are."

"I don't need them, but if it makes you feel better, sure." I conjure the same glamored outfit again.

The way she's ended our intimacy stings. I've given myself to her, let her control me, and the strangest thing is, no part of me regrets it. But she does. "Do you do that with all your claims?"

"Huh?"

"You've claimed me, and now you…"

"I told you I'm confused. The drugs—"

"You're healed. The drugs have worn out." I show her her own bite marks on my shoulder. The marks of a wolf, not a human. "I don't know how you burned them so quickly. Must be the high metabolism of your double beasts."

"Ronan, I… I don't know. Please try to understand this isn't easy for me."

I step forward and touch her face. "You used my name."

She smiles truly for the first time, a devilish smile that makes my heart lurch. "Did you like it?"

What a question. How do I answer it? Do I like to be used by her? Do I tell her that nobody else has ever brought me to heel like that, not even any of my lovers from amongst the fae? Do I tell her that the physical feeling of her body, while exquisite, is nothing to how she is able to command my heart, my soul? Do I tell her that I've known her for two days, and that already I can't imagine a life without her in it? "I—"

Aedan walks back into the clearing. He looks at us, at my hand on her cheek, and then narrows his eyes at the melted snow under where I'm standing. "Been having fun, have we?"

Divina doesn't even blush. "Good, you're back. We need to keep moving. They must be after us. Honestly, I have no clue how we haven't got caught by now."

"Have a better place to hide, your highness? One of your MC safe houses maybe where I can fucking make a fire without getting caught?"

She narrows her eyes pensively. "Actually, I have something even better."

TWENTY-FOUR
DIVINA

After Mom died, I swore I'd never come back here, but here I am.

Beast Clearing is exactly as I remember it, with its babbling creek and the huge willow tree in the center. It's still cold, but the snow is somehow lighter here, only dusting the grass, and the creek remains unfrozen. I remember this place from my childhood, running around with my sister, my father assuring us humans don't dare come here. It's where we can be ourselves without fear.

The name says it all. Beast Clearing. Where the Beastly clan comes to play. Wolves and bears, reindeers and lions walk side by side as friends, as brothers, as family.

Even demons and vampires are welcome here. A reservation of sorts. Away from the human eye.

I gaze at the willow tree, where the fate of the supernatural in Forest Grove has changed forever. Where the devil has made a pact with my clan and the vamps. A blessing and a curse all at once.

A three-hundred-year-old deal gives us the liberty to shift at will and live peacefully with our enemies. Gives us the rules that control our world. Yet the same deal gives Damien Pattison his mate. Isabella Ferro. The woman he's willing to do anything to keep. Like snatching two babies out of their mother's womb.

Rina and I used to climb that tree, mocking Damien, unafraid. Because Dad was there. Because Mom was there.

We used to play hide and seek and tag. Sometimes my uncles would chase us across the whole clearing while everyone else watched and laughed. Slasher and Inferno would play cops and robbers with my brothers, except it was supes and humans in our version. We used to be happy. We used to be a family.

My eyes itch threateningly at the memory. I won't let these two see me cry, though. My gaze shifts to the sky and the dawning sun. Aedan and Ronan take in the clearing with obvious admiration.

It's empty at this time of the day, which just works better for us. The last thing we need right now is more company, beast or human or otherwise.

I let them rest a little, but when the morning comes, I mention my father again. They shut me down and chat as though nothing is wrong.

Do they really think I'm going to just leave Dad there to rot? They have to help me. They can't just ignore it. Especially Ronan, after what has happened between us…he can't pretend he doesn't care. Not now.

He offers to take his turn finding us food, but I think he does it just to avoid me. He vanishes off into the woods, as if he and the trees are one and the same.

That leaves me the dragon. Great.

Aedan is lounging by the creek, as though he's sunbathing despite the cold, his hands under his head as he watches the sky. He's relaxed? Fine. All the better to get what I need out of him.

I sit next to him, facing him, my legs bent under me. "Aedan."

He doesn't even glance at me. "Give it up, your highness. We're not going back for your da. What we need to do is get out of town. You, too, not just Ronan and me. You helped two dangerous criminals get loose."

I grit my teeth but force myself to remain pleasant. "He's my family."

"And you're his, and that's why he sacrificed himself. Brave man. Doesn't change anything."

Wolf howls in my head. How can that Irish fuck just lie there, getting a fucking tan, while my dad may never see the sun again? "Are you serious? What if it was Bethany?"

His whole body tightens, muscles intimidating more than usual, and Reindeer reacts with fear, urging me to run. I stay put, and now his black-and-gold eyes, thin and lizard-like, glare at me. "Don't go there, Divina." I can tell by the way he uses my name instead of one of the playful nicknames that I've touched a nerve. "This isn't the same thing."

"How is it not? My family is trapped,

possibly in danger, and you expect me to sit back just like—"

"Just like I did?" It's not a question, but a threat, and it runs down my spine, making my body cold. *Danger,* warns Reindeer. *Fight,* snarls Wolf. "Are you accusing me of killing my sister?"

"No." I know I should placate him, make him less angry, but I'm furious too. "No. Look, Aedan, we don't need to go back to the prison. We just need to find Derek—"

"Your police shag will just as likely kill us as help us."

I jump to my feet, anger pulsing through me at the dismissive way he talks about Derek. How dare he? What does he know? "Derek is a better man than you'll ever be."

He sits up, his eyes flashing dangerously. "I'm not a man, Princess," he reminds me. "I'm a dragon. You'd do well to remember that."

Something inside me snaps. Is he really trying to intimidate me? Does he think that's going to work? Well, he can go to hell. "Are you threatening me?"

"Do you feel threatened?" he growls, showing his teeth.

Maybe if rage wasn't banging in my skull right now, I would, but I'm more angry than terrified. I've gone way too easy on these assholes. I guess after what has happened with Ronan, I am getting soft, but I want to thank Aedan for the reminder of what they really are. Fucking assholes.

I stand, turning on my heel and storming away. Once I am behind the trees, I kick off the shoes and remove the jumpsuit. Then I hang it over a tree branch and run. Wolf howls again, tired of her cage. As I get farther out, my strides get longer and the fur sprouts from my skin as I shift, freeing the beast. To help me run faster, get away from Aedan, get away from all of this.

A pang of regret sets in my chest because I don't get to say goodbye to Ronan first, but I run it off. My family matters more. My father needs me. If I don't leave now, I might not be able to leave at all.

"Get back here!" Aedan yells after me.

My paws are steady in the snow, taking long, loping strides into the trees.

"Divina!"

I run past tall trees that all look the same, but I can smell the direction of the town at the other end of the towering forest. Even though I don't have a precise plan of what I'll do on the other end, I know I have to get to Derek. Despite what he must be thinking of me now, he'll help me save Dad. I just need to keep running and stay out of sight. The miles are nothing to Wolf and—

A wave of heat blinds me, and a powerful wind sets my fur on end as a huge golden dragon lands directly in front of me, blocking my path. Aedan has fully transformed at last, and the result is…awe-inspiring.

He's taller than he is as a human, and he fucking glints. Each individual scale is like a gold piece in a treasure chest. His eyes are still black, but they are above a serpentine snout which houses a long, forked tongue. It darts around his lips and his too-large pointed teeth as if anticipating its next meal. His wingspan is huge, and his tail curls behind him as thick as the trunk of a small tree.

He's stunning. He's terrifying.

I growl low in my throat, planting my feet, my fur bristling, and my back arched in a display of power. I can't deny that I'm scared, but I can refuse to show it. I am the alpha here. The growl is a warning, telling him to let me pass.

He snorts, a curl of flame escaping from his snout, and growls in echo. I can imagine his voice with that annoyingly charming accent now, saying something like, *"Not a fucking chance, lass."*

Fine. You want to stop me? Fucking *try* it.

The snarl that comes from deep inside me in response is more than Wolf, it's something darker, something diabolical. His beady eyes widen in surprise, but it's too late.

I pounce, my teeth bared. I leap right for his long twisting neck, my teeth scraping the scales on the way past. He lets out a roar of outrage as I hit my mark, swinging one of his thick arms, swiping at me with his claws. He misses as I jump away, dodging his hit and rushing forward. The threat brings me to life, gives me the advantage. He might be big, but I'm fast. I could get to Derek without him finding me.

But he's attacked me.

Even if it's self-defense. Aedan dares attack me.

The sensible part of my brain knows I should just run. Aedan's reaction is instinctive, nothing else. The fury swirling in flames inside me begs to differ. There's bile heating my stomach, roiling and spitting and it's rushing at me now.

That darkness. That power. What I deny. What I bury. What I can't understand or control.

No matter how much I ignore it, it's always there, waiting for its moment to rise, and when it does, there is no Divina, nor are there Wolf and Reindeer. There is only power, dark and dangerous and deadly, and it doesn't like that this *upstart* thinks he gets to attack me without any repercussions.

So yes, I can run. But he's hurt me. He has to suffer for it. I need to teach him a lesson. I *must*.

I've never tasted dragon's blood before. Right now, Wolf and I are in agreement that he'll make a delicious meal.

I howl into the sky and turn back to him. Then I attack again. With a powerful sweep of his tail, he sends me flying. I let out a canine whimper as the side of my body connects hard with a tree, knocking the air out of my lungs.

He looms over me as he takes slow, earth-shaking steps forward. The heat of the fire boiling inside him waiting to be unleashed on his breath reaches me even this far away.

The darkness thirsts for the fight, but the part of me that is me, the part of me that can think and feel and understands what's happening, freezes.

This is a *dragon*. He's bigger than me, much stronger, and can breathe fucking fire. He could kill me now, and easily. I should have run when I had the chance.

Then he makes the mistake of pausing, just the slightest hesitation where his body isn't moving.

I dart to my feet and get behind him. He sweeps again with his tail, but this time I am ready, and I leap over it. His wings hit out in attack, the scales scraping hard against the flesh under my fur, but my teeth close over a chink in his scaly armor just behind one of his legs. I pull, ripping out a huge chunk of scales with me, his blood flying, the metallic taste sharp in my mouth.

I spit, the red-covered gold clattering to the ground. He may look like a lizard, but the blood that flows out as he stumbles and falls down is hot and warm and mammalian, and Wolf's attention can focus on nothing else.

The huge dragon lies flat on the ground in front of me. Of course, the wound isn't enough to kill him, but I've tripped him and made him bleed. My tongue darts out, lapping it up in my jaws, savoring the taste. It won't be hard to finish him now. I just need to bite his leg again, sever the tendons there. Then he'll be completely in my power.

He's roaring, furious, his noise shaking the ground I stand on, but that just inspires the bloodlust more. Once I've sliced his tendons, I can climb onto his back, dominate him.

Then my teeth will find his neck once more, except he's less able to defend himself. I still have to be careful, but if I stay this powerful, if he stays down, I can kill and devour him.

He's not Aedan. He's not even a dragon. He is my target, and I will *have* him. The darkness inside me flares in excitement, in anticipation, pushing at me, begging at me. This is not just the hunter's brain. This is something deeper, something murkier. It calls to me, coaxing me to dive into those black depths.

Is it so bad to be wild? To give in to the darkness? What are good and evil anyway? They seem like such petty concerns in this wild instant.

Is it so bad to be free?

My jaws close around the weak point on his back leg once more and make him ready to be my meal. I bite down, but I don't manage to split the tendon before I go flying backward as he roars and kicks out his leg.

I manage to right myself and duck, just avoiding the billowing flame that pours over my head. He's stomping toward me now, a limp on his damaged leg, his wings flapping furiously.

For a second, I picture Aedan staring back at me out of those lizard-like eyes. I hear his voice. *Don't do it, lass. Don't make me kill you.*

But there's another voice, deeper, smoother, more seductive. *Kill him.*

It reminds me of Marco, but without the cheer, a little of Inferno, too. It reminds me of my mother. It reminds me of me, the me I try to shove away every day of my life

I don't try to shove her away now. I let the darkness surround me when I pounce forward, agilely avoiding another tail swipe.

My claws find purchase in the spaces between his scales, one jammed in his flailing arm, the other in his side. I scamper, moving to his back, just out of reach. His skin is torn and bleeding under the protective armor. I dig my claws in deeper, clinging for my life as he fights, swaying and jolting and slamming against trees, breathing useless fire because his head can't reach where I am on his back, doing everything he can to dislodge me.

Kill him.

His neck is prone, calling to me. My fangs itching. The new power blinding.

I take a huge bite, and the scales rip from the flesh and clatter to the ground, leaving dark, exposed skin while he screams in pain, a noise somewhere between animal and human that will haunt me forever.

Not as a tormenting shadow, but like the

taste of ambrosia.

As I stretch my neck, my jaws ready, I fantasize about the sounds he'll make when I rip into that flesh and claim my victory. The wolf that conquers a dragon.

Just before my jaws snap closed, the scales vanish and a torn, bleeding, *human* neck is in the dragon's place.

I fall back, losing my grip with the size disparity and lack of scales, but I'm on my feet again in an instant. He staggers, Aedan, not Cináed, and falls on his back, his neck and leg bleeding heavily.

He lies on the ground before me, Wolf's face over him, my teeth bared, the smell of his blood tempting me beyond temptation, his life in my control. All it will take now is one bite.

"Stop," he groans.

Now, Wolf begs, drool forming at my jaws at this naked, helpless human, all ready for me. *Now,* calls the darkness, wanting to see the light disappear from behind his eyes.

"Divina." He's not begging. His black eyes are wide, not with fear, but with the look of a man sentenced to die with no way out. "Make it quick."

Wolf agrees with him. The darkness doesn't. It wants me to draw it out, make him beg as I rip the life from him, one agonizing attack at a time. To suffocate him, to make him suffer every hurt and agony I've ever felt, but on his flesh.

We want to hear him scream, beg, plead for his life as he dies. We want to deposit his still, mangled body in front of Ronan so that the lesson is never forgotten.

Ronan. Ronan, who has held me so gently, who has kissed me under the moonlight, who has flown in the air with me.

The darkness protests this line of thought. It wants to focus on our enemy. On the kill. On the urge.

On Aedan. On the strong man who would burn the world to protect his sister. On the scary-looking dragon with the cute freckles that hint at something softer. On the man with a dead girl's name on his blood-covered chest, asking me to kill him quickly. There's no fear or resentment in his eyes. He's prepared to forgive me for the monster I've become.

The blackness of his gaze swallows me in. There it is. The horror that lies in the power of taking a life. It reflects what I am. What I'm about to be forever.

I don't want to be a monster.

Isn't that what I've always said? Isn't that

what I've been fighting for? Isn't that the only thing that keeps my life, my jobs, my relationship with someone like Derek going?

Derek. How would he see me now? How would Ronan? How would my family?

The horrible voice, too strong, thunders, *Who cares?* They're nothing compared to me. Compared to what I'm about to become.

But I do care.

I do CARE.

I DO CARE.

Panting heavily, I move back away from him.

I shift into my human form, my stomach in agony; the wound from the dart, which has been mostly healed, is aggravated by the blow against the tree. It isn't bleeding, but bruises pattern my stomach, and a long scratch runs down the side of my arm from the blow Aedan landed on me, as well as scratches from all the scales. There's blood there. There's blood all over me, some mine, some his.

Breaths catching, naked, covered in blood and bruises, we meet each other's eyes again. The picture of him dead in my jaws, his lifeblood pulsing away won't stop flashing in my head.

He scrambles back a bit, pulling himself

only by his arms, away from me. His calm acceptance is gone. "You fucking eejit!" His accent is stronger than usual. It baits the animal inside me once more.

"Shut the fuck up," I snap. "I could have killed you. I didn't. You're welcome, asshole."

"Oh, I'm the arsehole, you stupid cow?!" He limps up on his injured leg. "You're the one trying to get us all killed! Where in the heaven and hell do you think you're going? What, you're going to howl your way into your darling *Derek* to help you save the day just like that? And your precious *Ronan* thinks you have brains!"

I hate the way he's said Ronan's name. Does he know what has happened between us? Is he trying to shame me? I'm on my feet, too, so much shorter than he is when he towers over me like that, but I don't care. I glare at him, the space between our bodies diminishing. "Shove it up your ass, Aedan. You wouldn't know a brain if one danced in front of you in a top hat."

He fucking smirks as if he wasn't about to die a few seconds ago. "Did you dance for Ronan, Divina? What would *Derek* do if he knew about that?"

"Don't talk about him, you piece of shit. I'm warning you—"

"What, are you going to shift again and kill me?" His eyes flash and he steps forward.

"Yes," I hiss, taking a step back, and another.

He keeps moving forward, and suddenly there's tree bark behind me. "Nowhere to go, Princess."

I could dart to the side and away easily enough, or I could shift and attack, but I stay there, he at my front, tree at my back, and blood pounding in my ears because he doesn't know how much it's taking me not to rip at that wound in his neck until he's lifeless.

My eyes train on his nakedness instead of the blood. The huge, rippling muscles making every inch of him. Layers after layers that make everything about him from his neck to his shoulders to his chest to his…everything broader, harder.

He leans down, his lips at my ear. I feel the heat of his body radiating against me, or is it my own? "Are you going to kill me?" he repeats.

I could. But it lodges in my throat for a moment when the hardness of his bare cock presses into my belly. I glance at it. Fuck. It, too, is huge, like everything about Aedan Oakberry, except his brain. I swallow. "I could."

"Go for it." There's a hunger in his voice. In fact, it sounds like a command. He isn't asking about fighting anymore. "Go on. I'd like to see you try."

He pulls back, surveying me with a cocksure grin that fills me with fury and sets my lower belly pulsing with a new urgency, delicious and fierce and primal.

"Do it," he says slowly. "I dare you."

The whole world freezes, holding its breath in anticipation.

I snarl, and he lifts me in his strong arms, his hands cradling my ass, backing me right up against that tree. It scratches my back, and I gasp, but the sweet pain just adds to the heated impulse. His lips crush onto mine, and he growls in his throat holding me more tightly, our mouths moving and tongues tangling and teeth nipping at lips with a need that harbors on desperation.

He pulls his head back, but holds me still. The air comes rushing into my lungs, only till he buries his head in the crook between my neck and shoulder, his red hair brushing at my face like a flame. He bites at the skin, licking, tasting, just where he would if he was going to tear me apart.

Shuddering, my arms wrap around his shoulders. He feels like an enormous, very warm statue. My nails dig into his back, his shoulder blade where the golden tattoo always reminds him of what he is. My legs tighten around him, pulling him closer, barely any space left to move between him and the tree bark now.

He nips at my earlobe. "I've been wanting to taste you for days, lass."

"Go fuck yourself, Aedan."

"I'd rather fuck *you*."

I throb with lust, with need, at the gruffness of his voice, the accent. I snarl like a desperate animal caught in a trap. My heart is hammering, and good God I want to feel him inside me already.

We're both covered in sweet, tantalizing blood. It mixes with the abstract tattoos all over his arms and chest, and I can't tell which is blood and which is ink. I'm sweating despite the cold, my nipples painfully hard, so fucking wet I'll come if he so much as breathes on me.

"Do it," I whisper as his teeth graze my collarbone. "I dare you."

He grunts, and then suddenly his arms flex around me, squeezing me. I'm not against the tree anymore. I am suspended against him for a moment before he practically throws me down, but the banging of the hard, frozen ground is softened by the snow.

He leans over me, his face over mine, and kisses me roughly and fiercely again. My clit pulsates in anticipation as he lines himself up, begging him to enter me, to fuck me, to *take* me.

His mouth tears from mine, his tongue running down my jaw, my neck, leaving little bites along the way. It leaves a trail of flame behind it that has nothing to do with him being a dragon. Everywhere his mouth touches me, my body is ablaze.

He reaches my chest, his mouth closing over one of my nipples, his hand on the other, pulling, twisting, stroking. I'm panting in a plea while his teeth graze, and his tongue flicks and suckles. Nothing exists but the heat, the feral need he's bringing out in me.

When he abandons my breasts, I whimper, feeling the loss, but he does it only so he can continue his trail downwards. He plants wet kisses on my mound, teasing me, and then he has one of my legs in each of his strong hands, lifts them over his shoulders, bending his head down to work.

He growls against my lips, loudly, hungrily, like a savage animal. His tongue is in me, tasting, devouring just like he said he would, and every hard sweep, every stroke, shakes me with flushes of ecstasy.

He lets go of one of my trembling legs and puts his fingers to work, slipping them deep inside me as his mouth focuses on my clit. I hiss and moan at the teasing of his tongue, and the nerves he's hitting when his fingers slide in and out of me. Then his tongue flicks harder, faster until its pace becomes relentless.

My vision blurs as I squirm, my moans getting louder, my pussy clenching around his fingers. He lifts his head just enough to shoot a mischievous glance at me, watching my face while I'm about to come for him. Then scales appear on the visible parts of his arms and back, all gold. With that, a beautiful dragon going down on me, his black playful eyes holding mine, and his fingers perfectly fucking me, I scream, the orgasm blowing my fucking mind.

He doesn't pull away as I come, holding tight to my hips as my body jerks, keeping his mouth against me, making it last as long as it can. I think I'm still screaming, but I don't know for sure because I can't hear, I can't see, there's nothing in the world but the pleasure Aedan— Cináed—is giving my pussy.

When the wave is over, I'm far from done. My body is throbbing with need still. I reach down, grabbing at his short hair pulling him up, telling him without words what I need.

He responds eagerly, leaning over me again, the glinting scales on his arms and face more stunning than the sun and the moon and the stars. He's so warm, as if the dragon's fire in his body is heating him like a boiling bath, and I just want to sink myself into it. His hard cock pokes at my opening. My breath catches. Mingling with his, we're creating a mini fog in the air between us.

"Still dare me, Princess?" he growls softly, and the vibration sends another hard pulse through my clit.

He doesn't wait for an answer. He just thrusts inside me. Rough, hard, long. He's stretching me like I've never been before, reaching places I don't know exist. My eyes squeeze shut with sweet pain. My hands grip his ass, pulling him in deeper, because this is what I need.

There's none of the gentleness there is with Ronan. Aedan fucks me hard, and I make him fuck me harder, satisfying the darkness inside me that needs to be fed. I might have managed to curb its need to kill, but I have no control over this desire. I should give it something to satisfy it for now.

I tremble with every jolt of pleasure, every

thrust of his rock-hard cock. He runs his tongue along my skin, biting harder than before, licking up some of the blood from our fight, letting out noises of pleasure as he tastes every part of me.

My hands roam his body, his ass, his back, his chest, his abs, the scales hot and rough, the lines of his muscles even more defined in this form. The sweat shines on his forehead and skull as he moves with fast strokes inside of me. His grunts get heavier, make me even wetter.

I nuzzle his neck as his pounding gets more urgent, his desire for me sends more quivers down my pussy. The blood trickling from the wound on his neck, and the scraped flesh call to me. I want to bite. I want to claim.

I claim Ronan and almost abandon him today. Should I claim Aedan, too, knowing we have no chance to stay together?

My teeth graze his neck as I move my hips to match his pace. He makes a little mewling sound that is almost a whimper.

"Do it," he moans.

"Do what?" I gasp, tasting his blood.

"Claim me, Divina."

My head lulls back so I can see his face. He slows down, and slides a hand under the back of my head, tangling his fingers in my hair. "I know you've claimed Ronan, your detective boyfriend, too. I don't mind. I don't fucking mind."

His lips crush against mine in a kiss that isn't just hungry. My heart skitters, and my breaths snag. "Aedan…I almost killed you a few minutes ago."

"But you didn't." He brings my head, my mouth up to his neck. "Take your claim. I want to see you come for me again before I explode in that sweet cunt of yours."

He plunges deep, pounding with frantic need. His hand tugs and plays with my nipple again, and I cry out. Between that and how hard he's fucking me, it hurts. I want it. I need it. Like it's the only thing anchoring me to this world right now. I want his cock. I want his teeth. I want his blood.

His teeth find my neck, too. "When I've tasted that cunt I've been fantasizing about for days, when I'm inside you like this, fucking you like this, I want nothing but to do just that for the rest of my life. Do it, Divina. I know how much you want it. So go ahead. Claim your dragon."

My eyes flutter at his words, and his teeth biting me, claiming me, without permission, shatter the rest of my sanity and restraint. I smile wickedly, digging my nails, wolf claws, into his ass.

"You witch," he gasps.

My jaws shift, too, and I let my fangs sink deep into his bleeding flesh.

It's his turn to squirm now. Quivering, he growls, his cock swelling in my pussy. The way he's stretching me along with the thrill of the claim, the taste of the blood, throw me to the edge.

"Yes. Come for me," he orders. "Now."

I do as I'm told, my teeth marking his skin, biting him over and over as warmth floods my body, a pulsing heat that rushes from the tips of my fingers to the end of my toes. It only gets stronger when he lets out an animalistic roar as his cock jerks and throbs inside me, too.

We ride out the orgasm together, clinging to each other, pulling, scratching, biting, holding on for dear life, the spurts of his cum so fucking hot as they fill my pussy.

Lying still on the forest floor, with him on top of me, my body is still pulsing, still sensitive, and every brush of the wind is too much. After a few moments, he grunts. I flinch when he pulls out of me, and then he flops on his back. We both lie there, spent, for a couple of minutes in total silence.

I've kissed Derek. I've fucked and claimed

Ronan. I've almost killed Aedan. I've fucked and claimed Aedan. What in the actual fuck is happening to me?

"I don't think Cináed likes you," he says.

I chuckle at the stupid name. "I don't think Wolf likes him either."

"And Reindeer?"

"Umm… Maybe a little."

He grins, and then he kisses me deeply before he gets to his feet. "Your clothes are back at the clearing." He holds out a hand, which I take, and allow him to pull me to my feet. I'm still shaking, and he pulls me against him for another deep, burning kiss.

His smile and the cute freckles don't match anything of what we've just done. "You're going to freeze. Let's go back."

"Why do the two of you always assume I'm cold? I'm a reinwolf. Double winter beast."

He brushes my hair off my face gently. "Well…You're still going back with me, Divina."

"Are you threatening me again?"

"Maybe."

"And if I don't?"

"You brought it on yourself, lass." He yanks me up in his arms, and I yelp. Then he throws me over his shoulder caveman style. "You're my captive now, and you're not leaving   my   lair,   dragon   princess."

TWENTY-FIVE
RONAN

Her—my—jumpsuit is hanging over a tree, and Aedan's is discarded on the ground nearby. It's not hard to figure out what's happening. They are either killing each other or having some intense mind-blowing sex in the woods. Either way, I'm not worried or jealous, not at all.

I fold their clothes neatly so they're ready when they return. Then I set to cooking the edible mushrooms, leaves, nuts, and herbs

I've gathered for our evening meal, despite the snapping winter cold making foraging harder than in the warmer months.

The sun is about to dip West when Divina and Aedan—Divina over Aedan's shoulder—come wandering back into the clearing, both stark naked and covered in blood, just as I serve the food on some rocks that I've cleaned off in the creek to serve as plates. There's nothing to say we can't be civilized just because we're on the run, living in the wild.

"Whose blood?" I ask.

"Mostly mine." Aedan's grin is big for someone admitting to a loss. Sure enough, he's limping, favoring his left leg. She's winded, too, clutching at her stomach again when he puts her down.

"Go clean that off in the creek, then come back here and I'll heal you both." I sigh. "And maybe don't tear each other apart and waste my energy again after this."

Aedan chuckles, but Divina can't meet my eyes, doing that awkward gesture with her lip. He heads straight to the creek, and she barely glances at me before she blushes and runs after him.

Her shyness, though likeable to most men, doesn't appeal to me. Her confidence and intelligence—and dark mystery—are what draw me to her. Perhaps she thinks I'll be jealous or upset or I don't like to share, but she is wrong.

Humans—and shifters and others like them—are so quaint. They get so tied up in sex and love, as if the two are related or exclusive. They don't understand their own capacity for both. It's possible to love one person with your whole heart or love five just as intensely. You can have sex with someone without love or you can sleep with someone and let your feelings guide you.

Like we…

I sigh, twirling grass around my fingers and yanking. Okay…she might be right just a tad.

I don't like that she has it with another man, even if it's Aedan, but I won't speak of it. I've already given myself to her, let her claim me without conditions. If one fae isn't enough for her…so be it.

Maybe it's just my pride, but I believe I'm just lying to myself. It's a lot more than that. More than I'd like to admit.

I dismiss the whole issue, promising myself to never bring it up again. Besides, she is good for Aedan. He's a different person around her. A better one. And he's my friend, who has suffered a lot. He deserves to have a taste of happiness. Even if it is for a few stolen hours.

When the two of them are dressed, it's time for my healing. Aedan first because knowing him, he's going to rip those wounds open again and make it worse if I don't deal with it quickly. "So?"

"So," Aedan points his thumb at her as I whisper the words that stitch skin together under my breath, "she was trying to run to the detective. Looks like *we can't do that* is hard to understand for the genius."

I've expected as much. He continues to grumble for a few more minutes as I finish his neck and leg. Then I turn to her, to her stomach so I can heal the wound there, too. She can do it herself, now, but it's quicker if my much more effective magic does the work.

She lies back, unzipping the front of her jumpsuit to allow me to do it properly. I don't need to touch her to heal her, but I do. When my fingers feel the softness of her belly, my skin tingles with her power over me. Her power as a female and as a marvelous supernatural. "The fight got…heated, I take it?"

She blushes again, and I don't take my eyes off hers. I might be a little upset, but Divina and I found a connection last night. Why would her sleeping with Aedan bother me? It doesn't change anything between her and me. No matter what, that connection isn't going anywhere.

Aedan just flashes that teeth-bearing grin he always does when he's smug. "Yeah, we fucked. Hard."

Her cheeks redden darker as she escapes both of our gazes. "Divina, it's fine." I keep my voice gentle, only putting the slightest power behind her name to make her look at me. "It's good even."

She's silent for a minute before speaking. "Can we… I just want to help my dad."

I exchange looks with Aedan. Then I take her hand between mine. "Look. I don't think it's too much of a surprise if I tell you that I feel something for you," I say in that same soft voice. Finally, it makes her find my gaze. Her eyes widen a fraction, and her lips part without words.

"I know it's only been a few days, but I think the feeling is mutual. And it's clear that you and Aedan have a connection, too," I add. "Why risk that, *destroy* that, on a suicide mission?"

"We can have a life." Aedan's voice is quieter than I'm used to. "The three of us. Ronan's my best friend. We can all get out of here, start again. We can be a family." He's got that tender look in his eyes, the one that only ever appears when he's talking about Bethany. I hope Divina knows how significant that is, for both of their sakes. "Let us take care of you."

I nod. "I know you're worried about your father, but he has friends, doesn't he? Colleagues? You mentioned your mother's other lovers, that one of them was his brother…"

"The MC," she murmurs. "The Blood Demons. Yes."

Perfect. "Then…let them take care of him. That's their job, isn't it? To look out for each other?"

Aedan grunts. "Your da wanted us to get you out of there, Divina. You don't want to throw that back in his face, do you?"

Her eyes flick between us both for a moment, and then she lets out a loud sigh. "You're right. You're both right. I should…I need to give up."

"Not give up," I encourage her. "Survive."

She jerks her head in what I think is agreement. Then she squeezes my hand and nods at the food. "What's for dinner?"

I hand her a rock-plate. "Mushrooms a la O'Shea. For your Reindeer."

She takes a taste and scrunches her nose. "Umm…herby. Really French."

I don't appreciate the sarcasm. She munches on raw bunnies just fine, but she makes fun of my exquisite food-making skills. "I can make them taste like butchered, bloody, maimed chicken if that's more appealing."

She chuckles, and Aedan slaps my back, finishing his plate at once.

As twilight turns to night, we chat about little things. I talk about stories from years ago with my brothers, Aedan his sister, and Divina her twin, all of us dancing around how each of the stories takes a tragic turn only a little further down the line. We focus on the laughter, on the happy memories.

When the darkness surrounds us, she falls asleep with her head on my shoulder. I gently lie down, careful not to disturb her. Aedan is on her other side, already snoring, sounding like a backed-up truck.

I smile to myself, feeling safe for the first time in years. I can get used to this. The safety. The friendship. The girl nestled between the two of us.

Yeah, I can get used to it very much.

I allow my eyes to flicker shut. I dream of freedom, of warmth and magic, of Divina by my side, of Aedan finding peace in our little family, happy at last. Of our beautiful future that awaits the three of us together.

Except when I open my eyes, it's all gone.

The hope. The peace. Divina.

She's left us in the middle of the night, and only a taunting, neatly folded jumpsuit and the faint scent of a reindeer remain.

TWENTY-SIX
DEREK

The Captain Kirk clock on my bedside table has his hour hand pointed at two and the minute hand near thirty, and I've been lying here awake since eleven. Every time I try to sleep, all I can see is Divina.

And what I think I've seen in the breakout footage.

She is a wolf. A wolf! What *is* that?

It's not just her. The big guy with his

dragon wings, the fire he breathes, the skinny dude with the glitter…and that animal I've never seen before…

I know now why she asks me about the supernatural. She's been lying to me for four years. The world isn't what I've thought. *She* isn't what I've thought. Unless the footage is part of the bigger plan, part of the trick, but even if that's the case, she still goes to the pen when she's not supposed to. She is still involved in their escape.

The inmates have got into her head; I know that. That's the only reason she'd be stupid enough to go back there by herself…at least, I think so. What do I know anymore? If this has been going on the whole time, what else is fake? Our friendship? Our laughs?

Our kiss? Is that fake, too?

I groan, pulling the pillow over my head, begging my brain to let me rest so I can even begin to process this shit.

A movement from the corner of my eye makes me remove it again, a shadow crossing my window.

I groan again and get out of bed. It's probably nothing. I live next to the woods; it's not exactly unusual for things to be moving around nearby during the night. But I'm a police officer, and when I get a feeling in my gut that I need to check something out, I can't just *not* check it out.

I pull on my robe over my pajamas, grabbing my boots. Then I pull them on, too, shove my gun in my pocket and head to the backyard.

There's a deer, no, a *reindeer*, like one that they have at the Christmas market attraction in December, standing right at the edge of the trees, staring at my house.

"Okay…" I approach carefully, quietly. I've never seen a real one close, and though she looks cute, those antlers aren't. "Are you lost?" I look around. Maybe there's a pack member somewhere. "Where's your Mama?"

She just keeps staring.

"Okay, wait here. I'm gonna call…someone." Who do I even call in this situation? Animal control? The ASPCA? Maybe I should just find a direct line to Santa Claus. None of this is covered in the Academy.

The reindeer struts toward my backyard and stops behind the fence. She's looking at me, not the house, me, a too-intelligent spark in her eyes as she watches me.

"Shit. Easy girl. You really shouldn't be here. I'm just gonna go inside, make that phone call. They will find your—"

The words gurgle in my throat and I stumble back, tripping, because the reindeer hunches and retracts into itself, its fur disappearing, its hooves turning into hands and feet, and an extremely naked woman is hunkered in my backyard before me, long, curly hair draping over her face.

"Fuck. I know that hair."

She lifts her head, and her pouty lips tremble with a smile. "Hello, Derek."

I just…stare. I've had dreams about Divina Beastly showing up to my house completely naked, but never in any of them has she been a reindeer first.

Am I dreaming? Yesterday's Derek is sure it's a dream, but today's Derek already has seen her tearing her clothes apart, turning into a ferocious beast and helping two possible killers escape a high security prison.

So…she's a reindeer now, too? Of course. That makes sense! Maybe the last two days have been a big fat hallucination? I thought that cheese tasted funny…

"Derek?" She reaches out hesitantly, her hand shaking, and touches my arm. I feel her warm skin against me with a shock.

This isn't a dream or a hallucination. This is real.

She is real.

And so very naked.

I shrug out of my robe and take my gun out of the pocket.

"Seriously?" she whispers.

Confused for a second, I grimace, but then I raise my brows and slip the gun in the pocket of my pants. "No. Of course not." Then I hand her the robe. "I'm just giving you this."

"Thank you." She pulls it over her shoulders, tying it at the waist, covering her gorgeous body. Despite the situation, I can't help the pulse in my cock. I swallow. "D. You're…alive. You're…a reindeer, huh?"

"Uh…" Her mouth twitches, and her eyes flicker to the door. "Reinwolf, technically."

I look at her for a few moments, and then shake my head as I look around, making sure no one is watching. "You can't stay out here. Come inside."

She ducks behind me as I lead her inside, and into the living room. I get her some spare clothes that have been going to waste in a box under my bed since my ex-wife left. Luckily, they're only a little big on her.

"Derek…I'm sorry I stood you up."

I blink. Yeah, like our date is the first thing on my mind right now. "I'll go make us some tea."

When I get back, I hand her the cup and sit next to her on the couch. She isn't drinking the tea, her attention straying to the door as though every second she's spending here is a second wasted. And she's not talking.

"What the fuck happened, D?" I finally break the silence. "Chief says he begged you not to go back, but you did anyway. You never waited for me or told me you were going. They're saying you're involved in some sort of…supernatural attack. That some sort of creatures killed that poor bastard at the pen, then *you* set them free. Tell me that's not true."

"They think I did this."

"You're surprised?"

"No." She shakes her head, and there's a tired sadness behind her eyes. "No, I'm not surprised. I just hoped, maybe, after everything I've done for the department, someone might have…I don't know, considered me collateral. Thought that maybe I'm not some hidden criminal who has just been waiting for an opportunity."

"Why don't you tell me exactly what happened?"

She does. It doesn't make anything any clearer. In fact, when she stops, my head is pounding, and I'm even more baffled than before.

So many things make sense now, though. The way she's pushed me away. The weird conversations I've overheard the very few times she talks to someone in her family over the phone. The way she seems to sometimes go into a trance at bloody crime scenes.

I shake my head. So the footage isn't fabricated. I say goodbye to that theory, along with my last shred of sanity. I mean, I guess that already goes when she has *shifted* from a reindeer in front of me. Fucking hell. Okay. She thinks the warden killed the guy to frame her four friends, all of whom are supernatural creatures, along with everyone in Ward E. Oh, and also her whole family, except her mother, which is why they don't get along. Right. Well, at least it's nothing *ridiculous*.

I try to keep my face neutral. "And this, all of this, is a conspiracy by a renowned warden to set humanity against supernatural creatures?"

She purses her lips. "You don't believe me."

"I don't know what to believe. Last time I checked people don't turn into animals, and magic isn't real. You've just waltzed in here, I'm sorry, *trotted* in here, to tell me everything I know is a lie."

"Not everything."

The guilt in her voice doesn't make me less shaken, or less furious. My hands ball into fists, and then I let out a slow breath and release them. "Were you going to tell me about *all the fur* before or after we slept together?"

Hurt etches on her face. Even though I'm angry and scared and confused, I'm awash with guilt because hurting her is the last thing I ever want to do.

"The date, the kiss…those were mistakes," she mutters. "I—"

"Just stop." My jaws clench. "That kiss was not a mistake. It was the best thing I've felt in years. You're not allowed to call it a mistake."

She averts her eyes, but not before I see the glistening tears. It tugs at my heart. I hate her tears. I hate this awkwardness. We've never been awkward, not even when she has been, sort of, rejecting me. Annoying, yes. Bickering, yes, but never awkward. It's one of the things I love most about being in her presence.

Rising to my feet, I put my cup and down and run a hand through my hair. "Look," I start slowly. "I don't know how I'm supposed to process all this, but I know it is…dangerous." This is about her family's safety and hers. She doesn't have time for my hurt feelings. "Why don't we get out of here? Go somewhere until it all dies down? We can prove you're innocent when we get back. And until then, we can—"

She doesn't even let me finish. "It's overwhelming that you're ready to risk everything and do this for me, but Collins has my father, Derek." She chokes on her tears.

Wincing, I sag back on the couch and wrap my arms around her. "I know." My eyes close as the smell of her hair fills my nostrils, and I kiss her head. "I know. It's okay. It's going to be okay."

When she draws back, she wipes her face quickly. "I didn't want you involved in this, but I didn't know who else to go to." She chews at the bottom one like she always does when she's conflicted. "I know what you said about supes when we talked the other day…creatures like them… like me…" She speaks to me carefully, like *I* am the animal, trapped and wounded, and she is trying not to hurt me. "But it's my dad, Derek. *Please.*"

I don't say anything. I can't say anything, and it feels like a physical blow to my gut that she's come to me for help yet my hands are tied. What am I supposed to do? Break a prisoner out like she has? Live on the run with her?

Well, when I put it like that it doesn't sound so awful. Living with Divina.

Shit.

After a moment, she sighs, putting her still-full mug on the coffee table and leaves my side. "I understand. I do. Just…please don't tell anyone I was here. Not just yet." Her shoulder lifts in resignation. "I understand if you can't do that either." She gives me one last regretful look and starts toward the backdoor. "I will—"

"Sit down." The image of what will happen if I let her go hits me hard. Divina behind bars. Divina still and silent with a gunshot wound in her forehead. Divina, gone forever, because my stubborn, proud, brave partner won't let this go until she knows her father is safe.

I can't risk it. Damn it.

A lump rises in my throat. "You won't find anything if you go to the pen, except maybe bullets. You're a target."

She stops in her tracks, but she doesn't sit down. She turns and stares at me with those big eyes of hers. The eyes with the gold flicks that I've always found so interesting. That have turned out to be magic. Her magic. "I can't just leave him. And I don't know what I was thinking coming here. I can't put you at risk as—"

I don't listen. My mind hums with one thing, and I jump to my feet, grab her arm and press my mouth to hers.

She gasps against my lips, her breath sending a shiver through my body. Her hands tighten on my waist, and she kisses me back without any of the reservation or restraint I've felt from her in our first kiss.

Fuck, this is good.

Mind-blowingly good.

I groan, my fingers in her hair, my other hand sliding down her side. Her skin is burning, and it's making me burn. My cock jerks, but I keep the distance between our lower bodies. If we go there, I don't think I can stop.

As if she hears my thoughts, she pulls away abruptly. "We can't do this. Not now."

"I know." I pull her in for another kiss, and she doesn't object. Fuck. I squeeze my eyes shut and tear my swollen lips from hers. "Sorry. Okay. Okay. Your dad… He's not at the prison. Ward E is empty."

"What?"

I reach for my bag, pulling out the bulletin that has circled the precinct today. It describes a new Supermax in Mount Hood. "Whatever is going on with your…friends, I believe they're all there now. The whole ward disappeared. If the conspiracy is true, they must have been moved to the new Supermax yesterday. The new prison you were asking about."

She sucks in a breath and snatches the bulletin.

"The official announcement goes out in three days' time, with the grand opening, but they're rounding up a list of people now. Apparently they want the place populated before they go public."

When she looks at me, there's fear I've never seen before in her eyes. Real fear. "Then it is true. It's not just my dad. It's all of us. My whole family. They're coming for all supes. Now."

Well, fuck. I guess I'm helping her after all. I have to. All this supernatural shit…I don't know how I feel about it, but right now I just see Divina, *my* Divina, scared and helpless.

"My dad was right all along, and he sacrificed himself for me." She wipes at her eyes. "Okay. I need to go there even more now, but I should never have come here, I'm truly sorry." She hurries to the door, intending to vanish once more.

I go after her and grab her hand. "Hey,

Divina, stop."

She turns to me, not pulling her hand away. "You really shouldn't be involved. This is a lot bigger than just helping an innocent man out. It's too dangerous for you."

"I *am* involved, you crazy wolf-reindeer-woman." I still can't wrap my head around it, but the face staring up at me is still her own, and that's all I need to know. I gently place my hand on her cheek. "I can't just let you leave. You came to me because you trust me. I'll help you. All this strangeness, I'll get used to it. And once we have your dad back…"

"I can't ask that of you." She waves the bulletin. "Not with that."

"You're not asking," I insist. "I've told you a million times. I'll always have your back." I lean my forehead against hers, staring into her eyes. "I love you, Divina. You know that, even if you wouldn't let me tell you before. I've loved you for years. Whatever you are, whatever you can do, I'll be here. I'll help you. After the escape, I thought I'd lost you. I'm not doing it again."

Her lip wobbles as though she's going to cry again, showing that sensitivity she only ever reveals around me. I brush away a tear with my finger, and gently kiss her forehead. "What do you need me to do?"

Trees rustle hard outside, and a heavy thud hits like something has landed hard in the backyard. I tense, every muscle clenching. Fuck. I look at Divina—my fugitive—and a raw panic fills me. Her eyes widen, and I grab her by the hand and drag her quietly to the stairs. I gesture for her to hide up there, and she nods once.

I get my gun out and hold it steady, slipping out the back door and into the woods.

Her footsteps hurry behind me just as I reach the trees. I'm about to snap at her to go back, but she sighs in fucking relief?

"It's okay," she whispers. "I can…smell who it is. They're friends."

What the fuck? The branches rustle again, and then O'Shea and Oakberry stand between the trees, the first annoyed, the other amused.

I have to blink, twice, to make sure my eyes aren't deceiving me. O'Shea's hair is glinting silver, the deep black gone, and the contrast with his skin makes him look like he's glowing.

"Detective," O'Shea greets with a nod, glancing at my gun. "Are you going to shoot us with that?"

Bristling at his tone, I have one arm protectively around Divina as I glare back at him.

"You're a pain the arse to track, lass," Oakberry tells Divina, as though that's a totally normal thing to say now. He's covered in gold scales on different patches of his skin, and there are fucking *wings* folded behind him.

I need a drink.

She shrugs off my arm and steps in front of me, staring at them both. "Why did you come?"

The two of them give each other a look and shrug simultaneously. "Because we're not leaving you," O'Shea says simply. He moves forward, touching her cheek, cradling it in his hand and making her look up at him. "I thought I told you that already."

"And because Ronan wanted to show off his glamor." I get the sense that Oakberry is teasing O'Shea. The way the *fae* man rolls his eyes confirms it. "You're lucky I like you, Beastly," Oakberry says. "I flew all the way here with him as he mutters his nonsense so we wouldn't be seen."

"You can turn invisible now?" she asks with admiration.

"No," O'Shea shrugs. "It was just camouflage. I called the name of the night to wrap around us, covering us up. It wasn't a great disguise. Anyone looking properly would have seen us, but apparently humans like sleeping at this time of night in little towns like this."

Oakberry grunts. "Invisible or not, your chanting is annoying as fuck. He didn't stop until we landed behind these trees." He winks at Divina.

She drops her eyes, and a flare of jealousy fills me. I don't understand what's going on between her and Oakberry, her and O'Shea, her and me.

She takes a step away from me, toward them both. "You didn't have to come. You made it clear you didn't want to help."

Oakberry rolls his eyes and pulls her into a big embrace that dwarfs her in comparison to his size. "Yes, we had to come, and we will help. Shut up."

I don't like this. I don't like any of it. "D, why don't you come here?"

She clears her throat. "It's okay. They're not dange… It will be a lot easier with their help."

"But—"

"Please," she beseeches me.

I shake my head, putting my gun down. Then I rub my forehead, blowing out a long breath. "Okay. So we're basically living in an X-Men comic, and I'm the human dragged in to help the mutants."

O'Shea looks at me incredulously, but Oakberry grins.

"You never said your boyfriend was a nerd. But he's hotter than most of the dorks I've ever met," Oakberry says. "I see why Connelly wanted a piece."

I let the boyfriend comment pass for now.

O'Shea studies me. My body. "You don't look so bad. Decent."

"Are you…" I raise a hand between us. "I'm not into men."

He shrugs. "I'm not a man."

Divina slaps him on the stomach.

He smirks. "What? You want us to share, but you can't?"

Oh, they're sharing? Her? "Uh… Okay. This is really awkward. Let's get inside before anyone sees." My eyes shift toward Divina. "Then we'll get your dad back and prevent a supernatural apocalypse."

The dragon keeps his silly grin on, and the fae nods curtly. His hand wraps around Divina's, and she holds it as if she barely even notices.

I avert my eyes. "I really need that drink."

TWENTY-SEVEN
GIANMARCO

They move us in the middle of the night. It's as good as any other time, but I'm rather upset by the interruption to my beauty rest. Of course, I don't need anything to make me look more attractive, but sleep is one of the few pleasures we have in this kind of prison—sleep and sex and, for me, messing around in the heads of some idiots.

They already steal the two latter joys away

from me as much as possible with these drugs and insistent lack of privacy. Taking my sleep too is just outrageous and cruel. I'm fairly certain there's a passage about it in the Geneva Convention.

I say as much to the armed guard who drags me out of the transportation van that opens straight into a tunnel like an airport gate. He responds by smashing the butt of his gun against my face, hard enough that my lip splits, and I stumble and fall backwards, colors dancing in my eyes.

I fall against someone, and the guards guffaw. Animals. My pain gets them off. Ironic, really. They should know what it's like to feed on *real* pain.

"Watch your mouth," Flynn mumbles under his breath. It's him I've fallen against, of course; he is directly behind me as we're led down the white plastic tube to our new Supermax home.

I straighten up. Each inmate has a guard. The one who has hit me and the one responsible for Flynn are busy laughing at making me bleed. I suppose they're too distracted to hit us for talking.

I want to wipe the blood off my mouth, but we're cuffed. Instead I run my tongue along my lips. One of the guards looks at me in disgust, and I wink at him as I taste my own blood. My nose feels off. It might be broken, but the pain is nothing new.

"It's quite all right, Flynn." I talk louder than I normally would, attempting my usual drawl, though the effect is a bit spoiled by the nasal thickness to my voice because of the injury. "The fellow is just upset because the Geneva Convention only applies during wartime, and he thinks my comparison is incorrect. However, given that the abyss I sense at the end of this tunnel is ten times as suppressing as Ward E ever was, I think 'war' on the supernatural is rather apt. Don't you?"

Flynn says nothing, which is probably a smart move, as the next second the gun is in my face again. This time I fall, and there's a crunch. It's definitely a broken nose now.

Dazed, my head pounding, for a moment I can't get up. The gun points at me, the weapon end inches from my eyes. "Listen, Connelly. Next time you speak, you slick bastard, it'll be a bullet, not a bruise. Got it, dickhead?"

He's threatening me, and I am thankful for it. It's the reason I'm not screaming in agony right now, the reason I'm able to get back to my feet after two blows which would have knocked out even a bigger man. He's getting off on hurting me, the dark swirling of his awful joy and pouring out of him. It feeds me, helps me keep the pain at bay and focus.

Still, I prefer not to get hit again. My face is something to be proud of, and I shouldn't push too hard and let him ruin it. Not until I know what we're up against, at least.

Instead of another smart comment, I just nod slowly. I'd hold up my hands, too, if they weren't in chains, but we work with what we have.

I can't wait to get out of here and watch as I make them all kill each other. I'll make it slow. Painful. Brick by brick, drug by drug, guard by guard. I'll be as Nero in Rome, playing the fiddle while this place destroys itself from the inside out.

If I get out.

If that's even a possibility anymore. This place, though…I'm beginning to doubt it a little.

A lot.

Fuck.

They shuffle us out of the plastic tunnel and into our new home sweet home through some sort of prisoner's entrance. We stand in the middle of a large, empty, ovular space. Harsh and false light blinds my vision. It takes my eyes a moment to adjust.

There's nothing on this floor but small doors dotted around—elevators?—and some corridors leading away. The area isn't as tight a squeeze as one would think, given there are fifty-seven of us, each with his own guard, and this is one room. We all fit.

We're kept in this containment area for now as everyone who has been in Ward E is being pushed in behind us. Then rough hands drag and push us into position.

I look up, and up. My head swims in vertigo as the ceiling doesn't seem to exist. My first impression is that the place is huge. A tower, reaching up into the sky, yet cut off from the sky. Endless metal rings for cell floors and no windows.

That's all I can see. Metal. Ward E and its white and gen pop and its gray are hideous, but at least they look like *something*. This? This is a metal prison with corrugated steel floors, dark iron bars on the far apart cells, sheet metal on the walls. There is nothing natural in here.

"Vetala," Flynn says under his breath with a nod toward a particular spot in the wall.

Vetala? The only kind of steel that kills vampires isn't exactly well known to humans, and it's here? Well, shit. What else do they have? Salt? Silver? Iridium?

They're shutting us off from the natural world, from sunlight, from the elements, from human emotions, from anything that might boost our power in any way. And they're using the right weapons to stop us.

They know. Not just how to inhibit us. They know how to *kill* us. They know more than I've ever thought, and the implications are terrifying. Ward E suddenly makes more sense. It's never been just a locking cage. They've been studying us. *Using* us. We, the inmates, intentional or not, are the reason they've managed to build this place.

Inescapable.

Supermax is a metal tomb where we will never see light again.

Inmates trip as they're shoved around, then get kicked or punched or hit for disobeying orders. There are screams, shouts, curses and protests about this awful place so loud I can't hear my own mind. Every time someone tries to riot, or speak, or even breathe, a whole host of the guards swarm on them, their guns and batons twitching and ready for action, swinging liberally at the slightest provocation. The negative energy swirling around is magnificent, but I can't enjoy it, the suppressant drugs and this place draining all the joy from it.

There's a loud hydraulic hissing as the last prisoner is inside, and the opening where the tunnel has been attached just...vanishes. The wall closes down over it, sealing so tightly it would be impossible to guess there is an opening there at all if I haven't just walked through it.

When the room seals, our only source of light is the halogen strips. The lack of windows is already obvious, but when the wall closes it's like throwing dirt on a grave. Taking us from the light forever causes a new wave of angry prisoners. Then I wince at a sharp pain in my arm; my guard has just unexpectedly injected me.

The same thing happens with the others; every one of them wears that glazed look when the suppressant takes effect. I'm lucky; the negative energy keeps me going, but my body still sags, my head still swims, and everything gets duller.

A double dose today. I hope it doesn't kill us. If this place is the last thing I ever see, I'll sue someone in the underworld. I'll complain directly to *Daddy* if I have to.

Now that we're all varying levels of zombie, the guards sort us into groups and lead—well, prod or smack—us in the direction they want us to go. Flynn and I and a few others are packed into a tiny elevator with our guards, who have to scan their badges and their fingerprints at each floor before we move on. The elevator finally opens onto the fourth floor to a small room that reminds me of an airlock with another huge metal door at the end.

One of the guards swipes his badge, scans his finger, and also says something into a speaker—voice recognition?—before there's a click, and the door opens.

As we're dragged into the hallway, I examine the cells now that I can see them better. They are not adjacent, each on its own wall without a neighbor, and the doors are offset so there's no peering across the hall—well, the gaping abyss.

Ahead of us, a figure waits outside one of the cells. He grins as he sees me, his eyes examining my face. "Got into a little tiff with my guards, did you, Gianmarco?"

I'm not surprised to see him, and for half a second I consider spitting blood on his face. Flynn is still behind me, though, and even though I can't see him, I can feel his warning glare. He's cautioning restraint. Yet another irony, considering he's in here for intentional homicide.

I grin. "Not at all, Warden. They just

wanted to do my make-up."

Collins glares. He doesn't like me to be smart with him. He wants me defeated. His eyes dart over my shoulder. "I see you looking over to that balcony, Killian. Are you thinking of jumping?"

I peer at the hollow void that centers the tower. The *balcony*. Trust the warden to come up with a fancy phrase for what's just an open hole in the middle of the prison.

"Throwing," Flynn replies in a quiet, dangerous undertone that reminds me why I am so attracted to him in the first place. Idiot. He cautions me over and over again, presumably in a gallant attempt to protect me, and then he does this? I chance a glance at him and am rewarded by seeing his guard's face clench and his fist ready for a smack.

The warden doesn't like that either, but he gestures at the guard to stop. Then he reaches into his pocket. For a wild moment I think he's going to shoot us both.

He just takes a coin from his pocket and throws it. It sails over the edge smoothly, falling straight down, but there's no clatter of it hitting the corrugated metal far below. Instead, there's a loud popping and fizzing, and a tendril of smoke rises from the center of the opening.

"Electric," the warden explains with a vicious smile. "So if any of you bastards are thinking of taking the easy way out, think again. It's not enough to kill you. Just the right voltage for some nasty scars before we fish you back to your cages. Death is too good for the likes of you."

Shuffling closer to the edge, I chance a look. The field, still smoking, hovers above where we were a few moments ago, like an invisible ceiling. Fuck. How have I not sensed it? It's been hovering above us this whole time. I'm supposed to be better at sensing things than humans.

Flynn must be furious. He's a simple man with simple goals and a dark, brooding personality. The idea that they have unknown traps hidden in plain sight will offend all his sensibilities. He needs to know what he's up against.

We all do. And if they're taking the very option of death from us, what do we have left?

I fake a yawn, but my mind is buzzing. "Did you want to continue with your supervillain speech, Warden, or may we go into our cell? I'd like a nap."

Flynn groans behind me. This time the gun hits me across the back of my head, sending me sprawling to the floor. The cool metal against my face is suddenly all I can see or feel, distorted mutterings behind me, somehow both too loud and too quiet.

My head thumps, and my legs feel like jelly. Someone grabs me by the back of the jumpsuit and throws me into the now-open cell. I'm vaguely aware of Flynn being pushed in behind me. Someone removes my cuffs, I think, and Flynn's, and I'm knocked over the head once more.

Flynn curses as he kneels next to me. The heavy metal door to our cell slams shut. All I can focus on is the sudden nausea threatening my stomach, the pounding of my head, the feeling of the matted blood in my hair, and how the floor seems to be rotating under me.

"Enjoy your nap." The warden's voice is the last thing I hear, muffled through layers of metal, before there is nothing at all.

TWENTY-EIGHT
FLYNN

I've spent what seems to be hours tending to Marco's face and examining the tiny box that is our new home. There are two bunks in here, one on either side, four beds total. Each of them is about as thick as a plank and as comfortable. Apart from that, there's the toilet in the corner and that's about it.

The walls reek of salt. Vetala and silver laced into the bars and door. This cell... It's made especially for us. And two other unlucky bastards joining us in the future.

The asshole finally opens his eyes. He stares at the bottom of the upper bunk, his bruised face contorting. The noise I make is somewhere between a sigh of relief and a grunt of irritation. He turns his head to look at me, wincing in pain as he does.

I get up from where I'm sitting cross-legged on the floor and walk over. "Congrats on staying alive on your very first night."

"Thank you, darling." His voice is still thick, his broken nose curbing the vowel sounds, making him sound like he has a terrible cold. "Were you scared? Did you sob over my lifeless body?"

I reach for the bowl of water and the cloth I've managed to get out of one of the guards after begging and debasing myself. Then I dab at his face again. "Keep that up and you *will* have a lifeless body."

Most of the blood is clean now. I hand him the cloth. There's nothing to be done about the rapidly swelling black eyes or the tangled mess in his hair. "Keep that on your pretty face."

"You think I'm pretty?" He attempts to flutter his eyelashes, and I roll my eyes.

"What were you thinking? You don't heal.

And even if you did, the amount of drugs they've got pumping around our system—"

"Are probably a good thing." He moves over, allowing me to perch on the tiny bed next to him. "With all the blood I've spilled, you'd be having me for dinner, vampire boy."

I snort, but then I brush my hand on his arm. "Just try not to get killed, please."

He grins at me, somehow able to still look dazzling despite the mess they've left him in. "You should be careful. Keep that up, and people might start to think that what we have is more than just sex."

Fucking bastard. I want to punch him in his smug face and make it bleed again. He's doing it on purpose, riling me up, making me pissed so he can feed off me.

It's why he got close to me in the first place. The conflict and darkness are what make him thrive. My anger over no longer being who I'm supposed to be. The hatred for the monster pair that did this to me. The longing for a life I can never have.

But he knows it stopped being *just sex* for me a while ago, and how that messes with my head. He must find my feelings hilarious. That's what I do, right? Fall for people I can't have? People who will never love me back. First Divina, then him.

Her eyes, her voice force their way into my head. Seeing her during the interrogation has woken a part of me I thought was long dead. I haven't been able to get her out of my head since.

I might have changed after the turn—and the double murder. I might not be Flynn anymore, but she is still Divina. My forbidden teacher. My unrequited love. All the feelings I've been trying to suppress are refusing to stay down anymore.

As much as I hate her for it, I love her. Even if she's a dream so far away.

As much as I hate how he uses me, I love him. Even if he's a demon incapable of returning any sort of affection.

They don't, or can't, or won't love me. Whatever *me* there is left.

Fuck me, right?

With a grunt, I move away but stop as he tugs at my arm. "Come lie down with me, Flynn."

His voice is soft, earnest, not his usual silkiness. Though I'm angry, and I know he's playing me, I do what he says with barely a thought.

We both lie on our sides, our noses almost touching, barely fitting onto the tiny slab they have the cheek to call a bunk. He wraps his arms around my waist, both to stop me falling and to pull me close. It's a gentle touch, but it's enough to make my cock twitch and my heart thump. Even with the black eyes, and the crooked nose, he's so…

Damn it.

"What are you doing, Marco? I'm not in the mood for this."

"Not in the mood for what?"

I gesture between us, my hand brushing his shoulder as I do, and I let it rest against his arm. I know better, but I can't help it. "This. I know I'm a snack for you and you're injured. But I don't want your games right now."

"And yet you lie down next to me anyway?"

Yes. Because I'm an idiot.

He smirks, and then one of his hands moves from my waist. It's only to run his knuckles down my cheek in a gentle caress. My eyes close without my permission, and a soft groan escapes me at the contact.

When I open my eyes again, he's staring at me intently. Then he cups my cheek, forcing me to look into his eyes and not away. Like I can look away. "This is a prison, Flynn. We are criminals. We do things that are mutually beneficial and then we get out. And I…I'm a *demon*. Do you know what that means?"

"It means you like to fuck with my head."

"Yes. In my case, it also means that my father is the literal devil. I'm not… good."

I lick my lips as my eyes dip to his. "I'm the one in here for a double homicide."

His mouth quirks with amusement. "That's true. Perhaps we're both not good. But I'm dangerous. You're not."

I snort.

"You're not," he insists.

"Why are you telling me this?"

"Because I want you to know your feelings are absurd."

My jaws set. Fuck this. I didn't—I don't need to be lectured. I know who I am. What I am. I don't need to be mocked because I'm a stupid asshole who can't control how much I spiral when I have feelings for someone, how lost I am after—

"And so are mine," he adds.

My heart skips a beat. What's that supposed to mean? I know he spends most of his time in my head, but the bastard doesn't need to make fun of me for having emotions, too. Is he messing with me? I'm pretty sure he is teasing me for daring to feel something, and the urge to punch him in the face nags again.

He interrupts my raging thoughts by pulling me even closer in a slow, intense, yet gentle kiss. I have to be gentle, too, so as not to hurt him. We're never gentle, and it adds a layer of sweet passion I've only felt before in my dreams.

Oh.

That's what he meant. If it's true, then he isn't teasing me at all.

I sigh into his mouth. "What are you saying? Do you have feelings…for me?"

He raises an eyebrow. "Oh, darling. Do I have to spell it out for you? Haven't I made it clear enough?"

A shudder runs through me, my lips opening for him as his tongue meets mine. My hands cling to him while his move down my back, running over each of my muscles, the lightest touch making me crave more.

He nips at my ear and then grazes my jaw, his hand sliding to my front to unzip my jumpsuit. I moan because I fucking want him, but I make him stop. I should be happy right now, but all I feel is scared. I'm not even sure if what he says, what he means, is the same thing I do. "I don't know about any of this. We should stop. Maybe we should just stop doing this entirely."

His smile drops. "Is this about the girl?"

My stomach lurches. "What girl?" As if I don't know. As if her face doesn't spring to my mind right away. As if I don't spend my nights dreaming of her rare smile and the curves of her body.

"Beastly." The gentleness is gone from his voice. "Divina. You need to get her out of your head, Flynn. You can have any woman you want, but not her. She's a curse. She's dangerous."

I move back, as far as the tiny bed allows, an angry wave starting in my belly and swelling upwards. "What's that supposed to mean? You were all over her before—"

"Before she helped those bastards escape and got us locked in Supermax?"

"That wasn't her fa—"

"You don't know what I know." He pushes past me, rolling off. Then he's pacing the tiny cell while I sit on the edge of the bed. "You don't know who she is. *What* she is. I made a mistake, talking with her. I should have run the second I knew."

My lion is sleepy after the double dose of drugs, but he roars a protest deep in my gut. He wants to defend her, and, despite the conflicting feelings I have for her, so do I. What does Marco know? What is he talking about? "What is she?"

He stills. For the first time since I've known him, those brilliant green eyes look haunted, all sense of humor gone. "Darkness," he whispers. "Danger. Death."

"What are you talking about?"

He runs a hand through his hair. "When they come here to get us tomorrow, to run their experiments, to hurt and use us, think of your Divina. If it wasn't for her, we wouldn't be here at all."

"It's not her fault. You know O'Shea was planning something, you know—"

"I'm not talking about the escape. I'm talking about something bigger. Worse."

His tone is like ice, and I brace myself against the cold. I get up, walking over to him. "What… Marco, come on. What is this?"

Without a word, he pulls himself up to the skinny top bunk and covers himself with the thin blanket, his face turned away from me toward the wall.

TWENTY-NINE

DIVINA

My heart is in my mouth as I wait for them to return. All three of them insisted I stay put. I'm not stupid enough to argue. I know it would be too dangerous and would kill any chances we have left.

Waiting back here, even with Aedan for company, is sheer agony, though. My beasts are both restless. *I* am restless. We've already wasted a day planning, and now I'm waiting on Derek and a glamored Ronan to return with the necessary intel. Every second we spend safe in Derek's house is a second my father rots in the Supermax supernatural prison, being tortured or experimented on or who knows what else.

"Stop pacing, and stop chewing your lip before it bleeds," Aedan commands.

I don't know how he looks so relaxed, lying across Derek's couch and flicking through his TV as though there are no problems anywhere in the world.

"Unless you want me to have to taste your blood again," he adds.

I glare at him but remove my teeth from my lip, wiping my mouth with my hand. He's such an asshole. Why am I so attracted to him?

"And stop ringing your hands like that," he adds again.

I glance down. I haven't even realized I'm rubbing my hands together nervously as I pace. Frowning, I unclench them, but suddenly I'm too aware of my whole arms, not sure what to do with them.

"If you need something to occupy your fingers, I'm right here, Princess." He gives me a lecherous wink.

Of course that would be his answer. The

six hours we've been here alone, he's managed to suggest more sex either implicitly or explicitly about twenty times. We do it. Twice. Hoping that distracting myself with his body will be enough. Although it is pleasurable, it does nothing to stop my worry.

What if Derek gets caught? What if Ronan's glamor stops working? What if they're both locked up right now while we're here discussing our next fuck? All of that, and the day of the Supermax's grand opening is approaching closer with every passing moment. "Shut up, Aedan. I—"

The front door opens, and Derek walks inside followed by a nondescript, young Asian boy around seventeen or so. When the glamor fades, the dark-skinned, silver-haired beauty stands before us once again.

I run forward, embracing Derek, relief washing down on me like a physical feeling. "You're all right."

He holds me tight, stroking my hair. "All good."

"Yes, me too." Ronan pretends to be annoyed at me running to Derek instead of him.

I know him well enough by now to be sure he's far from angry. It's only been a few days, but I feel like he and Aedan have been in my life for years.

"I did as you asked and scouted the building on the outside. It's a metal hellhole. It stinks of iron and silver, Vetala, iridium, and salt," Ronan says.

Shit. "What about suppressants? Is it the same as Ward E?"

"Much stronger. It extends outwards over the whole tower."

"And? Is it magic or tech?" I ask impatiently.

"It seems to be magical."

I pull away from Derek, excitement pulsing in my chest. "Which means you can siphon it?"

Ronan flashes a heart-melting smile at me. "Absolutely. I can siphon anything. One day you'll understand how powerful I am." He shrugs. "It'll take a while, though, so you were right about needing a distraction. Something loud and flashy."

Aedan snorts from the couch. "Loud and flashy is what I do best. Our wee princess can help out, too, yeah? She's got quite the devilish streak."

I freeze for a second, and then I clear my throat. He has no idea how true that comment really is. "Yes, of course I'll help. This is my father. My family. In fact, with what they're planning, it's all of our kind. I'll do anything."

Derek reaches into his bag and pulls out a USB stick. "Well, hopefully cashing in twelve different favors to get these blueprints for you can make that *anything* as less drastic as possible."

He strides over to where his laptop sits on the coffee table, opens it, and plugs in the stick. A few seconds later, 3D schematics appear on the screen.

My belly lurches. "This is the prison?" I move closer. Ronan does, too, and even Aedan sits up. "It's…huge. How will we find my dad in all that? Holy shit."

"Fortunately, there are only certain cells occupied right now." Derek clicks something, and about sixty cells light up in red, most concentrated on the third floor and a few on the fourth. There's a single cell right on the basement floor, pulsing. I guess, from how it's separate from the others, it's where new or holding criminals would usually go.

"From what I've worked out, the fourth floor is where the most dangerous inmates are held," Derek explains. "Based on the notes on this file, I'm betting your friends Killian and Connelly are there. Your dad might be, too, but I don't think so."

"Why not?" I'm pretty sure my dad

qualifies as dangerous.

"Because his name isn't on the roster. Anywhere. But they do have someone down in holding who's only marked as *New Guy*, which tells me someone in admin should probably be sacked." Derek points at the separate cell. "I'm betting it's your dad, and he's in here."

"Dad." I touch the screen, as though my finger against the blinking light will somehow bring me closer to him. Then my fist clenches. I can't wait another second now that I know where he is. The things they could be doing to him as we speak…

"Thank you, Derek. These certainly help." I turn to the boys. "Okay. I think we're ready to go in."

Derek tilts his head toward me. "But Divina, it's not going to be easy. This place…it's rigged against supes. Against *you*. You aren't going to be able to just stroll in there and take him. Outside, there's an army of guards with weapons fitted for supes. Inside, there's voice recognition software. Electric wiring on the floors. Keycard elevators. Badge scanners…which reminds me," he reaches into his pocket and brings out a card, "I stole you a visitor's card just in case, but I don't know how you're going to get in in the first place."

I chew on my lip. He's right. We could die, all of us, on a suicide mission to save my father. Derek is risking his career and future. Ronan and Aedan have never even met Dad, and they're willing to put themselves back in the prison they only just got free of. A prison that could kill them.

They're willing to die.

For me.

I look into all their faces. I can't ask that of them. "This is my father. Not yours. There's still time, if you want to go—if you want to get away from all of this—"

Aedan snorts. "Like we'd let you do this on your own, lass."

"Your family is our family, Divina," Derek adds quietly. "All I meant is that if we just had more time…"

"I'm not leaving my dad in there for one more second than I have to." My heart swells at the significance of what they're doing for me. "But that doesn't mean you all have to run head-on into danger. Ronan, you pride yourself on being clever. Don't risk yourself for me."

"I wouldn't risk myself for anything else." He says it so simply without a speck of hesitation that tears prick at my eyes.

I breathe out. "Derek…you've worked so hard to be a detective. I can't just—"

"You're my…partner, D. I was involved the second you showed up at my door. I'm not backing out now."

"It's not about backing out. It's about how this isn't your fight," I insist. "It's my fight, my battle—"

"Which makes it mine. If the world is at stake, and you're at stake, then I'm not really sure what other motivation you think I need."

Derek is too good. Too good for me. Too good for this fucked-up world of supes and villains.

I look at Aedan, and I'm ready to come up with another protest, but he interrupts. "Divina." He's using my name…to show me how serious he is. "I let Bethany down. I won't do the same to you."

The comparison to his sister, how important I am to him—to all of them—breaks me. I take a moment to collect myself, wiping my eyes from tears of gratitude, of fear, of anticipation.

They're all watching me, waiting for me to tell them what to do, putting all their trust in me. It's a dizzying feeling, but an empowering one. These men, all of them, trust me. They want to help me. I cannot let them down.

I straighten up, nodding to myself. "Okay. Ronan, you're on siphoning. Can you do that from a distance? We can't risk you touching the tower in case it's electric or triggers some alarm."

He's got that cocky look on. "I can do anything. However, it'll be harder. You'll need to have all their attention on you because I still need to be close. My best shot is if I fly and siphon it from above. That means you'll need to keep their eyes on the ground. They know we fly so they probably monitor the sky, too."

"I think we can manage that." I swallow. "But Ronan…I know this will incur debt. What do you need in return? I don't have much, but I—"

He sets his index finger on my lips, hushing me. That pride in his eyes I always see when he's listening to me is tangled with something warmer, something more. He brushes my hair away from my face, the simple gesture making my heart swell. "Whatever you need, Divina, anything you ask of me, I will do for you. All I want is to know you'll come back to me in one piece when this is all over. Can you promise me that?"

I snort. "You mean rather than leaving my head behind in the prison?"

"How about you don't leave *anything* behind? What you can give me in return is all of you. Safe and sound."

Seriously? That's all he wants? Me to promise that I'll be safe? My skin tingles, maybe by magic or maybe just nerves. Ronan O'Shea never ceases to astonish me, and I wonder if I'll ever understand this man—well, fae.

I swallow nervously. "I…I can try. I mean, if I'm alive at the end of this, I'll come back to you in one piece, I promise."

Something happens as I speak. A rushing feeling as if my heart is going to burst out of my chest. The word promise has never held such a weight.

He looks into my eyes, and something in our souls clicks together. I'm breathless for a moment, unable to understand what this bond is, unwilling to talk about it out loud.

"You promise," he echoes, the words like a wheel turning to seal a vault. The relief in his voice is palpable. The promise has weight for him, too.

Are promises taboo, like he tells me thanking is?

"Ronan…the word promise. It's a big deal for you, isn't it?"

He just smiles in answer.

"So why…why am *I* allowed to just use it like that?"

He leans close to me, and I feel his breath in my ear. "Because you're a big deal to me, too."

My body flushes because the way he says that, the surety in his voice…feels like a declaration. The bright purple of his eyes and the soft expression on his face when I gaze at him only confirm it.

"Are you telling me what I think you're telling me?" I whisper.

"You've always been so smart, Divina Beastly."

Lightheaded, I just stare back into his eyes, his magic, every inch of my skin prickling with it. I can't think about the L word, not now, not yet, but if we survive tonight we're going to have a lot to talk about.

Derek looks less than thrilled with my exchange with Ronan. He folds his arms across his chest and looks away from me.

Aedan, on the other hand, grunts. "And the rest of us? If he's getting your one piece, what are we getting?"

"A slap if you keep talking about me as an object," I warn. Then I smile. "I'll come back to *all* of you in one piece. We're a unit now."

Derek gazes at me again. "I can't say I

expected you to follow your mother in this way."

The mention of Mom sets me on edge, but I can't blame him. This is all bizarre. Only a few days ago, I was denying myself any sort of relationship, and now look at me. "Derek…lots of people lo—have feelings for multiple people at the same time. If you think it makes what happened when we kissed any less real, you're wrong."

"I guess I never thought about sharing." His voice has the cadence of a joke, but his eyes are hard. "It's not something I know if I'm capable of."

My stomach clenches. "What do you mean? What are you saying?" Is it that he doesn't want me anymore? There's a big chance I die tonight, and if the answer is yes, I don't know if I can bear it.

He lets out a long, slow breath. "Now isn't the time, D, all right? Whatever happens, I'm on your team. All I care about right now is you getting in and out safely."

He's right, though the selfish part deep inside me would rather deal with it now. It takes me a few moments to stuff this emotional turmoil down. "Okay. Yes, okay." I shake my head, turning to Aedan, distracting myself. "I need you inside with me."

"You need me inside of you? Now? All right. Just give me a minute to warm up."

Derek groans, and Ronan rolls his eyes. I'd laugh if I wasn't fighting tears. Aedan doesn't mean any harm. This is just his way of coping. My dragon isn't good at feelings, and in his own way, the joking is just as enforcing as Ronan's confidence and Derek's dedication.

"And me?" Derek starts. "I know you want me to stay here, but—"

"Go back to work. Pretend everything's normal," I interrupt before he can say more. "I promise we'll call you if we need to, but I need you with the police. Let us know if anything changes and gather information for later. This is just the start. We need to stop this conspiracy before it turns into an all-out war."

Because war is what it will become if we can't prevent the supes from being rounded up. We have beasts and magic, they have bombs and metal weapons. If the two are used against each other, the death toll will be catastrophic.

That's not why I'm asking him to stay away, though. Even if he doesn't want me, I need Derek safe. If anything happens to him, I can't live with myself. I'd rather die.

But I won't tell him that.

The look in his eyes tells me he knows anyway. His mouth pinches, but he nods. Then he hands Ronan a slip of paper. "Like you asked, these are all of the duty guards' names and photos. I don't know what you're going to do with them, but they'd better come in handy with how much effort I've spent to get them."

Ronan takes the sheet. "I appreciate it, Detective Bright."

Derek gives Ronan and Aedan a hard glance, not meeting my eyes anymore. "Keep her safe."

"We will, lad." Aedan's voice is unusually serious. "I swear on my mum's grave."

Then the three shake hands, which might be the weirdest thing that's happened in the last week, including all the murder and intrigue.

I gaze around Derek's house, suddenly struck by the feeling this might be the last chance I ever have to see it. There's so much that I should say, so much that I should do.

Ronan and Aedan seem to feel the change in the air and back off a little, giving us a bit of privacy before we have to go. Derek and I look at each other, and words suddenly feel so…difficult.

"Derek." My own tone is strange in my ear,

uncertain and nervous like I haven't been since I was a kid. "I need to tell you—"

"Tell me when you get back." He pulls me close and plants a kiss on my forehead. A pang sets in my chest, and when I look up at him, for the briefest moment, I see tears in his eyes. Then he releases me and glances back at the computer. He clears his throat, tapping the screen.

"So...as well as the magical protection Ronan sensed, there's your standard electric fencing, and some invisible fields between floors, too. The ceiling opens, too, but it can only be controlled from the security checkpoint."

"So we could fly out?" I ask. I raise my voice, calling over to where Aedan and Ronan are lurking just out of earshot. "Aedan, do you think you can burn through a slide-open roof if you have to?"

Aedan snorts, stepping forward again. "Aye, I think I can manage that."

Derek grimaces. "The problem isn't getting out, then. How are you planning on getting in?"

"Getting in is going to be the easy part," I promise.

"What's cooking in that clever mind of

yours, your highness?" Aedan asks.

A smirk tugs at the corner of my mouth as I turn to Derek. "Do you still have that prison jumpsuit?"

THIRTY
AEDAN

If it was anyone else who has come up with this stupid plan, I would have told them they were off their fucking nut. But when Divina says it, when she has Derek go get that fucking ugly jumpsuit, I just nod and agree to put it on. The woman might be a witch. She's certainly got me under her spell.

I suggest shifting, burning the place down, but she just gives me a look. The kind of look women give when they're right, and you just need to shut the hell up.

So that's how we're here, Ronan hanging back in the trees doing his magic siphoning thing, and Divina and I ambling toward the towering metal block before us.

It's ink-dark. Great for Ronan. He can do his sky trickery and glamor some camouflage of the night to keep him invisible while he flies about on those little fae wings, sucking the magic off this place.

Surrounded by wired fencing, the prison stands in the middle of a clearing, looking for all the world like some creepy cock-like art installation. Despite the darkness, the metal seems to gleam as we approach it. The tower is an eyesore, reaching up in smooth metal, fucking the sky like an ugly dildo.

Cináed doesn't react well to it, recoiling. What metals exactly have they got in there? This place is wrong. Feels wrong. Smells wrong. My every instinct screams at me to run away.

But we just…stroll up toward the front door.

The spotlights swing onto us immediately. My ears ache as the sirens blare, but, hand-in-hand, Divina and I just keep walking.

Angry voices scream for us to stop. Someone fires a warning shot. They don't want to hit us in case we're civvies or something? I want to just run inside, but Divina keeps my hand in hers and squeezes it tightly, reminding me to walk slowly and drag this out.

Guards speed toward us now, their guns drawn. The idea of being caught again has both me and Cináed boiling, but it'll be worth it if by the time we're dragged inside Ronan has had enough time to finish the job.

I'm not a praying man, but as the guards reach us, all I can think is *please*.

When they recognize me and the suit I'm wearing, the two guards who reach us first jump on me, calling for back-up, and a third arrives to hold Divina.

"You shouldn't have come back here, Oakberry," one of them taunts as the three of them drag us inside past the security office and into a little antechamber, their guns pointing at us the whole time.

The prison is freezing, as cold and bleak and metallic inside as it is out. I don't understand, though; there's no door except for the one we came through. How are we getting to the cells from this room?

"There's no escaping now," the same guard says.

"Aye, you're a fucking genius," I snarl,

glaring at my girl. "I can't believe I let you talk me into this, you stupid bitch."

"We had to come back," she sobs. I'm impressed. She's a better actress than I've reckoned. Tears stream down her face as though this hasn't been her plan the whole time. "He has my dad."

A hissing noise stuns me as the whole wall opens up in front of us, revealing the covert first floor. Then the guards push us through. They radio the warden, telling him they're propelling us toward the holding cell. Just as Divina guessed they would. Smart lass.

The first floor is empty and bleak. They push us inside an elevator with no buttons. I've been in tight squeezes before, but none like this. Even for someone half my size all these people in here would be too much. It's claustrophobic to the point my skin is itching.

The elevator moves downward, pulling us into a dark basement. When it opens, the guard shoves Divina out. She skids, hitting the floor on her knees. Bastards. They try it with me, but it takes all three of them to get me to move.

They open the door to the one cell here, kick us inside and slam the door behind us. The elevator rattles away, leaving us below in this big metal semi-sphere with just rows of benches, where there's only one occupant.

Divina scrambles to her feet and hurries to him, taking him by the arm. "Dad! Oh my God."

He's just sitting there, not even reacting to new people being thrown in. I don't even know if he's noticed.

Her eyes flicker at me and then back at him. "Dad, can you hear me? We're here, we're going to get you out. You're safe."

He looks up at last, and she throws her arms around him in an embrace. "Divina," he says.

That isn't the voice of a man happy to see his daughter. In fact, Terror's voice is trembling as he says, "Divina, get out of here. Go."

I wait for Divina to tell her dad what's happening, but Cináed growls inside me. Something is horribly wrong here.

"Not without you." She's stubborn, unable to hear the anxiety in her father's voice through her determination. "Aedan is going to shift and fly us out of here."

The plan is for me to shift and break out of this cell now that the magic has been lifted, assuming Ronan has done his job right. He's assured us again and again that he'd take less than ten minutes. It's been at least twenty. He must be done by now.

"Shift?" he scoffs. "There's no shifting in here."

"No, Dad, Ronan is siphoning the magic barrier. Look."

Divina tenses next to me, that familiar tension that comes with a shift, but a few seconds pass, and it's still her human self, standing there, all blue eyes and brown curls. She tenses again, and then a third time. What the fuck? Nothing is happening at all.

"I can't shift," she murmurs, as though saying it quietly will make it less true.

"Relax," I tell her. "Why don't you try something smaller? Bring out the claws or whatever. Maybe Ronan hasn't finished his voodoo yet."

She nods and tightens her fists. When she opens them, only her pale human fingers and nails are there.

Worry shoots through me. Something must be wrong with her. Her nerves in this place must be getting the best of her. I can't blame her.

Never mind Divina's weird failure. I'm going to shift and I'm going to snap the necks of anyone who tries to get in here and stop me once I do.

Cináed is ready to play. I roar, and—

Nothing happens.

Ice fills my veins as I stare at my human fingers, put my hands to my back to feel wings that aren't there.

Has something gone wrong with Ronan? That can't be right. Things don't *go wrong* with Ronan. Ronan is a bastard and an arsehole, but he's smart, he's talented, and he doesn't make mistakes.

What the fuck is going on? If she can't shift, if *I* can't shift, there's no way out. None.

The idea of being trapped in this hell forever...

"Fuck this shit!" I snap.

Divina is pale. "Dad, Ronan must be running late. We can still do this."

She doesn't believe it. I can see it in her face, hear it in her voice, and so can he. The way Terror looks at his daughter makes me want to throw up. There's no hope there. He believes this is it.

We're fucked. There's no other word for it. I'll never see the sun again. I'll never see Ronan again.

I stare at her. In her eyes, my fear echoes back at me. Fear for herself, fear for me, but mostly she's terrified because she promised to get her father free and now we're going to be stuck here with him for all eternity.

This can't be it. Has Ronan run? Has he abandoned us? He's many things, but not a traitor. I'll kill him if he's just escaped without us, but part of me also hopes that's the case because if it isn't—

There's a slam as the door flies open. I spin around and growl at the new intruders. There are three of them, two guards and the fucking warden, all just outside the now-open door of the cell. They stand there as if they've just won a bet.

"I told you she'd come back." The warden gives Divina a smile that makes me want to bite his head off. "You don't know how long we've been waiting for you, Professor." Then he nods at me. "Now we don't have to go to the trouble of finding you both. Much appreciated. It's good to know there's not a single one of you that will be loose when we're done."

Fists clenched, Divina moves away from her father. She stands in front of him as though she can protect him, side by side with me and ready to fight. "We're leaving with my father, Warden Collins. But we will be back. To bring this place down and expose you for what you are."

"Oh? And how will you do that?" he asks. "After all, we've already caught your fae boyfriend."

The color rushes away from her face. My every muscle clenches and fury rips at my skin. If he's hurt Ronan, I'll burn this motherfucker and every single member of his family alive.

One of the guards steps aside, and a beaten, unconscious Ronan is tied up, his wrists bound in iron, behind him. They must have dragged him here by the arm.

Divina gasps, her hands covering her mouth, and I stare because this can't be right. Ronan doesn't *fail*. I can't believe it. I won't. But there he is, and he's hurt.

Fire flares inside me as I picture their screaming bodies and the taste of their blood as their skin cleans my teeth.

"You really didn't think we'd rely *only* on magic, knowing you had O'Shea with you?" the warden asks her, amused. "Do you think we learned nothing while we had them locked up in Forest Grove? Do you think we haven't planned anything? I'm disappointed in you, Divina. I thought you were supposed to be clever."

"But…but how…" she stammers.

One of the guards chuckles, and I growl. I try to shift again, though it's just as hopeless as the first time.

The warden smiles tauntingly. "O'Shea was easy. He still has the tower's magic tearing up his insides, but our tech prevents any nasty little surprises. I guess that's why he tried to touch the building instead of just giving up when he realized he was fucked. Idiot. The inhibiting electricity got him like a bug zapper. He fell right out of the sky, and that's when my boys hit him with six, seven darts from a distance. If he lives, he's going to have a hell of a headache." He shrugs. "If he doesn't, one less of you scum to feed."

Divina's face contorts in horror. "You…you knew we would come. This whole thing was a trap."

The warden's fucking smile grows into a shit-eating grin. "You thought when your beloved Detective Bright was here scoping the place out earlier, we wouldn't know? I also knew O'Shea would be lurking around, too. So I let down the tech wards for his little exploration, just until you'd come back."

"Tech wards?" I snarl through gritted teeth.

He doesn't lose the grin when he looks at me. "Ah, yes. Quite the simpleton, aren't you, Oakberry? See, magic isn't the only thing that can keep you animals at bay. We have the technology to replicate its effects, to create an entirely inorganic field that stops you and your cursed powers in your track."

Holy fuck.

"Derek," Divina gasps, and it's as much fear as it is fury. "I swear to you, if you hurt him, I will murder you. Shifting or no shifting."

The warden laughs. "I'd love to see that. Would you bite me apart with your human teeth? Perhaps you'll poke me with your nails? Or will you just whine me to death?"

Dia ár sábháil. That fuck is an absolute *bodach* and waste of his mother's womb, and he's been breathing for far too long. Divina is right. Shifting, no shifting, I don't care. He needs to die.

I don't need Cináed. I'll tear them apart with my bare goddamn hands.

I rush forward, but I don't get far before a dart is in my neck and the world goes dark.

THIRTY-ONE
DIVINA

The dart that hits me isn't as strong as the one that gets Aedan; it's enough to make my arms and legs heavy as lead, but I am still conscious, flailing, trying to get away.

They throw Ronan in the cell, but they have other plans for me. I don't know why they want me to stay awake. I'll use it, though. I hit and kick, my useless limbs betraying me, my body weak. I scream for my father over and over. One of the guards has his arms on him, and Dad can do nothing but cry out for me.

Warden himself drags me by a handful of my hair, forcing me out of the cell and along the wall toward another elevator. The guards have locked the cell with Ronan, Aedan and Dad inside, and are walking with us now. I'm struggling with all my might, desperate to get back. All I can see is the fear that flickers in Aedan's eyes when he realizes he can't shift, the blood all over Ronan, the defeat in my father's eyes…

"What are you going to do with them?" I demand, the drug pulsing deeper into my blood, lulling me towards helplessness. "If you hurt them, I'll—"

"I'm not going to hurt them." He swipes a badge at the scanner, and the elevator opens. Once I'm shoved inside with the guards, he steps in and speaks into the voice recognition panel. When the doors close, his shoulder lifts with a cold shrug. "Not much."

Along with my heartbeat, his disgusting laugh echoes, as though it's the funniest thing he's ever heard. "They'll be moved to a regular cell like the rest of the prisoners. Your father served his time as bait. Now he can rot with the rest of the scum."

I shudder, torn between disgust and terror, not for myself, but for the men I've brought into this with my own idiocy, those who trusted me and just wanted to help me. For my father, captured to save me, yet here I am. And for my people, every single supe, the people Collins sees as *scum,* who are going to be captured and killed, or worse.

Because I failed.

He presses a button, and the elevator moves up. I'm paralyzed by the horrible events and my swirling conflicting emotions. I want to collapse, but I stay on my feet out of pure spite, glaring at him. "Where are you taking me? You haven't even enrolled me. I'm still in civilian clothes."

"The fourth floor is where I keep my special pets," he says, disgustingly pleased with himself. "I think you'll remember some of them. Killian. You knew him, didn't you? We know a lot about him, too. Like, for example, how dangerous he is and how much he wants you. He has problems resisting his…urges."

"What are you talking about?" I back away, but there's nowhere to go in this elevator, especially with so many of us crammed in. "What does Fl—Killian have to do with any of this?"

He just smiles. "And then there's Connelly. Satan's bastard. Though a disappointment to his father, I imagine he must have picked some things up in hell. With you being *you*, Professor, I think it's going to make him want to *devour* you."

One of the guards snickers.

A wave of nausea hits me hard. "Are—are you throwing me to them so they'll—"

"They'll use you, Professor, and teach you what happens when you can't leave well alone." Warden's hands tighten around my hair again as the elevator dings, and he yanks. My skull screams in protest, but I refuse to cry out. I even try to resist, but he grabs my arm and pulls me out. The guards follow behind us. We pass spaced-out doors which I imagine must be hiding more sad, desperate prisoners. Like my father. Like my friends.

My teeth clench, grind, aching to bite him. As Wolf or as me, I'm not picky. "You killed Sean Chisholm. It was all an excuse to set…this…in motion."

"Very good. But, then, we knew you were smart already." He looks to one of the guards, "Wasn't I saying that just recently?"

"You were, sir," the guard replies. "You were saying Professor Beastly has a whole wealth of information in that pretty head of hers."

"That's right. The professor who has spent years preaching about the nonexistence of monsters when she is one herself. And never got caught. Well…until I came." Warden agrees. "I admire you, Beastly. I really do. But even you can be outsmarted."

The way he taunts me makes my stubborn side indignant. His mocking admiration irritates yet fuels me. He thinks he knows who I am. He doesn't. It's time I reminded myself of it, too.

Yes, maybe I've been too arrogant to see this coming. Yes, I've lost this time. But this is one battle. There's a whole war ahead. I'll get out of this. At least, I'll make sure everyone else does.

Then I'll kill this bastard myself, even if it's the last thing I ever do.

We reach the door that must hide Flynn and Marco. He pauses as he reaches to swipe his card. "You got one thing wrong though, Professor."

I grit my teeth. "And what's that, Warden?"

"I didn't kill Chisholm." He lets go of my hair, but it's only to pull me by the arm close to him, holding me too close to his disgusting mouth. For a terrible moment, I think he's going to force a kiss on me, but he just holds me there, staring into my eyes as though he can intimidate me.

His guards are watching, waiting for me to flinch.

I don't.

I stare back with equal force until his pupils dilate and the corners of his eyes twitch. "Then who did?" I demand.

He lets go of my arm. His racing heartbeat reaches me from here, but he flashes his repugnant smile. "Oh, you'll know soon enough."

Reaching past me to unlock the cell, he pushes me so I fall inside when the door opens. "Have fun with your treat, boys."

I scramble to my feet, the cell door sliding shut behind me, clicking and sealing into place, Warden's laughter echoing behind it.

"What the *fuck* are you doing here, Professor?"

I turn slowly at the harshness in Flynn's voice. He's staring at me, his silver eyes gleaming. If he's surprised to see me, it's muted by the coldness of his tone. I break my gaze and look behind him.

Marco is standing there, leaning against the wall, foot resting against the metal, arms folded. He's just…watching me, like one would look at a colorful bug. My insides curl at his ominous gaze.

"Well," I say, managing somehow to keep my voice steady. "He put me in here because he thinks you're going to beat and rape me. You aren't, are you?"

Marco lets out a smooth, devilish laugh, and my gut clenches.

Flynn gives him a dark look. "Of course we won't," he promises me.

"You speak for me now, Flynn?" Marco pushes off the wall. His eyes are stormy as he starts slowly toward me.

What the fuck? Is he really going for this? Is he going to hurt me? Use me, like Warden says?

I recoil. "Are you really that stupid, demon? I'm a cop and a reinwolf. I can take you down in a heartbeat."

"You're not a cop. You're a teacher." He doesn't back down. "And in here, your beast is worth nothing."

"You're wrong. You don't know me. You don't want to test me. Besides, I don't have drugs in my system as much as you do. If you come for me, I'll win. So don't try anything. I don't want to hurt you," I warn.

Marco gives that devilish laugh again and keeps walking forward.

Fine. Have it your way. A delicious surge of

dark force engulfs me as I ready myself to fight.

THIRTY-TWO
RONAN

My head hammers with uncontrolled magic as I wake up, the rest of my body screaming with physical pain. Aedan stands over me with his face contorted in absolute fury. I haven't seen him like this since the clinic.

Slowly, I come around, and when I am able to sit up, he barks what has happened. How I'm captured. How we're tricked.

In the center of the room, Terror sits on a

bench, a shell of a man. Aedan says he's been like that since Divina was dragged away. My skin prickles at the thought of what they might be doing to her.

Aedan snaps the cursed iron cuffs and tears them off my burnt wrists. The first thing I do is try every trick in my arsenal on the door and…nothing. No matter how I push with my magic, the metal won't budge.

All this overcharged magic in my body, ripping my soul apart, desperate to be set free, and there's nothing I can do to get us out of here. Not when my head feels like mush, and I feel I weigh more than a boulder.

I am useless. For the first time in my very, *very* long life, I'm absolutely helpless. The thought should make me furious and terrified. Without my power, I am nothing. Like a human. Less than a human. And worse, getting out of here isn't the only thing at risk anymore. The magic I've siphoned has to get out. If I stay backed up like this, I could implode.

I could die.

But I can't even get my emotions to work right. These fucking new drugs are leaving me hollow.

I sit listlessly on the ground, listening as Aedan swears and roars and hits the lethal walls, the doors, raining human punches on them as if they'll be effective in any way. He stops, hissing in pain as his hands smoke from the burns that spring up.

Great. Before the monstrous magic kills me, I'm going to just watch my best friend kill himself trying to get out because I can't heal him. And then there's Divina, my Divina, the only girl in hundreds of years I…

She's in danger. She's being hurt, or abused, or…worse. I don't move. I don't think, either, because if I do, I'll start thinking about what that evil shit disguised as a human being is doing to her, and when I think of that, and how I'm sitting here unable to act—

The door opens, and three guards tell us to follow them. Aedan spits at them and gets a whack across the jaws for his efforts. I think he's going to fight for a moment, and I don't have the energy to stop him. Is this how we die?

He glances at me, and something in my expression convinces him to deflate. We're cuffed. One guard grabs each of us individually. Then they pull us through the door into an elevator. All six of us are pressed together like sardines in a can, as a guard speaks the command into the metal, and the elevator rattles and moves slowly upward.

"Where is Divina?" Terror asks. It's the first time he's spoken since I woke up, his voice low, gruff.

One of the guards has a twitch to his face and can't seem to keep his expression steady. It's him who speaks. "Women are on the second floor for now. We're going to the fourth."

"Shut up, Tom," another guard barks. He elbows Terror in the gut, causing him to let out an *oof* and double over in pain. "You too, asshole. Nobody gave you permission to speak."

I'm surprised that Aedan doesn't say anything to that, but when I glance at my friend, he's staring straight ahead, his black eyes somehow even darker than I've ever seen them before.

When the elevator doors open, we're half-led, half-dragged in silence along the edgeless floor and around a bend. They throw us into a tiny cell with two sets of bunk beds against the walls shrinking it even further. There's a toilet in the back. Apart from that, nothing at all.

The second the guards leave and we're canned in, Aedan rounds on me, the anger missing with the guards flaring to life. "You said I wouldn't be caged again, O'Shea!"

"I know," I say tiredly. "I failed you. I failed us. I failed Divina. I'm—"

Terror interrupts us. "You two don't get to complain. You belong here, but my girl? You fuckers got my girl wrapped up in this shit."

Aedan glares at him. "She'd have been wrapped up in it anyway. It's all of us they're after. And from what she told us, she wouldn't have even taken the case if you hadn't made her."

Terror blanches. "Fuck you! You're blaming me?"

Aedan squares his shoulders and takes a step toward him. "Yes, arsehole! Let me tell you something, *Terror*. Your daughter *begged* me to get involved to save your sorry arse."

"My daughter would want nothing to do with a prick like you," Terror snarls, his fists clenching. Shit. Are they going to fight? I need to stop this.

Aedan laughs without humor. "It wasn't like that when she was begging for every inch of my *prick* on the forest floor."

Just as Terror makes his swing, I step between them, catching his hand before it connects with Aedan's jaw. The force propels me back a little, but I stand my ground. "Stop, you idiots. You're giving them exactly what they want. Don't you have a brain between you?"

"What the fuck are you talking about, Ronan?" Aedan keeps his voice level, but he hasn't looked away from Terror yet, and he's still ready for a fight.

"Why do you think Collins put us together?" I ask. "He wants us to tear each other apart. How in the world are we going to help Divina if we kill each other?"

For a minute, I don't think my words are going to work. But then their expressions change. Chagrinned, they are suddenly unable to even look at me or each other.

The silence stretches, and I press the point. "We need to work together. For her."

Terror growls, but there's acquiescence in it. "Fine. So how do we get to her?"

I look around the cell and see nothing but metal. What am I supposed to say now? That it's truly hopeless? We're going to die here, we're going to lose everything, and his daughter is doomed?

There has to be something we can do. If we're going to die anyway, we might as well try to save the girl we all love.

There, I said it. I love Divina Beastly more than I'm ever willing to admit.

Except that now, I want nothing more than to admit it to her.

I can't just leave her. I can't let go without seeing her one more time, without watching her face the first time I confess my love to her in words.

My eyes fall on the door, and my mind sparks as the beginnings of an idea blossom.

"Aedan, Terror," I say slowly. "How much noise do you think you can make if I need you to?"

Terror frowns. "This is a metal cage. A lot, I guess."

"Bet I can make more," Aedan challenges. "What are you planning, Boss?"

I don't say. Not yet. I need to think. I need information. I need to concentrate. The problem is how I do all of that from here.

I have no other choice, though. It's do or die tonight.

Hang in there, Divina. Hang in there, my love.

THIRTY-THREE
GIANMARCO

I back her into a corner, enjoying the taste of her fear. She deserves it, for everything. Her heart is hammering, and she stares at me like a trapped rabbit. Or deer.

"Move back, Marco," Flynn warns me.

Warns me! As if he could hurt me. He might be big, but I can take him any time I want. "Stay out of it," I tell him, my eyes never leaving hers. "This is between me and…Divina Beastly."

Her body calls out to mine, even now. That part of her that wants me to step closer, even in her fear and anger. I grit my teeth because part of me wants to as well. Still.

I move ever-so-slightly, my heart banging in my chest.

She clenches her fists and moves her feet into a defensive stance. She really seems to think she can fight me. That she could win. She really thinks I'm the warden's lapdog, and that I'll just use her to make him happy?

I wasn't expecting *that*, despite everything. A sudden disgust fills me at what she seems to think of me. What the fuck? Who cares what she thinks? What the heaven is happening to me?

I hate her even more now.

"One more step and you're dead," she hisses.

"Oh please. I can think of a million better uses for my dick," I deadpan. Then I turn my back on them both, storm over to my bunk and throw myself onto the bed. I keep my back turned to them, staring at the wall. Fuck the pair of them.

The last thing I need is that bitch in this tiny, shitty pit with me. I'm more pissed off than I have been. I can't believe she has the gall to turn up and ask us if we're going to hurt her. To *rape* her. As if I need to take without consent. As if I'm the warden's slave.

As if she doesn't want to sit on my pretty face.

And Flynn, defending her like that? Please. He has no fucking idea who she is. What she is. He thinks she's just another shifter, his old esteemed teacher, and his hot fuck fantasy girl. He doesn't have a clue of her danger.

As I stare at the wall, my back to them, Flynn keeps talking to her in a low voice then coming back to me, trying to *reason* with me.

His words fall on deaf ears, and I won't tell him what I know. It's not up to me to tell him his new girlfriend is eviler than the literal demon he's been fucking. If he wants to throw his lot in with her, after I've warned him she's bad news, then he can enjoy his own funeral. I won't be losing any sleep over it, feelings for him or not.

There's a tap on my shoulder, and I roll my eyes, rolling over. "Flynn, I don't want to talk—" I chop off my words when I see it's not him. He's sitting over on the other bunk, and Divina is the one standing next to me. I grunt and turn back around.

"Wait. *Marco.*"

I bristle. "Don't try to manipulate me again. It won't work."

"I'm not trying to manipulate you. Why are you acting like this now?" she demands. "What have I done to make you hate me? Is it because of the prison break? Because I assure you, I had nothing to do with that."

"Oh, you're all so fucking innocent, aren't you?" My hands tighten into fists. I won't be drawn into this game with her, not now. "You know what? I thought I could work with you, but I know better now. I knew as soon as I realized exactly what was going on in that place. How you ended up on this case. Why they chose now to move us. It's *your* fault, and you're going to dance on all of our graves."

Her eyes narrow at me in that infuriating confusion, as if she doesn't get a word of what I'm saying. "I'm not… Marco, you said we had a common enemy. Has that changed?"

I laugh. "Oh, it has, Divina, but not in the way you're implying."

"I don't…"

I snort. "You've tasted it again, haven't you, since you left? The darkness? I can smell it all over you. My father is calling to you, and you're going to answer."

She pales, tension coiling her body. "Marco… Damien Pattison has no chance in hell—"

I'm about to snap something back, but the

second she says his name, her body seizes up, as though she's having a fit.

I can't help it; I move automatically to catch her before she falls and hits her head off the metal ground. She lies unconscious in my arms, not responding to anything.

Flynn runs over, staring at her twitching body in horror. "What the fuck did you do?"

THIRTY-FOUR
DIVINA

I don't remember falling asleep. My eyes do not open yet, but I am awake, in a bed. My hands brush the mattress cover and are met with the smoothness of silk sheets. It's warm, the kind of comfortable warmth that comes on a day by the ocean when the sun is streaming in your face. It reminds me of the time my mom took us to Hawaii. Is that where I am now? Am I on vacation? My eyes flicker open, and someone is next to my bed. "Derek?" I say hopefully.

"Hello, sweet one."

The voice matches the sheets, but when my eyes stop blurring, and I see the face in front of me, my heart sinks. It's not Derek. It's not Ronan, or Aedan, or even Marco or Flynn.

My whole body, every cell, is burning, trying to get away from this place, but I can't. Eyes bulging, I want to scream, and I want to cry. No matter what, Damien Pattison stands next to my bed, grinning at me. "I've been waiting to talk with you for such a long time."

I have spent every day of my life, running away, trying to avoid this very moment, trying to be free…and yet here he is. Looking at me, talking to me, fucking smiling at me as though this is normal. Damien. The devil. The malice that tried to steal me from my mother's womb.

The darkness.

"Get out of my head!" I yelp, reaching for the nearest thing— the pillows— to throw in his direction. But they're not pillows anymore. I'm not in a bed. I'm not anywhere; there's nothing but darkness and blazing heat surrounding me. Darkness and heat and Damien. Hell. "What—where—"

He tsks. "You weren't supposed to break

the illusion so quickly. I was only trying to make you comfortable," he says disapprovingly. "Don't worry. You're still back in that awful prison with my useless son and his cocksucker. I just thought we should have a chat. Do you want to chat with me, Divina?"

"Go to hell," I snap.

"Will do. Right after we finish up here. Now, I don't think you're very happy at the moment, are you?" He leans closer to me, and I step back into the nothingness, wanting as far from him as I can get. "Has either of my inferior bastards you're acquainted with told you about the amazing power seeping out of you? I know you've felt it in the past few days more than ever."

"Leave me alone."

He shakes his head, ignoring me. "You're a human, but not as much as you'd like. You're a shifter, but that doesn't explain everything either. That darkness swirling inside you, do you know what it is? Do you know what it means?"

"I don't care." I set my jaw, but my curiosity burns me against my will. I know what he means; Marco has mentioned it, yet I haven't had the guts to ask.

And I have felt it, curling within me,

threatening to break loose.

Would it... Can it be so wrong to just...listen? It couldn't hurt to get the truth once and for all.

But no. I don't want to know. I don't want to hear it. I've been trying since birth to get away from this, all of it. Whatever the devil sees inside me, I don't want it. I don't want him to tell me.

The only profile I'd like to remain incomplete is mine.

He's watching me, and whatever he sees grows his smile even wider. "You do care. That's why I'm here. To tell you everything...so you can finally come with me. Now, where to start, where to start?" He taps his chin, clearly enjoying himself.

"I don't want to hear it!" It's true, I don't. But at the same time, I'm lying. He knows it.

He holds one finger up. "I know. Let's start with your brothers, shall we?"

My heart swoops. "Stay away from my brothers, you fucking monster. I'll kill you if you hurt them. I will. I don't care if you can't fucking die, but I'll find a way, and I'll *kill* you."

He feigns hurt. "Hurt them? Why would I harm my own grandson? Or you, for that matter. You're practically my granddaughter.

Half-granddaughter? Whatever."

I flinch. I know my brother, Inferno's son, is Damien's grandson, but the reminder is…unpleasant.

"No, my grandson and your other brother are quite safe. It's a shame, though. I go to all that trouble for mediocrity. The demon child isn't even a demon, just half of that again. Weak. And the other, the vampire's…do you know what his kind is called?"

I don't care what he's called. He's my brother. My blood. But I know the answer. Half human, half vampire. "Shadowborn," I grate. What does my half-brother being what he is have to do with me?

"Shadowborn," he repeats as though it's a dirty word. "Such a fanciful term for a creature so inferior. A dark human like your mother and a vampire, and none of the best parts of either. Such a waste."

He's suddenly standing right before me, and he reaches out, touching my cheek how a family member would to a newborn baby. I shake my head to dislodge him. "Don't touch me."

He just smiles. "But you, Divina, sweet Divina, are something else. Your sister, too. Don't worry, we'll get her with us later."

At the mention of my sister, I want to hurt

him. "Stay away from my sister." I throw out my fist. He catches my hand easily, the blow nowhere near landing.

"Like you have in recent years, you mean?" he asks me, still smiling. "I do admire your feistiness, Divina. It's one of the reasons I came for you before her."

I yank my fist out of his, my chest heaving with a hissing, blazing fury that can't wait to burn this asshole.

"I think it's your father to blame. Certainly, the way you and your twin were conceived says that was the difference. And then there's your mother, an unholy excuse for a human. Sometimes I think she was more monster than any of her lovers."

"Don't talk about my mother! Don't talk about any one of my family! Leave us the fuck ALONE!"

"So the pairing of dear evil Vixen, and your abomination of a father, conceived as he was, drowning in darkness himself, gives us unholy parents," he continues as if I've said nothing at all. "Add that to the unholy conception. Oh, that taboo threesome with the two brothers was really hot. Eeek."

"What in the actual fuck?"

"And then the third condition to seal the deal…" He taps a finger on the tip of my nose playfully but removes it quickly before I shove it off me. "The devil's touch."

I still want to tear him apart, but his calmness and the way his words flow sedate me into a pause.

"I delivered you and your sister. My hands, the hands of the devil, were the first to touch you. They sealed your fate."

I swallow, my eyes fixed on him, waiting. He's about to reveal it, and I'm powerless to stop it. All my resistance, my struggle is for nothing. I'm here, the devil in my head, and he won't stop until he says it. The truth that's going to trigger it all. What I can't run from anymore.

Now that it is right in front of me, there's no point to stop it.

"And what is that? What is my fate?" I ask, my throat dry.

He looks thrilled that I asked, and the lazy smile that crosses his face is like a cruel mockery of Marco's grin. "*Darkborn.*"

There's a beat. The word seems trivial, but it makes my skin crawl. It sets something to rise in me, baying in agreement, eager to be free. It's not Wolf. It's not Reindeer. It's something else, that something that flared when I've touched Marco. When I've attacked Aedan.

The darkness.

"*You* are Darkborn, Divina Beastly." His voice is soft, mesmerizing. "You are fated for more than this pathetic life. My kingdom awaits you, sweet child, not as a prison, but as home. No more pretending to be a human. No more trying to shed the ridiculous shifter guise. You would be as a queen in my domain. All I need you to do is agree and to come with me now."

Darkborn. There is a word for me. For what I am, and of all people, Damien is the only one to tell me the truth. Does my father know? Did my mother? Her other husbands? Is that why they haven't fought harder to make me stay after my mother left?

And my sister, what is she? Is she the same as I am? Is she in just as much danger?

I want to tell him it's not true, but I can't because it is. I know it without needing any proof because I've always, always known that I fit nowhere. Except, apparently, in hell. I'm something worse than a demon and a vamp and shifter combined. Maybe worse than the devil himself. I've been running all this time, but I've been running from the wrong thing. My beasts aren't the problem. It's the darkness. It's always been the darkness.

I have always been the darkness.

The devil wants me, needs me, because I am a tool for evil. Suddenly, all the running is pointless. This is…what I am. I have nothing else.

No.

A presence looms behind me. I glance over my shoulder, and Marco stands there, staring at me with horror. His father doesn't seem to see him. I pretend I can't either.

The confusion in my brain snaps, and the rest of Damien's words filter through my system. A queen? He tries to tempt me by calling me a *queen*?

"Bullshit," I snarl. "You already have a queen. Isabella Ferro. Your barren eternal mate you tried to steal me and my sister for. And what you're saying now is just a version of the same thing you told my mother. You couldn't get Mom…and you can't have me. Now what do you really want?"

He looks pleased as he lets out a devilish laugh. "Clever. Very well, let me explain. You are a child of pure darkness, all of it brought together at once, taking up your very soul. It is in you. It fuels you. Makes you more powerful than any of my bastards or their offspring. Any of your shifters or vampires. And humans…are nothing to you."

My heartbeat pulses in my ears. "I'm not—

"

"You're embroiled by the darkness whether you like it or not. Just like your beasts, if you keep denying it, it's going to consume you whether you like it or not. Don't you think it's better to embrace it? To use that ultimate power within instead? Come with me now, Divina. Embrace what you are. Let me help you channel it into something powerful, something beautiful. Let yourself become free. Free of cages. Free of expectations. Let yourself be *you*."

His words, his whispers wrap around my head like a warm blanket. It's...more tempting than I'd like to admit, numbing me, shattering my resistance one word after the other.

I know what he is, what he's trying to do. The epitome of evil, the king of the underworld. I can't let myself fall. Not now, not ever.

But just for a moment, the thought of freedom is enticing. My whole life I've been looking for somewhere to belong, the acceptance my own mother, despite what my family says, has never given.

What if this is it? What if Damien Pattison is the parent I deserve, and his kingdom is where I belong?

Home.

No. No, his home is not my home. He is not my family. I am *not* his toy. I shake my head forcefully, dispelling those thoughts. "No."

"No?" He raises an eyebrow. "No, you don't want to be free? You don't want to experience your full power? You don't want to feel what it actually means to belong? To be accepted?"

"Get. Out. Of. My. Head."

He waves a hand, and I gasp as another figure appears. Instantly, tears fill my eyes. She stands before me, smiling softly like she used to, warm and…alive.

"Mom." My voice comes out small, broken. She doesn't answer. I don't even know if she can hear me.

"Mommy dearest," the devil whispers. "That's right. Do you know why she died, Divina? Why didn't she let them change her? Do you know why she *left* you?"

I lift my chin because I won't let my tears fall now, not in front of him. "The darkness," I whisper. "It was in her, too."

He smiles dangerously. "That's right. It runs in your family, sweet one, mother to daughter. The conditions of your conception and birth brought it to its peak. She, however, was still human. Weak. But you…" His eyes hold me with enchanting admiration. When his fingers touch my face this time, I don't cringe. I allow it. "You are the one destined to help me win the war against heaven, to bring freedom to a world filled with prisons. Your power is the key to everything."

He glances at the conjured image of Mom. "She was supposed to be a part of it, too, witness it, enjoy it. Live it. But she chose to die, holding on to morals that shall no longer be relevant, abandoning her family without a shred of care."

I sink to my knees, tremors running through my whole body. His voice is thundering, too loud to ignore, the rage he's awakening too powerful to bury.

I want to scream, at him, at her, that face, that smile, those eyes. She taunts me even in death, pushing me to the edge.

"But you don't have to do that. You can protect your father. Your sister. Your brothers. You can even take care of your lovers, the fae and the dragon, the shifter-vampire and my useless son. You can save all of them."

My head whips up toward him. "What did you say?"

"Everything, everyone you want is yours."

He points at my mother's ghost. "Even her."

My heart thuds. "Mom? You can bring Mom back?"

"Of course," he croons.

I shake my head in shock. "She isn't in hell, is she?"

His everlasting smile vanishes. "No. She's eluded me even after she's gone. But," he takes a deep breath, "when we win the fight, with your help, you and I, together can do anything, my sweet child. And you will have your mother back."

My tears stream now as I gaze at her, my fingers desperate to touch her again. As angry as I am at her, I love her and I miss her so so much. "Damien…"

"All you have to do is say yes," he whispers in his silky voice, holding his hand out to me. "Take my hand, child, my sweet Divina."

I stare at it, my mind, my senses, my instincts all knocked out, much worse than the effect of the awful drugs they've injected in me. I want to take his hand. I want to forget all of the pain. I want to let myself be who I am. I want to absorb the darkness. I want to save my family. I want my mother back.

My hand stretches of its own accord, my

fingers shaking toward the devil's…

No, baby girl. You got it all backwards. It's her…

Dad's image yanks me out of my own despair, his voice echoing in my head. That conversation I've never let him finish. The words he still has to say.

Damn it.

My eyes widen in horror at my fingertips that are less than an inch away from Damien's, and then at the apparition of my mother.

Rising to my feet, I drag my eyes away from her face, my heart ripping in my chest. Then I stare at the devil, our eyes level.

"Come, Divina. Come, my child."

My eyes flicker back at Marco, who is just standing there, staring straight at me, his once tanned face paler than Aedan's. Then I jerk my head toward his father. "Not today Damien. Not today."

"What?"

"I said fuck you, Damien Pattison."

He bursts into laughter. "Very well then. I suppose I'll see you later, my child."

"I'm not your fucking child. My father's name is Terror. My mom is Vixen Legend. The abomination of a shifter and the woman that beat your ass. My name is Divina Beastly.

I am *their* child. *I* will beat your ass once more."

THIRTY-FIVE
GIANMARCO

Darkborn.

She doesn't just have darkness coiled tightly around her soul. She is darkness.

Properly trained and with the right help, if she gives into it, she could destroy worlds with a thought. If the evil takes her over, if my father has, no one can stop them.

Yet, faced with that temptation, armed with knowledge most couldn't handle, she turns and tells Damien Pattison to go fuck himself.

That wasn't her darkness. That wasn't her power. That was *Divina*, the person, the confused, scared, white-faced girl in my arms right now.

Her strength, not power, is a force I've never expected, one my father could never understand.

Maybe…I'm wrong about her. Wrong to blame and hate her.

She raises her hand to her temple. "Ow, my fucking head."

I take in her face as if I'm seeing her for the first time. "You just told the devil *fuck you*. I'm impressed, darling."

"I'm darling again now?" She squints up at me. Her head must be pounding, but she manages a cheeky smile. "And all it took was saying no to your daddy?"

There's a sharp jolt that runs from my chest down to my groin as our gazes lock. "I'm not used to people standing up to him like that," I murmur, suddenly aware how close she is, cuddled in my arms like that. "I have to say, it was rather fetching."

She cocks an eyebrow. "Fetching? Does that mean hot?"

Flynn mumbles a curse behind me and plops off on his bunk. Such a touchy boy. My focus is only for Divina now, though. I can't bring myself to hate her anymore, not after what I've just witnessed. She's beautiful, anyone can see. I've wanted her so badly before, and I want her now even more. It's not just about her beauty as a woman or as a dark creature. She's bold. Brave enough to stand up to Satan himself. There's cunning in her expression, hidden behind a false sheen of innocence.

With all that strength, though, lies struggle. Even now, while she's smiling and biting her lip, when my cock is twitching for her, and I can tell by the slight part to her lips and the blush to her cheek that her thoughts are moving the same way, the strongest feeling I get from her is conflict.

Human. Shifter. Darkborn. She doesn't know what she is. She doesn't understand. She wants to be all. She wants to be none.

She wants me to go ahead.

She wants me to stop.

Divina Beastly with her tormenting conflict and seductive darkness, the cords that bind her, and bind me to her… The thought of it makes me drool.

A pleasant zap runs in my skin, and my cock aches as I think of feeding on such a feast, tasting such dark depths and power.

"Yes," I stretch out the word into something long, seductive. "Yes, I mean hot."

Her teeth show as she chews on that damn fleshy lip again, hard enough to leave marks I'm filled with the urge to kiss away.

"Do you think I'm hot too?" I tease her, my eyes glued to her mouth, though, of course, I know the answer.

She makes her decision, and it's not the one I want. She pulls away from me, breaking the tension.

I lean forward, won't let her go just yet. I know she wants me, too. The heat springing back up between us, just like in that interrogation room, when she's let me into her head, confirms it. "Don't you want to kiss me?"

Her lashes flutter, and I lean in farther, filtering out Flynn's irritated grunts, my breaths dancing on her face.

She shakes her head, moving away from me. "No."

"No?" I raise an eyebrow. "Is that a challenge, darling? Do you want me to make you? You know I could."

"Probably," she agrees. "But you won't. It'll hurt your pride if I don't say yes by myself without your compelling whispers."

I laugh. "Like you don't want it."

I get off the floor, still riled up from her, from that darkness, from the proximity of her body just a moment ago. I need to let it out.

My eyes dart to where Flynn is lying with his back to us, facing the wall. Well, she's not the only tight ass in the room.

He's angry. I feel that even before I lie down next to him, pressing my body up tight against his back. I moan at the delicious anger. I will use it on him. I want him to remember who is in charge. How much he loves that I'm in charge.

"Go away, Marco," he grumbles.

My hand slides over his chest, inching downward in an agonizingly slow movement, my fingers dancing. "Say no if you don't want it," I whisper.

He doesn't say anything, but he pushes my hand away. I put it back, let it slide down only to stop at the join between his legs. He pushes me away more insistently, but I'm back on him once more, turned on by his half-hearted protests. His cock isn't hard yet, but it springs to life at my touch in an instant, even through his clothes. My hand works him, waking him, coaxing him to join me.

"What are you doing?" Divina demands from the other side of the room, a catch to her voice. I can feel her eyes drawn to us.

She's enjoying this as much as I am.

"Tell me to stop," I instruct Flynn.

"Fuck off," Flynn snaps, and I shudder pleasantly. Behind me, Divina lets out a little gasp.

I squeeze him, firm but not hard, and he sucks in a sharp breath. My free hand finds the zipper of his jumpsuit and pulls it down slowly. I touch his skin, first his deep brown chest, then his belly, my other hand never leaving the firmness of his erection. I don't try anything yet, just stroke and tease and play, feeling him get harder, enjoying my power.

"Last chance," I whisper. "If you don't want this, say no now."

He growls and spins around, throwing us both off the tiny bed, the metal floor freezing through the thin fabric of my jumpsuit. He's on top of me, and his lips crush against mine, his tongue relentless, his hands impatiently pulling at my zipper. I chuckle into his mouth and let him touch me, let his feelings flow into me.

We both shrug out of the sleeves of our jumpsuits and toss away our undershirts, his impatience affecting me. The second our bare chests touch, he whimpers. I roll, bringing myself on top, back in control.

I sit up, my ass grinding against his dick,

my nails dragging teasingly down his chest. I dip down, kissing him again. Then I nibble at the piercing in his earlobe. When we get out of here, I'll buy him some nice earrings…a belly and a cock ring, too. My wild lion. His piercings are so sexy, and I can't wait to see them with the actual rings they've taken away from him.

"Fuck, Marco," he groans.

"In time, darling," I tease between nibbles of his neck. I don't look at Divina, but her emotions are pulsing. Her stuttering, heated breaths fill the room. She's watching, and she likes what she sees. She feels guilty about it, and that's only turning her on more. She wishes she was the one with my teeth and tongue on her neck. "Do you want me to taste you?" I ask Flynn, but it's intended for her, too.

When I look up at her, she pretends she isn't watching. I smirk and return to Flynn. He grunts in affirmation. I work my way downward with my mouth and my tongue and my teeth, pulling away the rest of his jumpsuit as I go, and then his underwear.

He lies naked before me, his cock hard and ready for me, the little mark where they made him remove the piercing stretched against it. I bend and lick it teasingly. He lets out another *fuck.*

Divina's emotions pound, too, and I sense the wildness rising in her, the eagerness to watch this play out, the growing temptation to join, to touch. It makes me harder because I want them both.

Because I want them both to want me.

"Damn it, Marco, just do it already." Flynn is always so tense. It makes getting him riled up like this easy, allows me to take my pleasure when and where I need it. Right now, I'll get the most joy from watching him squirm under my power. My hand cups his balls as I move my head, lowering my mouth over him and taking him in.

"Oh my God. You guys are unbelievable," Divina protests.

I look up at last and see her, her mouth slightly parted, her hands hanging loosely by her side as she stares.

"It's the only freedom we have left," I say. "If you don't like it, don't look."

"I do like it. It's so fucking hot," she whispers almost inaudibly, and then she swears.

It's coming from her in waves. How she can't look away, how she wants to be part of this, how watching us like this is turning her on in ways she didn't know were possible until now. I watch her for a moment and grin.

"Get up," I command Flynn.

He doesn't question me. As he rises to his feet, his eyes flick back to Divina. She's watching him, too, staring at his hard, throbbing cock, her thirst so fucking delicious. Would she feel the same when she sees mine?

Her eyes trail over his muscles. My Flynn is all muscles; his strong arms, his taut legs and rippling, tight ass. I stop to admire them too. I love that strength, how it flexes when he holds me, how I can rule him even if his arm is as thick as my head.

Pointing to the bed, I tell him to sit, watching with enjoyment as he obeys and walks to the bunk. The symbolic flowers and swirls on his back, the delicacy of the tattoo inked from his shoulder to his elbow portrays the softer side of him. It makes me pulse as I long for him more.

I sit next to him, one hand stroking his dick, teasing it. He writhes, and she gasps again. "Would you like to join us, Divina?" I *whisper*.

She blushes a delicious bright red. "No. No. I can't—I won't do this. I can't give in to this. Not when—not after—"

I stand up once more and approach her,

enjoying the whirling horniness and darkness and everything else in her heart. When I am right in front of her, her eyes are transfixed on my bare, bronzed chest and the black and red thorn whorls I have tattooed on my collarbone.

I lift a strand of her hair from over her ear and lean close to whisper. "I know you've always wanted Flynn, haven't you? But he is taboo. Your student. You let your morals get in the way of him." I gesture back at Flynn. "Of this."

Entranced by the way her hungry gaze follows my hand and darts to his hardness, I continue. "You're just following in your mother's footsteps. She did it too, didn't she? She couldn't resist. Why should you? Why deny yourself? It's not wrong." I'm leaning close to her now, and my tongue darts out, briefly meeting her ear.

She shudders as it hits her soft skin. I pull back. "See, Flynn and I are going to do this now. You can sit here and watch, or you can let us touch you, too. Touch us. Feel what you want to. Take that pleasure you've always wanted. It's not just your forbidden student. You can have me too. Your body deserves the attention of not just one, but two hard cocks ready for you. Two sets of hands and lips touching and kissing every inch of you. Two hard, sexy bodies grinding yours between them, giving you everything you ever wanted."

She trembles. "Marco…"

"Our bodies are yours if you want them. I promise it will be a pleasure like you've never known. Flynn can be the feral party boy I know you've been waiting for since you first saw him all those years ago. And if you'll let me, I can taste your deepest desires, be in your mind when you orgasm, and make it feel like it lasts forever. Give in, Divina. Just give in."

She pants, her chest rising and falling, showing off those sexy tits. I drop her hair and move back, my fingers lingering on her cheek for just a moment.

"Or don't give in," I say pleasantly. "Up to you."

THIRTY-SIX

FLYNN

Sometimes I hate Marco. Right now, watching him talking Divina—Professor Beastly—into a threesome with him and me is one of those times. She's standing in that loose button-up shirt and some oversized pants, locked in a fucking cell, her father in one too, and he's coming onto her as if it's the most normal thing in the world.

Fucking asshole.

Gets me all horny and then does *this* with

my teacher?

I glance at her, aiming to apologize, but fuck, that blush looks good on her cheeks. It reminds me of a simpler time when she used to stand in the classroom, move her hair out of her eyes before she wrote the next quote on the board. The little secret smile I saw when someone gave a great answer.

I've never wanted anyone more than I wanted her, not before or since. I've had more lovers than I could count, but none of them except maybe Marco started to live up to the dreams I had of being with her.

Now I'm naked, hard, and sitting on a bed waiting for my boyfriend—cellmate—to suck my cock while she watches with a blush.

Not exactly the kind of thing you mention at tutoring sessions. Fuck.

I know, after everything, our old relationship shouldn't get to me, but the tiny part that's Flynn-the-person is…shy? Embarrassed? So fucking horny at the taboo? Because this is Professor Beastly. The woman of my wildest fantasies. My secret forbidden crush. And as Marco saunters over and kneels at my feet to suck me off, her eyes are on mine. On my cock.

My teacher is getting wet for me.

Marco plunges down and takes my erection

in his mouth. His skilled tongue works me, my skin prickling from his heat, but it's her eyes that I see. Those big, luminous, blue eyes, wide, sparkling in gold, staring with longing in a way I've only ever seen in my fantasies.

"Tell her," he says between licks. "Tell her it's her lips you want around your cock."

My eyes squeeze shut. "Fuck…Marco, stop it."

"She wants it, too. She's picturing it right now."

My breaths hitch as my gaze flickers back at her, but I can't hold it for long. She must be upset.

But she's not saying anything in protest. She's just staring, her breaths speeding like me. Is she picturing it like he says? Is that really what she wants? My cock between her lips. Between her tits. Inside her pussy.

Oh fuck me.

Marco's honey-blond hair bounces as he tastes me, licking along the shaft then deep throating. Fuck, he's so good at his job. My fingers dip into his beautiful hair, my free palm braced on the bed, my nails digging in the blanket. His wet lips and tongue driving me to the edge. Between him doing that and how Divina is looking at us, at me, I just about nut right now.

My moans pour out of my chest, my whole body tense and sweltering. Then I choke up because she's walking toward us, slowly.

Marco looks up as she approaches us, and the most devilish grin stretches on his face.

She glances at me, and something darker crosses her face. "It's true."

I moan again, blinking. Is she saying what I think she's saying? "What is…" I keep moaning, my eyes rolling back.

"I've always wanted you," she admits, in the same tone she'd confess a crime.

My heart skips a beat.

"Marco is right. You were there, in the back of my class, and some days all I could think was how much I just wanted you. Every time you flirted with me, I just… I wanted to drag you to my office and… You were so young and hot and…off-limits, but I wanted you, Flynn. So much."

It's too much for me. She says she wants me, something she's told me a million times in my head. Hearing it out loud is way too much.

Marco winks at me and gets hard at work, tasting me, stroking me, cupping my balls. I'm so hard I feel like I'm going to erupt. Then the bastard stops.

"Come on," I groan, but it comes out as a whimper.

He sits up, still on the floor, and reaches for Divina, pulling her down to his level. She goes with him willingly.

"What about me, darling?" he whispers. "Have you secretly wanted me, too?"

He's such a dick and likes to tease, and I want to fucking bust his balls right now, but this question, this tone, this look in his eyes, all of them are genuine. The fucker is holding his breath.

My gaze lifts to the ceiling, my feelings a tangled mess. Good or bad, aren't we all just a bunch of suckers desperate to be wanted and loved?

She licks her lips. "Not secretly."

I glance down at her fast to find his lips on hers.

He kisses her deeply, not in the hungry way he usually kisses, but taking his time, soft, sweet, and it's pure agony to witness. She moans into his mouth. It's not just him. She's tasting me on his tongue, too.

His fingers flex on her back, victory in his expression, a deep growl in his throat. I know that sound. He's been waiting for this, dreaming of this, and now he has her. Or maybe now she has him.

She pulls away, off his lap, and finds her own spot on the floor in front of him but it's only to watch while his tanned hand returns to my cock.

He reaches back and pumps me again. His free hand unbuttons her shirt, and then tugs at her bra impatiently to get to her nipples. When he finds them, he pulls, pinches and circles his thumb around them while she squirms.

He bends his head from where he's sitting in front of her, his mouth and tongue and teeth taking over so that his hands can remove the shirt and the bra properly. She whimpers, her back arching, pushing her chest out, encouraging him to play more.

When she wriggles out of her shirt, I stare at her whole tits. My teacher's fucking naked tits. "You're so beautiful."

"You're beautiful, too." Her back arches again, and her tits bounce with the movement. "Both of you."

His tongue flicks across her hard nipples, and then she gasps, turning her head and staring at me. "Do you like it, Flynn? Watching your professor naked while your boyfriend sucks her nipples and you're fucking his hand?"

"Holy fuck…yes." My palm slams the bed. "Yes, Professor."

Marco moans against her tits. "You're dirty,

Professor Beastly. I fucking love it."

She looks from my face to my cock with hooded eyes and moans. That look, that sound and Marco's hand moving on me… Shit. This time, I make him stop.

When he releases me, I slide off the bed toward her, kneeling at her side while he touches her. She pulls me into a deep kiss, and my whole body shudders. It's a kiss I've waited on my whole life, a kiss that outdoes every pair of lips that has brushed mine. I never want it to end. I need more. More of it. More of her.

She doesn't allow it. She breaks away from me, the faint scent of her, shifter and human and something more, hitting my senses in a way the drugs have prevented for so long.

"Your smell," I say.

"Is it upsetting your vamp?" She pants, reaching for the button on her waist. "I mean you stink a little, too, but with your lion's scent I can bear it."

"It is irritating to my vampire, but the shifter… I don't understand what's happening. This is the first time I could smell you."

"And I can still smell you, too."

"Now, it's not the time for this." Marco beats her to the button, pulling her pants off in a practiced movement. She stands, quickly wriggling out of pants, and underwear like being clothed right now is torture.

Fuck. She's beautiful, more than I've ever let myself imagine.

Marco gives a low whistle. "You're hotter than hell."

She laughs under her breath as she gets back on the floor with us. I want to make her laugh like that too, but I can't even begin to form a coherent thought. I fantasize about this, just seeing her exposed, fully naked in front of me, and now here she is. Smooth. Stunning. Perfect. There for the touching. There for the taking. The breaking of the ultimate taboo.

He's about to draw her back onto his lap, but she bats him away and grins with mischief. He takes her smile as an invitation, and reaches for the bottoms of the jumpsuit, slipping them off along with the prison-issue underwear underneath. He is bare and glorious like a green-eyed Roman god. Lean, chiseled and huge.

His cock is hard, the veins pushing at the skin, the whole thing swollen to such a huge size that there's a swoop in my gut as I imagine it inside me. The same thing that happens right before we're about to fuck.

Her jaws part. Her brows shoot up. Then she murmurs a curse before she rearranges her face back to neutral. "Not bad. I've definitely seen worse."

"Bigger?" Marco asks with a wink. "I doubt it. Would you like to take it for a test drive?"

Jesus. They're bantering. "Uh…the three of us are naked right here, and we're making jokes? Two very hard cocks, and I hope one soaking wet…" My stare drops to her bare pussy, and I hiss. "Could someone please touch…or suck something already?"

She does exactly that, kneeling and lowering her head to suck him. Marco's eyes widen first in surprise and then in bliss. He gives me a hard look and then his hand is on my cock again, working me as Divina does the same to him with her mouth, her beautiful full lips running up and down his throbbing length. His groans vibrate through me.

Fuck it all. I can't bear this.

His hand feels so good on me when he's so worked up like that, but watching her do this, watching her suck him, wanting her lips and tongue on *me*…

I'm going to tell him to stop. I'm going to get my own back, but it's too late. My cock jerks hard, and the release is one of the most forceful I've ever had.

Divina stops blowing him, looking up as I groan loudly, and Marco bends down and takes it all in his mouth as I come, swallowing before licking me clean before her transfixed eyes.

"This is so hot," she gasps.

Well, Professor, guess it's our turn to teach you something.

She's about to return to her work on Marco when he pounces, and he's leaning over her, her back on the cold floor, her hair spread everywhere. He kisses her, her neck, biting her there, then licking her nipples. His mouth leaves a wet trail down her stomach and stops right before her pelvis.

She squirms underneath him. I growl, my lower half stirring again. It's going to take a few minutes before I'm hard again. Less, if she keeps panting and he keeps groaning like that.

Marco moves back, giving me a look that screams *after you*.

Really? I don't stop to wonder too long, though. I want her more than I've ever wanted anything before.

My eyes hold hers so I can be sure she's okay with the switch. Any doubt is gone when she grabs my hand, pulling me to her. We both shudder when my opposing halves mix with her shifter scent. It's becoming stronger and more overpowering with every touch, every kiss. My lion wants to devour her. My vampire instincts want me to snap my teeth closed around her neck, drain her dry and remove the threat.

She feels me up, studying my body, the muscles on my shoulders, my chest, my abs, my thighs, her eyes glowing hungrily. "Your body is incredibly hard. So sexy," she snarls, clinging harder, gouging the skin on my back. I don't think her fingernails are human anymore.

I don't care, though. My hands explore every part of her I can reach, her hair, her neck, her arms, her hips. One of her hands clutches the thick locks hanging loose where they flow down the nape of my neck—they've taken my tie before we're moved here—pulling and causing my scalp to prickle with pain and pleasure. Her other hand scratches at my back, marking the tattooed flowers as her lips press against mine.

The smell of her blood from where my claws must be piercing her is driving me insane. Claws? Have I shifted a little?

My paws at her hips, her claws on my shoulder and the glow in her eyes confirm it. Is she a wolf now? Am I human? Lion?

Vampire? I don't even know anymore, and I don't care.

I feel the weight of her tits in my hands and squeeze. Then I press them together and suckle at both her nipples. Her nails dig into my back again, and I groan. My cock throbs back to life against her hips as she grinds them up.

How much of this is natural shifter-vampire instinct and how much is Marco getting into our heads, ratcheting up the tension, making us angry, horny, unable to control ourselves?

I don't give a shit. All I want is her. The taste of her skin, of her blood, of her pussy. My teeth sink into her arm. It bleeds, and I lap up the blood. She growls and pulls me closer. I need to hear her scream.

Marco makes a small thirsty noise, his hands stroking his own dick as he watches. "You're shifting," he mewls.

We are. We shouldn't be able to, and it just electrifies me more. "How?"

She pulls back, and stares at him, though her hands don't leave my body.

"It's her," I grunt, though I have no real evidence of that other than the fact that I can smell her so strongly despite the drugs when nothing of the sort happened back at Ward E.

Her touch is setting me on fire, and her closeness is bringing out my magic.

I don't know how or why, but I know she's stronger than these drugs. It's intoxicating. Lion is roaring, and I am growling, and I need to take her. Now.

"It *is* her," Marco says, and he tilts his head, dangerous hunger in his eyes, his voice. "You continue to surprise me, Divina. You're so…special." He stops stroking himself, his gaze taking in all of her. "Such darkness."

"Come here. I need you. Now." Marco's growl is accompanied by a push. He takes my place and grabs her by the hips. Then he flips her over and pulls her back, positioning her with her ass in the air, ready to fuck her.

She squeals, but there's laughter in it. Then she adjusts herself on her knees to help him get her into place.

I'm about to punch him off, but seeing him holding her like that, seeing her ready for him sends a sweet shudder down my spine. I want to see this, but while he's going to fuck her I'm not done giving her pleasure, giving her pain.

One of my hands holds her hair, forcing her head to stay put, while my other finds her clit just as he plunges into her, rough and without any preamble. A loud moan escapes her as he fucks her hard right from the outset.

Fuck, she's so wet. For him. For me. My thumb circles her clit. He rails her so her whole body moves with each thrust and slides, soaking against my fingers. She gasps and moans with pleasure, fully on board if the way she is bucking is any indication.

"Yes," she groans, writhing in front of me as he pounds her from behind, and I press my lips against hers forcefully. I didn't say she could talk. I am the teacher now.

He slams into her again and again, hard and fast, each stroke making her cry out more, louder. My finger rubs at her clit, vibrating, and she lets out a wild cry, rocking against us. I'm hard as fuck again, but I won't do anything about it until she's screaming our names.

Letting go of her hair, I have a new target. Her head falls forward as my now-free hand trails down her cheek, brushing her neck and then stroking the globes of her tits.

Then I squeeze her nipples and pull roughly. My teeth grit as she flexes and reacts to my touching and his fucking, each whimper reminding me I have to claim her as my mate so I can have her whenever I need, make her whimper like that whenever I want.

"Jesus fuck, I've dreamed about this," I

mutter, filling one hand with the swell of her tits and the other with her juices.

"Oh yes. Y-y-e-s." She bites hard on my shoulder.

Shit. Shit. Shit. My balls swell with the intensity of her bite. Her fucking claim. Blood swells, and she licks at it desperately. Her repellent smell, my pain from her bite, both acting as an aphrodisiac. She bucks against Marco's cock and my hand more insistently, using us both for her pleasure.

It's crazy but hot as fuck. I can't believe she's just claimed me while Marco is fucking her pussy. His face contorts, and he cries out that he's about to come.

Divina's mouth drops open and her breath comes faster. She screams with him as he explodes. He falls forward against her, panting, but she just keeps going with him covered in sweat against her back, still inside of her, and my fingers flick her clit.

I press hard on it, while Marco holds her ass and gives her the little he has left. Until she screams at the top of her lungs, and my lion roars in triumph.

Her orgasm seems to last forever, and I've never seen anything more beautiful than Divina's face while she comes. I guess he's making it last longer, using his power just like he tells her he will.

She falls forward when it's done, into my lap, her lips next to my hard cock. I want to shove it in her mouth, but she's panting, exhausted, still shaking from the aftermath of the orgasm. She looks so vulnerable. I want to kiss her. I want to attack her.

"You're still hard," she says when she looks up, Marco leaving to the bed.

"Hard again," I correct, stroking her hair with both hands.

Her tongue darts out, tasting me, tasting where Marco's lips were moments ago, and a million fantasies of a young man watching his professor at the board, daydreaming about the things they could do to each other, come true at once.

Shit.

I twitch, and that makes her smile. She moves her head, pulling herself to her feet. "There's something I always wanted to say to you while you were delivering those dumb lines after class."

My hand moves of its own accord, reaching every inch of her skin I possibly can, as if I stop touching her, she'll disappear. I need her here. With me. next to me. Always.

She moans softly as I touch her, her eyes fluttering closed, her head tilting back, and the little smile on her face is spellbinding.

"What did you want to say to me?" I ask.

She looks at me again and moves my hand away. "Just shut up and fuck me already."

I purr and pull her up in my arms, and then I throw her on the bed. She squeals, and I tighten my grip around both her wrists and pin them above her head. "You got it, Professor."

With my free hand, I spread her legs. "Time for me to claim you." Then I push my hips forward, my cock slipping inside of her wet pussy that is filled with Marco's cum.

My eyes flutter closed. The feeling of her pussy around me is just…I can't explain it. I've fucked plenty of women, and men, and none of them—none—felt like this. It's like her pussy is made for me, and as I pound, she moans openly.

"God, you feel so good, Flynn. So fucking good."

I mash my lips against hers as I thrust. My beautiful teacher has her legs spread for me, and she's finally mine for the taking.

Marco is watching, his breaths loud in the cell. When I look at him, he's already hard again.

She notices, too, a fresh gush of her wetness on my cock. I let go of her wrists and grip her hips, fucking her harder.

"I want to see you suck my taste off Marco's cock," she says between gasps.

"Fuck, Professor. You really are dirty," I groan as Marco stands next to me.

He grabs my hair, pulling me to his cock. I don't stop fucking her as my lips wrap around him. He tastes like Marco always tastes, but sweeter, drenched in her wetness. I lick the soft skin of his hard dick, tasting them both. My hips grow jagged as I pound into her with that amazing sensation.

I raise my mouth from a now grunting Marco just for a moment, slamming against her with all my strength. "You taste so fucking good. Now tell me you like it, Professor."

Her eyes roll back. "You're the best student I've ever had."

I grin and take Marco's cock back in my mouth again. His legs are wobbling, so he grips at me to stay upright. The taste of him and her at once in my mouth while I pound her with my cock drives me out of my fucking mind. How she moves in response while he groans my name is the hottest thing that's ever happened in my life.

Divina drags Marco toward her, moving her head to his neck. Her sharp teeth, a wolf's teeth, bite him hard, claiming him as much as she's claimed me.

I've never heard Marco moan like that. We all groan simultaneously as we're bound together by flesh and lust and blood. And when she lets go of his neck, her pussy clenches around my cock tightly in a much more forceful orgasm than the one I've felt on my hand.

The sounds and the face she makes will be carved into my memory until the day I die. My teacher is coming hard for me.

When she's done, I suck Marco again, not leaving her pussy, and he and I go at the same time, my cum spurting into her, filling her as his shoots into my mouth. It takes all my concentration not to bite down on him through the rush.

The three of us collapse, sweating, panting, but somehow still touching each other. "What now?" I say after who knows how much time has passed.

Divina lets out a low laugh and looks at Marco. "Are you able to use my…whatever…to, I don't know, boost yours?"

"After that display?" he asks with a snort. "Certainly. There's something about you, Divina. That…power," his mouth waters audibly, "it's stronger than the inhibitors. It brings out the best in us or maybe I should say the worst." He strokes her cheek affectionately. "Why?"

"I need to talk to Dad. We have a conversation to finish. And then we need to talk to Ronan." She breathes out. "Your father isn't the only one with power. If we can get in touch with Ronan, with his magic, if we all work together…we can get out of here." She softens, and I see her eyes dart between the bloody marks she's left on both of our necks. The claim she's made on us both. "Together."

THIRTY-SEVEN
RONAN

I have one hand on Terror's arm as I siphon the dormant magic from deep within him, hidden under the suppressant. "Come here, Aedan Oakberry."

I intone his name as perfectly as possible. If I can use Aedan's name, if I can activate my powers, my plan might actually work.

It's a simple plan, using the list of names Derek gave me. If I'm successful, it'll solve two problems at once.

First, it will give us a way to compel and control the guards, and maybe get us out of this cell.

Second, it will give me a way to let out the magic overload threatening to destroy my body.

It's risky, though, because to do it, I'm taking in more magic. If this backfires... Well, it will be like an overloaded pipe with a valve released too quickly, except rather than forceful water, it will be my body imploding.

Aedan shrugs, sitting on his bunk. "You're going to have to do better than that, lad. I feel just dandy sitting here."

I scowl. I don't like it when I underperform. I also don't like the way Terror is looking at me, as if this is nonsense. He thinks me incapable. I cannot tolerate that.

Closing my eyes to focus, I gather my power, feeling the energy pulsing at my seams, and then I force it all into my voice as I try again. "Aedan Oakberry. Come *here*."

The power slams through me and there's a *bang* in my head like a backfiring car exhaust. I let out a long stream of curses in the Old Language as I fall backward. Terror steadies me by the arm before I hit the floor. I grip my head, forcing the explosion back down, forcing the weakness away before they can see.

When the wave is over, I am cold, shaking. Aedan is *still* sitting on the bed unmoved.

I'm failing. We're trapped, and Divina is gone. "Fuck," I mutter in English, wincing as my head pounds once more. "Fuck!"

"Maybe you should stop for now," Aedan suggests, but the concern in his voice just emphasizes my frustration even more. I don't want his sympathy. I don't want anyone's sympathy. I am better than this, drugs or no drugs, magical backup or not.

"I. Can't. Stop." My voice comes in pants as the power loops through my veins, rushing faster than blood, threatening to burst them all.

My body disagrees. I sit heavily on the floor, all of the momentum I have left focused on stopping my body from being torn apart. I bury my head in my hands, refusing to believe this, here, is how I die. Thousands of years, and it ends in a cell of iron with no air, no grass, no sun.

My mother would be ashamed.

I am ashamed.

"Come on, O'Shea, pull it together." Terror's voice is gruff, but there is something of Divina in it as he speaks. He has that same stubbornness, that same gentleness hidden deep within the roughness of his exterior.

I laugh wildly, and the very action makes me ache. "I *can't* pull it together. I thought I could get us out of here. I was sure. All I need is a guard and his name. Some noise from you two to attract just one by himself and a simple compelling. It would be easy. It should be easy. But I *can't do it*."

Terror crouches in front of me. Is this how he used to talk to Divina when she was small and worried and scared? She must be scared now. Because of my fucking fuckup. "And why not?" he asks.

"My powers. I should be able to access them, even with these damn inhibitors. I could before. But…they've learned new tricks. And the magic I siphoned from the building, it's…" Trapped. Ready to explode. Life-threatening. "It's stopping me from releasing it and using the compelling power the way I usually can."

He frowns, then stands, offering me a hand to help me to my feet. "Try me, then. He's a dragon. Take his power. Use my name." Terror doesn't sound certain, but I suppose for his daughter he's willing to try anything.

I pause for a moment. Then I grip his hand, letting him pull me up. "What is your birth name?"

"Luke."

Luke Beastly. "You're…Divina said her mother's name is Vixen Legend. Is that the same Vixen Legend that… Of course. I've no clue how I missed it all this time." Something—someone from hell—has been messing with my brains so I won't remember.

He blinks, obviously surprised. "You knew my wife?"

"Not personally, but I've heard of how two brothers associated themselves with a human and nearly had their children ripped from her womb by the devil himself." I speak in a careful monotone. I don't want to seem accusatory, but I need to know for sure.

Terror—Luke— just grunts. "Vixen is gone." There's raw pain in his voice, even all this time after her death. "Divina is more like her than she knows. My daughter is—"

"—Special," I finish for him quietly.

He nods. Does he know how special she really is? Back during the interrogation, when all that power I can't yet understand has piqued my interest. When she speaks with me and captures my heart over and over with barely any effort at all. When she uses my name with a power matching that darkness and strength behind her eyes.

Yes, Divina is special, more special than I've ever imagined. If she allows it, she can be more powerful than even me.

That also leaves her exposed, prone to temptation, and without guidance…

If he comes for her, if she's not prepared, she could be in more danger than I've considered until now. My jaws clench at the thought, at the threat, and despite the pain, I nod at Terror. "All right. Let's do this."

Aedan jumps to his feet, holding up a hand. "No. Look at the state of him. He's going to die if we keep this up."

"I'm going to die if we don't," I mutter, ignoring the pain lancing through me. I look at my friend. "Help me." It's hard, but I swallow my pride and add, "Please."

Aedan doesn't look happy, but he lets me lean against him. As soon as we touch, I feel the frisson that means I've connected with the power deep within him. He can't shift, but the dragon is there. All I have to do is reach out to it. Sure enough, I feel it stirring.

Terror moves away from us far enough that if I call to him, he'll have to walk forward a few steps again. I take a breath, concentrating the power. "Luke Beastly. Come here."

He stiffens when the sound hits his ears. His eyes widen ever so slightly, and for a beautiful moment, I think I am successful.

But he doesn't move.

He looks at me, disappointment in his eyes, and with a crushing invisible blow to my chest, I know it's over.

I sink to the ground, resting my elbows on my knees, burying my head in my hands. Aedan's hand is on my shoulder, his version of comforting me, but the sympathy just makes me hollow.

"Hey, O'Shea, can it with the despair," Terror's footsteps echo on the metal, and then a loud thump hits. Aedan runs over to him. I look up, startled, to see Terror lying prone on the floor as though in a dead faint.

I scramble over to him, too. He's barely moving, but his lips are forming a familiar shape, the only word running through any of our minds right now. "Divina."

"What in the name of the holy ghost happened to him?" Aedan isn't touching him, obviously not sure what he should be doing. Aedan is more used to knocking people out than reviving them. "Did you do this?"

"No." I speak in a clipped tone as I kneel next to Terror, cursing myself and my inability to use my healing magic to work out what's going on. I reach for him, attempting mundane human first aid, when his eyes snap open. He bolts upright, gasping. There are tears in his eyes, and they fall unchecked down his cheeks.

"Divina. My girl. She…she contacted me. She was in my head…there's a demon. She's safe. She's—" His voice breaks, and he stops talking, rubbing at his eyes. "Fuck. My baby girl."

Aedan and I look at each other, and the relief in his eyes at the word *safe* echoes the warmth flowing through me now. "Connelly?" he asks, and I nod. She must be with Gianmarco, and probably Flynn too. Which means she's…well, not safe, but in a better state than I've feared she might be.

"What did she want?" I ask terror. "Why did she contact you?"

"Unfinished business," Terror answers shortly. "She's okay."

"Good." The lightness I'm feeling at knowing she's okay is going to my head. Aedan isn't saying much—not that he ever does—but there's a softness in his dark eyes. Although he hides it, I can see it, that barest glimmer of hope that he won't acknowledge in case he's wrong.

"Let's…take a break." Five minutes of rest won't be the end of the world. Maybe it'll help. When Terror and I have collected ourselves, I can try his name once more.

Aedan nods, and I move to my bunk, flopping down as if it's a comfortable king bed rather than barely more than a covered plank.

My mind is too active, the power still pulsing too strongly in my body to allow me to fall asleep properly. But eventually, after a little time, I drift into something close to it.

I'm not in the cell anymore. I'm standing in a clearing in the middle of the forest with a bubbling creek and a willow tree. Gianmarco stands underneath the tree, arms folded, his sly grin on his face.

"Nice of you to join me, O'Shea. At last," he greets. "You look like shit."

"I feel like shit," I answer, taking a step toward him. "Am I dreaming?"

He winks. "Do you often dream of me? I'm not surprised." Then his expression changes to something more serious. "Did Terror pass along my message?"

I nod. "She's with you? Where are you?"

"Not in this clearing, unfortunately. I think we're fourth floor neighbors, though. Our cell is the sixth from the elevator. East side. Do you know where yours is?"

"I was unconscious when I was dragged here, but my cellmates weren't. I can ask. But first, is she okay? Divina?"

I see it then, though I don't think he realizes. That flash in his eyes when I say her name. It's the same look in Aedan's eyes when she stands up to him. A reflection of the feeling in my heart when she says something clever with that smart mouth of hers. It's what hides behind the agony in Flynn's eyes when he tells us he doesn't know her. And it's the softness in Derek every time he glances her way.

Divina Beastly has us all under her charm now. And we are all her willing subjects.

Gianmarco doesn't know he's given anything away. He answers my question as though nothing has changed. "She's fine. As fine as she can be. She…" The clearing gets darker, and he lowers his voice. "She got a visit."

The power. The rumors. "From your father?"

Gianmarco's smile is thin. "You know more than you let on, O'Shea. Yes, from my father. He tempted her, told her about her power. You know about it, don't you? You know what she is?"

I do, though I can barely believe it. *Darkborn*. I never let myself think it until this second. I've lived a hundred lifetimes, and until this moment it was one of the few things I believed was really just make-believe. But I have met her. I have felt her. "Yes. What did she—"

"I'm using her power now. It's how I can contact you." He grins widely. "She told him to fuck off. She thinks we can all work together and get our pretty asses free."

Hope, beautiful, wonderful hope surges through me. At the same time, the magical pressure on my body, suddenly, slowly, is releasing. I hold out my hands and let my power spread free. My enchantment touches the subconscious world Gianmarco has created. The atmosphere lightens, and the sky glitters with stars. He looks around, unimpressed.

"You're a bit of a show-off, O'Shea," he comments.

I can't control my smile. "It takes one to know one. Now, does she have a plan to get out of here?"

"Yes. Here's what we're going to do." Gianmarco leans forward. "We—"

An abrupt jolt bursts through, and I am no longer in the clearing but sitting up on my own bunk back in the cold cell. My head pounds when the connection shatters. I rub at my forehead as if it will reconnect the broken strands. "Gianmarco. *Gianmarco!*"

Aedan and Terror look over to me, their expressions moving from confusion to fear and worry in half a second. Aedan's whole body tenses. "You talked to Connelly?"

I drive the heel of my hand into my forehead. "He was right there. He had her with him. We were…she wanted us to…" It's like someone has doused me with ice water as it hits me what must be happening. The only reason he'd pull away so quickly, the only way he'd sever our connection before telling me what he comes to say. Either he is hurt, or…

"Divina." The hope that has been swelling inside me crashes like an angry wave, and I am dragged under the surface once more. "They have her."

THIRTY-EIGHT
DIVINA

A loud crash breaks through the cell. I jump at the sound. My stomach drops when three guards slam open the cell and enter.

"Hey," Flynn snarls, leaping to his feet and moving in front of me. His muscles taut, he's in position to fight if he has to.

Marco's head snaps around.

No. *Marco, keep going.* If he stops contacting Ronan now, we might never have the chance again. I can't say anything out loud, and I don't think he even acknowledges the pleading look I shoot his way.

Fuck.

The three guards ignore Flynn and stop just short of him. "Professor Beastly, you're coming with us," one of the guards commands.

It's my title, but I'm disgusted by his false respect. I'd rather he just uses my first name. I'd rather he doesn't use my name at all.

"She's going nowhere with you," Flynn growls. Marco moves next to him, both shielding me. "What do you want with her?"

The middle guard signals with his with hand, and the one on the left has his gun out and levels it at Flynn's chest. "You won't heal from this bullet, vampire." He has a wicked grin on his face, and fear lances through me at the possible image of Flynn's cold blood and petrified body on the floor. "Move aside."

A flare of power pulses in me, and Marco is staring at him intensely. Is Marco trying to use my boost to get inside these guards' heads?

The gun-holding guard's eyes droop, and he sinks to the floor. The middle guard runs to help his friend up, and Flynn pounces, punching the lone one in the temple. That guard goes down straight away.

The one under Marco's control stands, turning his gun on his own friend that's trying to pull him up. Startled, the third guard swoops to disarm him, knocking his gun to the side, but it goes off anyway, embedding a bullet in the wall. The third guard throws a punch, and then both of them are brawling.

Fists and feet and blood and screams are all I can see or hear. Marco watches them with a smirk as he controls this. Flynn keeps beating on the one on the floor, and—

Bang!

Marco's bellowing swear bounces off the walls of the tiny cell, shaking me deep to my bones. He staggers, landing heavily on the bunk, clutching his bleeding arm, his face bone white. I scream, Flynn springing up and rushing to Marco's side.

My whole body shaking, I turn to the door. Warden Collins stands there with a small gun, a trail of smoke coming out of it, pointed at where Flynn is seeing to Marco, who is still hissing in agony. Collins smiles at me as if we've just met in the street. "Rock salt bullets. Now, are you coming or shall I finish him off?"

I gulp and glance at Marco bleeding onto his bed. Being so weak looks odd on him, and if the gun fires again I may lose him forever. I can't allow that. I won't.

The guards are shaking their heads now, clear of Marco's whispers, and they're tending to their unconscious friend.

I take a step toward them.

"Divina. Don't," Flynn growls.

I fake a reassuring look. "Take care of Marco." Then I walk to Warden. "Let's go. Just don't hurt them anymore."

Collins laughs. "Such a good girl. Predictable." His gun is still trained on Marco, so Flynn doesn't dare move. Collins keeps it there as the two conscious guards drag the third out of the cell, and I follow them. Only when we are all out does Collins lower the weapon and slam the door shut.

One of the guards waits with his unconscious friend after they call for backup, and the remaining one snaps a tight pair of cuffs around my wrists. I stand tall, pretending I can't hear Flynn crying out my name as the guard and Warden, each with a hand on one of my shoulders, steer me to the elevator.

Warden seems amused by something as he proceeds with the scanning and voice recognition security measures. Then he presses the button with the number ten on it. The elevator rises. Where the hell are they taking me? Enrollment? Interrogation? Worse?

The elevator shudders to a halt, and the door opens to the tenth floor.

The space in front of me is huge. There are no cells here. It's been hollowed out entirely. There's a quarter shut off from the rest, hiding behind a huge window. Through the glass, I can see comfortable chairs and tables with fucking drinks on them. What the hell is this? Movie night?

The guard pushes me, and I stumble forward. I put my hands out to stop the fall, but the cuffs just over-balance me. I land on my knees.

He and Warden chuckle as I jar against the harsh metal. "She doesn't seem all that special," the guard says with a cruel laugh.

Warden replies with something, but I'm not listening. My eyes focus away from the viewing quarter toward the wall the window faces, and the silver chains hanging there. There are metal shelves near them, a variety of instruments on top—knives, scalpels, and surgery pliers. It'd look like medical equipment if it wasn't for the shackles gleaming in the glow of the halogen bulbs.

These aren't instruments to heal. They're instruments to hurt.

Me.

I am the movie they're going to drink beer and eat popcorn while they watch. Genre: horror.

The flicker of hope that has sparked in me since Marco helped me reach out to Dad and Ronan dies at once as I stare at those shelves, leaving coldness and despair in its wake.

They're going to torture me.

They're going to chip at my flesh, at my soul, until there's no Divina left. They're going to hurt me until I'm begging for death, and Warden is going to sit behind that glass and watch.

I look for Wolf and Reindeer, but they're smothered deep. I can't shift without Marco and Flynn here. Somehow, just as I boost them, they boost me.

Even if I could shift, the silver will make it useless.

I try to swallow, but my throat is too dry as I realize my chances to get out of this are zero to none. Will this guard be the one to do it? I doubt it'll be Warden. He's too much of a coward.

The guard pulls me to my feet once more, and the door to the quarter with the chairs opens. A hooded man walks through, staring at me through the holes around the eyes in his mask. My head swims, and bile fills my throat.

My torturer.

I can't make out his face. His eyes and mouth are the only things visible. The dark-blue eyes are familiar, the pupils wide, fanatic. He's excited about what he's about to do. When he approaches, the guard passes me to him like I'm a toy. The hooded man smirks. "Are you ready?" he asks like he's asking me if I'm ready to go to a theme park, rather than threatening to torture me.

I've heard this voice before, but I can't place it. Damn this fucking place. I can't think straight in here. I start a profile anyway.

He doesn't like to be looked at in this persona, probably keeping an opposite lifestyle outside the prison. As a person, he blends well with the masses unnoticed, insignificant and perhaps even ridiculed.

He's either ugly or insecure. Or both. Most likely, an impotent that only gets aroused by power play. Sadists like to be admired for their work, but not all can handle the guilt. The hood gives him the illusion of control and power he lacks.

However, the way he speaks, the way he smiles…his eyes, the eager strut to his walk… This man isn't just ordered to torture me. This is personal.

He knows me.

His gloved hand cups my jaw roughly. "I said are you ready?"

I flinch at his snarl, at the feeling of leather on my skin. At this moment, my body has stopped reacting how I want it to. All I feel is the paralysis of a deer faced with a predator.

He wants something from me. In fact, the pride and anger in his voice say he thinks I should be grateful for what he's about to do to me.

I don't answer and stare right into his eyes to see if he'll hold it. His nostrils flare under the hood, and the next second he looks away. Then he growls, his hand squeezing my throat and pushing me against the wall.

The guard and Collins walk away into the viewing room, leaving me alone with this psycho. I can't even manage to scream.

My heart thrashes, but I don't need to be scared. I need to focus. I need to push, need to find out what he wants beyond just doing his job to hurt me. If this is personal, maybe I can talk my way out of this.

The darkness swirls inside me. It thinks I should act differently, and that frightening power threatens to break free. My eyes focus on the blades on the shelf, the tempting bloody things I can do to him if I get to those shelves. I could smash his face and gouge out his eyes. I could stab him twenty times and watch him bleed out slowly and then take my pound of flesh. I could chop his dick off, make him watch while I make a ceviche out of it and feed it to him—

No. *No*. I will *not* give into this. I don't want to succumb to that darkness. To Damien Pattison. It doesn't matter if it's going to be self-defense. If I attack that man, the others will come, and I'll have to hurt them, too. With the way I feel, the way I *want* to hurt them, there's no going back. The darkness will have me. Damien will have me.

A few cuts, bruises, and broken bones to avoid the fall seem like a cheap price to pay.

"When I ask you something, you answer. Understand?" the hooded man instructs.

I just nod, playing along.

There's loud laughter from behind the window across the room at my meekness, and even a cheer. Revulsion roils in my gut. They're enjoying the show already? Popcorn out yet?

He runs his fingers down my cheeks, a cruel mockery of a lover's touch. "So pretty," he murmurs in a modulated voice. "Those clothes aren't regulation here." He takes out a key and undoes the cuffs the guards put on me.

They clatter to the ground as he takes out a knife of his pocket, and with quick, dexterous strokes, pops the buttons on my shirt.

The material flutters to the ground. My breaths snag in my now exposed chest, my upper body covered by nothing but my bra.

He lifts my hands over my head. I want to scream, hit, scratch, do something to defend myself, but I'm paralyzed with the idea that if I attack him now, I won't be able to stop.

I suck in my yell at the sizzling burns the silver makes against my wrists. He doesn't get that satisfaction yet. Not before I get a better idea of who he is.

The snap of the shackles suspends me against the wall. Then he kneels, pulling off my shoes and pants, holding my legs so I can't kick at him. I shudder as his hands brush the skin of my thighs. My skin crawls at each touch.

"Stop." My voice is weak, trembling. I need him to think he's in control. "Please, stop. Please."

"That's right, make the bitch beg." Warden's voice is loud and clear even behind the glass. He savors me pleading just as much as my torturer does. He's hurting me just as much. He might not be holding the weapons, but this is on him. Just like Frank Goldstein and Pete Yates. Just like Chisholm's murder.

The begging works, leaving the hooded man satisfied for now as he leaves my panties where they are and stands up, surveying my naked, bound body. I can't see his expression, but the satisfaction radiates from him. I can feel his darkness, not as the criminal psychologist who has been around the darkest souls, but I can literally feel it. Even taste it.

It's filling his soul, drowning his heart, pouring out of every space in his body. I could use it, I think, just like Marco and Flynn have used me for a boost. I've clawed up in that cell, which means, like them, I was getting a boost from something.

The only thing I could think of, the one thing the demon and the hybrid have in common, the one thing that is seeping from my torturer and dulling my pain, is the fucking darkness.

If I take his, will it just add to mine? If I make him boil from the inside out, slit his throat and watch him bleed—because that's all I can imagine right now—will it be a victory? Or will it just bring me closer to give Damien Pattison everything he's ever needed to have me?

The hooded guard walks over to the

shelves, pondering the devices there. His hands caress and explore each weapon with the same sick sensuality as his touch on my skin. He settles on a small, silver knife, barely bigger than my finger.

When he approaches me, he slits the join of my bra, and then the straps, and the ruined contraption joins my shirt on the floor.

I tug at my chains, burning my wrists even more, as my breasts tumble free, exposed for the pleasure of these motherfuckers. I can hear them laughing, whistling, jeering at the sight of my nakedness. Then this fucker kneels at my feet, his free hand on my hip, his lips inches from my belly. "You're so beautiful," he whispers again. "I don't want to hurt you."

My stomach clenches in a tight knot. I close my eyes for a second to control my temper, something I've always been good at, a skill necessary to hide among humans, but it doesn't come easily now. I cry on purpose. That isn't difficult. Some of the tears streaming down my face are real. "Then don't." My voice betrays me, the fury clear.

Fuck, that was too aggressive. I can't get to him if I get angry. I take a breath and force the weakness back into my tone. "Please."

"I like it when you beg," he says sensually.

Then there's a cold sharpness that swiftly turns into a horrible burn sliding down my body as the blade slices my skin.

Rattling my chains, I scream. The pain is fucking real enough that I barely stay conscious.

The sick bastards applaud. "It's not human!" one of them yells, though it hurts too much to make out if it's Warden or his goon. "Show it real pain! Make it scream more!"

Bolstered by their applauding, cheering and whooping, he drags the knife down my skin, slowly, languorously. It leaves blood and agony in its wake. I scream, my body bucking, straining at the shackles as I try to recoil, but the knife keeps flashing, painting a gruesome bloody picture on my stomach.

It seems to go on forever, and then he pulls back. He lifts the knife to his own face and runs his tongue along it, tasting my blood. "Huh." His voice sounds a little more familiar, but I'm bleeding too much, my skin prickling with pain, to finally place it.

"Your blood tastes like copper. I expected more, given how you people seem to thrive on the stuff," he says.

I struggle against the chains again, the welts on my wrists nothing compared to the sharp stinging fire of my lower torso. "*My* kind," I hiss through the pants, "aren't the monsters here."

The knife clatters to the floor. Then he slaps me, hard, his hand across my cheek sending my head back and clanging it against the wall. "*Your* kind? *Your* kind? You still think of them that way? Divina, you don't belong to them. You belong with me. You belong to *me*. He said so."

What in the actual fuck?

My vision blurs from the hit, but I see him storm over to the shelves again, "Wh...who did? What are…" I slur.

There's a hissing noise. I will my eyes to focus, trying to work out where it's coming from. He holds a tool in his hand. A long rod with wires hooked to something, and the end is glowing hotter and hotter.

"It's a process called electrocautery," he croons, sounding as excited as a child at show-and-tell. "Once it's finished heating, the tip can reach up to 2000°F. I can use this tool to draw on your skin, whatever pattern I want. Instant third-degree burns. Permanent scarification. I'll mark you, just like he marked me when I gave him my soul." He rolls up his sleeve to show me the burn on his forearm, but he covers it too fast for me to make out the shape. "And I'll mark you again as mine when you're given to me as my reward."

His lord, who marked him. His lord, who claimed him.

I don't need to see the mark to know who his lord is.

The fucking devil himself.

The prick brandishes the tool at me. I twist and shout at the top of my lungs, desperate to get away. It barely touches my leg, and the whole world explodes in a blazing anguish. The shrieks ripping from my throat as he permanently brands me don't sound human, or even beast, but something made in hell.

He doesn't stop, he keeps going. The cool beckoning of unconsciousness is about to give me some relief.

When he pulls the tool away, he slaps me hard again, refusing to let me faint, making sure I feel all of his precious work. My leg is throbbing, and I can't see it properly through the tears and the swimming lights, but there is a mark there now that I don't think will ever fade, even with a shifter's healing.

I'm wheezing now, even breathing hurts. I'm pretty sure they're having a blast in the other room, but I can't hear them anymore. I can barely see or hear anything. He lifts his mask to his nose and grabs my hair. Then he yanks my head forward and presses his lips to mine, holding my head there. I thrash and lean back as far as I can to get away, but his filthy mouth crushes into mine anyway.

"See," he says when he's done. "That wasn't so bad, was it? Better than the vampire? The demon?" His voice hardens. "Yes, I know what a slut you've been. But I'm willing to forgive you."

My eyes twitch as I take in the exposed part of his face and link it to the more familiar voice.

His disgusting breaths hit my face. "I love you."

My memory stirs, and the image of a friendly guard at Forest Grove pen fills my mind.

Spiraling, my whole body slumps, sags. My lips quiver with a bitter smile. Then I choke on a humorless sound that is supposed to be a chuckle. "Graham Wilder."

"Yes, sweetheart. It's always been me." He kisses me again, and I think I'm going to vomit. "That's why I did this, all of it. And once you do what my lord wants, we'll have power and love forever, you and I."

Clarity hits me like a sledgehammer through the pain. *This, all of it—* Chisholm's murder, the investigation, this prison, everything—is nothing but the devil's plan to claim me.

I can barely speak, but I gather whatever strength left in me to say a few words. Now that my profile is complete, I need to provoke Graham, to push him a little harder. "It was you, wasn't it? You killed Chisholm. Collins ordered it, but you…you were the hitman. A pathetic tool for both of them."

His palm rings on my cheek, almost breaking my jaw. "I'm not anybody's tool! And it wasn't a fucking *hit*. It was a sacrifice. For a cause you're only beginning to understand."

He's silent for a long moment as I swallow my own blood. "But I know you're smarter than this, Professor. You'll come around. You might think you still have your family, your friends that will come to rescue you, but soon enough you'll know *I'm* your only family and friend left. I'm the only one you can trust."

"Then why…why are you hurting me?" I don't know how much of it is an act anymore.

He reaches for his hood and yanks it off, finally revealing his face, and the little strength I have remaining crumbles away as I look into the eyes of someone I once thought I could trust, as I realize how much of a stupid fuck I've been.

"Because you needed to *learn,* Divina," Graham says, his eyes wide, his voice earnest as though he believes every word. "You needed to learn that you've been bad. It's okay though. I'm here to help now. I'll fix you."

My body shakes with dry sobs. "You need serious help, Graham. If you just get me out of here, I'll stay with you. I'll help you myself."

"I don't need help!" he snaps. "*You* need help. You teased me, told me you loved me, and now you treat me like this?"

Great. He's delusional, too. Probably an obsessive stalker because this can't be just about my rejection at the pen. It goes way back before the murder.

"I thought you knew me better than this," he blames me, waving the brander again. "I sat in one of your classes once. I thanked you for the lecture afterward, and you said it was a pleasure to have me. A *pleasure,* Divina! The things I've done to try to get to you since then, to allow us to be together. You ungrateful bitch!"

The rod connects with my other leg. My throat burns as I shriek again, praying I could just pass out, or maybe even die. God, just please let me die.

He drops the tool and grabs my chin,

making me look into his eyes. "Yes, I killed Chisholm. I took him to the exercise room, and I told him about the Great Plan. He begged, just like you were begging, but I tied him down. Every cut, every tear, was in service to my lord. In service to you. When I tore his guts from his body, it was for *us,* Divina. For our love. For our future."

He tugs at my chin and forces me to kiss him once more. My body is limp, sweating, cold. His lips travel down my cheek to my jaw, his hands even more searing than the brander and the silver together when they squeeze around my breasts.

Tears spill from the corners of my eyes. "Please stop."

He does, but only because the door behind him opens, and Warden and the guard walk out.

"That's enough for now." Graham's voice holds an ugly promise of more later. "We're going to go visit your *friends.* Just remember, anything that happens to them is your fault."

THIRTY-NINE
DIVINA

The gift of unconsciousness comes at last. It's the only break I can get from the pain, the agony that every breath is causing me. My wrists ache. The blood has rushed from my arms. There's not enough leeway to allow me to sit, but I'm so exhausted that I sleep anyway.

The second I do, he's there waiting. I'm not surprised this time. It's the only thing that makes sense, that the second I am free of the pain, the devil awaits me.

"Hello, Divina."

"Hello, Damien." I sound dull to my ears, just like all the color has vanished from my world.

"You look like you could use some help." He speaks to me in a fatherly tone.

The image of my real father flashes behind my eyes. *You've got it all backward, D.*

I've never let him finish, never let him explain. But today I learn he is right.

I did get it all wrong.

Dad's voice echoes back in my head. "Your mother wasn't afraid of being a supe because we are bad. It was her human darkness she was scared of. She refused to turn so no one would blame a supe for the evil a human can bring.

"She couldn't risk it with a new side she would have known nothing of. She stayed human because it was the only side she could control. So you, your sister and your brothers can live knowing there's nothing wrong with being *you*. So you would believe that, beast or no beast, darkness or no darkness, if you tried hard enough you could be good too.

"She made that choice so you, baby girl, can someday choose wisely too."

Choose wisely? How am I supposed to do

that?

I've tried to live as a human. So fucking hard. The result is a huge lie. No matter how hard I make believe, I don't belong there.

I don't fit in the shifter world either. Look at where I've ended up when I thought I did.

I've even tried to combine both of those worlds, and all it's resulted in is pulling Derek, my family and everyone I've ever loved into all this pain, putting humans and supes in danger.

The answer, the wise choice can't be any of this. That leaves me with only one path to try.

My gaze travels back to Damien. When I look into his eyes, I no longer see a monster. I see myself.

He smiles benignly. Does he know? Does he know how tempting it is for me now to just give in? To escape the pain, to stop trying. To go to him. To be free of this, of everything. I could save Flynn, Aedan, Ronan, Marco. I could save my people. Derek. My father.

I could bring my mother back.

Did he mean that? Can he really do it?

Because if he can, there's nothing I want more now than to feel her arms wrap around me one more time, listen to her tell me everything is going to be okay.

"I don't need your help," I lie, clinging to the last shred of sanity left in me. I have a power I barely understand. I don't want to be the one responsible for handing it to Damien. I don't want to give into this. Even though all that awaits me when I wake is torment…I don't want to fall.

"The boy is going to come back soon," Damien tells me softly. "He hasn't had his fill of you. He's only just started. He wants you. He intends to take you."

"Yeah, thanks to you." I don't know where the snark comes from, but my hopelessness hardens inside me and comes out in a rush of hurt and rage. "You *gave* me to him. Like I'm a toy! Everything is a toy to you. A game. All of this is your doing in a pathetic attempt to make me give in to you." I snort. "You are pathetic."

Damien shrugs, unrepentant. "I tried to play nice, sweet one. But you scorned me, over and over. You know I'd do anything for someone as precious as you, no matter how much it takes. It's what fathers do."

The dark rage flares again. "You are not my father. And I don't want your deal."

Liar, my subconscious scolds me. *Liar, liar. Think of the power. Think of the freedom. Think of your mother. You have no other way out.*

He's watching me as though he can hear my thoughts.

"That guard is going to rape you and cut you and beat you. He's not going to kill you, so he can come back and do it over and over again. Collins is going to round up every supernatural creature in the country, including your uncles, the men who raised you and your siblings. He's going to torture your boyfriends. Derek. Your father. Your whole family. He'll bring them in front of you so you can listen to their screams."

"Shut up!" I close my eyes against his whispers, but it's useless. I know what he's saying is true, and he's making the images dance in my brain. My father covered in lacerations. My lovers, my family begging for the pain to stop. And I just watch, useless, weak, just waiting for my next turn at the torture. "Leave me alone." The firmness is gone, and my voice breaks. "Please."

He approaches and touches my arm comfortingly. It reminds me of my father, and I hate Damien for trying to take that role. "Just call my name and ask for my help if you change your mind."

He vanishes, and I'm in another dream. More of a memory. The conversation I had when Marco let me into my father's head.

My father smiles, tears streaming down his face, and he strokes my hair. "She loved you, D. So much."

"I love her, too. Is it true? About the darkness?"

"Yes. But you must believe me. She would have done anything for you. I loved your mother with all my heart. We all did. And that's why we understood, even though her choice damn near destroyed us."

My eyes stings with tears I won't allow to fall. "I've spent so many years angry for no reason. Maybe she should have given in. Maybe it's who she was. Who we are. Dark. Evil."

Dad shakes his head. "No. You still got it all backward, baby."

"What are you talking about?" My head swims. "Dad…I don't…what are you…"

A sharp slap jerks me awake. I jump, my wrists tearing against the shackles. Graham is staring at me, furious. "I didn't say you could sleep. Why weren't you waiting on me, Divina? Didn't you miss me? I thought of you all this time, and you just snooze?"

All the pain rushes back in. The scarring on my legs is still burning, the cuts on my stomach red, weeping, and my jaw and cheek are swelling with bruising from where he keeps hitting me. Being awake is torture. Being *alive* is torture.

When I look at this fuck, that rage I feel toward Damien spins in my stomach, rushing through my veins, fueling that darkness I've spent so long trying to deny.

And for what? So I can be left here to rot, naked, for the pleasure of some sick psychos?

I spit in his face, the saliva mixed with blood. He raises his hand, wiping his cheek slowly, and then he's hitting me again. Not just a slap, but punching, kicking, every blow a new ache.

When he finally stops his attack, he grabs my hair, yanking back so I'm forced to look up at him. Then he lowers his free hand, hooking his fingers around the edge of my panties and tugging.

"No. No, Graham, don't, please, don't—"

He silences me by crushing his lips against mine, forcing my mouth open, making it more of a claim than a kiss. He pulls, and my panties tear.

He grabs my back, pulling my naked, bleeding body close to him, pressing me against him. A terrible shudder runs through me as I feel how hard he is. I kick him and shove my knees up at his crotch, screaming, but it just makes him harder.

With a smirk, he pushes me to the wall, squeezing my neck, rendering me immobile. "I'm sure my lord won't mind if I have a little taste now. Since I've worked so hard."

His fingers reach for the button on his pants.

No.

No.

No.

Nobody can help me now. Dad. Marco. Flynn. Aedan. Ronan. Derek. All of them would be here if they could, but they're suffering too, and I can't help them either.

We're alone, all of us, and nothing can stop this.

Graham has his pants off and makes a fist around his erection. I squeeze my eyes shut, moaning a sound at the back of my throat. I can hear him move closer, and he kisses me again, his fingernails digging, leaving marks on my breasts.

I snarl against his lips, biting hard. He barks, and I open my eyes. When he tears away from me, there's blood pouring down his face.

Staring at me with mingled fury and lust, he wipes his mouth with the back of his hand. I stare back, imagining what it would be like to wrench my arm free, to use these chains and wrap them around his neck, to hold them tight against him as his face turns red, then purple, then blue, as the air leaves him forever and he chokes his last breath.

But the chains hold, even when I try to tug free once more. He leans in close to my ear. "I'm going to fuck you now. And you're going to tell me how much you like it. Okay?"

I spit again. "Never."

"We'll see." He squeezes me harder, and I cry out in pain. "Aren't you going to ask me to stop? I like it when you beg," he whispers.

My breath trembles with my body. Behind him, Damien stands, watching with a blank expression.

Graham grabs my butt and lifts me up so he can spread my legs. I glance one last time at the door where no one is coming. The next second, Graham's fingers are inching between my thighs.

I'm out of time, out of options, out of hope.

"Damien, help me."

FORTY
RONAN

I dream of her. We are lying naked together under the stars, the moonlight bathing our skin in shining silver. Her head is on my chest. My wings are spread out behind me. There's no sound but the rustle of the leaves in the slight wind, the lapping waters of the lake, and her gentle breathing. I know Aedan will return soon, but right now it is just us, alone together and happy.

She sighs contentedly, a sigh that sounds

like the first rain after a drought, gentle and life-giving. "Ronan, will we stay here forever?"

I run my fingers through her long curls. "Do you want to stay here forever with me?"

A sudden coldness ripples through the air. Her body tenses against mine. When I look down, she is weeping, her tears staining my chest. I can't hear the trees or the lake, only the anguish in her cries. "I can't," she sobs. "I can't."

I hold her close, calming her, whispering her name, whispering soothing sounds, desperate to stop her pain. "Why not?"

Brutally, she's not in my arms anymore. I'm alone in the snow, under a clouded dull sky. Her voice rustles in the trees. "Because I'm gone. Because you left me."

The cold wind blows harshly. The trees are gone. There's only me now, standing alone in a void. Not far from me, there is a small, pale shape with long flowing brown curls, and as I approach it, I see it's a body, cold and still, no life left. Her voice comes again in a terrible accusatory scream. "You left me!"

I bolt awake with a shout, sweat on my brow. A dream. It's just a dream. A nightmare.

"What the fuck are you yelling about?" Aedan paces back and forth restlessly along the center of the cell. He doesn't look like he's slept at all.

Terror sits up from where he was dozing on the other bunk. "What is it? Is it Divina?"

It's just a nightmare.

Isn't it?

I shake my head to clear it, to get rid of the image of her still body in my mind's eye. But it persists, and her cry still permeates my brain. If I let anything happen to her, if she's hurt, it's my fault.

You left me.

No. No. I'll never leave her.

I layer my voice with as much magic as I can manage, infusing it with my fear for her, and my love for her. I've lived thousands of years, but without her—without being able to love her—they will all have been worth nothing.

My stare lands on Aedan. I'm not siphoning anyone now, but I don't need to because magic is my soul, and *she* is my soul. "Aedan Oakberry, come *here*."

Aedan's eyes widen in surprise for half a second, and then he walks toward me.

"What the fuck?" Terror mumbles slowly.

"Raise your hand," I command.

Aedan does.

"Sit on the floor."

He sits.

Terror is staring. "Holy shit. Are you doing it?"

I break the compelling and Aedan blinks, rising back to his feet. "Fae bastard. You've been holding out on us."

"Not anymore," I say. "Ready to make some noise?"

The two of them look at each other and grin.

They're true to their word. My ears might be ringing for the next five years from the amount of noise they manage to produce with just their hands and feet and mouths and what's in the cell. They clang the metal rods of the beds, scream and yell, crash against the walls, and it doesn't take all that long before someone comes running.

It's just one single guard. Perfect.

"If you convicts are going to kill each other, do it quietly," he snarls, throwing the door open and leveling a gun at us. I recognize him right away. His red hair made him stand out on the list Derek gave me with the full names and passport-sized photos of each of these bastards.

I take a note of his voice, too, storing it in my memory for later. The bag at his hip is familiar. The same they used at Ward E to carry the drugs. If he gets near us with that, we're doomed.

Aedan and Terror both bulk up, ready for a fight. I hurry over to them, not threatened by the gun pointing at them, and put a hand on both their shoulders, drawing whatever I can. "Eric Stanley. Put that gun down."

He looks at me for a second. A horrific second that lasts a lifetime. He just stares. I stare back, and yet he's not moving.

The tension from Terror and Aedan floods into me. No. No! I can't fail now. It has to work. It has to fucking work. "Eric Stanley," I say again sharply. "Put the gun down."

Slowly, his eyes droop. Then he lowers his weapon to the floor.

We can finally breathe.

"Eric Stanley, give us your badge and your weapons."

"And the drugs," Aedan grunts.

"And the drugs," I agree.

Stanley does as I command, handing everything to Terror, who gives the badge to me and straps the drug bag securely around his waist.

"You aren't going to raise the alarm, Eric Stanley. You're not going to protest when the door locks. You're just going to sit on this bunk quietly for the next few hours. When they find you, you're not going to tell them you know how we escaped. Do you understand?" I tell him.

He walks to the bunk and sits, moving like a sleepwalker.

"Tell me you understand, Eric."

"I understand," he says.

"Go," I tell the other two, keeping my eyes on the guard as I back away.

Terror and Aedan rush out of the open door of the cell. Then when I'm out, too, I close the door. It locks with the now-familiar hiss.

"Now what?" Aedan demands. "We don't even know where she is."

"Detour," I say, nodding across the hollow gap to the other side of the fourth floor. "We're going to pick up a couple of friends."

FORTY-ONE
FLYNN

The cell door lock hisses, and in the few seconds it takes to fully open, I've come up with a hundred ways to kill whatever unlucky piece of shit walks through. If they have Divina with them, I'll make it quick. If they don't, they'll suffer. If they do, and she's hurt… Well, I might not be able to shift, but that doesn't mean my lion will be denied a meal. Or that all that blood should go to waste.

Marco scampers to his feet next to me, pale from the bullet, a piece of my blanket haphazardly tied around his arm to stop the bleeding. He hasn't said anything at all, but his eyes are focused on the door, too.

In a hunting crouch, I brace myself to attack. I'll tear them apart before they know what has happened.

"Try it, wee man," a gruff, harsh voice says. "You'll be in for a bad yin if you do."

I scowl, straightening up. "Oakberry?"

The dragon is watching me as if he's not sure if I'm going to attack still. Maybe he'd kind of like it if I did. I can feel it pulsing from him; he's spoiling for a fight.

O'Shea stands a little farther back, a keycard dangling from the end of a lanyard twirled around his finger. He wears this unbearably smug look on his face. I kind of want to punch him, though by the state of him, it looks like someone already has, so many times.

And behind them…familiar blue eyes and pouty lips. "Mr. Beastly?" I guess.

The man snorts. "Terror."

"Or Luke," O'Shea adds, amusement in his voice. Oh, he's bragging about being on a first-name basis with Divina's father? They're good friends now? Motherfucker.

Terror rolls his eyes at him, though, and I smirk. You got nothing on us, glitter dude. Her father doesn't like you. You're not going to win any free points with our girl.

"Terror," Marco repeats, as though he's savoring the sound. His eyes trail over the man's body. "Well, you certainly are…terrifying."

"Are you fucking kidding me? He's her dad," I whisper angrily.

Marco just shrugs, ever smirking. Of course. He's a demon, for fuck's sake. He doesn't care about such naive things. Fuck the girl and her father together? Yeah, no problem.

Though…I must admit Terror is really hot. To have a guy and girl who look like that together is just… I shake my head violently and glare at Marco. "Fuck you. Stop messing with my head."

Marco puts his hand on my shoulder, squeezing slightly. "Gentlemen." I don't know how he keeps his voice so annoyingly calm, like he has been expecting this the whole time. "How pleasant. Is this a prison break?"

"Not until I get my girl back," Terror says. "Where is she?"

Marco's laconic smile drops, a deep frown taking its place. "They took her. I don't know where. A few hours ago."

Oakberry snarls and kicks at the wall.

"How are we supposed to find her in this fucking mausoleum?" I demand, anger flaring up in me. Anger at the warden, anger at the guards, but mostly anger at myself. I should have stopped them. I should have protected her.

O'Shea is quiet, his mouth set in a hard line. I'm not sure what he's thinking, but it doesn't look pleasant. Terror, meanwhile, looks like fury incarnate, but there's real desperate fear in his eyes.

"He's right," Terror grunts. "Even apart from the drugs, this place is a repellent. We can't track her like we normally could, not even me, and I know her scent better than any of you." His fist clenches. "My own daughter and I can't even pick up a hint of her trail."

I want to laugh through the onslaught of dread and rage and horror surging through me. Marco's demonic powers must be having a field day with all of us in this state.

When it hits me, it's like a lightning bolt directly to my brain.

Marco's *powers*.

"They must be hurting her. She must be scared," I say slowly, and all of them are glaring at me with expressions ranging from incredulity to hate. I don't care. At least they're listening.

"This may surprise you, Killian, but we don't particularly want to dwell on her pain." O'Shea's voice is hard and sarcastic.

I wave him off. "Me neither. But someone in here can."

We all look at Marco as one, and he stares back, surprise written all over his face. "I…don't know. There are still drugs in my system, and this whole building is rigged to stop us from doing, well, anything. I don't know if I can—"

"But I shifted a little," I tell him eagerly. "When we were—when Divina was—there's *something*. Just try, Marco. Think of her. This place is teeming with misery, but if they're hurting her, I'm betting she'll stand out."

O'Shea's eyes are on me now. "You're smarter than you look," he tells me, as though that's supposed to be a compliment. Cocky bastard.

Marco kisses my cheek. It's such a casual, intimate gesture that I've never experienced from him. Until now. Until tonight. The night we've made love to each other. To Divina Beastly.

"Put the moon-eyes away and let's go." Oakberry is impatient. "Unless you want to wait for the next dickhead guard to come looking for his pal."

Terror is the first to move, and all of us follow him out of the cell into the hallway. Bodies litter the floor, guards that Terror and Oakberry have no qualms about claiming as their own kills when Marco queries.

Ronan points to the cameras. The only things in this hole that aren't made of lethal metal. He's enchanted them. We're basically invisible to anyone watching as we pick our way through right now.

When we reach the elevator, it's obvious that between me, Oakberry, and Terror, there's no way in hell all of us are fitting inside along with O'Shea and Marco. We're just too big.

Marco assesses the problem in an instant. "Teams, then. It will allow us to search the place faster anyway." He steps forward into the elevator. "Flynn, Terror and I will start at the bottom and—"

He freezes in place.

"Marco?" I say, but he doesn't even answer me. Instead, he looks straight up through the roof of the elevator, as though he's a dog that's caught a scent. "Marco," I repeat.

"New plan." His tone is clipped, urgent. "We all get to the top of this hellhole. Right.

Now."

"What is it?" O'Shea asks as Terror and I join Marco in the elevator. "What do you sense, Gianmarco?"

Marco swallows. "Darkness."

FORTY-TWO

DIVINA

Damien moves forward, a blade shining in his hand. The victorious grin on his face is very, very real.

It's time to give in. The darkness calls, and it's time to answer. It hurts, but it's sweet, too. Everything in me longs to sink into it, to surrender to its depths.

"Nobody can help you," Graham murmurs into my ear, moving so close that his breath leaves droplets on my skin, his fingers crawling between my thighs. "Whoever you're calling for, they're not here. Nobody is coming."

I silently say my goodbyes as I contemplate what I'm about to do. Goodbye to my human life. Goodbye to my coffee in the morning, to the way I laugh with Derek over sushi. Goodbye to my sister, who I might never see again. My brothers, who may never know what happened to me. Goodbye to my uncles and the men who raised me with my father, the men who see me as one of their own, whom I abandoned because I thought I could outrun it all. Goodbye to my father, who gave me everything, who lost my mother, who's going to lose me too.

A tear rolls down my cheek. *Goodbye.*

Damien places the blade in my shackled hand, and I nod at him. His hands work fast to unlock my restraints...

Ding.

Graham looks up as the booming sound of the elevator distracts him. I don't bother to see who's coming. It must be the rest of the fuckers who want to watch. I only focus on the rattling of my chains, waiting for the moment to be free so I can put this asshole fuck in my place and take my time with the blade.

They can watch that. I'll make them. Then they will have their turn against this wall.

It's when Graham takes a few steps backward at the roaring coming out of the elevator that I look.

Dad?

I shake my head to make sure I'm not hallucinating. Three men are coming barreling toward us, my father leading the charge.

He's on Graham in an instant, punching him across the jaw and knocking him to the floor. He crouches over him, beating him over and over. While Graham screams, Flynn and Marco hurry to my side.

"Oh my God," I pant. "You guys are really here. You came for me."

Flynn is gazing at the blood and damage to my body, looking sick, but he attempts something like a smile as he quips, "Jesus, Professor, we can't leave you alone for a minute."

Marco delicately bends down next to where my father is beating the life out of Graham and fishes in the guard's pocket, coming up with a tiny silver key, and then he goes straight to my cuffs.

But Damien was about to get those undone. I look to my side and up and around wildly, but the devil is nowhere to be found.

When my hands are finally free, a wave of dizziness takes me, and I stumble. Both Marco and Flynn are there to catch me. "Where…where's Damien?" I ask.

"Damien?" Marco demands, steadying me with his good arm. Is it my imagination, or has he gone a little paler? "You don't mean…"

I glance at my hand, at the blade still in it, but I hide it quickly behind my back. I don't want him to know, don't want any of them to know I was about to give in. "He's gone. It's over. Damien is gone."

They hold me close, both of them, Flynn delicately kissing my disgusting hair, Marco stroking my cheek, both breathing slowly, calming themselves, as though my presence is a balm to their wounds. Being in their arms, being alive, being with them, it shakes me with happiness. It's finally done. I'm safe. We're together at last.

The elevator dings again, and Ronan and Aedan are here, both of them making loud noises of dismay at the state of me, at the blood everywhere.

Aedan's fury contorts his face as he rushes forward and helps my father with the beating. A loud snap echoes around the room. Aedan grunts from the floor, releasing Graham's head. "Oops. You didn't want that alive, did you?"

He's grinning at me. Even now he's joking, trying to make me smile in his signature macabre way. My heart pounds for this huge, scarred, freckled boy who loves so deeply it hurts him. I am so glad he's with me now.

Dad pulls Graham's stained jacket from his body and hurries to me, placing it over my shoulders. His hands are stained with Graham's blood, but I don't care as he hugs me as gently as he can so he won't touch my wounds.

I nestle into his warmth, allowing myself, just for a moment, to be that little girl again. Dad's little girl, safe from everything in the warmth of his arms, protected from the world by my brave, terrifying father. He pulls back, looking into my eyes, tears flowing silently.

I don't want to cry, too, so I just let the blade drop and slip my arms into the dead fucker's coat, buttoning it up, grateful for the extra warmth.

The bloody pulp on the floor that has been Graham is now lying with its dead head at an unnatural angle, the neck clearly snapped by Aedan. His face is unrecognizable, the whole body savaged.

I stare at it, and ice forms in my veins. This

man, who is now a human body, lies dead before me, mutilated beyond recognition. He's beaten me, cut me, threatened my people and tried to rape me.

I should feel something, anything.

But all that exists is cold.

The darkness is pleased.

I lift my eyes to the boys. "Let's get out of here."

Dad lets go of me. Ronan approaches and hugs me tight, saying nothing at all. I hug him back, ignoring the pain of my wounds when I do. I understand. Words are what the fae use for their magic, and what Ronan is feeling is beyond even that now.

When Ronan and I finally let go of each other, Marco loops an arm around my waist, supporting me, and helps me along as we all make our way back to the elevator.

I can't believe it's over. I take another swipe around the place to make sure Damien is really gone. We've won. We're getting out of here, and I get to keep my—

The elevator doors open, and we all stop to a halt. Because Warden Collins and his guards are flashing their weapons at us, snatching the victory I thought we've just had.

The warden laughs. "Come on. Don't tell me you didn't see this one coming."

FORTY-THREE
RONAN

Gianmarco's unearthly scream jars me to the bones when the rock-salt-infused silver bullet connects with his already-injured arm. Terror dashes for Divina as the bullets rain, pushing her away from Gianmarco and out of harm's way.

I throw myself to the ground, narrowly avoiding a hit. Aedan grabs me by the scruff of the neck and pulls me to the side, away from the direct line of fire.

Flynn gets in front of the demon to protect him as the guards pour out of the tiny elevator. There are six plus the warden, with guns, darts and iron knives.

Three guards point the dart guns. It's them I focus on when I call out the air's name, commanding it to form a solid barrier between us and those weapons, freezing the darts midair before they hit us.

They will *not* take my magic. Never again.

I cry out the name of iron, even though it burns my tongue, and send the dart guns crumbling to dust in the guard's hands.

The others fire the bullets. Aedan lets out a long list of Gaelic swears as one of the bullets grazes his leg. He manages to jump and dodge the silver dagger the warden swings toward him.

Aedan grabs one of the guns we've stolen from the dead on our way here and levels it at one of the guards, firing directly into the man's skull. Then he hits another guard, then another, their blood and brains flying everywhere.

As soon as the blood spray begins, the warden retreats out of our reach, out of the line of fire. Coward.

A flood of armed guards rushes from the other side of this floor, circling us in no time.

Gianmarco clutches his arm, waving one of the scalpels he's taken from the shelves despite the damage. He hisses at the new ambush. There are another five—ten—of them. They all bear enough darts and weapons that could incapacitate us in a blink.

"What do we do, Boss?" Aedan asks, his black eyes narrowed, fire behind his pupils. "I'll tear them with my human teeth if I have to."

Fists clenched, Flynn crouches down next to Marco. Terror pulls Divina as far back as possible, telling her to stay put as he rushes back to join the fight. The five of us are all that stands between her and them hurting her again

I won't—none of us will—allow harm to happen to her again. Something glints in Terror's hand. He throws it before I can even see.

There's a frozen moment where everyone watches a knife sail through the air. It can't be more than two seconds at most, but it seems to last forever as it perfectly arcs through the air before embedding itself in the skull of the foremost guard dashing our way.

It takes an eternity for him to fall.

His body makes an odd clattering sound against the metal floor. Another frozen second passes…and then they all charge.

We grab whatever weapons we can. Knives, pliers, chains, guns. If these don't work, we still have our fists. I still have my magic.

It's chaos when we attack while we dodge, desperate to avoid the darts and bullets. I grapple with one of the guards when another approaches me from behind. I don't see him but the cloying scent of iron fills my nose.

Aedan roars and tries to fight five off at once while an already-injured and weakened Gianmarco tries to shield Divina. I can't see Terror, but I hear his yells and Killian's loud swearing.

I don't know how long we can keep dodging, so I burn my tongue on the name of the iron again to squash the dart guns. If any of these hit, it's over.

Only then, a horrible squelching noise pierces my back.

A sharp, iron blade bears down on me. I rabbit-punch the one whom I grapple, knocking him out. Then I twist onto my back, staring up at my oncoming death. If I am to die, I will at least have the pride of looking the man who kills me in the eye. The knife sinks in and protrudes out my chest.

This is it.

My eyes dart around for Divina. I want to see her for the last time, but I can't find her anywhere.

I gurgle, falling to my knees, my eyes shutting down and—

A loud snarl. A dark shape pounces over us, its teeth closing over the neck of the guard with the knife and dragging him away. The warm blood splatters over my face as he is knocked clear.

Blinking away the blood and the pain, I see the gray fur, and the wolf tearing at the guard's throat, ending his miserable life. She turns to me, a spark in the golden eyes as our souls recognize each other.

Divina.

A full wolf, bloody muzzled and ready for the next fight. There's something…different about her, a strength that radiates from her, an aura of power that glistens on her fur and surges off her body in waves, washing over me, over all of us.

I don't understand, but I don't have time to think. I just have to believe in it, believe in her. My love for her boosts me to new heights despite the iron sticking out of my chest, despite the drugs, despite the inhibitors.

I call the name of the air.

It responds to me, dancing to my tune,

jumping to my command in a way that makes me want to weep with happiness. In the lake, the air has helped me breathe. This time, I ask it to do the opposite for the guards.

Two of them turn blue in front of my eyes as the air refuses to reach their lungs. Their choking sounds are like music to my ears. I concentrate on them, not allowing their breath to keep going, until they fall and stop twitching.

As I allow myself to take a breath of my own, to regroup before finding my next victims, Gianmarco shouts to the others. "Shift, idiots. She's helping us! Do it! Now!"

With a flash of gold, Aedan's wings erupt from his back, ripping through his jumpsuit as though it is paper. His claws sprout. Cináed roars, accompanied by a bout of flames the guards attacking him jump to the side to avoid. One of them isn't quick enough and goes down screaming, flames leaping from his body, blistering every inch of exposed skin.

A lion's roar erupts from my left. Flynn tears through the gathered guards, teeth unnaturally sharp and pointed even for such a beast. He fights side-by-side with the reinwolf monstrosity that is Terror. Each of them has a guard's arm in their mouths. They pull, each taking half of the unfortunate man with them.

The stench of blood is all that exists anymore.

Still gripping onto his twice-injured arm, Marco is gazing intently at the two guards closest to him, waving their weapons threateningly. His forehead creases in concentration. The guards stiffen, and then they have their guns raised at each other's foreheads.

Two simultaneous shots bang, and the guards' viscera decorates the wall, the floor and all the people around them.

I understand now, as I call the air once more to target another two nearby. It's in Gianmarco's vibrant expression, the glow in his eyes as he looks for his next victim. It's in the effervescence of Divina's loping movements as she pounces, deftly, avoiding weapons to tear at guards' throats. It's in Terror's attacks and in Flynn's roars, and in every powerful surge of Aedan's flames.

It's Divina. It's all Divina. We call it her darkness, the power the devil wants so badly, the part of her she denies with all her might. The part that gives her the strange draw I cannot resist. She is fueling us all.

Her power boosts my soul, and my feelings for her, her feelings for me, they bolster it further. She has given back her father, Aedan, Flynn, and herself the power to shift, and

Marco the power to whisper, just by being herself. Her urge to defend us, to save us; that is where our power is coming from.

The devil and his demons may call it darkness. Divina may fear it. But it is *her,* and it is beautiful.

As a fae, it should repulse me. It *is* dark, unnatural, the opposite of everything my heart and my magic stand for. But I feel quite the opposite. I can't be repulsed, not by her, not by anything she can do. Her power isn't something to be shamed. It's up to all of us who love her to help her understand it. Is this what Terror was trying to explain? Is this what he needs her to understand?

That darkness, to me right now, tastes just the same as blazing hope. Guard after guard falls, weapons clatter to the ground. Aedan lets out that dragon cackle of his as fire fills the room. I take the iron blade out of my chest, huffing and groaning but certain I'll heal.

We've won.

We'll kill them all. Then Aedan and I will get us out of here. He'll melt the ceiling, and we'll both fly free and clear.

Finally, we'll burn this place to the ground.

Now, I dare to believe it's really over.

I scamper to my feet, but more

reinforcements arrive. The sixteen original guards are down, but we're not done yet. The new ones arrive simultaneously; six more elevator guards with six more guns, and ten, twenty, *thirty* more men from the other side, all rushing toward us.

I hate death, I hate killing, but I ready myself to do more of it. I'll go down slaughtering them for what they've done to us. To Divina.

They have more weapons this time, and there are just too many of them. I back up, avoiding a swing from some sort of thick iron rod. But the man I spot out of the corner of my eye is what sends a shiver of fear down my spine.

It's him. He's standing in a corner, separate from the action but very visible, wearing a smile on his face. The warden stands next to the blond man in the suit, smug and proud. Aedan sees him too, and Gianmarco, and Flynn. All of them wear the same lost look on their face that I feel in my heart.

When Terror notices him, he howls. Because if that man is here, if we can all see him, it means it really *is* over.

Damien Pattison will watch us all burn and play with our ashes.

FORTY-FOUR
DIVINA

The world moves in slow motion as I look up from the mangled throat of my latest kill, and the new squadron arrives to mow us down.

Marco's scream is loud as a bullet hits him in the leg, crippling him to the ground, and the same gun is at his forehead.

My father and Flynn are circled, trapped, being borne down on with silver and Vetala. Flynn's primal screech tears at my ears as one of the weapons connects with his flesh. My father, trying to be a hero, pushes him out of the way, in vain.

There's no way for them to escape the circle now.

Silver chains rope around Aedan, binding his wings, and the golden scales that have erupted over his skin sizzle everywhere the chains touch. The guards are gaining on him now, blades in hand, ready to kill.

Ronan chants furiously, stealing the air from the lungs of two of our enemies. He doesn't see the attack before it hits him. An iron dart spears his throat. Burns flare along his neck. He croaks as he suddenly can't use his voice.

It falls on me like a heavy rock that no matter what I do, I can't save them. No matter which path I take, some of them are going to die, if not all.

My father. The men I love.

I can't save them.

Yes, you can. Only if you give in.

I hear his whisper before I see him, but I don't need to look to know Damien is here. There's nowhere else he could possibly be right now.

The bolt of realization wrenches at me, electrifying my limbs. It should make me weak; it should make me scared, but maybe this is how it has to go.

Maybe this is how it's always had to go.

I don't want to do this. I don't want to sell my soul to the devil. But now, at last, it's my only choice. I can't let them die. I won't. If falling to save them is a sin, then maybe doing right isn't all it's cracked up to be.

My fur retreats, my back straightens, and my teeth shrink. I stand there, human, bleeding, hurting and naked, and I have never felt more powerful. I feel it now, the darkness dancing in my head, my heart, my soul. It is no longer my enemy.

I know who I am.

What I must do. What I have to become to save them.

I am Darkborn. This is my fate. I've tried to run from it, and maybe in another world, another Divina could have run forever. But I cannot, not when their lives are on the line. Not when it's a choice between me and my loved ones, me and every one of my kind.

Damien stands next to me now. "Give in, Divina." His soft whisper entices me. I don't even need the temptation. Not now.

My father looks at me and snarls. "Divina! Don't do it. Stay away from him!"

The time it takes him to yell is all the

distraction the guards need. A silver bullet flies directly toward his chest.

Panic flares up in me mixes with the hell seething in my soul at the thought of them taking my father from me. Then numbness hits. I glance at Damien, steady and calm. "Just do it."

There's a bright flash, and I stand in that room again, the one that reminds me of Hawaii. There's no blood, no fighting, no aching in my body, just the soft silk bed and that warm comforting air. My modesty is returned to me through a simple white chiffon dress. I look like a bride. No, I look like someone about to be baptized. In a weird reverse kind of way, I suppose that's not inaccurate.

Damien is in front of me, that warm fatherly smile on his face. He's played me. Despite myself, I must admire it. All of this, all the pain and the blood and the death, all the tricks and the promises, and here I am walking directly into his arms without a pause.

"I knew you would come to me, my sweet child." His words are practically a song with all the joy in his voice.

"I'm not your damn child. Let's be clear about that. I'll work with you. I'll do what I need to. But *only* when I know they're safe.

My friends, my dad. Derek needs to be protected, too. I need to see him before I come with you." I take a breath. "And the rest of the supes, the ones who got transferred from E, I want them out of Supermax. And then I want the place destroyed."

His smile grows. "Destroyed how, sweet one?"

"Dragon flame. Hellfire. I don't care, I want every trace of it gone." I tighten my fingers into a fist and say, "Warden Collins, too. I want him to burn."

Damien laughs, a silky-smooth laugh that sounds like Marco on steroids. "Such darkness. It's delightful. So I save your friends, your people, your father, destroy a prison, and you are mine?"

"The conspiracy. You're trying to set humans against my kind. I need you to stop that. It can't happen. I need it so it never existed."

"Done. Anything else while you're listing demands?"

I swallow, but there's no backing out now. "My mother," I push. "You said you could bring back my mother."

He chuckles, reaching for a strand of my clean hair, curling it around his finger. "I can. And I will. Once we've won our battle against heaven. So patience, my child. Do we have an agreement?"

I think of them, all of them. How much they've been willing to sacrifice, how much they've given for me.

It's not a hard choice.

It's not a choice at all.

Yet something deep down is still holding on to dear hope. My instincts. My sanity. Maybe, miraculously, I'll be rescued again and—

Another flash, and we're back at the battle. I guess Damien must sense my hesitation and is impatient.

Time seems to be frozen, and they all stand exactly as I've left them. Dad staring and pleading with me, the bullet so close to him. The others being dragged under as the tide turns against them.

Time starts again, and the bullet flies forward. My dad screams at me again for the last time. "Divina. No!"

I swallow and stretch out my hand. "Goodbye, Dad."

FORTY-FIVE
DEREK

I've been up all night, waiting for their call, waiting for some sign that they're all right. That *she's* all right.

They should be out by now, they should be in touch, but there's nothing. I'm not sure what to do. My head hurts from sleep deprivation as I drive to work, my radio turned to full volume on the off chance some news reaches me that way.

What if they've been captured? What if…

Gulping on coffee, I tell myself I can't think like that. I'll lose my mind. I just have to get to work. At the precinct, I'll be able to come up with something to help.

Chief waits in my office, which is a surprise. Before I even take my coat off, he asks me if I've heard from Divina. I don't hesitate; the lie is smooth and easy, and I'm stressed enough that it isn't hard to sound annoyed. "My partner of four years has orchestrated a prison break, sir, and she's not human. If I hear from her, everybody will know because she will be here wearing my cuffs."

Chief snorts a laugh. "You're a good kid, Derek. I wish you hadn't got too mixed up with her."

Cold runs down my spine. "What does that mean?" I can't keep the defensiveness out of my tone.

He holds up his hands. "I know you have a thing for her, supernatural or not. But Beastly can try to pull away from it as much as possible, but she is what she is. Just be careful. She's not worth the risk." Then he shrugs and leaves my office.

Something in his voice tells me he knows more than he should, not about my helping her, but about Divina herself. Something more than I even know.

I shake my head to clear those thoughts. I can't deal with it right now. I can worry about it later. Finding out everything I can about what the fuck is going on in Mount Hood is top priority now. Maybe someone has heard something. Maybe there's something over the radio…

A box which sits amidst all the paperwork I have yet to do grabs my attention. The small package is addressed to me. I put down my coffee and pull open the edges. The USB drive that falls out is as unremarkable as the box.

It's against protocol to plug this directly in the computers, but my gut screams at me I need to see what's on this drive right now. Confidentially.

I grab my laptop and plug in the stick. There's one video file there. I open it, and it's some grainy footage of… My eyes narrow. Is this Sean Chisholm?

The vic throws a ball over and over at the netless hoop on the wall in that desolate exercise room. He hits every shot until he's distracted by the click of the door opening. Two men walk inside, both of whom I recognize. Wilder, the guard D likes from the pen, and with him is Warden Collins.

Everything becomes clear at once as Wilder brutally smashes his baton against Chisholm's temple, sending him sprawling to the ground. He turns to Collins, who tells him something I can't hear, a large slasher smile on his face. Graham wears one to match, then reaches for his pocket, bringing out a blade.

I study the slaughter as much as I can before it's too much even for me. It's too early in the morning for even my hardened detective's stomach to deal with this. I switch off my monitor and sit, cold and clammy, processing what I've just seen.

Finally, we got him. Them. Even if Divina is trapped in the Supermax, I can get her out.

I pull the USB from my computer and head directly to my sergeant. I've never seen a warrant issued so fast.

Divina and her…whatevers…are right about this conspiracy. After what I've just watched on the screen, I'm not sure which side are the real beasts anymore.

It's still early morning, the sun not even at its high point yet, when the squad races to Mount Hood, me in my own car bringing up the rear. The blue lights and sirens blare ahead of me. I grip my steering wheel, hoping Divina and the guys are nowhere near the place. Hoping they just forgot to call.

I'm still a couple of miles away from the prison when I spy the first load of smoke rising above the horizon. I have no evidence, but the twisting in my gut promises: she's in danger. They all are.

The squad stops, and men get out of the cars for a quick inspection, but I can't waste that kind of time. I swerve to turn down the narrow icy forest path that leads up to the Supermax clearing. The sky in front of me is filled with billowing smoke and a brightness that eclipses even the sun.

The tower on the far end of the forest ahead of me is in flames. They blaze, licking the sky, devouring the clouds, greedily feeding on the building. It doesn't look like normal fire. It's brighter, hot enough that the snow on the trees has thawed.

I press down hard on the accelerator and plead with my car, the lovingly named Millennium Sparrow, to fly like her namesake. I need her to survive this path I'm definitely not supposed to be driving on, to get me to that towering inferno before Divina is gone for good.

The second I'm in a running distance to reach the fence, I skid into a park. Part of the squad has arrived, too, and as a unit we run toward the burning tower. The heat is unbearable. I cover my eyes and push my way through the trees to the center.

Guards dash from the building, screaming, covered in hideous burns, one or two collapsing onto the now-melted snow right in front of my eyes. I keep my arm up over my face as I run ahead, the energy from the flames like a physical repellent keeping me away, but Divina is in there. I need to be as well.

Abruptly, one of the fleeing guards seems to smack hard against mid-air and fall backward. More approach, each of them meeting the same invisible resistance. The checkpoint exits are wide open, yet none can get through.

They scream, slamming this invisible force with their hands, unable to get past. One of the guards cries out as he sees us, calling for us to save him. However, the squad can't get through. They're staring, frozen in horror, unable to understand what's happening.

"Help!" someone screams from the exit close to me. I look up at a guard I recognize, clawing desperately at seemingly thin air. Rivera from the pen. I rush forward on instinct, holding out my hand, but it feels like it hits a brick wall. We both stare at each other, and my head pounds worse than it has this morning. All I know is that this man is going to die right in front of me.

There's a loud creaking noise, and a hunk of metal comes hurtling my way. I dive to the side, scraping my shoulder and hip on the ground, the heat from the flaming chunk scorching my face even from this distance.

My body aches from the impact, but I pull myself up quickly before I become the target for the next chunk. Rivera is in pieces. Melted skin and an arm several feet from the rest of his body. Metal dotted over him like gruesome body piercings.

There's another flash. Something golden in the sky, shining in the light of the flames. A dragon.

Oakberry.

He perches atop the tower, protecting the exit he's just made.

A few seconds later it's followed by a humanoid figure with silver glittering wings. He leaves a trail of dust behind him as he seems to carry someone else and flies to the woods.

The guards scream more as the tower creaks again, and the rest of the cops try to get them through the wall with everything they have. I turn and run for the woods to where O'Shea has landed.

Gianmarco Connelly sits on the ground, covered in ash, coughing, while the fae has his hand on his shoulder, silver wings still glittering.

I have a million questions, but only one matters. "Where is Divina? What the hell is happening? Where *is* she?"

O'Shea looks away, not even bothering to answer me. Connelly mutters in a low voice, "Flynn." He clutches his side, his arm, and I notice the blood for the first time. He's been shot. Several times.

The fae takes off in flight again. I head to Connelly's side, reaching into my pocket and pulling out the tiny first aid kit I always carry on duty. He wheezes a laugh but lets me fuss over him.

When O'Shea is back, Flynn Killian and a man with Divina's eyes, limping, covered in blood and soot, use each other as crutches. Killian shoves me roughly as he takes my place at Connelly's side. I don't question it, handing him the kit.

My gaze is on O'Shea, demanding an answer. I open my mouth, but he speaks first. "What are you doing here, Bright? Why the force?"

I tell him in short terms about the footage. When I'm finished, Oakberry, who only has golden wings now, lands, laughing. "Right again, O'Shea."

"I'm always right," O'Shea mutters. "Derek—"

Whatever he's going to say vanishes as a man runs for his life, screaming, and hits the invisible force field. I hurry forward because I'm a cop. Helping people is what I do. Even if I don't know how I'll get this man through the wall.

I stop short when I recognize him. It's Collins, the bastard who started it all. I falter for half a second before I reach him. It doesn't matter how evil he is. He's still a human being. I have to help him. I'm a cop, not a judge, jury, or executioner.

Among the flames licking the ground and chunks of metal falling, two figures walk out hand-in-hand, untouched by the fire, undamaged at all. I stop short again.

She looks like a demonic angel, her hair covered in blood and gore, streaks of it on her white dress. The man holding her hand is perfectly coiffed and calm, wearing a finely tailored dark suit, a sardonic smile on his face.

She reaches where the invisible wall seems to stop and stills.

"Divina," I gasp.

As if I don't exist, she lets go of the

smirking man's hand and grabs Collins, pulling him close to her with a snarl. "Hello, Warden." It's her, but she sounds…different somehow. She's calm as ice despite the flames, and her tone reminds me of a snake about to strike.

"D!" her father cries out, raw and gruff and beseeching. "Look at me. Don't do this."

The rest of the inmates hurry behind me, Connelly, too, even if his breath is coming short and pained.

She doesn't acknowledge anyone. She raises one finger, a single pointed, thick wolf's claw, and bears it toward Collins' throat.

He's not a good man. I wouldn't weep for his death. But I can't watch her, my Divina, do this. "Divina. No. You're not a killer."

"Divina!" her father yells again, banging the air.

She pauses, just for a second, and I push my case. "This isn't you. I know you hate him; I know he's evil. I *saw* what he did. We're here to arrest him. He'll rot in a cell for the rest of his life. He'll be punished for everything he did. But please, D, not like this."

"You don't have a clue what he did since you last saw him, Derek," the smirking man says calmly. "Divina does. See those scars shining through that pretty dress, now vanishing on her belly? A few hours ago, Collins had Wilder slit her open. Mark her flesh. *Touch* her."

"To please you! I did everything you asked of me. You promised me power!" Collins shrieks at the man. "You swore it!"

"And the son of perdition keeps his promises," the man replies easily. "I gave you power. You squandered it. It burns behind you now. That is no fault of mine."

The son of perdition? Tedious hours of Sunday School rise to the front of my mind. But that can't be right. He can't be claiming to be…can't think he's…

"Do it, Divina," the man whispers to her. "He deserves worse. Feed your darkness. Take your pound of flesh. You deserve it."

"Divina, get away from him!" Connelly's broken voice calls from behind me. I glance over my shoulder. He's leaning heavily on Killian, his face pained as he gazes at the man with pure hatred. "I don't know what he promised you, but he's lying. You know better. You think they call him the father of lies for nothing?"

The man—the devil, the actual fucking devil—laughs. "Father of lies? Father of yours, even if you want to forget it. I'll deal with you later. This is between me and my new daughter."

Terror snarls. "She's not your daughter. Keep away from her, Damien, you sick bastard." He thrusts forward threateningly, but the wall stops him. He bangs his fists against it again. "D, don't do this."

I can't believe this. Fuck me, weren't the shifters and faeries and vampires enough? Now, the literal devil, Damien, has my girl, calling her his new daughter.

Her claw grazes the warden's Adam's apple. He swallows hard. A little trickle of blood runs down his throat.

"Divina, no, nonono!" I reach a hand as if I could stop her.

"Life is sacred," O'Shea says. There's real, deep pain in his voice, something haunted and ancient that sends chills through my body. "Taking a man's life like this, while he's unarmed and afraid and at your mercy…isn't something you'll recover from as smoothly as you think. The Divina I know, the one who risked everything to free guilty criminals just because part of them is innocent, would never do this."

"This is the real Divina, little fae," Damien croons. "Just like it was her mother. The darkness created her. It will make her slice this man's throat. In front of all of you. In front of this human."

Collins screams as Divina's claw digs slightly deeper.

"Stop it, Professor," Flynn snaps, desperate. "Remember what you've always taught. Ethics, justice. Truth. Don't run from that now."

Aedan grunts. "I want to see him dead as much as you do. But Bright is here. He'll take care of him. Be better than the rest of us. You *are* better than us."

"Please, D," I whisper. "He won't get away, I promise. Just let him go."

She stands there for one moment that feels like an eternity, clutching the whimpering, bleeding warden by his shirt.

"Baby, *please*." Terror's voice rattles with a sob.

She looks up at last.

Then she releases Collins, disgust in her face as she throws him to the ground.

The devil sighs and rolls his eyes, looking for all the world like an impatient teacher. "You'll get better at killing with time, I suppose." He kicks at the warden's whimpering figure that is still crouched on the ground between them. "I was hoping you'd make a show of it. Maybe I shouldn't have sent your boyfriend that footage after all.

Anyway, you've seen the human. Let's go."

"What? Go where?" Is he saying *he* sent me the footage? How? *Why?* I don't understand any of this. Why is the devil standing with the girl I love? What does he want with her? Where the fuck is he taking her?

I hold up a hand, and she does, too. "D." I can't touch her, but our palms rest on either side of the invisible wall. "D, what did you do?"

She looks away from me, though she doesn't move her hand. Her eyes slowly trace their faces. Her father. The other four. "What I had to."

Something in me breaks. I don't know what's happening. It's like a canyon has ripped my heart apart, and I don't even know why.

"Divina!" her father howls, furious and terrified, an animal stuck in a hunter's trap. "You can't do this. You have to come back!"

"Dad, take Rina and get out of here until you know for sure everything has blown over." When she speaks, her voice is cool and steady. "I can't risk her too."

"Stop this," Connelly begs. "Darling, you *can't*."

She doesn't say anything, but it is in her eyes. I bet they can hear the finality of that silence like I do.

Goodbye.

She takes the devil's hand. He smiles lazily at her. "Let's go, baby girl. Did you like my wall? Locking everyone like this? I think it was a stroke of genius."

"Don't push it, Damien. And don't ever call me baby girl. Besides, you still have to get the rest of the prisoners out."

"Yeah, yeah, and stop the conspiracy." He fakes a yawn. "Remind me, all of that in exchange for what?"

She doesn't flinch. "I'll fight your battle with Heaven, and I'll belong in your kingdom forever."

"That's my girl."

Her father screams after her, the other men, too. But I can't talk. I can't think. I can't breathe. It's like all the air from my lungs has been knocked out.

The devil has just taken away the only woman I've ever really loved.

Forever.

FORTY-SIX
GIANMARCO

It's still mostly dark when I wake up. It takes me a few minutes to recall everything. I'm in a bed, Flynn's heavy breathing in my ear as he sleeps next to me. There's an actual pillow under my head and a comforter over me. I lie there for a moment, marveling at the softness. This is the kind of comfort I've forgotten about after all those years in Ward E and the Supermax.

The Supermax. The memory of smoke fills

my nose. The creaking, flaming tower flashes behind my eyes as it crumbles apart while Divina vanishes with my father.

Our Divina. Gone.

I sit up, sharp pain in my head. Fuck. *Fuck*. She saw us in danger, all of us, and she gave in without a second thought. She let the darkness consume her, let my father take her, for us, for supes everywhere.

She became a sacrifice to the dark.

I am a demon. I thrive on the negative, on the cursed and murky, on the bleakness and agony. But now, as I imagine her there in hell, imagine such a force of goodness becoming overwhelmed with evil…it brings nothing to me but heartache.

On my right, there's the soft glow of an alarm clock shaped like some sort of spaceship. I let out a breath that would be a chuckle if everything didn't hurt so much. Derek is an odd one, all right. The numbers display six thirty, so we have at least an hour, maybe longer, before the sun deigns to rise.

I experimentally move my arm, There's hardly even an ache. I feel much better than I should after being shot repeatedly with salt and metal. I guess there's something to Ronan's fae healing magic after all.

Carefully, I slide out of the bed. Flynn

deserves to rest. I look down, and I'm thrilled to see sweatpants and a cartoon shirt. It's the kind of outfit I wouldn't be caught dead wearing, but after years of jumpsuits, it feels like the finest suit.

The damn door creaks as I open it, and Flynn bolts up immediately. "Divina?" he asks roughly.

I turn back to him, barely able to see his face in the dark. "No. It's just me. Go back to sleep."

He swears, and then stumbles out of the bed. His feet are heavy on the floor. He moves to me with zero grace, zero precision, still half asleep. Then he blindly reaches out and grips me into his embrace.

My heart thuds. The pain of losing Divina, Flynn's need for contact, for comfort…I have no idea what this swirl of emotions is doing to me. All I know is that I love him, love him in a way I didn't know was possible for a demon, and seeing him hurt like this on top of my own pain is true agony.

We don't say anything as we walk out of the room and down the stairs. The kitchen buzzes. All the others are already awake, gathered around the table while Derek makes coffee.

"Morning boys." The attempt at my usual

tone falls flat.

Aedan has a black look on his face, the kind that sends people running before they even know why they're scared. Ronan sits next to him, his expression carefully neutral, but I can feel the pain, the panic, spinning around him.

Terror stands propped against the wall nearby. If I think Aedan's expression is scary, it's nothing compared to Divina's father now. For a moment, I am nervous. What if he blames me? It won't be the first time I am held responsible for my father's actions. Is he even wrong if he does? I told his daughter about her darkness, I brought it to the forefront so I could taste it.

I don't even realize I'm speaking until the words have already fallen from my lips. "I'm sorry."

They all look at me, Derek frozen with the coffee pot in mid-air. Flynn squeezes my hand, but I pull away. I don't deserve his affection. I don't deserve him. I certainly don't deserve her.

The person who speaks is not who I expect.

"It's not your fault." Terror doesn't sound like he wants to comfort me. His tone is hollow, raw, but he forces the words out anyway. "My daughter can't be told what to do. Being what you are doesn't make you responsible. You're not a bad kid. Just like your brother."

"Your da is a cunt, though," Aedan comments darkly.

I snort as Derek hands me a steaming coffee mug. "You got that right."

Derek passes out coffee to the rest and takes a seat himself. "Now what? How do we get her back?"

I stare into my cup. "We don't."

"What do you mean *we don't?*" Flynn snaps. "Marco, this is Divina. We can't just leave her in hell!"

"Yeah, but what can we do?" I put down my cup, refusing to look up at any of them. "She made a deal with the devil. You don't just walk away from that. Even if we get inside hell and kidnap her, the deal still stands. She will be dragged back there by the force of that deal. There's nothing we can do about it. Nothing."

Aedan roars and shoves at the table, sending it crashing to the floor. The steaming liquid goes everywhere, the cups smashing on the ground. We all jump back as one. Aedan doesn't even look back as he storms out of the door, slamming it open so hard it might leave a dent in the wall.

Ronan pinches his nose just below his forehead and follows. Derek looks at the mess on the floor, then at Terror, then at me. I follow Ronan outside in case Aedan decides to dragon up and burn down the whole of Forest Grove in his rage.

It's freezing. The winter morning darkness makes the world even bleaker. After all that time on the inside there's still a beauty to it, one that I would feel if it wasn't for the ache of her loss.

Aedan stands a little far from the house, and Ronan whispers something urgently to him. The dragon seems to be calming down ever so slightly.

The other three amble to the yard as well. Terror looks up at the sky. "I'm sorry, Reindeer," he mutters. I'm not supposed to hear that, so I pretend to be very interested in the fading stars. "I tried to protect her. I thought I could make her understand, but I pushed her away." His lips purse. "You gave up your life to save her, and I couldn't even make her stay." He goes on his knees, breaking, crashing into tears. "Our daughter is gone, Vixen. It's all my fault."

Flynn swears under his breath, a stream of curses so unbroken that I can't even make out the individual words. Derek, lost, human, holds Terror's shoulders as he crumbles on the grass.

I search the skies, unsure what I expect to find there. The stars blink out in preparation for the sunrise. Humans love the sunrise. They think it erases the darkness. They don't realize all it does is hide it for a while.

Then I find it, shining brightly against the blackness. It's the exact right time before dawn that the planet Venus glints above me. The Morning Star.

My fucking father has so many alternative titles. Satan, Lucifer, the Fallen One. But he revels in the planetary grandeur of the Morning Star. A creature of darkness, named for light. It's a duality that's haunted me my whole life.

I don't remember much about my mother, but I remember watching the stars with her in early winter mornings, waiting for Venus to show herself. She was sick even then, but we'd still watch. She'd point to the Morning Star and whisper lovingly in my ear, "Gianmarco, *vita mia*, always remember that from darkness comes light and light comes darkness. One day I'll leave you, but never allow the darkness to eclipse your ability to love."

She'd hold me tight and kiss my forehead, and I'd feel safe. When she died, when I was sent from home to home, unwanted, unloved, I'd seek out the Morning Star before dawn. It is named for my father, but my mother is in it, too, watching me, guiding me, kind and gentle despite the darkness that surrounded our lives.

What would she do now? What would she say?

I know. Since she's not here, I must say it for her. "This is unacceptable." My words are quiet. Nobody responds. I speak louder, clearer. "This is *unacceptable*."

Silence stretches as they all stare at me. Then Derek nods. "Agreed, but you just said there was no way out. So let me ask again. What are we going to do about it?"

I sweep my hair back from my forehead. "I don't know," I admit. "I don't—once someone belongs to my father, that's usually it. I don't know how we're going to challenge it."

Terror glances at me with bloodshot eyes. "I'll call Inferno. See what he knows about this. He stood up to Damien once. Maybe he'll know what to do."

Ronan's eyes flash, and he moves closer to me. "What did you say? *Belongs* to your father?"

I shrug. "Sure. When he makes a deal, there's usually a big point about the subject and their soul being his. It's kind of his thing. You all heard it. He calls her his daughter. That's even more deep shit than we're already in."

Ronan stares at me, his violet eyes suddenly bright purple. Then his mouth curls into a fierce grin. "How quickly can you arrange for a meeting with your father?"

FORTY-SEVEN
DIVINA

Time doesn't exist in hell, not in any way that I'm used to. There is no distinction between night and day. I sit on the special throne Damien has built just for me. I am not his queen, of course, but I sit at his left hand, his most trusted lieutenant.

Not so shabby.

Flayed creatures that have been once human are dragged away in chains. Burns and viscera and blood and gore fill the place.

Screams are mostly all I can hear as I watch desperate soul after desperate soul dragged before us and sentenced to sufferings beyond my imagination.

I should feel horror. I should feel revulsion.

Mostly, I feel empty. There are cold black caverns in my heart, hollowed out by the loss of the ones I love. There has been a huge one already there for my mother, but now I mourn so many more.

Yet there's nothing there now. No pain at all.

Except the one caused by Damien's love for psychedelic pop. I mean, how many times can anyone listen to *Where Evil Grows*? It's the national anthem around here. I'd kick souls that haven't been sentenced yet in the Pit myself for some Rihanna.

As I sit on my throne and observe the latest damned being sentenced to the Pit, there's something else where the emptiness usually consumes me now. Something darker. Something gleeful.

When Damien offers the next one to me, explains the man's crimes and that I will choose his punishment, I condemn him to lashings and a dip in the flaming river without a blink. The darkness likes that, purring like a cat. Damien looks at me with a proud smile.

I want to yell at him, to tell him not to look at me like that, but a louder part of me enjoys his validation to the core. Is it so wrong, really? These people are in hell to be punished, so how is it a crime if I let my darkness take over, let myself hurt them, let their screams nourish me?

It's basically the same thing I did when I used to be human. Just a tad darker.

This me is dark, dangerous, a cloud of poison ready to strike at my moment. It should terrify me, but it doesn't. In fact, I like it. So fucking much.

When I condemn, when I revel in their bleakness and hopelessness and ache, those caverns finally stop feeling so empty. The black sludge of evil fills my whole body, replacing my blood, and it's like a sick balm, healing my ravaged soul.

It isn't what my mother wanted before her death, but what did she know? She made her mistakes, and they all still think she was a saint. Why should my choices be any different?

Who are any of them to say what is dark is what is evil?

The thing I'm changing into is content. I am alive like I don't remember feeling since I was a child. Surrendering to it is the best way, the only way, to finally find a place where I feel right.

The darkness is what I am now, all of me, and I relish it.

"Damien." I grin. "Can I have the next one, too?"

Damien returns my grin. "Of course, my child." He beckons the next unfortunate soul forward.

I lean toward him, ready to act. This is where I'll finally belong.

FORTY-EIGHT
AEDAN

I'm all for just ripping his head off the minute I see him, but Ronan tells me I must have patience. I don't really feel like it, but I'll wait. For now.

Terror makes a couple of phone calls before the six of us head to Beast Clearing.

The devil is there when we arrive, lounging on a fallen tree trunk not so far from the willow tree like it's a throne. She stands beside him, pale, silent, dressed in the same white, lace dress she wore at the tower, but this one is blood free.

My chest aches to see her like this. I just want to rush forward and grab her. Only Ronan's warning hand on my arm holds me back.

Terror is clenching and unclenching his fists as we approach, but he manages to stay back, his eyes pinned to his girl.

"Well?" Damien says as soon as we enter the clearing. "What can I do for you?" He trails his gaze over all of us. "The bastard. The angry dragon. The lost fae. The vampire-lion, the abomination…all of these I expected." He focuses on the end of our little line-up. "But not the human. Have you brought me a plaything?"

Divina stands there without a word, her stare cold, looking right through us. Her blue-and-gold eyes are gone, replaced with blackness. It's not coal black like mine. It's a void, covering her pupils and the whites too, taking all of the joy from her expression.

"We came to take, not bring, *Padre*." Connelly's voice is smooth and calm. "Divina. Will you listen to us?"

She doesn't even respond, doesn't even look at him, at any of us. She's gazing in our direction, but it's as if she sees right through us.

Damien chuckles. "I see. Very well then. Say your piece, for all the difference it will make." He leans back on the wood and gestures for us to go ahead.

"You need to come home, Divina," Derek says immediately, taking a step toward her.

She finally looks at him. It's as if she's separated from him through thick glass. "I am home. At last. You should be happy for me."

"Happy? D, you don't belong in hell. I know you. This isn't you."

"You don't know who or what I am, Derek. You barely even know supes exist. I can take that away if you want. It'll be easier. You can forget all of this, just like all the rest of the humans."

"Forget? How can I forget? Why would I want to forget? All I want is for you to come back. We all do."

She smiles, a cold, cruel smile. The light dims behind Derek's eyes as his expression crumbles. Connelly is pale, drawn, Flynn looks ready to kill, and Ronan, my genius unflappable friend, looks truly lost for the first time since I've known him.

It makes me flinch. Fear for him, fear for her. Fear *of* her, or whatever this creature is that's wearing her body. "Stop this damned game, lass, and get your arse over here." She turns her face to me, and I scowl back at her calmness. "Enough is enough."

She chuckles darkly, the sound echoing around the clearing. "I'm not Bethany, Aedan. You can't save me."

Pain flashes through me. It hits me like a physical blow so hard that I stumble backward a bit. My baby sister. Divina. Both of them gone under my watch. I'm such a fucking arsehole that I've just let it happen.

"You think none of us know what it's like," Killian speaks up. "But what do you think I am? I'm half shifter half fucking vampire, for God's sake. A few years ago, I was a human, and now I'm not. I *still* don't even know what I am for sure. Before I saw you again, I'd given up on life. But I'm finally accepting that I'm alive. All my parts whatever they are. I'm still *me*. It's *you* who made me realize that. You gave me. Hope. Love."

"And me," I say gruffly.

"All of us," Connelly adds.

"And I have faith in you. I've spent four years watching you work by my side, falling in love with you. You're many things. Everything. But not that," Derek insists, his voice firm.

"That's why we're here," Ronan finishes.

"Because we believe in you. You're stronger than all of this."

"Stronger?" she repeats with an icy incredulity. "You want *strength,* Ronan?" She holds out a hand, and a nearby tree slowly shrivels. Black mold starts at the top and runs down to the roots, leaving the wood bleached and white and dead wherever it touches, shrinking the grand oak down into dust.

"And that's just a tree." She smirks. "Imagine what I can do to a person." Her eyes are black pits, sucking the life from the world. "The darkness *is* my strength. It is me. I've just finally accepted it. You say you have faith in who I am? This is who I am."

"You're lying to yourself, baby girl," Terror whispers. "Come home, Divina. Your real family needs you. I need you."

She looks away. "Damien, let's go."

The fucking devil smiles and holds out a hand. She's about to take it when Terror steps forward puts his hands on her shoulders, making her look into his eyes. "I'm not leaving here until you come with me."

"Dad, I have to go," she says as a warning.

"Haven't you been listening to me at all, baby girl?" Terror sobs, no attempt to hide it from his voice. "Yes, there's darkness in you, like there was darkness in your mother. But you don't need to push it away or run from it. Your mom was born human, and that's all she knew. All she had to accept and control. But you…you're different. Supe. Human. Darkborn. You can only control any of your sides if you accept all of them."

She shakes her head, a small tremble in her hand that still wavers inches from Damien's.

"You can't just surrender to one side, whatever that side is. Or else the others will never stop haunting you. They're *all* you, D," Terror tells her gently. "That's where your strength comes from. That's what you need to understand. What we all need to understand."

She stares at him, her black eyes wide, drinking in his words, so many conflicting emotions on her face.

"You need to come home. I know you're strong enough, baby girl. I believe in you. We all do."

Quiet stretches over the clearing. Divina's expression hardens once more. "No. You're wrong. Damien has given me power. When I fulfill my purpose, he's even going to bring Mom back. Don't you see? This is the best way, the *only* way—"

Gianmarco laughs. "You haven't changed since Eden, Padre."

Divina looks furious and shocked at being

interrupted by his laughter, but Terror speaks again before she can react. "And you believed him? Baby, Damien is the devil. When he tempted Eve to take the apple, who did that deal favor? When Faust gave in to Mephistopheles, did he and his woman live a happy life? The devil's deals always go wrong. They always go his way."

Her eyes squeeze shut. She holds up her hands as though his words are stones being thrown at her.

"Even if he did tell the truth, even if he *can* bring your mother back…do you think she'd want that? Like this? At this cost?"

Divina's eyes shoot open. They're still black, but there's an uncertainty in them now that sets Cináed on edge.

Damien, getting to his feet, slowly claps. "Bravo. What a show! Unfortunately, all of your words don't make any difference. Divina here made a deal. She's mine."

Ronan smiles beatifically and takes a step forward. "Actually, I think you'll find she's not."

"What?" Divina and Damien demand at the exact same time.

Damien narrows his eyes. "She made a deal with me, little fae. That's binding. You of all people would know that."

"I'm glad you brought that up," Ronan strolls forward, like a lawyer about to win in some court movie. "Because when she said she'd be yours, that wasn't hers to promise anymore." He holds her gaze. "Divina doesn't belong to you. She belongs to *me*." He pauses for effect, the showy bastard. "To all of us."

Damien growls. "Your treacherous games can work on someone else. Her soul is mine!"

"No." Ronan's easy charm vanishes. The air crackles as his power gathers. "Divina made a deal with me first. In exchange for returning to me in one piece, complete, I offered to help rescue her father from the Supermax. I fulfilled my end of the deal. After all, Terror stands right here. Now she is bound to fulfill hers." His smile is chilly, enough that even I shiver. I sometimes forget how scary he can be. There's a reason our partnership works so well. "She promised to return to all of us in one piece, soul included."

Ronan holds out his hand to Divina. "Now," he says softly. "Your end of the bargain."

Divina stares at him for what seems like an eternity. We all wait with bated breath.

Motorbike engines rumble nearby. The trees rustle as they make their way through closer to the clearing.

Damien howls in outrage. "If you take his hand, Divina, you're dooming yourself. All of your kind. The conspiracy won't be hard to reignite. Rogue supes, committing a murder then destroying the only place humans could control them? The humans will come baying for your blood. For your lovers, for your family. For your sister you want to protect so much. Nobody will be safe."

"I wouldn't try to use me like that, if I were you," a girl says as she steps out from between the trees, her voice like a breath of warm spring air. Her hair is short and blonde, her eyes a bright amber. Flanking her are two young men. One has the same exact hair and eye color of Damien and Connelly, the other pale with long, jet black hair and silver eyes.

Damien freezes in place as he looks at them, his stare fixed on the blonde girl.

"The cavalry arrives," Connelly says delightedly. "You were right, Terror."

"Hello, Uncle," the blond boy teases him, and then shoots Divina a reprimanding glance. "Sister, what the fuck are you doing?"

"You really think we feel threatened by the likes of him? C'mon, D." The pale one folds his arms. "Anyway, Prez and the rest are on their way here now, but honestly, Mom raised you better than this."

The girl, Divina's twin, rushes forward, stopping right at her. "Divina," she cries, and then they're both sobbing.

The sister pulls back, brushing Divina's hair to the side with a smile, and looks into those black eyes. "You've always been the strong, levelheaded one. It doesn't matter what he does. He can't have me. He can't have us. Isn't that what she's always said? We believe in you, Sis. You already left us once. Don't leave us again. Please."

Divina stares at her twin and between her brothers. As she does, her eyes flicker and the black void retreats. Then there's the bright blue and the shining gold that I've come to love once more.

Then, slowly, she sighs and places her hand in Ronan's while she reaches for her sister with the other. "I won't leave you. Any of you. Never again."

"You're a fool," Damien snarls. "You're condemning all of them. You'll regret this."

There's a cool, calm expression on Divina's face as she meets his manic stare, hand-in-hand with Ronan and her sister. "Maybe. But I know, one day, no matter how long I'll wait, with my family, with the people who truly love me for who I really am, I'll be the one who teaches you what regret means."

As if a barrier has just been broken, we all dash forward at once, surrounding her with our embraces, our kisses, touching and holding her. All of our arms and bodies overlap but we don't care as we cheer and we celebrate and we're together at last as we should be.

When I look up from the giant group embrace, Damien is gone.

"He'll be back," Connelly mutters in my ear.

I snort. "We'll be waiting."

FORTY-NINE

DEREK

Divina insists on seeing me safely home while her family rides with the rest of the MC to reach as many supes as possible. Divina's other guys go with them. They want to alert as many people as they can before the conspiracy hits and they become hunted again. The plan is to round as many as they can and hide them somewhere safe, but she can't tell me where.

I unlock the front door, and she walks

inside with me. "Does that include you?"

Her eyes are sad. "Yes, that includes me. I need to hide with the rest of them. I need to help them through this."

What about me? "What about your jobs? Your house?"

She smiles, as if she knows what I'm really asking. "I'll keep in touch as much as I can, but I can't promise anything. Not until I know it's safe."

I nod, taking off my coat and hanging it on the rack. My stupid eyes itch with tears. I know it, of course, but hearing her say it hurts more than I bargained for. Work won't be the same without her. Life won't be the same without her.

Work.

"Divina, Chief…said something weird. About you." I tell her about our conversation. "You don't think—"

"—he's involved?" she asks, quirking an eyebrow.

Cold settles in my belly. "Nah. He can't be. I'm being stupid. He wanted you away from the case."

"Did he?" she asks patiently. She waits for me to solve this puzzle. Always a teacher, my Divina, even now.

Could our Chief be in on this conspiracy?

How deep does it go? Who else does Damien have in his grip? "I don't understand. You mean he was really in on this? But then why—"

"Because he knows me, Derek. How stubborn I am. He knows that refusing me was the only sure way to make me go."

I stare at her. Then I square my shoulders, taking her hand. "I'll get him. He'll be locked up, and he'll rot alongside Collins for the rest of his miserable life," I promise. "Whatever I can do from my end, I'll do it. I'll keep you safe."

She reaches up and kisses my cheek. "You're so good, Derek." The heat builds between us like it has so many times before, but things are different now. Everything is different now. "All this supernatural crap…you accepted it without blinking. You put your job, your life on the line for me and my father. You know I have…something…going on with the others, and I don't expect you to be okay with it, but—"

She's cut off as I pull her close and kiss her lips. She melts into my embrace, her lips parting for mine, our tongues dancing together. Her arms wrap around my shoulders as I lift her, her legs around my waist.

We move blindly back toward my living room, not stopping for breath. I can't stop kissing her. I won't. Her lips, the feel of her hands on my neck, in my hair, that is the whole world, and nothing else matters.

"We shouldn't," she murmurs against my lips.

I kiss her harder, panting against her lips. "We can stop."

"Don't you dare stop."

I laugh a little as I place her gently down on the couch. She reclines, and I lean over her, kissing her eyes, her cheeks, nibbling at her earlobes, licking the join between her neck and her collarbone.

We don't talk. We've said enough. She helps me as I remove her dress, her bra, her panties. Her deft fingers undo my shirt buttons and pull it off my body, then my pants and boxers. We're both completely naked. I fall onto her once more, my lips returning to her, crushing her against me.

"You don't know how long I've been waiting for this," I whisper between kisses. "You're so beautiful. So beautiful."

The feeling of her breasts against my chest as I hold her is electrifying. Her legs wrap around my hips as our body heat mingles. I kiss her chest, her nipples, her belly. My hands explore her, all of her, touching every inch of skin, eager and hungry for her. Her hands and eyes are roaming my body, my muscles, grazing my back, gripping my ass. She wants me as much as I want her.

We need this. We need each other.

Every touch, every breath, every sigh is incredible, every brush of her lips a prayer. My hands travel behind her thighs and up to her beautiful ass, squeezing the flesh while my mouth devours her wetness.

Her gasps get louder, her fingers diving in my hair, pulling me even closer. "Detective Bright, you've got some serious lady-pleasing skills. How did you manage to stay single for four years?"

My tongue laps over her sweet pussy one more time. "I fell in love and have been waiting for her to love me back."

"Stupid. You should have just eaten her like that four years ago. She would have fallen in love with you right away." She pants a laugh. "By the way, she, too, loves you so much, Detective Bright."

I release her clit for a moment, my heart throbbing with happiness I never thought existed. "I love you, too, D."

Her amazing smile brightens her face, and I work harder at her pussy. My fingers enter her. She's already soaking now, moaning as I slip two fingers and then three, while my tongue flicks her clit.

My cock jerks, harder than I remember ever being in my life. I twitch my fingers and she cries out, and I'm rewarded with another flow of her wetness.

She groans my name. The sweetest sound I've ever heard. "Derek, just fuck me. Now. I need you. Please."

I want to make this last forever, but I'm only a man. She's writhing naked under me, saying she needs me, begging for my cock, and I'm so hard it's painful.

Fingers out, I line up on top of her, unable to get enough of her lips. Then slowly, I push into her.

She gasps as she takes my cock, and as I fill her up. I've never felt so complete, so hot, so right. She reaches for my hips, her nails digging in as she grips me, guiding me deeper, pulling my body closer to hers.

My pace is slow, steady, and her grip tightens, urging me for more. I hold back, though. She's moving against me. It makes it so fucking hard not to come straight away, but I won't, not yet. We've both been waiting so long for this.

I slowly thrust into her and out again, softly

at first, but each stroke gets harder and more forceful. She gasps and groans, her hands all over me. I pick up my speed because she's asking for more, begging for harder.

Panting now, I plunge my cock as deep as it can get, fucking her so hard. Her fingernails dig into my ass. "Fuck, Derek. Your cock feels so fucking good. Fuck me, baby. Harder, please."

She sounds like an animal, starving, hungry for it, hungry for me. I thrust into her with all my strength, the pain of her nails turning me on more as I give her everything I have.

She jerks up to kiss me. My tongue plunges into her mouth as I pound her. I pull back from her face, just in time to see as her eyes flash gold. She screams in bliss. Her pussy contracts around my cock. Her legs hold me in place so she can rub against me, use me, as she rides out her orgasm.

Fuck me. That's the hottest, most intense thing I've ever seen. But it's not just the fucking—though damn, it's a really good fuck. It's something else, something more.

At her peak, her eyes change. It's the blackness again, the void from the clearing. I stop moving, and as she looks at me, surprise on her expression, they change back to blue once more. "What?"

"Your eyes… They were black again for a moment."

She swallows. "I know. That's going to happen now. The darkness is still part of me. I'm human. Shifter. Darkborn. Not more of any one of them. Can you accept that?"

Can I? Can I share the girl I love with four magical creatures? Can I accept she can turn into animals? Can I bear the thought she'll always have this darkness inside her, pulling her to the devil, to hell? That she won't even be by my side for a long time yet?

We're both covered in sweat. Her breathtaking breasts rise and fall with each heavy breath as she waits. She still holds me inside her wetness, her damp legs around me, and her hands on my ass. I lean down and kiss her fiercely. "Of course I can." Then I move against her once more.

"Don't just say things because you're inside me now."

"Trust me. It's not just that, D. No matter what you are, you're *you*. You fill my heart. I want you. Always. I'd do anything for you. Loving you makes this more than anything I've ever felt before."

She helps me, pulling me deeper, holding me tighter. "Fuck, Derek. I love you."

That's when I let go, and I growl as I come,

the heat rushing from me and into her. Every cell in my body is on fire with her, every pleasure I've ever felt until now dull in comparison.

My forehead rests on hers, and I taste her lips one more time while I still can. "I love you, too. I love you, D."

She wraps her arms around me, holding me close, comforting me, my face nestled between her breasts.

We doze off for a while. When I wake up, I lie on the couch alone, covered by a blanket. She's dressed again, fixing her hair. Her smile greets me when she sees I'm awake. She kisses me once, deeply, and strokes my cheek. "I have to go."

Catching her hand, I sigh. "I know." I press it to my lips, tears stinging my eyes. "Tell those guys I said to keep you safe or else. Your other boyfriend is a cop."

She laughs. Her eyes are wet too, but she doesn't let the tears fall. Strong until the end, my Divina. "I meant it when I said I love you, Derek. I'll be back one day. I promise."

I smile, glancing up for a second so she won't see me crying. I should make this easy for her. She has a long way to go. A war we never know when it will end. I force a bigger smile when I gaze back at her. "I love you, too. I'll be here when you need me. No matter how long it takes."

She kisses me once more. It lingers, but then she turns and leaves the room. I lie there until I hear the front door open and close.

No matter how long it takes.

FIFTY

DIVINA

I can't believe we need to run, but it's for the best. At least for now, our priority has to be keeping our kind safe.

"You all right, lass?" Aedan asks over his shoulder as we get out of the car half a mile away from Beast Clearing. "Cop give you any trouble?"

"He'd better not have," Dad growls.

Despite the whirlwind of emotions in my brain and heart, I can't help but laugh.

Aedan offers to carry me to help protect my delicate feet. I slap his arm in response. Dad cackles.

The good news is word has spread fast. Supes everywhere are retreating into hiding, making their way to safety until all of this is over. As the three of us enter Beast Clearing, I'm overwhelmed by how many of them have found their way here.

Hundreds of supes are jammed into this little secret place. Adults and children, shifters, vampires and demons galore. Silence falls as we enter. They're all staring. At us. At *me*.

Ronan, Marco, and Flynn separate from the crowd, each taking a turn to embrace me. Marco whispers in my ear, "I told them about you. About how you stood up to the devil himself. How you're a survivor."

"They liked the story," Flynn continues. "A lot. All that shit about accepting all parts of us…turns out it goes over really well with a crowd like this."

"Is that why they're all staring?" I ask, and Aedan snorts a laugh. "What?"

Ronan gives him a look of disapproval. "You didn't tell her?" Aedan shrugs, unrepentant. Dad doesn't react at all.

Ronan sighs and turns to me. "Yes, that's

why they're staring. Because you inspire them. Because you inspire all of us." He offers his hand and leads me a little farther into the crowd.

I am nervous among the whispering, gazing supes, but it doesn't matter when I see my sister. My precious twin who has saved me in the clearing even though I've avoided her for so long. For reasons that feel so distant now.

She brightens at the sight of me. "Divina!"

In the distance are my brothers, my uncles, Slasher and Inferno—all of them grinning at the sight of us Beastly twins being reunited once more without the devil anywhere nearby.

Rina brushes my hair to the side and rests her forehead against mine. "Who knew you'd be the one to lead a revolution?"

I stare. "Wait, what?"

My dad's hand is on my shoulder. "Like the fae told you, D. You inspire all of us. We don't know what's ahead, but we know one thing. We have you. Damien doesn't."

I blink up at him. "What…I don't…"

"We need a leader, Divina." Aedan approaches, amusement in his eyes. "Someone who can give hope to all of these arseholes. Someone who told the devil to fuck off and lived to tell the story. That's you. Congratulations, your highness." Then he looks off to the side and points his thumb. "Also, if you're serious about this 'joining humans and supes' thing, you'll be thrilled to see the visitor who just arrived."

Derek walks out from amongst the trees, embarrassed when all eyes swing on him. Then he stalks in my direction through the cheering of the crowd.

I gape at him as he approaches. "You can't be here."

"Sure he can." Rina grins. "Isn't that kind of the point? Him being here is exactly what we need." She lowers her voice. "Besides, his stink is all over you. Nice hunting, Sis."

Heat rises to my cheeks as I punch her arm.

"Hey. Sorry. I really meant to do what you asked," Derek says. "But I can't just…wait. I want to help. Whatever it takes."

My heart swells at his sweetness. I can't help but smile and take his lips between mine.

The crowd roars, and now his cheeks burn.

"He's so hot. Would it be terribly wrong to ask to share with the rest of the pack?" Rina whispers again.

"Oh fuck off." I push her away.

"Possessive alpha bitch," she giggles.

Derek chuckles, scratching the back of his head. "Your sister is really nice."

I punch him in the arm, too. "Well,

welcome to the jungle. Literally."

With my hand in Rina's, I turn to the awaiting crowd, evening my breath. "Okay. Let's do this."

"Damien Pattison thinks he's won by setting the humans against us," I start, my voice surprisingly steady and clear. "But all he's managed is doing us a favor." I step forward. "There are good people out there, strong people. Humans can be accepting and loving and kind." I point at Derek. "Like Detective Bright has...like Vixen Legend has."

My heart flutters at her name. Rina sniffs. My brothers share a rare moment of affection as one wraps his arm around the other's shoulder. Tears glisten in my siblings' fathers' eyes, and Dad squeezes my arm.

Finally, I understand. Mom started building a bridge between humans and supes, and she left it to me and my siblings to finally complete it.

"For thousands of years, we've been living in the shadows, afraid to show who we really are. Not anymore," I explain. "From now on, we'll learn to accept each other. And when that happens, we won't need to hide. We will be able to live free, as ourselves, not in the shadows, but *amongst* the humans."

The crowd murmurs, and Rina gives me an encouraging nod. I breathe out and then continue. "We're different, it's true. That doesn't mean we become someone else to fit. If I've learned anything from what happened to me, it's that I have to stay true to myself and embrace all the parts that are me, the bad before the good." I glance at Dad. "My mother knew that. My whole family. My friends, human and supe alike."

Rina squeezes my hand, and I continue. "Their faith in me, in what I am—all of what I am—saved me from hell itself." I gesture out to them. "So yes, we have to hide now. Yes, it's going to be hard. Yes, we will have to fight a lot of prejudice to stay safe. But it won't be forever. We'll recuperate. We'll regain our strength. We'll accept who we are, and *they'll* accept us back. Human, supe, or otherwise."

My father, family and boyfriends walk forward and stand by me. "One day, I promise you we'll all be united by our faith in each other. That's the day we'll take down Damien and his reign of evil forever."

There's a moment of silence, and then a cheer swells from the ground, expanding over the horizon, filling the air. My boyfriends have my back, and my family is beside me. Derek connects me to humanity. My darkness is nothing to be feared. It is part of me, just like Wolf and Reindeer.

I am not ashamed. I will not run anymore, not from any of it.

If all these supes, all these people, need me for this new world free of fear, then so be it. I will be their inspiration as they inspire me. I will serve as the bridge between our kinds. If Damien wants a war, a war is what he'll get.

We stand here, all of us. Creatures like my father that are called abominations. Demons, fae and dragons. Wolves, lions, vampires. Shadowborn, bastards and tinged shifters. Humans like Derek, like my mother.

And me. Darkborn, shifter, human. Daughter of Luke Beastly and Vixen Legend. A misfit that has finally found a home.

We are all of us united.

If he wants to hurt us, Damien can bring it. We'll be waiting.

We'll be ready.

Together.

THE END

Thanks for Reading!

I hope you enjoyed reading All the Teacher's Prisoners as much as I loved writing it. I put a lot of hard work, tears and sleepless nights in this book.

If you haven't already, get All the Teacher's Bad Boys, the story of Vixen Legend and Terror, Divina's parents and the Blood Demons MC.

To know more about Damien and his mate, and why he wanted to steal her some babies in the first place, get the first book All the Teacher's Beasts

There are some Irish terms and sentences that may sound odd or have missing words, but they're NOT incorrect. The story is in present tense, so some flashbacks are TOLD in present to keep it consistent stylistically, while some are in past tense for better impact. As the author, I CHOSE this style. I hope you've enjoyed going on this journey with me. I certainly enjoyed creating every letter and emotion in it.

Write a review on amazon or Goodreads

Sign up for my Newsletter on njadelbooks.com

Read the series finale, All the Teacher's Little Belles, to know what happens to Divina, Damien and all the supes.

ALSO BY N.J. ADEL

Paranormal Reverse Harem

All the Teacher's Pet Beasts

All the Teacher's Little Belles

All the Teacher's Bad Boys

Reverse Harem Erotic Romance
Her Royal Harem Series

Her Royal Harem: Complete Box Set

Contemporary Romance

The Italian Heartthrob

The Italian Marriage

The Italian Obsession

Dark MC and Mafia Romance
I Hate You then I Love You Collection

Darkness Between Us

Nine Minutes Later

Nine Minutes Xtra

Nine Minutes Forever

ACKNOWLEDGMENTS

My readers, as always, I FLOVE YOU. You don't know how much it means to me that you're sitting here, reading these words. Thank you. For reading my book. For every review, comment and message. I treasure every single one.

Mooney, thank you for putting up with my manic feats.

My street team, thank you for every post and recommendation. Thank you for bearing up with my crazy.

My family, as always, there are no words to say to your continuous support.

Rina, you are in my every book.

About the Author

N. J. Adel, the author of All the Teacher's Pets, The Italians, Her Royal Harem, and I Hate You then I Love You series, is a cross genre author. From chocolate to books and book boyfriends, she likes it DARK and SPICY.

Bikers, rock stars, dirty Hollywood heartthrobs, smexy guards and men who serve. She loves it all.

She is a loather of cats and thinks they are Satan's pets. She used to teach English by day and write fun smut by night with her German Shepherd, Leo. Now, she only writes the fun smut.

Made in the USA
Middletown, DE
02 May 2023